CLAIMING HIS BABY AT THE ALTAR

MICHELLE SMART

CROWNING HIS LOST PRINCESS

CAITLIN CREWS

MILLS & BOON

CLAIMING HIS BABY AT THE ALTAR

MICHELLE SMART

MILLS & BOON

CHAPTER ONE

THE FLASH OF cameras was blinding.

Flora Hillier kept her gaze fixed ahead and ignored the questions being shouted at her by the horde of jostling reporters. A microphone brushed against her cheek. Another jabbed her neck. She would not give the vultures the satisfaction of reacting.

The dozen or so steps she climbed to enter the centuries-old building were wide but short in depth and she prayed not to trip.

At the top of the steps, the double doors were opened for her. A court guard took her arm and swept her inside.

The low-level hum of noise inside the court building was a welcome contrast to the shouts and hollers she'd just endured. Flora removed her sunglasses and placed a hand to her aching lower back. The pain had been strong enough to wake her that morning.

Filling her lungs with air and fortitude, she put her bag on the tray to be scanned and stepped through the body scanner. She wondered if this level of security had long been a part of Monte Cleure's criminal court or if they'd installed it specially for Ramos. She imagined there were any number of people out there who would be happy to form an orderly queue for the opportunity to do harm to the Spanish bastard. She'd be right at the front of it.

He was here, in this building. Soon, very soon, she would see him again. More importantly, he would see her.

She approached the curved reception area and handed her passport over.

The lady checking it raised an arched eyebrow before inputting the details into a desktop computer. 'Look in the camera,' she said in English, pointing up.

Flora lifted her stare to the domed device on the ceiling. Less than a minute later, a lanyard pass with her name and picture was handed to her.

'Go to room four,' the lady ordered.

'Thank you.'

Sliding the lanyard over her head, Flora headed down the wide corridor until she found the room.

Justin was already there, huddled around an oval table with his small legal team. He greeted her with an exhausted smile.

She held up a sympathetic hand to him and then sank gratefully onto a chair one of the legal team pulled out for her, and rubbed again at her aching lower back.

Today was the start of a trial expected to last two weeks. When found guilty, Justin could expect to spend two decades behind bars.

Monte Cleure allowed reduced time for good behaviour only in the most exceptional circumstances. Funnily enough, those exceptional circumstances only ever seemed to apply to the fabulously rich. Justin was no longer rich. Ramos had made sure of that. Ramos had also made sure the evidence against Justin was watertight. Ramos had chosen Monte Cleure to press charges against him deliberately.

It pained Flora beyond reason that the case against Justin was watertight only because Justin was guilty of the crimes he was about to go on trial for. Theft of a million euros. Fraud had been added to the charge for good measure.

Which room was Ramos currently holed up in? The one next door? Further away? No doubt he too would be huddled around a table with his legal team. Maybe two tables to fit them all in. His team would vastly outnumber Justin's. What was the atmosphere like in that room? She doubted it was the resigned, subdued atmosphere permeating this one. Most likely, anticipation and expectation.

Anticipation and expectation that Justin Hillier be not only punished but destroyed.

If Flora had any tears left in her she would weep for her brother but the last year had spent her of them. There came a time when they would no longer form. Her tear ducts had simply dried up.

A knock echoed on the door. An official stepped in.

It was time.

Flora heaved herself back to her weary feet and stared into her brother's gaunt face. She straightened his tie even though it was already perfect, wiped away a fleck of imaginary flint from the lapel of his suit jacket, and kissed his cheek.

'I love you,' she whispered to the man who'd been more of a father to her than theirs had ever been.

His smile was sad. 'I love you too.'

There was nothing more to be said.

The hum of noise when Flora had arrived was now a buzz, the corridor bustling with bodies. It was a rare event that Monte Cleure's criminal court was the setting for such a high-profile crime. The principality was used to the press swarming for the goings-on of its rotten royal family and the fabulously wealthy people who inhabited the glamorous, sunlit place, and when Flora was led to the front of the public gallery overlooking the court, the press were already crammed into their section like eager expectant meerkats, faces bobbing in all directions for the star attraction's appearance.

They didn't have to wait long.

The prosecution team entered. Amongst them strode the tall figure of Alejandro Ramos, suave and gorgeous in a navy suit and tie and grey shirt. Today, he was clean shaven, his thick dark hair cropped short.

The last thing Flora expected was the jump of her heart into her throat at his appearance.

She placed her trembling hands on her belly and breathed deeply, telling herself the jump of her heart was only to be expected considering the last time she'd seen him had been when he'd passionately kissed her goodbye.

Much better was the spike of hatred that came when he sat amongst the prosecution lawyers on the prosecution bench. The spike pierced her to see him as one with them. In England he'd be nothing more than a witness.

Look at me, she silently urged him.

The smooth-looking man seated beside him whispered in his ear. Ramos tilted his head to hear more clearly then nodded with a grin.

How could he smile when he was condemning his best friend to decades of imprisonment?

Look at me.

The Justice of the Peace entered the court from his private room at the back.

An order was called out. Everyone rose to their feet.

The Justice took his seat and indicated for everyone to follow suit.

Flora, her stare fixed on Ramos, stayed standing.

Look at me, you bastard.

As if he could feel the weight of her stare, he turned his face up to the gallery. To her.

Flora had chosen her clothing that morning with care. She'd selected a simple, short-sleeved cream summer dress with tiny buttons running its length that fitted snugly over her form. She'd wanted nothing that could detract the eye from the huge swelling of her stomach.

For the briefest of moments Ramos's eyes locked on hers then flittered away as if he hadn't seen her.

A wave of longing crashed through her, as unexpected and as frightening as the jump in her heart at the sight of him had been, but she swallowed hard and remained standing.

Barely a beat passed when she caught the sudden stillness in his frame.

Slowly, he turned his gaze back up to her.

Clenching her teeth tightly in an attempt to keep any emotion from showing on her face, Flora pointed both forefingers at her belly.

If he was looking closely enough he would see the bulge where their child had just kicked her.

If the situation weren't so desperate and heartbreaking, Flora would have found much amusement in the first hour of the trial. The leading prosecutor rose and made his opening speech, not a word of which she understood as it was all conducted in French. Ramos would have understood but she was willing to bet not a single word penetrated his head.

The supremely confident, arrogant man who'd walked

into the courtroom looked shell-shocked. Poor diddums. Her heart bled for him. It really did.

Only when the prosecutor sat back down did any animation show on his handsome face, and he whispered into the ear of the man beside him, who in turn whispered down the line until the whispers reached the prosecutor, who got back up and shuffled over to Ramos. The pair of them whispered frantically between themselves. The whispering culminated in Ramos scrawling onto a piece of paper that was immediately handed to the Justice, who read it, rose to his feet, addressed the court, and then swept back into his room.

The buzz in the courtroom as everyone filed out was strong enough for Flora to feel it on her skin. The excitement coming from the press box and the many glances being thrown her way told Flora her stunt hadn't gone unnoticed. It couldn't be helped. She'd tried everything else.

Rather than join the exodus, she stayed seated and closed her eyes. The muscles on her face hurt from the tight, unmoving position she'd held them in and, now that she relaxed them, emotions she'd contained just as tightly rose to the surface and threatened to choke her.

Rubbing her belly, she concentrated on breathing in and out. Something was going to happen and she needed to be calm and in her zen zone to cope with whatever that something would be.

Would Ramos decide to ignore her obvious pregnancy just as he'd successfully ignored her these last eight months? Ignore was the wrong word. He hadn't ignored her. He'd ghosted her. He'd seduced her, kissed her *adios* and then cut her dead.

Or would he acknowledge her pregnancy but think it a jest? Or assume another man was the father?

She would put nothing past him.

If he ignored her or denied paternity then so be it. She was mentally prepared for that. She had the trial to get through and she needed to stay strong for Justin's sake.

She'd done her duty and ensured her baby's daddy knew their child existed. The rest was up to him. For Flora, best case scenario would be Ramos acknowledged their child, offered child support—she really didn't want to have to go the legal route for that—and limited his involvement to the odd visitation. He wouldn't want to be a full-time father, that was for sure, not with his lifestyle. A baby would definitely cramp his style.

'Mademoiselle?'

She opened her eyes.

An official beckoned her.

She summoned a smile and heaved herself to her feet. She hadn't realised how exhausted she was until she put one foot in front of the other. That silent confrontation with Ramos had drained her. She supposed it was because it had been so long in coming and she'd built it up so much in her head. The ache in her back felt more intense.

As she left the viewing gallery, she was about to head to her brother's designated room when the official touched her arm and pointed in the other direction.

'Mademoiselle? Come.'

Immediately pulled out of the zen zone she'd calmed herself into, Flora hesitated before following.

Okay, so it looked as if Ramos wasn't going to ignore her.

The official pushed a door open. It was a waiting room with a coffee machine and plump sofas and, though she'd expected to find him there, her heart still leapt back up her throat.

He was sitting on a single sofa, leaning forwards, hands locked together.

His dark brown eyes penetrated her from the first lock of their gazes.

Flora had imagined this moment so many times. She'd planned how she would act and what she would say. Act nonchalant. Speak only in practical terms about their child. Do not do or say anything that would make him think she felt anything for him but contempt.

The reality was very different. Enough emotions zoomed through her to make her nauseous with their strength. Hate. Fury. Despair. Longing. The last of them was the worst.

How could she long for him after the way he'd treated her?

How could she have fallen under his spell in the first place?

Flora had known Ramos since she was eleven years old and he and Justin eighteen-year-old students. The young Spanish man had been a regular presence in the Hillier home. He'd even joined them for Christmas a couple of times.

Her brother's closest friend, a veritable hunk in impeccably tailored clothing, a classically chiselled handsome face women swooned over...and, boy, didn't he know it. Flora had been determined not to become one of those swooners. The way Ramos and her brother treated women had nauseated her. They might as well have set up a deli counter and handed out numbers to the 'lucky' recipients who would be discarded in turn before they got stale.

Ramos had discarded Flora even quicker than he'd discarded the others.

His set jaw loosened enough for him to say, 'You should sit.'

Thirteen years she'd known him. That his lightly accented voice had a real depth and richness to it were qualities she'd only noticed the night they spent together.

Now, it fell like velvet on her ears and it shook her enough for her to force a laugh to cover it. 'That's the first thing you have to say to me? *You should sit?*'

'You look like you're about to collapse.'

Aww, he was concerned about her welfare. Such generosity of spirit.

Easing herself carefully onto a leather two-seater, she wished her huge size hadn't made her movements so ungainly and graceless when every inch of him reeked of sophistication. It was just another of the discrepancies between them, all weighted in his favour.

Until today, she'd rather enjoyed being so obviously pregnant. The number of smiles she would see as people clocked her watermelon belly lightened her heart. There was something magical about the late stage of pregnancy that people responded to and she liked that it made her feel less alone in a world where her mother was dead, her father an unreliable, useless deadbeat and her beloved brother incarcerated.

Now she felt none of the magic, only a weight in her chest that her precious child should be saddled with such an unworthy and undeserving father.

Ramos's full but firm lips were tightly compressed as his uncompromising gaze scrutinised every inch of her. He really did have beautiful eyes, so dark they could be mistaken for black, and with such depth that a woman could lose herself in them.

Flora had avoided looking into those eyes for years and a pang ripped through her heart to remember the night they had gazed at her with such intensity and then melted with something more than naked desire, something that had filled every cavity in her chest and seen her fall into their hypnotic pull.

'When is the child due?' he asked.

She blinked the unwelcome memory away and forced her voice to remain steady. 'In three weeks.'

He exhaled and inclined his head. 'I am to assume from your stunt in the courtroom that it is mine?'

'Yes.'

If he asked how she knew it was his, she would throw her bag at him.

'And I am to assume that your stunt was designed to bring attention to this to the whole world?'

Her mouth dropped open. Incredulous, she shook her head and laughed. 'Seriously?'

His jaw clenched again. 'What else am I supposed to think? A note to a member of my legal team would have been as effective.'

'I would have done that if I thought you'd read it.' She wished she could sit straight with ease and cross her legs, project the image she wanted him to see rather than the reality, which included swollen feet and ankles. Instead, she had to use her elbows for purchase to straighten. 'I've spent seven months trying to tell you.'

He raised a sceptical eyebrow.

Quelling the burst of fury this provoked and determined to speak without a hint of emotion, Flora leaned forwards as much as her belly would allow and eyeballed him. 'You blocked my phone number and email. I called two of your homes and spoke to two of your housekeepers. I spoke to your PA three times. I wrote you four letters. *Four.* I told you in every single one of those letters and the messages I left for you that I was pregnant with your child, but it wasn't until I made another call to your office and spoke to a temp that I was told you had instructed all communications from me in whatever form they came to be ignored or destroyed and that anyone who so much as whispered my name to you would be fired for gross misconduct. You cut me off dead and refused to have my name spoken in front of you, not just a refusal but a specific order—*that's* why I had to show you publicly. It was the only way to guarantee you'd notice.'

Ramos's hands were still clasped together but now the knuckles had whitened. The tension on his handsome face was such that the flick of a pebble onto it would see it shatter.

Low in Flora's belly, her baby shifted. It was a movement she adored, and had the effect of staunching the anger that had been building in her. She rubbed in big, sweeping motions and was rewarded with a foot or a hand poking against her palm.

She didn't want to get angry and lose her temper. Trying to maintain a zen edge for her baby's sake while her life was falling apart at the seams had, at times, felt impossible, but from the moment the pink line appeared on the pregnancy stick, protective love for her growing baby had overridden all the other emotions engulfing her. That love was primal, strong enough to douse the terror of a future raising a child alone without the mother she'd loved with all her heart and the brother who—for all his faults in his personal life—had always been there for her; a rock for her to lean on. Flora had found an inner strength she'd never known she had and she was not going to let Ramos undo all that hard work, especially not so close to the birth.

But it was so hard. Being in the same room as him

for the first time in eight months was awakening memories she'd spent eight months trying her best to forget...

Waking in his arms, their mouths fusing together and then the fusion of their bodies before Ramos woke enough to drag himself away for protection...that memory came in a rush of vivid colour. The passion she'd experienced with him, the utter rightness she'd felt in his arms.

She pulled the strap of her bag over her shoulder. If the pain in her back hadn't sharpened, she would have hauled herself to her feet. She wanted out of this room and away from the man who'd taken her to heaven and dropped her into hell.

'Well, you know about the baby now,' she said, speaking tightly through the pain. 'Let's get this trial over and done with and then we can talk about your future involvement.'

He leaned his muscular body forward, animation returning to his eyes, his movements like those human statues she'd seen on the Embankment and Trafalgar Square. 'Future involvement?'

'If you want to be a part of his or her life...' She pinched the bridge of her nose, knowing he would likely want no involvement at all. 'Entirely up to you, but I will need child support. The sooner the better.'

Distaste flashed on his face. 'So that's what that little scene was all about. You're after my money.'

Flora clenched her teeth and swallowed back a fresh wave of anger. 'You're the father. You had a right to know, but your insistence on having Justin tried in a country where every criminal trial is prosecuted whether or not the defendant pleads guilty has wiped me out financially.'

The clenching of his jaw was pronounced.

'*Someone* had to help him.' The pain had lessened enough for Flora to straighten her back, the act of straightening her spine injecting another dose of steel into it. 'You chose to prosecute him in a country that doesn't have legal aid and made sure all his assets were frozen. Well, *I* paid for his legal fees, by remortgaging my home and taking a loan on my business and I am now skint, so yes, I want your money, as much as the law entitles me to but only so I don't have to raise our child in poverty, and if you want to think me a gold-digger for that then be my guest. I couldn't give a fig what you think of me. I care about two things—my brother and my child. You've already ruined my brother and I will not let you ruin my child too, and if you want to fight me about money then fine, when the press next swarm around me, I will talk to them and I will give a statement and I will tell the world how the father of my unborn child seduced me when I went to him pleading for mercy and then cut me dead, and I will name and shame you.'

His bronzed skin darkened with every word she said, a tight contortion of emotions playing on his face. And then he smiled.

It was the cruellest smile she'd ever seen.

'Will you tell them how you prostituted yourself too?'

CHAPTER TWO

RAMOS'S ICILY DELIVERED words hit Flora like a slap.

A burning flush crawled up her neck and covered her face.

'You talk of me seducing you…?' He shook his head, the smile twisting. 'What a selective memory you have. Let me refresh it for you. *You* came to *me*. You shared a drink with me and while your mouth was pleading with me to show mercy to your brother, your big, beautiful, seductive brown eyes were eating me alive. You were as sweet and seductive as chocolate. A hot little *bombón*.'

His voice had developed into a cruel, silken caress.

'You leaned into me for that first kiss. You put your hand on my chest *right here*.' He put a hand to the spot. 'And then you touched my face.'

Flora covered her flaming cheeks and squeezed her eyes tightly shut against the invading memories of the moment she'd finally fallen into the hypnotic spell of Ramos's eyes.

'You waited until we were both naked before you saw fit to mention that you were a virgin.' His laughter was bitter. 'You must really love your brother to sell your virginity like that.'

'It wasn't like that and you know it,' she whispered.

God help her, it had been *nothing* like that. It had just happened. One minute they'd been talking, the next...

No, she didn't want to remember that. Not that. Not the most thrilling, heady moment of her entire life.

Flora had spent years actively avoiding the Alejandro Ramos deli counter and then when she'd woken in his bed in the most delirious bubble of happiness, she'd been stupid enough to believe that what they'd shared had been so wonderful and beautiful that it had moved him as much as it had moved her.

For a few short hours she'd been stupid enough to believe that he felt something for her that went beyond sex.

An edge formed in his voice. 'Yes, *querida*, it was like that. You came to me with the implicit intention of seducing me into mercy and you so nearly got away with it.'

She snapped her eyes back open.

His top lip curled and he shook his head disparagingly. 'I read the message from him.'

'What message?' She didn't have a clue what he was on about.

'From your brother. In the morning. While you were sleeping. I went downstairs. I wanted to surprise you with breakfast in bed.' He shook his head again. 'Your bag had spilt over the coffee table.'

It had toppled when Ramos had lifted her into his arms to carry her upstairs to his bedroom and her foot had knocked the table. Her heart throbbed at the memory of it.

'The message flashed on your phone when I picked it up to put it in the bag for you. Do you remember what it said?'

Flora remembered little of that day. She'd been floating too high on her delirious Alejandro Ramos bubble of bliss for anything else to reach her.

The evening had been a different matter. When she realised he'd deliberately stood her up, the bubble she'd been floating in had plummeted so hard and so fast the landing had bruised every part of her.

'It said, Any news, Flo? Did your charms work their magic on him?' He laughed, a horrid, bitter sound totally unlike his usual throaty laughter. His top lip curled again. 'I should have guessed when you turned up at my door dressed for seduction that Hillier had sent you.'

'I can't believe you've interpreted it that way,' she said hoarsely, her brain reeling. 'And Justin didn't send me. He knew what I was doing because I told him, but me coming to see you was *my* idea.'

Flora had driven her hire car from the Monte Cleure prison over the border into Spain and then on to Barcelona with her brother's gaunt face lodged in her retinas, desperately wondering what words she could say to make the notoriously unforgiving Alejandro Ramos show mercy to his best friend.

Justin deserved punishment, she knew that, but he needed help too.

Her brother had always been there for her: the boy who humoured his baby sister when she demanded he play dolls with her, the young adolescent who walked her to school, made her packed lunches and helped with her homework when their mum was working, the adolescent who patiently taught her to play chess and made himself late for his school leavers party so they could finish a game of Scrabble, the young man who taught her how to drive and then forgave her when she reversed his precious car into a lamppost.

He'd always been there for her and she would always be there for him, even if the guilt and shame over what he'd done didn't hang over him like a shroud.

'Did your charms work their magic on him?' Ramos repeated the quote in a snarl, and for the first time Flora saw real anger rise to the surface.

'Do you really believe I traded my virginity to save my brother's skin?' The horror of it turned her blood to ice.

He just stared at her, only the tightening of his lips betraying his thoughts.

Dear heavens, he *did* believe it.

Ramos thought she'd gone to him with the deliberate intention of exchanging her body for her brother's freedom.

Justin's message—his phone was the one thing the Monte Cleure prison authorities had allowed him to keep—had been a form of gallows humour she now remembered. He'd thought her mission to beg for Ramos's mercy a fool's errand.

Despair had her throw her arms in the air. 'I *never* expected what happened between us to happen. I came to you not knowing if you'd even open the door for me.'

'But I did open the door to you,' he said, unmoved. 'And *you* made the first move...you, who had always treated me with such disdain.' His nostrils flared, the anger that had slipped back beneath the handsome mask showing itself again. 'Whether you intended it to go as far as it did...' He inhaled deeply then shrugged, his large body relaxing. 'Play with fire, expect to be burned.'

'So that's why you ghosted me?' She was hardly able to form the words over the dizziness in her head.

She'd assumed it was because their night had either meant nothing to him or his hatred of her brother overrode any feelings he might have developed for her or because she'd been such a boring lover that he'd rather fire all his staff than see her again. Or a combination of all the above.

She'd been wrong on all counts. Ramos had ghosted her because he thought *she* had used *him*.

He hooked an ankle over a thigh, his voice returning to its normal velvety timbre. 'You tried to play me for a fool, what else did you expect?'

A fresh swell of pain in her lower back struck and all she could give in the way of denial was a hissed, 'I *didn't*.'

He raised another sceptical eyebrow and studied her with that intense scrutinising look that burned through her skin. She could practically feel him thinking what his next move would be, and when his handsome features loosened into a sardonic smile and he folded his arms across his chest, fearful anticipation of what came next had her holding her breath.

'It no longer matters,' he dismissed decisively. 'You came to me for your brother's freedom—I am sure this is not the way you thought you would gain it, not back then, but it has worked. Congratulations. I am willing to drop the charges against him…'

His words hanging between them, his smile widened. 'But to get that freedom for him, you will have to marry me.'

The room spun around her so quickly and so suddenly that Flora had to grip hard on the arm of the sofa to spot herself back into place.

Her vocal cords were paralysed.

Ramos laughed. A less bitter laugh but one that still landed like nails on a chalkboard. 'I see that I have shocked you into silence—that must be a first. But that's okay. You can thank me later.'

That unfroze her vocal cords! '*Thank* you?'

'Your brother gets his freedom and, as my wife, you will have access to more money than you could have dreamed of. I will have a prenuptial agreement drawn up, of course, but you will be very well provided for.' He flashed his teeth at her. 'See? I can be generous. Be nice to me and I can be *very* generous.'

She shook her head, utterly dumbfounded. 'I wouldn't marry you if you were the last man on earth.'

He shrugged as if he didn't care. 'If you want your brother to be freed you will.'

'But why, when you hate me so much?'

'I like to think of it as self-preservation.' His dark eyes glittered. 'Sometimes it is wise to keep your enemy close.'

'But…why marriage? Why something so drastic?'

Rising to his feet and removing his phone from the inside pocket of his suit jacket, he smiled as if she were a simpleton. 'Because, my little *bombón*, I know how much you hate me. I want you where I can keep an eye on you and make it impossible for you to keep our child from me and poison them against me. Now excuse me one moment. I need to update my legal team.'

With that, he strode to the other side of the room, turning his back on her at the same moment a sudden tightening down low in her abdomen sucked the air from her lungs.

Breathing hard until the cramping pain subsided, Flora tried her hardest to find her zen and kill the panic that was hitting her from all directions.

The abdominal pain she'd experienced was only a Braxton Hicks, she assured herself. She'd had a number of them in recent weeks. It was her body's way of preparing itself for the birth.

And Ramos was just playing with her. Punishing

her some more for the crime he believed she'd committed of sleeping with him as a ruse to soften him to her
brother's cause.

It devastated her to know he believed that of her, but
it explained so much. If she had learned anything about
Alejandro Ramos over the years it was that he held no
forgiveness. He'd been cutting people—friends—who
he considered to have abused his trust from his life without mercy and without hearing their defence long before
Justin's betrayal.

In a minute he would tell her it had all been one big
jest and then he would sweep out of the room and continue his destruction of the man who'd been his closest friend.

She could scarcely believe this was the same man
who'd made love to her with such intense passion and
awoken such intense passion in *her*.

Flora's feelings for Ramos had always been intense,
from the minute he'd first walked into her childhood
home with the swagger of someone who'd been a regular visitor his entire life.

He'd been eighteen years old, gregarious and gorgeous. She'd been eleven and resentful at having to share
the precious time she had with her brother, who she'd
missed terribly since he'd left for university. Her resentment grew when Ramos tagged along to many more of
Justin's visits home and mushroomed at her brother's
sycophantic behaviour.

If Ramos cracked a joke, Justin would laugh as if it
was the funniest thing he'd ever heard. If Ramos gave an
opinion on something, Justin would treat his words with
the same respect he would an academic philosopher.
Hillier and Ramos, they called each other, like something from a bad police television programme. Buddies

on the university rugby pitch, drinking and pulling buddies off it. Sometimes they even remembered to study.

Resentment and jealousy turned markedly darker when she turned thirteen and went to stay with Justin for a weekend. By then, he'd moved into the six-bedroom house with its own basement games room that Ramos's billionaire father had bought his only child. He'd promised their mum that Ramos would be spending the weekend with his father in Barcelona and that it would be just him and Flora at the Oxford house. He'd spoil her rotten, taking her around Oxford's plentiful art shops and museums, and treating her to dinner at a posh restaurant. He'd even bought her a plethora of embroidery supplies. Even back then, Flora had a love of embroidery and a vague plan to turn her love into a career.

When she'd woken the next morning, she'd been sleepily opening her bedroom door when the door on the other side of the vast square hallway opened. She'd frozen on the spot.

Ramos had come out, laughing over his shoulder, leaned over and picked something off the floor then strode back in and closed the door behind him. He hadn't noticed his buddy's baby sister watching him.

He'd been naked.

The hot, sticky sensation that had flushed over and through her skin at the sight of his nude body, all muscular yet lean with a smattering of dark hair in the centre of his chest that ran down to his abdomen and tapered until it thickened at the place where his large *thing* was, had confused and disturbed her, and she'd hidden under her bed covers until Justin had come in to see if she was awake.

Later, after an awkward breakfast with Justin, Ramos and a pretty blonde woman wearing a dressing gown that was far too big for her, Flora had overheard Ramos apologise to Justin.

'Sorry, Hillier,' he'd said. 'Forgot your sister would be here. My father took a last-minute break to our villa in Martinique so I flew back and hooked up with Miranda. Sorry if she was too, err, vocal.'

She hadn't heard her brother's reply because the hot, sticky sensation had flushed through her again. She'd been growing up. She'd known exactly what Ramos had meant.

For over a decade, something about Alejandro Ramos had put her perpetually on edge and made her insides feel all swollen. Whatever those feelings were or meant, be they loathing or something more dangerous, she was now only weeks from giving birth to his child.

His smile was smug when he ended the call and strolled back to her. 'Good news,' he said, perching on the arm of the chair he'd been sitting on. 'We can marry right now.'

'You what?' she said dumbly.

'We can marry now… Well, in an hour. I've got the team drawing up the prenup for us, so we'll need to get that signed first, and sign a declaration that we are unencumbered and don't have other spouses hidden away, but other than that we are good to go.'

For the first time she realised he was actually being serious. 'But…we *can't*.'

'Monte Cleure law says we can. We both have our passports here. We will marry and then I will have all the charges dropped and your brother will be a free man.'

'Ramos, will you slow down a minute?' she begged. The room was starting to spin again.

'When you are my wife, you will call me Alejandro.'

'I've called you Ramos since my brother brought you home thirteen years ago.'

'You called me Alejandro the night we conceived our child,' he corrected silkily.

Heat filled her head to remember how she'd cried out his name when he'd brought her to her first ever climax, and she pressed her palm to her burning forehead to blot the memories away.

She sucked in a long breath. 'Are you really prepared to drop all the charges against Justin?'

'If you marry me, yes.'

'Can you do that?'

'Without me, there is no case. I will withdraw my testimony and all the evidence.'

'The prosecutor might still go ahead with it.'

'He won't.'

Frustration had her raise her voice for the first time. 'But how can you know?'

'You will just have to trust me.'

'Yeah, right. Get the charges dropped and then I'll marry you.'

'Do I look stupid?'

'I know you're not stupid, but it's the fairest way of going about it.'

'Possibly, but the sad fact is, my pretty little *bombón*, you are not to be trusted, so it's marriage first, charges dropped second or no deal. And if you think you can marry me and then divorce me as soon as your brother's set free then I warn you now, the charges will be slapped back on him and he will spend the best years of his life in a prison cell. There will be no divorce.'

As languid as a panther, he stepped to her and lowered his face. His spicy scent seeped into her airwaves and before his hypnotic stare could capture her, Flora closed her eyes tightly and held her breath.

He whispered, 'One hour, and then your nightmare will be over. Your brother will be free and you will have all the riches you could ever want.' He traced a finger lightly over her cheek.

His touch made her stiffen.

It also set her pulses surging.

All her nerves strained as his face moved closer. His breath whispered against the sensitive skin of her ear, sending tingles dancing through her.

'It looks like your selling of your soul to the devil has paid off,' he murmured. 'I congratulate you. Your brother will be very proud when you tell him how you bought his freedom.'

The air around her swirled as he walked away.

Flora kept her eyes tight shut until she heard the door close.

Once certain she was alone, she wrapped her arms around her belly and expelled the breath she'd held for so long, and tried to clear the fuzz in her head enough to think.

Thinking proved impossible. Her head was too full.

This was crazy.

How could he still affect her like this? It shouldn't be possible, not after everything he'd done.

But he thought she'd slept with him for her brother. He thought she'd used him…

There had been a moment—only a brief one—when she thought she'd seen hurt flash in his eyes.

Oh, this was all so confusing! As *if* she could have hurt him. The man had the hide of a rhino.

But even if she had and if he'd genuinely misinterpreted her brother's message, that didn't excuse him ghosting her, not after the night they'd shared, or from kissing her goodbye the way he had and making promises to see her he'd never had any intention of keeping.

If he'd genuinely believed that then why hadn't he confronted her about it? The answer to that came quickly—that was what Ramos did. Wrong him and he severed you from his life without thought or hesitation.

He *couldn't* mean to marry her.

Another tightening cramp low in her abdomen cut her panicked thoughts off sharply. Pressing a hand to the underside of her belly, frightened to find that her belly seemed to have sucked itself in and that she could feel the outline of her baby even more clearly, she gritted her teeth and breathed through her nose.

By the time it eased, her forehead was damp with perspiration.

How long had passed since the last one? Twenty minutes? More? Less?

She forced herself to think clearly and take note of the time. She'd had four Braxton Hicks total, each days apart. None had gone on as long as those two. None had been as painful.

Was her baby coming now? It couldn't be! It was too soon. She wasn't due for another three weeks.

Her back was aching again. It hadn't really stopped aching, just ebbed to a dull ache. It wasn't dull now.

Her tear ducts had started working again too. There was a hot sting in her eyes and she wished with all her heart that her mum were still here. She needed her desperately, for advice and comfort over the coming hours.

But her mother had been dead two years and there was no one else she could turn to for advice, at least no one whose advice she trusted, and, feeling more alone than she'd done since Justin's arrest, Flora began to rock lightly, backwards and forwards.

Marry Ramos and set Justin free.

Marry Ramos and—

'You are required to read and sign this, *mademoiselle*.'

Flora blinked. She hadn't noticed the door open.

The suited woman handed a document to her.

Flora cleared her throat. 'What is it?'

'For you to sign.'

'Helpful,' she muttered. She'd taken in only that it was a prenuptial agreement when the next contraction hit.

Her fingers tightened around the document but she gritted her teeth tightly and kept her gaze fixed on it, refusing to allow so much as a moan of pain leave her mouth.

'Are you okay, *mademoiselle*?'

She nodded and managed to make a noise that sounded a bit like *ahuh*. Once she'd ridden the pain out, she glanced at her watch. Ten minutes since the last one.

Don't panic, she told herself. *Don't panic.*

The door flew open. Ramos appeared.

'Are you ready to sign?' he asked.

She took a deep breath. 'Have you got the papers retracting your evidence?'

'It's in hand. As soon as our marriage licence is signed it will be lodged.'

Flora closed her eyes briefly then focused them on the document in her hand. Figures with lots of zeros flashed before her but she paid them scant attention. All she needed to check was that it dealt only with the financial side of their marriage and it did.

'Can I have a pen, please?' she asked the woman.

A pen was produced and a table pushed to her.

Marry Ramos and set her brother free.

Marry Ramos and tie herself to the most loathsome man on the planet.

Justin won.

Flora signed.

Ramos's smile was pure satisfaction. 'Time for us to marry.'

CHAPTER THREE

IGNORING RAMOS'S OUTSTRETCHED hand of help, Flora hoisted herself onto her feet.

Her baby was coming.

She'd get the farce of a wedding done with, ensure Ramos kept his word about Justin, and then she would tell him he was going to be a father imminently.

Plenty of time, she assured herself. Ten minutes between contractions was fine. Her English midwife had told her she probably wouldn't be admitted into hospital until the contractions were four minutes apart. That would likely take hours. Right now, she needed to concentrate on Justin's freedom. She had no idea how Ramos would react to her being in labour and didn't dare risk telling him just yet.

She was in labour!

A zing of pure excitement flooded her. Her baby was coming!

Soon, very, very soon, she would meet her baby.

'I assume the financial package is to your liking,' Ramos observed as they walked up the corridor.

The tone of his voice made her curious. 'Sorry?'

He shrugged. 'You were smiling.'

'Oh. Right. You assumed I was smiling about the money?'

'In a few minutes you are going to be a very wealthy woman.'

His cynical assumption barely doused the excitement still rippling inside her. *Her baby was coming!*

'Just set my brother free. That's all I care about.'

And that my baby is born safe and healthy.

'Sure.'

She stopped walking and faced him. 'Believe what you like, Ramos…' oh, she did enjoy the tightening on his face when she addressed him by his surname '…but I'm marrying you for Justin's freedom. You will never—'

Her intention of telling him he would never be a husband to her in the true sense of the word was cut from her tongue when another contraction hit.

Luckily she was close to a wall and slammed a hand on it to steady herself, and managed to focus on her watch. Uh oh. Nine minutes.

'Flora?'

For the first time she detected concern in Ramos's voice.

She waved her other hand at him and rode the wave of pain. 'Heartburn,' she managed to gasp.

As soon as she felt it start to abate, she breathed deeply and got walking again. 'Where are we marrying?'

'The civil court in the building next door.'

'Okay.'

Just breathe.

'Are you sure you're all right?'

'Yep. Let's get this done.' She upped her pace. She had eight or nine minutes until the next contraction hit.

As luck would have it, there was no need for them to go outside as there was an internal passageway adjoining the two court buildings.

'I need to use the bathroom,' she said once they were in the civil courts, and headed for the door with the sign for the ladies on it.

She closed the door right at the moment the next contraction struck.

Once it had subsided, she splashed water on her face and looked in the mirror. Immediately, she wished she hadn't. Her shoulder-length chestnut hair, usually so glossy, was lank, her usually golden cheeks flush. Even her eyes—alien eyes, her brother always called them, on account of them being so large—had lost their sparkle.

And no wonder.

She was in labour and about to marry Ramos.

Flora had never imagined herself marrying. Men didn't hang around, something she'd known since she was small. Women were disposable. For Ramos, as with her father and her brother, this was especially true.

And if she had imagined it—and she'd be a liar if she didn't admit the odd idle daydream of a wedding day had sneaked up on her over the years—the faceless groom had been someone who worshipped her, who swore to never stray, who swore to love her as she got older and her looks faded. Someone she worshipped in return.

Not this: coerced into a shotgun marriage where the only emotion between the bride and groom was mutual loathing.

It wasn't loathing that had led to their child's conception...

She cut that thought straight off.

Ramos was waiting for her outside the bathroom door. He looked at her closely.

'Come on,' she insisted before he could say anything. Her brother's freedom was minutes away. 'Let's get married.'

The next contraction struck seconds after the 'ceremony' began. This time she was seated next to Ramos, the official on the other side of the desk busy directing all his conversation at him, so she was able to ride through it without either of them noticing.

All Flora was required to do was hand over her passport, give some details about herself and her parents and then it was time for her to repeat some words—the ceremony itself was conducted in English—just as Ramos had done, and sign the wedding certificate.

It was as she leaned forward to sign that a contraction hit her that was so strong she was helpless to stop the groan of pain from escaping.

'Flora?' This time there was alarm in Ramos's voice.

Not daring to look at him, she squeezed her eyes shut and gripped her fingertips onto the table. When it had passed, she grabbed the pen and signed.

Only then did she look at Ramos.

'We're done,' she said hoarsely. 'Now free my brother.'

Not taking his eyes from her face, he said something that sounded like an order to the official, then murmured to her, 'Let me get you some water.'

'Free my...*oh*.'

She focused on Ramos's face. Properly focused. Gazed into his worried eyes. And then she looked down at the puddle of water forming between her feet.

Another contraction hit and this time panic hit with it.

The time between contractions was coming too quickly and she couldn't stop the fear from showing when she met Ramos's appalled stare.

'It is coming now?' he asked faintly.

She nodded.

He sprang into action.

Jumping to his feet, he flung the door open and shouted out an order into the corridor while simultaneously putting his phone to his ear and barking an order at whoever answered it.

In what felt like hours but was in reality a couple of minutes at most, Ramos had an arm around her and was gently helping her into a wheelchair.

'An ambulance is on its way,' he said in a soothing tone she'd never heard him speak with before. 'You're going to Monte Cleure's best hospital. Its top obstetrician is on his way and will have everything ready for when you arrive.'

She focused on his eyes and nodded jerkily.

She could do this. She could do this. She was prepared. She could do this.

Soon she was being wheeled into the back of an ambulance breathing into a portable gas and air tank.

Ramos hung back to speak to a paramedic and then the panic really hit her.

Her baby was coming. Throughout the pregnancy her midwife had spoken about the importance of a birthing partner but Flora had shrugged off her concerns and brightly assured her—and assured herself—that she could do it alone.

The truth was, there had been no one to ask.

She loved her brother but the thought of him being in the birthing room was too icky to contemplate, even if she had thought he'd be free to be there. Also, Justin was spectacularly squeamish. Same with her deadbeat father, who'd probably turn up a week after she called him. Her extended family had turned against Justin and so turned against Flora for supporting him. Her old tight-knit group of school friends all had busy lives and now all lived too far away to reliably be there. She'd made a few new friends since her move to London but there was no real closeness, no one she could turn to.

So she'd prepared herself to go through the birth alone just as she'd had to swallow her fears and prepare herself for raising her child alone too. She'd truly thought she was mentally ready for it but, now that the moment was here, terror at what lay ahead struck and as soon as Ramos was back by her side she removed the tube from her mouth and grabbed his hand.

'Don't leave me,' she begged. 'Please, don't leave me.'

A furrow formed in his brow. 'You want me to come to the hospital?'

Another contraction gripped her and she shoved the tube into her mouth and breathed in and out with it, squeezing Ramos's hand so tightly in the process he winced at the strength of it.

'Please,' she panted when the worst of it was over, uncaring that tears were rolling down her face. 'I don't want to do this alone. Please, Alejandro, don't make me do this alone. Please.'

He studied her intently a moment longer before his features softened. Smoothing her hair off her forehead with the hand not being squeezed to death, he placed a kiss to it. 'I won't leave your side. I promise.'

And just like that, the fear that had snuck up on her and come close to smothering her lessened and she flopped her head back.

'Thank you,' she breathed with relief.

'Shoot me,' Flora begged Ramos in the birthing room when the latest contraction subsided enough for her to speak. 'Please. Get a gun and shoot me.'

The midwife smiled sympathetically. She'd heard it all before.

Ramos kissed the fingers gripping his hand so tightly. His other hand was rubbing her lower back. 'I know it hurts, *querida*. You hold onto me, okay? You can do this.'

'I *can't*.'

He kissed her fingers again. 'You can. I have every faith in you. You're beautiful and brave and strong, just hold on a little longer. You're almost there.'

Two hours later, Ramos gently placed their son back to her breast and pulled the visitor's chair as close to her bed in the private room she'd been moved to as he could get. His eyes were shining with wonder and pride. 'He's perfect.'

High on the precious little bundle whose precious little face was nuzzling into her skin and high on the release of hormones flooding her system, Flora felt her chest swell with so much love she thought it might burst out of her.

She gazed at Ramos and took in his stubbly jaw, creased shirt and dishevelled hair. She'd never seen him anything but immaculately groomed before and the sight of him like this and the knowledge of *why* he was like this filled her chest even more.

He was all dishevelled because he'd spent six hours right by her side, four of those being used as her human form of pain relief.

The pain was already a distant memory.

'He looks like you,' she said dreamily.

He traced his fingers lightly over their son's head. 'Do you think?'

She nodded and smothered a yawn. 'Just like you.'

His broad shoulders rose and he gazed into her eyes with the same sense of wonder he kept staring at their son with. 'I'm so proud of you.'

Feeling a blush form on her cheeks, she tried to make light of it. 'Aw, shucks, it was nothing.'

He snickered but then the amusement faded and the wonder in his stare returned. 'Thank you for letting me share that.'

'Thank you for being there.' He'd been wonderful. It was an unselfish, giving, empathetic side to him that she'd forgotten existed, but she had seen that side of him before, in the months leading to her mother's death. Ramos's regular visits had never failed to bring a smile to her mum's face.

'Sorry about your fingers,' she added sleepily.

The grin returned. 'My own birthing war wound.'

Another yawn crept up on her before she could cover it, a wave of exhaustion hitting her like a sledgehammer.

Ramos noticed. Lifting their son from her arms, he gently said, 'Sleep, *querida*. I will wake you when he's ready for another feed.'

Her 'thank you' had barely left her lips before sleep claimed her.

'Have you chosen a name for him yet?' Ramos asked soon after his return from a quick shopping trip for baby clothes and provisions. He'd bought so many cute little outfits that there was no way their baby would wear them all before he outgrew them.

Night had long fallen. Their little boy had just been fed and was now sleeping in his daddy's arms dressed in an adorable romper suit.

Happily exhausted, Flora nestled her cheek deeper into her pillow and gazed at her husband and son.

Her husband and son...

This was going to take a lot of getting her head around.

'I always thought if it was a boy I would call him Benjamin for my grandfather. Do you have any ideas?'

'You did all the hard work. You should choose. If you want to call him Benjamin then I have no objections.'

'You're his father. You should have a say.' And the way he'd been during the birth and the way he was behaving towards them now showed he wanted to *be* a father. This was something she hadn't dared hope for her child, not after the way Ramos had severed her from his life, but, having grown up with her father on the periphery of her life, Flora would always choose for her child to have more if it was possible. She'd forgotten that the man who could be so vengefully cruel when crossed had a generous heart when touched, and it made her chest swell to see that heart so touched by his own flesh and blood.

For a long moment he just stared at her before a wry smile spread on his face. 'I am struggling to get my head around being a father. This whole day has been…' He shook his head, clearly unable to find the right words.

'A roller coaster?' she suggested. That's exactly how it felt for her. At least she'd had a good seven months to prepare for motherhood. Ramos had had little more than seven hours to prepare for fatherhood. Yes, it was his own fault but, in her softened, hormonal baby state, Flora could appreciate how overwhelming it must be for him.

'*Sí*. A roller coaster,' he agreed. 'This is not at all how I expected my day to end.'

'I didn't expect my day to end like this either. I thought I had three weeks left before this little one came along, and I definitely didn't think I would end it as the wife of my mortal enemy.'

The wry smile turned into a grin that in itself evolved into a snicker. 'A rather extreme method of calling a truce.'

'Who said anything about a truce?' she said lightly. 'This is a mere suspension of hostilities.'

'A ceasefire?'

'Exactly. And it's a ceasefire I think we should do our best to hold, for this little one's sake.'

'I'm glad you think that. I don't want there to be war between us, *querida*.'

Understanding flowed between them that, for their son, they were both prepared to make the best of things.

Flora dragged her stare from him and settled it on their son in his arms.

She sighed.

She had to be careful and remember who she'd married.

Sharing the birth had bonded them—how could it not have?—but she mustn't let the hormones and euphoria flooding her cloud her judgement or soften her too much against him. Whenever there was a high, a low was sure to follow. These magical first hours with their baby wouldn't last. Ramos was still Ramos.

But, for now, it was the three of them cocooned together and she was glad her little boy got to bond with his father.

'Are there any names that are special or meaningful to you?' she asked. 'What about your father's name? Rafael, isn't it?'

He pulled a dismissive face. 'No.'

That surprised her. She knew little about Ramos's father other than that he was supremely wealthy and went through wives as if they were going out of fashion, but she'd always had the impression father and son were close. 'Why not?'

'Just, no.'

'Oi.' She stretched an arm out and jabbed a finger to his arm. 'We've only been married a few hours. You can't start keeping secrets from me yet, you know.'

Melting dark eyes held hers before crinkling and looking down at their son nestled so securely in his strong arms. 'My father is selfish. He's always been selfish.'

She gave a sympathetic smile. 'We finally have something in common.'

His gaze fell back on her. 'Yes. We both have selfish fathers.'

There was little of Flora's life Ramos didn't already know. He'd been an intrinsic part of it for many years.

'What was your mother like?' she asked. For obvious reasons—the obvious being that she'd spent more than half her life actively avoiding conversation with him—she knew little about his childhood and home life apart from the things Justin had mentioned. She knew his mother had died of sepsis when he was ten, the only story Justin had ever related to her about Ramos that had made her heart pang for him.

'Bossy.' His mouth made a swirling motion. 'Very bossy. And very good at getting her own way. Like a sensei. She would make me put my toys away or straighten my clothes just by looking at me.'

She smiled. 'My mum could be like that too. With Justin. Not me. I always put my toys away.' Flora's mum had more than made up for her useless father.

'I remember,' he said drily. 'You were always such a serious child.'

'Not always.'

'Always when I saw you. And disapproving of me too—I would walk into a room and your little nose would go in the air.'

He was more perceptive than she'd credited. Ramos was so staggeringly arrogant she'd assumed he'd never noticed her hostility.

'I thought you were a bad influence on Justin,' she admitted.

A shadow immediately fell on his face. 'No one can be a bad influence on him,' he denied tautly.

'You were.'

'No.'

'He was always trying to impress you.'

He shrugged. 'Most people try to impress me.' The shadow lifted and a smile played on his lips. 'You are one of the rare exceptions.'

Unsure whether he was complimenting her or not, unsure whether she wanted it to be a compliment or not, she cautiously asked, 'Where is he?'

'Hillier? Probably celebrating his reprieve in a hotel bar with a woman or two on his arm.'

She ignored the slight on her brother's morals. They were traits he'd picked up from this man, but, with her body and emotions softened from her newborn baby, not something she wanted to think about right then.

'So he is free?'

'That was the deal.' An edge had come into his voice. 'Hillier gets away with stealing from me and can resume his life as if nothing happened.'

'Hardly. His life is ruined.'

His eyes turned cold. 'He has no one to blame but himself.'

'He knows that.' She swallowed. 'He's desperate to make amends with you.'

'He could start by repaying the million euros he stole from me but seeing as he stole from my casino to repay debts incurred at my rival's casino, I will never see that money again.'

'He was in over his head and not in his right mind,' she reminded him quietly. 'You know how badly Mum's death affected him.'

He knew too how close and protective her brother had been of his mother and sister, the self-proclaimed man of the house since the age of seven when their mum had kicked their dad out. All those weekends Ramos spent in the Hillier family home were because his party animal best mate needed to satisfy himself the females in his family were well.

Justin might have hidden the depths of his despair at her death from Ramos, but Ramos knew all about it because Flora had explained most of it to him the night she'd turned up at his home.

He'd heard her out. His expression had been inscrutable as she'd explained how Justin had developed a gambling addiction and how the owners of the casino he'd been secretly going to had continually extended his credit until he owed them a few grand shy of a million euros. The dark swirling in Ramos's eyes had convinced her she was getting through to him, but she'd never had the chance to lay everything out because the dark swirling had intensified and...

And she didn't want to remember what happened next. It had been madness. Heavenly madness.

Jaw clenched, Ramos tilted his head back and fixed his gaze on the ceiling. When he eventually spoke it was through teeth that were clearly gritted together. 'My mother died when I was a child. I didn't use that as an excuse to lie and cheat and steal, and I cannot believe that your mother would accept her death as an excuse for Hillier to do all that to me.'

'Mum would be devastated about it,' Flora agreed. 'He's behaved terribly but he wasn't in his right mind, I swear, and if you would agree to see him and let him—'

'I will never see him again,' he cut in, dropping his gaze back on her with a stare that brooked no argument. 'And Benjamin is to have nothing to do with him either, is that understood?'

'He's my brother,' she reminded him lowly.

His nostrils flared. 'I'm not going to stop you from seeing him but he's a liar and a thief and I don't want Benjamin anywhere near him.'

For a moment, Flora eyeballed him back, but only for a moment.

This was the most momentous day of her life and she didn't want to ruin the magic of her son's birth for a battle she was unlikely to win. Not yet, anyway. Maybe one day.

There was a tightening in her chest to realise she'd committed herself to many days as his wife. Thousands of them. For her beautiful, precious boy's sake, she would do her best to spend them in peace.

'Benjamin?' she whispered softly.

Ramos's dark eyes narrowed in suspicion before the glare on his face melted away and he bestowed her with a smile that made her heart expand. '*Sí*. Benjamin. It's a good name. I like it.'

She couldn't believe how much this pleased her. 'Then you should choose his middle name.'

'There is one obvious choice for that.'

'Which is…?'

'Alejandro,' he answered smugly.

CHAPTER FOUR

THE NEXT FEW days spent recovering in hospital passed in a blurry whirl. Ramos didn't leave their side, going as far as to cram his tall frame into a single foldable bed provided by the hospital every night. Anything Flora wanted, he made sure she got, whether it was a cup of tea or a bowl of her favourite comfort food: macaroni cheese. He gave her an arm to lean on when she needed to walk across the room to the bathroom or wanted to sit outside with their son in the shaded pretty hospital garden. She drew the line at him helping her to bath, however, and got the ever-helpful nurse assigned to her to assist instead. Birth had stripped her of any dignity she had, but that had been an exceptional circumstance and one she had no intention of dwelling on.

The little bubble the three of them formed was never destined to last though, and on the third morning Flora was filled with sadness when she and Benjamin were discharged. She was also filled with resolve.

She and Ramos had proved they could get on. They'd proved they could be effective parents together. She would start her married life with a positive frame of mind and hope that they could make their marriage work as best it could under the circumstances of its founding.

She had no illusions about the man she'd married but would take it one day at a time.

Ramos had had her dress dry-cleaned. He'd also conjured up a hairbrush for her, which was just as well as the second they stepped out of the hospital's main door they were greeted with the blinding flash of cameras and questions being lobbed from every direction.

Instinctively, she clung to Ramos's arm and pressed herself close to his side. He carried Benjamin in the car seat he'd had delivered to the hospital earlier that morning, and wrapped his free arm protectively around her.

Barely seconds could have passed before the jostling crowd was pushed back by four no-nonsense man mountains, but they didn't move back far enough for Flora not to hear their shouts. Most of them were in French and Spanish but she caught a few English ones too.

'Is the baby yours, Alejandro?'

'Are you going to have a DNA test?'

'Was this a trap to get him to drop the charges against your brother, Flora?'

'How long have you two been lovers?'

'What do you think of the footage of Aimee crying, Alejandro?'

'Did you forget to tell Aimee you were having an affair, Alejandro?'

And then she was being ushered into the back of a huge black four-by-four with darkened windows, the doors closed and the only sound her son's cries.

Flora soothed Benjamin as best she could while Ramos secured the car seat between them. When he was done and Benjamin was strapped in the seat, he tapped on the screen dividing them from the driver and bodyguard up front.

The car slowly crawled away.

Benjamin's cries soon quietened. Only when she was certain that he was asleep did Flora turn her stare to Ramos.

'Who's Aimee?'

The silence before he answered went on so long she could have boiled a kettle and made herself a pot of tea.

If he had answered immediately with, 'My girlfriend, but it's over, I'm married to you now,' Flora would have been fine. Or so she liked to think.

The reality was very different.

'Aimee was my mistress.'

Revulsion was instantaneous. 'Pardon me? Your *mistress*?'

He inclined his head.

'What do you mean by mistress? Isn't a mistress a married man's lover?'

'Not always.'

Her heart pounding, she waited for him to elaborate.

'Well?' she said when the silence grew.

'Well, what?'

'Are you going to explain it to me?'

'For what purpose?'

'Oh, let me think… Because I'm your wife and I deserve to know?'

'Or so you can judge me?' he challenged, finally turning his stare on her.

'I wouldn't.'

His top lip curled. 'You're judging me now. I can tell. You have always judged me.'

She clamped her lips together, unable to deny this latest evidence of his astuteness.

What she didn't dare tell him was that she'd never really judged him from a moral perspective, but more from an instinctive revulsion that she had only ever experienced for him and never her brother, who'd got through women with the same reckless speed.

His eyes narrowed and firm lips tightened at her silence. 'You used to give the impression you didn't think me worthy to breathe the same air as you. The first time you looked at me as if I wasn't something your cat had brought in was when you came to me to plead for your brother. That was the first time *you* instigated a conversation. I made every effort with you but you always made it clear you didn't care for my efforts. I wasn't good enough for you to look in the eye or talk to until you wanted something from me.'

Her stomach twisted.

Desperation to free her brother from a foreign prison had driven Flora to Ramos. Desperate times called for desperate measures and if she'd had to get down on her knees and beg him to drop the charges against Justin and come up with a way of punishing him that wouldn't have him sentenced to twenty years of imprisonment, then she would have done it.

Even so, she'd had to summon all the courage she possessed to announce herself at his gate. Five minutes it had taken for permission to be granted, and she'd felt every second of it. Then she'd had to find the courage to knock on his door. When he'd opened it, she'd pulled out one last scrap of courage to look into the eyes of the man whose gaze she'd spent years avoiding.

He'd stared at her without speaking for the longest time.

She'd been unable to speak too. Her tongue had become tied. Everything she'd planned to say had spirited out of her brain.

And then he'd blinked, run his fingers through his hair, and invited her inside.

He'd been barefoot, she remembered with a pang.

It made her skin burn to remember how she'd walked out of the same door the next morning feeling as if she were floating on a cloud only to end the day in despair.

The promise to meet in the lobby of the hotel she was staying in had never materialised. She'd made two calls that evening, one to his mobile, which hadn't connected, the other to his house. The person on the other end had curtly informed her Señor Ramos was unavailable and that she mustn't call again.

Nausea swirled in the pit of her stomach to know why he'd stood her up and cut her from his life. To know he still believed that of her.

Forcing herself to maintain eye contact, she whispered, 'What happened between us... I didn't sleep with you for Justin's sake, I swear.'

Ramos's jaw clenched. There was a long pause before he challenged, 'Then why did you?'

'You were there.' She swallowed. 'You know why.'

It was because she couldn't not.

At the time she'd thought it was because he couldn't not too.

His chest rose sharply. She could feel him trying to probe into her brain. She wished she could delve into his mind too, and scoop out his memories of their night together and see if it had meant anything to him. Anything at all.

Frightened at how badly she wished it *had* meant something to him, Flora cleared her throat and strove for lightness, desperate to break the charged silence. 'So... Was Aimee your lover...when we...' she couldn't bring herself to call it making love even though that was how it had felt at the time '...slept together?'

Eyes not leaving her face, he rested his head back.

'She was my mistress, not my lover,' he corrected. 'A mistress is a woman kept by a man. I paid for her apartment and gave her an allowance and in return…' He raised a shoulder.

'And in return she kept herself available for you?' Flora guessed hoarsely. Her stomach rippled violently in the same way it had when she'd seen those paparazzi pictures of him and Justin sailing the Mediterranean on Ramos's yacht with a dozen topless, beautiful women sunbathing around them.

He gave a slow incline of his head.

'Were you faithful to her?'

'There is no exclusivity between a man and his mistress. That is the whole point.'

'Then why has she been crying?' And why did *she* feel like crying?

'Because she's an actress—a professional one—seeking attention. Playing the wronged lover is a role she can get her teeth into.'

'Or, maybe, she's genuinely upset.'

'Very conveniently when the paparazzi are there to witness it,' he rebutted drily. 'We have been over for a long time.'

Noting that he'd avoided answering if Aimee had still been his mistress when they'd slept together, and on the verge of asking if he still intended to take lovers now they were married, she was cut off by the sound of his phone ringing before she could voice it.

Grateful for the interruption, Flora turned her face away to gaze out of the window and breathed in deeply.

Of course he would have lovers. Alejandro Ramos was a Lothario with the looks and wealth to live exactly as he pleased with no need for thought or consideration for anyone else. Any woman who kidded herself into believing otherwise was on a hiding to nothing but heartbreak. She'd been stupid enough to fool herself once that she might be different from the others, and he'd mentally cut her from his life before she'd got out of his bed. She would not put herself in the position of making that mistake again.

She was going to have to keep her heart sealed in titanium because this was a marriage she wouldn't be able to escape for many years. He'd already warned her of the consequences should she divorce him but, now that Benjamin was here, she was prepared to give their marriage a proper chance for their son's sake, because Ramos was his father and, most importantly, *wanted* to be a father to him.

She really hoped that Aimee woman's tears were fake. As repulsive as she found the whole mistress thing, she wouldn't wish harm or pain on anyone.

They'd reached the Spanish border.

She wished they could be back in the private hospital room, the three of them cocooned without any intrusion from the outside world.

The rest of the two-hour drive to Ramos's villa in the Pedralbes area of Barcelona was spent in silence broken only by the low murmur of his voice as he made numerous calls. Benjamin slept the entire journey. Still exhausted from the birth, Flora slept much of it too.

She didn't expect her heart to thud when they drove through the electric gates to his land. She'd only been here twice before. Both times it had been dark, the three-storey villa designed in the style of a French mansion aglow with soft, romantic nightlights. The last time, she'd parked her hire car against the high privacy wall and climbed marble steps, freshly awed at the ornately created wrought iron balconies each front-facing window was adorned with.

This time it was daylight, the sun high above them and casting the white exterior with a warm glow. This time, she was driven into a brightly lit underground garage in which seven other vehicles, including a motorbike, were already parked.

As if he had an internal radar, Benjamin's eyes opened. And then his mouth opened and the silence officially ended. Flora unclipped him, lifted him into her arms and carried him out of the car.

'I will show you to your room,' Ramos said as they stepped into an elevator.

Her room?

He must have registered the shock in her eyes for he smiled faintly. 'I thought you would prefer your own space while you settle in and recover. You will be in the guest room next to mine so I will be close by if you need me.'

Her stomach plunged but whether in relief or disappointment she couldn't tell.

With everything that had happened these last few days, the sleeping arrangements here were not something she'd allowed herself to think about but on some subconscious level she must have assumed she would share Ramos's room, because wasn't that what married people did?

The elevator door opened into the same reception room she'd first stepped into three years ago for his twenty-eighth birthday party. Directly ahead, through a wide, open archway, was the main vast living area with a ceiling so high she'd had to crane her neck fully back to see it. Her entire childhood home, floor to roof, could fit in a third of that one space. The other side of the living space led to the outdoor entertaining area where the party had been held.

With an unsettled Benjamin in her arms, they headed straight up the wide winding stairs to the first floor. Flora followed Ramos along the open galleried section of the landing that overlooked the main living area and held her breath as they neared the bedroom where she'd so willingly, foolishly, given herself to him.

If she hadn't seen Ramos's bedroom, she would have gasped at the splendour she'd been appointed. Her room—or suite, as it should really be called, but even that was to do it a disservice—was breathtaking. A princess of royal birth would be delighted to call this her own, and if she weren't feeling so low and if Benjamin's cries weren't becoming more vocal by the second, she would be bruising herself with pinches to believe this was to be hers.

A crib had been placed next to the emperor bed that in itself was approximately half the size of Ramos's own bed.

'I assumed you would want him to sleep with you while you are still feeding him,' he said.

Flora nodded. Benjamin needed feeding right now. She'd had no problem feeding him with Ramos around in the hospital but it felt different here in the intimacy of a bedroom, and as she realised this she realised he must have anticipated she would feel like this and that was why he'd given her her own private space.

He must have sensed her awkwardness for he bowed his head. 'I will leave you to it. I will show you the nursery and everything else when you are ready. Shall I get Madeline to bring you tea?'

'Who's Madeline?'

'My housekeeper.'

'Yes, please.' But as she spoke a tear rolled down her cheek. She had no idea where it came from or why it was followed by another, and another, but before she knew it her cheeks were sodden.

'Hey.' Ramos crouched in front of her.

She managed to wipe her eyes clear.

He brushed a strand of hair off her face. 'What is the matter?'

She sniffed but it did nothing to stop more tears from falling. 'I don't know.'

And she didn't. Flora didn't have a clue what she was crying about.

'You don't like your room?'

She managed a laugh. 'It's beautiful. I think maybe this is what they call The Baby Blues.'

Sympathetic understanding lit his face and he brushed another lock of her hair. 'You concentrate on taking care of Benjamin. Let me take care of you and everything else. Okay?'

She bit into her wobbling bottom lip as she breathed in deeply and nodded.

The whisper of a smile quirked on his cheeks before he gently kissed her forehead. 'I will get the tea organised for you.'

And then he was gone, leaving Flora touching the scorching mark on her forehead made by his lips.

There was a tap on her bedroom door.

Flora, her stomach churning, braced herself before calling, 'Come in.'

Ramos appeared, suited and booted and looking all hunky and fresh. 'I'm going now.'

'Safe travels,' she said brightly, determined he

should think she wasn't in the slightest bit bothered about him leaving.

Ramos owned an international chain of mammoth hotel casino complexes. He'd taken three weeks off work to be there for her and Benjamin, and now it was time for him to return to the working world. He was easing himself in gently. Today was the start of only five nights away in Rome.

Only.

He lifted Benjamin from her arms and said, 'The press have gone.'

He smelt as fresh and spicy as he looked and her despondency grew. She was still in her pyjamas. She hadn't even run a brush through her hair. She must look a right state.

And Ramos, who she knew for a fact hadn't had sex in at least three weeks on account of him not leaving the villa, was heading to a city filled with some of the world's most beautiful, sophisticated women.

She must not think like this. Ramos could do what he liked.

'Good,' she answered. And it was good. The press had been camped outside the villa's grounds since she'd arrived. She guessed they'd finally moved on to a fresher story.

'There are bodyguards to escort you when you're ready to go out,' he told her. 'Let Madeline know and she will make the arrangements. If you need anything at all, speak to her.'

'Okay.' She kept the nonchalance in her tone by the skin of her teeth. Her heart was feeling bluer by the passing second.

He kissed Benjamin's cheek then carefully passed him back to her, dark eyes scrutinising.

For one silly moment Flora held her breath in anticipation that he would kiss her cheek too. Other than the
brushing of arms when lifting Benjamin between them,
he hadn't touched her since that comforting kiss on her
forehead when she first moved in.

He took a step back. 'If you want me to stay, I can
rearrange things.'

Lightly stroking Benjamin's back, she injected even
more brightness into her voice. 'Don't be silly. We'll
be fine.'

'You are sure?'

'Haven't I already told you that a thousand times? Go
on, shoo. Rome is waiting with bated breath for you.'

She managed to wait until he'd closed the door behind him before bursting into tears.

Benjamin was sound asleep.

Flora wished she could drift off too but her head, so
hot and heavy from newborn baby sleep deprivation,
was too full of Ramos to sleep. She couldn't stop herself
from wondering where he was and what he was doing…
And who he was doing it with.

He was on his third business trip in two weeks. This
time he'd gone to London, just mentioned casually the
day before he left that he'd be visiting his Mayfair casino for three days. She'd held her breath waiting for
him to invite her and Benjamin with him to her home
city, but nothing.

She supposed a wife and newborn baby would cramp
his style.

Those early days and weeks when they'd found a har-
mony together were nothing but a distant memory. She
often wondered if she'd dreamt them because, since he'd
returned to work, in the much reduced time they spent

together conversation had become stiltedly polite and only ever concerned their son.

Wiping away more tears that had sprung from nowhere—she wished she didn't cry all the time but could do nothing to stop them—she gave herself a good talking to.

Flora had married Ramos for her brother's freedom. Ramos had married her for their son. That was all there was between them and she had better get used to it. When he was home he was a good, hands-on father. She must stop torturing herself about the women he shared his nights with. No good could come from it. All it would do would make her bitter and she had no right to be bitter, not when she was raising her son in a luxury she could never have dreamed of for him.

If Ramos had presented this marriage to her from the outset; a marriage where they had separate rooms, where he worked away for the majority of his time and where relations between them were cordially polite when home, she might not have needed to be blackmailed into agreeing to it.

These baby blue hormones would pass soon, she assured herself, and, when they did, all her emotions would return to an even keel and Ramos would mean nothing more to her than the man she shared a child and a roof with.

CHAPTER FIVE

FIVE MONTHS AFTER giving birth and moving to Barcelona, Flora finally felt like her old self. She'd come out of the baby fugue. She hadn't cried in at least a month. It helped that Benjamin now slept through the night, meaning she slept soundly through the night too.

With sleep deprivation a thing of the past, she began to see and feel things more clearly. Her love for her son had formed when the pregnancy stick had shown the positive sign and swelled from there. In the fugue after the birth she'd carried that swell of love every second of the day but now it had become more defined, encapsulated within the certainty that she would sooner throw herself in front of a speeding train than let harm come to a single hair on his precious head.

Unfortunately, her awareness for Ramos had become more defined too.

The days he was home, all the tiny atoms that made her became fully charged, creating a buzz in her skin and a burr in her brain. Her heart would thump painfully. The very air she breathed tasted different.

If her presence had any effect on him, he hid it well, but why should she affect him when he had any number of women to keep him entertained when he was away on business, women who didn't bear the scars of a belly that had so recently been swollen to the size of a watermelon? And he was away on business far more than he was home. It was probably why he'd not bothered moving her into his room or made any intimations to make their marriage anything more than two people who shared a child and a roof.

She never asked him about the women. It was none of her business, she reminded herself staunchly and often. It was obvious their marriage was in name only and, with all the stupid effects he had on her, that was just as well.

Not that the opportunity to ask about his women ever arose. Not any more. In the month since she'd stopped feeding Benjamin herself and moved him into his nursery, communication between them had deteriorated further. Now, when Ramos was home, she passed their son into his willing, capable hands, filled him in on anything new or that he'd missed, and then made her escape, usually to her suite, until it was time to hand over again.

It was safer keeping her distance from him, but the distance was not having the effect she so needed it to have. Right now he was over halfway through a two week visit to his majestic hotel casino in Las Vegas, his only non-European enterprise. He'd never been away so far or for so long before and, far from her rejoicing at this extra distance, her stomach had been tied in knots for every minute he'd been gone.

All she wanted was to find an emotional neutrality with him to get her through their marriage until Benjamin was old enough to flee the nest. She would flee straight after. Ramos would have no reason to keep her.

But that was years and years away. The child who would one day grow into a man was currently a five-month-old baby who loved swimming, and it was for this love that Flora smothered Benjamin in sunscreen, and then put him in a swimming nappy and a one-piece swimsuit that gave extra protection to his delicate skin from the sun's rays.

Hoicking her swim-bag over her shoulder, she carried him downstairs, through the main living area and out of one of the three sets of French doors that led into the rear garden where her favourite of the three swimming pools was located. Well, her favourite to take Benjamin swimming in. She didn't particularly like the memories she had of it, but it had a lovely sized shallow end.

Leaving their towels on the sandstone tiles that surrounded the pool and the sprawling terrace area, she carried Benjamin into the shallow water and put him in an inflatable ring.

'Coming for a play?' she cheerfully asked Mateo, the young pool attendant. Of all the staff, Mateo was her favourite.

He looked over his shoulder and shook his head.

'Did you get into trouble with Madeline the other day?' He'd joined them in the pool for ten minutes and had made Benjamin squeal his head off with glee.

He pulled a face and looked at the ground.

The housekeeper ran a very tight ship with the staff. Unobtrusive decorum was expected at all times. It was a mystery to Flora why Mateo had been employed. She'd never known an unobtrusive, decorous eighteen-year-old in her life. She imagined he'd taken the job expecting to be pool and bar attendant to wild parties with *muchos* semi-naked ladies like the one Flora had briefly attended, not for the only excitement in his working week to come from the new *señora*'s daily swim with the baby.

He would have been in heaven if he'd worked here when Ramos held his twenty-eighth birthday party.

'Madeline cannot tell you off if *I* give the order, okay?' she said, speaking slowly.

The look he gave her told her Madeline could and probably would.

Flora smothered a sigh.

When she'd moved in, she'd been physically and emotionally fragile from the birth, and so been glad of Madeline's cool authority. She'd become gradually less glad of it because it had become patently clear that the housekeeper had *all* the authority. The *señora* of the house—Flora refused to refer to herself as the mistress—had none.

Since the baby fog had lifted, Flora had become certain Madeline reported on her to Ramos. She hoped it was just paranoia on her own part.

'Okay, no getting in the pool, then. Can we practise my Spanish?'

That was something no one could scold Mateo for. No one else had time to teach her.

'Castellano,' he corrected, sitting down on the pool's edge. He dragged his fingers into the water and flicked it at Benjamin, who giggled.

'Castellano,' she repeated. She'd considered learning Catalan rather than Spanish—Castellano—but then realised Ramos was conversing with Benjamin in the latter. She didn't want it to get to the stage where her son and husband talked between themselves and she couldn't understand any of it.

She pushed Benjamin's inflatable ring back and forth while Mateo continued to flick water at him, laughing and repeating words in Spanish over her son's delighted squeals.

'You all look as if you're having fun.'

Flora didn't think she'd ever seen someone get to their feet as quickly as Mateo did at Ramos's deep rumble. And she didn't think her heart had ever thrown itself as hard against her ribcage as it did then either.

She lifted Benjamin into her arms, then, pulses racing, turned around to face her husband.

Painfully aware that even using Benjamin as a shield didn't hide the lumps and bumps on her body that her plain black swimsuit couldn't disguise, Flora managed to find a pleasant smile to greet him with and speak over the staccato of her heart. 'You're back early. I wasn't expecting you until the weekend.'

'Obviously.' He fixed his laser stare on an obviously frightened Mateo and barked an order at him.

The young lad scuttled off.

The laser stare zoomed back on her. 'We will talk about this when Benjamin is sleeping.'

'Talk about what?' she asked, confused at the dark fury on his face and confused about why it was directed at her.

His face contorted. He held up his forefinger as if to gesticulate before shaking his head. 'I will not be made a fool of in my own home, Flora.'

And then he stalked away, leaving Flora staring at his retreating figure in shock.

How was she supposed to have made a fool of him? If anyone had been made a fool of it was her. There was no way Ramos would return four days early from a work trip and not inform the household. No one, including him, had seen fit to tell her, his so-called wife.

Once they were both dry, she took Benjamin to the kitchen for some lunch. She'd recently started weaning him, something he'd taken well to, but today he kept his mouth tightly closed and shook his head so wildly she couldn't get the spoon near his mouth, never mind in it.

Flora understood his fractiousness. She felt it herself, her own fractiousness rising when she heard footsteps approach.

'Shall I try?'

She took a deep breath before jutting her chin and acknowledging Ramos's presence.

He'd changed out of his business suit, now wearing a pair of tan canvas shorts and a short-sleeved black shirt opened at the neck. He looked and smelled as fresh and gorgeous as if he were about to step into a photoshoot for a magazine specially featuring hunky, virile men, and her senses were totally overwhelmed with the potency of the whole Ramos package.

It only made her more conscious of her changed figure, and she thought miserably of the Vegas showgirls and other beautiful women he'd have just been surrounded by.

She wished she'd brought some clothes down with her and used the outside changing rooms to change into them. She wouldn't feel at such a disadvantage now, with only a beach towel hiding her ugliness.

Ramos's features were more relaxed than they'd been by the pool but his stare was still dark with anger when he trained it on her. It softened when he turned to their son.

Perching himself onto a stool next to Benjamin's high chair by the huge kitchen island, he chucked their son under the chin and spoke to him in Spanish before reaching for the plastic bowl with the mashed banana in it.

Benjamin opened his mouth and let the spoon go in.

Flora didn't know whether to laugh or cry.

Ramos lifted his gaze to her and dismissively said, 'I will finish feeding him. Go and put some clothes on.'

As Benjamin's back was to her she had no compunction in hitting Ramos with her most lethal stare, then sucked it away to kiss her son's cheek before finding even more venom to throw at the man who called himself her husband.

Fury propelled her up the stairs and to the sanctuary of her room.

How the hell did Ramos have the nerve to talk to her like that? To treat her like that?

He thought he wanted to talk to *her*? Oh, he'd better wait. It was nothing on what she wanted to say to *him*.

Wriggling her way out of her swimsuit, she stomped past the rolltop bath and into her shower room without looking at her naked reflection. She hated looking at herself nude. Hated it.

When she'd been pregnant, she'd loved the changes pregnancy had made to her body. Even when she'd been at her biggest with permanently swollen feet and ankles she'd seen it as a rite of passage, leading to the day she met her child.

Now, whenever she caught sight of her post-pregnancy body, her stupid brain conjured up the women she'd seen pictured on Ramos's arm over the years, a parade of beauties with perfect complexions and perfect curves. Imagined Miranda, the impossibly beautiful woman who'd hung on his every word over that excruciating—for Flora—breakfast eleven years ago.

She wished she didn't care that he'd seen her nearly naked. Wished she didn't care how repelled he must have been to see the changes pregnancy had wrought.

And she wished she knew what had made him so angry.

She didn't have to wait long to find out.

She was in her dressing room wearing only her knickers and bra, dithering over which dress to wear, when her bedroom door opened.

Her room was similar in design to Ramos's. Off the main sleeping area were two archways set at a right angle. One was the gateway to her bathrooms, the other to her dressing room. Heavy drapes could be closed to give privacy if wanted. Flora had never needed to close the drapes because Ramos rarely came in her room and when he did, he always knocked first and waited permission.

Whipping around, she saw the tall figure emerge. She yanked the closest item to hand off the rail to cover herself with, and scurried to the wall hidden from his view.

'Get out!' she half squealed, half shouted.

A deep, disembodied voice called back in a grim tone. 'After we have talked.'

Heart pounding hard, she pulled the item, a summery cream strapless dress, over her head. It was a dress she'd bought with a plan to shrink into it. She hadn't shrunk enough and, despite its supposedly forgiving elasticated, floaty design, looked and felt far too snug around her waist and hips. The bra she was wearing also looked ridiculous with it but no way was she taking that off.

The wall she was hiding behind had shelves of shorts and rails of T-shirts and tops she'd also bought with vague plans of shrinking into them. She found a pair of high-waisted denim shorts that landed mid-thigh and pulled them on under the dress. At least they did up without her having to breathe in too much, so that was a nice surprise. Flora then grabbed a loose lime-green kaftan and shoved it over her head. Only then did she pull the dress down to her feet and step out of it, and only then did she turn around and notice Ramos's reflection in the walled mirror on the far side. He was sitting on one of the plush rounded armchairs in her sleeping area.

He'd watched the entire charade.

With nowhere to hide, cheeks blazing with humiliation, she had no choice but to front it out.

Throwing herself into the armchair set at an angle next to his, she glared at him. 'Have you never heard of knocking?'

'I have indeed.' His features were poker straight. Not even his eyes were giving anything away.

Flora wished she could be as controlled. 'Then why didn't you?'

'A man doesn't need permission to enter a room in his own home.'

'This might be your house but this is my room and you coming in without my permission is a gross invasion of my privacy.'

'Go and complain to someone who cares. Have you allowed your puppy dog in here?'

'What puppy dog?'

'*Your* puppy dog. Mateo. I understand you two have developed a certain…closeness.'

Understanding hit her. Flora's mouth opened but the understanding was so abhorrent that it took a few beats for anything to come out. 'You cannot be serious? I mean, seriously? You think I'm having an affair with Mateo?' Shaking her head, she laughed, not with humour but sheer disbelief.

'Are you?' An edge came into the tight control of his voice.

'Your mind belongs in the gutter.'

'Flora, I have asked you a question. Answer it.'

'Of course I'm not having an affair! He's a friend. Or am I not allowed friends?'

'He's an employee.'

'So what?'

'He was flirting with you.'

'Don't be ridiculous,' she snapped. 'He's nearly seven years younger than me.'

'And you are seven years younger than me. What's the difference?'

'I've just had a baby, that's the difference.'

'I saw you with my own eyes. Laughing together…'

'Oh, we were laughing, were we? Must be having an affair, then. No other reason for it. Well done, Poirot. Case solved.'

'You think this is amusing?' he asked dangerously.

'I think it's hilarious.'

'You have spent five months keeping to yourself, always using the excuse you are too tired to join me in anything—'

'I *have* been too tired. It's taken me all this time to feel like my old self.'

'I let it go because I knew you were recovering from the birth and adjusting to motherhood,' he continued as if she hadn't just interrupted him. 'And then I come home from a stressful trip and find you half-dressed and laughing with another man.'

'I was in a swimsuit and he's not another man. He's Mateo. And I think it's hilarious that you think a fit eighteen-year-old lad is going to flirt with a frumpy nearly twenty-five-year-old woman with a post-baby belly.'

'I don't know the meaning of the word frumpy but by your tone I assume it is not complimentary, so let me assure you: you are not frumpy. Post-baby belly or not, you are an attractive young woman. An attractive, *rich* young woman.'

Flora gritted her teeth to hide the spear of pain that shot through her chest at his qualifying her attractiveness.

She wished so hard her senses didn't bound with delight to be so close to him. Even with all the tension and anger simmering between them, her skin was buzzing and her heart thumping painfully.

'Mateo has been helping me learn Spanish,' she informed him icily. 'I've got no friends in this country, and Benjamin's too young for me to leave and visit my brother…'

The tightness of his features at this only enraged her more.

Justin, who'd been living in her London house since his return to England, was a subject Flora and Ramos never spoke of. Not that they spoke much about anything other than their son.

'I have already given you my word I won't let Benjamin have anything to do with him,' she said, trying hard to keep her tone moderate. It had been a promise that had broken her heart to make. 'I'm not going to take him with me to England, but there's no way Justin's stepping foot in Spain—he's convinced you'll set a hitman on him or something—so I'm basically alone here. Mateo's the only member of your staff willing to have a conversation with me. The rest treat me like a houseguest. They don't consult me about *anything*. Even my bodyguards answer me with grunts. You know damn well I'm not having an affair because they all watch me and report back to you, and how you have the nerve to get all macho and possessive about the possibility of me having one, even though the idea is preposterous, is pathetic.'

Ramos's sensuous lips pulled into a taut line before he smiled tightly. 'Why is the idea preposterous?' he asked silkily.

Flora rolled her eyes. 'Why do you think?'

His eyes glittered. 'Spell it out to me.'

Jutting her chin, trying hard to adopt her own poker face, she pointed at her post-baby belly.

His gaze drifted down to it then back to her face. He shrugged. 'I don't know what you're seeing but it is not what I see. You are as beautiful as you have always been. More so now. But I will tell you why I have the nerve to be macho and possessive about you having an affair and that's because you are my wife.'

'Your wife in name only,' she hit back, her brief flare of happiness that he'd called her beautiful doused with fury at his double standards. 'I don't want to have an affair but I don't see why I'm expected to stay home all chaste and pure when you can take all the mistresses and lovers that you like.'

His eyes narrowed. 'Oh, I can, can I?'

'There is nothing to stop you doing whatever you like and sleeping with whoever you like.' She folded her arms across her chest and tucked her hands into her sides so he couldn't see the tremors in them. 'But while we're on the subject I might as well ask you to show some discretion in your affairs—one day Benjamin will be old enough to read and he might find it upsetting to find details of his father's sex life splashed everywhere like happened with Aimee and all the others before her.'

Proud that she had managed to say all this without her voice choking, Flora forced herself to maintain eye contact with him.

But it was hard. There was something swirling in those melting depths, more than the toxic anger shrouding them, but she couldn't decipher its meaning.

A long period of dangerously uncomfortable silence

ended when he coolly clarified, 'You are comfortable for me to have lovers?'

'Absolutely.' She wished that weren't a lie. 'Fill your boots.'

'You wouldn't find it upsetting?'

'Why would I?' she challenged.

'You don't want your husband to be faithful to you?'

'If I was married to a man I loved and had a proper marriage then of course, but even if we did have a proper marriage, I'm not naïve. Leopards can't change their spots. Some men are incapable of being faithful and you're one of them.'

His features darkened but his tone remained coolly moderate. 'You seem quite the expert on me.'

'An expert on men's infidelities. My dad's a serial philanderer, Justin too.'

Flora had been a baby when her mum had kicked her dad out. She'd been the same age as Benjamin was now. How her poor mum must have suffered, discovering her husband in bed with another woman, a much younger woman just to add insult to injury. She'd never bad-mouthed him to Flora but the fact she'd never dated again proved how damaging it had been to her. It pained Flora to acknowledge that, in this one respect, Justin was just like their father...or, he had been. Since his release from prison he'd lived quietly and, at her urging, joined Gamblers Anonymous.

Ramos steepled his fingers together. 'Let me see if I am understanding you correctly. Your father and brother are cheats, so therefore I am a cheat too?'

'Oh, come on.' She forced a laugh. The last thing she wanted was for him to think she cared what he did or who he did it with, but, as she'd learned, Ramos was far more observant than she'd ever given him credit for.

She couldn't bear to think of him knowing how much it shredded her insides to imagine him with other women. 'I've been on the periphery of your life since I was a kid. Justin never mentioned you with the same woman twice. I never saw you with the same woman twice.'

Blonde Miranda again floated into her mind. And the women on his yacht and all the other women photographed with him she'd seen before she'd trained herself only to use social media for work purposes. And the women at his birthday pool party that she'd stupidly let her mother talk her into going to.

She pushed away the images she'd always reacted so violently to and prayed it didn't show on her face.

'I have had many lovers, I do not deny that and I will not apologise for it, but I have never lied and I have never cheated,' he stated flatly.

'You told me your mistresses always knew you wouldn't be faithful to them, that it defeated the purpose of *having* a mistress.'

'There was no cheating because that's not how the arrangements worked. My father cheated on my mother, many times. I know first-hand the damage affairs can do and, quite frankly, I find it insulting that you assume I'm like that.'

'If I have insulted you then I apologise,' she said stiffly. 'That was not my intention.'

'I would consider accepting your apology if I believed it, but I thank you for allowing me to *fill my boots* with whoever catches my eye. I will bear your open-minded generosity in mind.'

'You do that.'

'I will. Me however…' He shook his head, the flashing of his eye belying the moderacy of his voice. 'My own mind is a little less open and my generosity does not extend to permitting you the same.'

Flora's mouth fell open before she found her own voice. '*Permitting* me? Who are you to permit me to do anything?'

His nostrils flared. She could sense his temper hanging by a thread.

'Your husband, that's what I am, and, in case you need reminding, there is no statute of limitations on Hillier's crime in Monte Cleure. I can have the case against him reopened and prosecuted whenever I so desire.'

Words uttered five months ago floated in her head. *Be nice to me and I can be very generous.*

'Are you threatening me?'

'I never make threats, *querida*. Only promises. Consider it a warning.'

'Okay, well, consider *this* a warning...' Leaning forwards, Flora looked deep into the molten eyes glimmering with fire and ice. 'All the money you've given me is sitting in an English bank account that you can't touch, doing nothing but accrue interest until the day I need it. There's more than enough in there to pay for the best legal representation for Justin to fight you every inch of the way.'

CHAPTER SIX

FLORA BRACED HERSELF for the explosion of rage that was sure to follow her threat in using Ramos's own money against him.

His generosity as a husband could not be faulted. The allowance she was given had allowed Flora to pay off her mortgage and the bank loan she'd taken for Justin's legal fees. Other than clothes and toiletries, she spent nothing on herself and was growing a nice nest egg.

She had no idea how long she awaited the explosion. So many emotions flickered over his face that they passed like a blur, the only unyielding feature the darkness of his eyes fixed tightly on hers.

The last thing she expected was the low chuckle that escaped from his widening mouth.

He settled back in his chair, folded his arms across his broad chest and shook his head. 'You really are back to your old self,' he murmured appreciatively. 'I had seen the changes…' He raised a shoulder. 'I had hoped.'

Taken aback at his change in demeanour and at something that was delivered sounding like a compliment, Flora was completely unable to think up a response.

'I knew recovering from birth could take some time but I didn't expect it to take quite so long for the Flora Hillier I have known all these years to come back to life.' With a subtle wink, he added, 'Let us hope it never comes to my money paying for both the prosecution and the defence, eh?'

'Well…quite.'

Eyes now gleaming, Ramos straightened and flexed his fingers. 'Correct me if I am misunderstanding you, but you are unhappy with how my staff treat you?'

Now confused at the change of conversational direction, she nodded and cleared her throat. 'They treat me like a houseguest. Apart from Mateo, who doesn't flirt with me but does treat me as a human being deserving respect,' she felt compelled to add.

He touched his fingers to his forehead. 'I apologise for misreading the situation.'

She thought her eyes might pop out in shock. 'You do?'

'I do.' His lips pulled into a grimace. 'It has been a difficult few weeks.'

'Why's that?'

His dark eyes held hers. 'I have a family now. I felt the distance. The first thing I saw when I arrived home was my beautiful wife, who I have not seen laugh since she moved here, laughing with a good-looking young man.' He raised his shoulders. 'I should not have jumped to conclusions.'

And her heart shouldn't be leaping that Ramos had called her beautiful again and had practically admitted to jealousy. Or possessiveness. Or something along those lines.

Most likely any possessiveness on his part came from her bearing the title of his wife. It was his arrogant pride that was possessive.

'Now, am I right in thinking you want the staff to

treat you as the mistress of the house?' he said in a lighter tone.

That knocked the confused thoughts out of her, and she blanched. If she never heard the word mistress again it would be too soon. 'I want them to respect me as your wife.'

His gaze held hers for a time that stretched so long Flora found herself holding her breath again and fighting not to lose herself in the melting swirl.

'They do respect you, *querida*,' he said.

'They spy on me,' she whispered.

'They watch you, yes,' he agreed. 'On my instructions. But it is not easy for them to respect you as my wife when you do not act as my wife. A marriage is the union of two people and so far there has been no unity between us. I blame myself for that—I should never have put you in this guest room. I only put you in here because you were fragile from the birth and needed time to recover and adjust to our new life, but I see now that was a mistake. It allowed you to hide away. I was trying to do the right thing by you but that time allowed too much separation between us and caused much distrust, as what just happened testifies.'

'But there hasn't ever been trust between us,' she replied shakily. Dizzying heat was filling her head at the direction in which she could sense Ramos was taking them.

'Then it is time for us to build some, if only for our son's sake, and time for us to build a proper marriage.'

Her mouth ran dry. The thuds of her heart deepened with a violence that matched the churning in her stomach. 'What do you mean?'

But she knew.

Ramos stretched an arm and took hold of her left hand. Turning it palm up, he traced a circle over the sensitive skin.

Flora was helpless to stop the shiver that rippled through her at the sensation.

He shifted closer, his knee now pressing against hers, and traced the length of her wedding finger. His velvet voice dropped to a murmur that was as seductive as the melting swirl in his eyes. 'You are my wife and I am your husband, and it is time for us to build a real marriage together with you in my bed and my ring on your finger.'

His scent was filling her senses. Memories of the night they'd shared were clamouring for release and, though she fought desperately to contain them, she couldn't contain the remembered caresses of his hands and mouth. They sprang so vividly she could feel the sensation of them on her skin, powerful enough to send a pulse throbbing deep in her pelvis and bring her hurling to her senses.

She snatched her hand away and shoved her chair back, far out of his reach.

Horribly aware that she'd been a whisker from falling under his spell again, painfully aware that her face was crimson, she managed to say with just the right amount of indignation, 'Excuse *me*, but you can't just suddenly demand I share a bed with you.'

Far from being perturbed, he appraised her with a knowing smile. 'I demand nothing, but you made your choice when you signed our wedding certificate. You signed up for marriage without caveats, and so did I.'

'That doesn't mean you can just take your conjugal rights now you deem me well enough for it!'

'Who said anything about conjugal rights?' he asked

innocently. 'I merely said you would be sharing my room and my bed, nothing more than that.' He rose to his feet and winked. 'I'm sure you'll agree though that sharing a bed should help kill the irrational jealousy we both seem to suffer from.'

'I'm certainly not jealous!' she spluttered. Where on earth had he got that idea from? Hadn't she just practically given him carte blanche to have all the affairs he wanted? Would an irrationally jealous person do that?

He raised a disbelieving brow then said, 'We will choose a ring tomorrow but everything else changes from now. I will instruct Madeline to move your possessions into my room when we go out tonight.'

'Out?' she echoed.

His eyes pulsed. 'Yes, *querida*. Out. On a date. Just me and my beautiful wife. I have let you hide away for too long, from me and from the world.'

Then, with long, languid strides, he disappeared from her room, leaving Flora shell-shocked from all the grenades he'd just detonated and the palm of her hand still tingling manically from where his fingers had caressed it.

In her five months living in Barcelona, Flora had never left the villa without her son and it was with a huge dose of trepidation that she kissed his sleeping face goodnight.

It was with even greater trepidation that she stepped onto the galleried landing. From her vantage point she could see Ramos waiting for her on one of the deep blue velvet sofas in the living area. Dressed in a snazzy navy suit with a black open-necked shirt, his ankle hooked over his thigh, he had a glass of bourbon in one hand and was reading something on his phone with the other.

Her breath caught in her throat, the thuds of her heart echoing loudly in her ears.

He really was the most beautiful man alive, from the top of his cropped dark hair to the tips of his long toes. There was not a part of her that didn't long for him, and not just a longing to punch him.

God help her, how was she supposed to share a bed with him without losing her mind?

Her shell shock from his grenades had slowly worn off, leaving her dazed at how easily he was able to turn any situation to his advantage. It would be impressive if she weren't the one in the firing line of his sharp brain.

Gripping tightly on the glass balustrade, she remembered begging him to slow down when he first demanded she marry him. By that point he'd probably mapped out their whole future in his head.

When Ramos made up his mind to do something, he wanted it done yesterday. She could hardly believe he'd waited five whole months to make her share the marital bedroom, not if his intention really had been to move her into it from the start.

One minute they'd been arguing about his irrational jealousy over Mateo—though why he'd accused her of suffering from irrational jealousy too, she didn't know, the idea was ridiculous—the next her whole idea about their marriage was being upended and decided on.

Emotionally, her recovery *had* taken a long time. She'd given birth to the most precious child in the world and had felt the loss of her mother, who would never meet her grandson, as keenly as when she'd first died. Ramos had sensed this, she realised. Impulsive and vengeful he might be, but he was also capable of empathy and that only made her heart swell even more for him. Only added to the danger she was in.

Flora wasn't like his other lovers. She could never be like them. She just wasn't made that way. As an adolescent, she'd hated the way Ramos and her brother treated women, feeling it too much like the way her father treated them. Gradually though, she'd learned the women they went with were of the same mindset. They were women who didn't care for commitment either.

Now she was even less like those other women. She'd had a child. Her body bore the evidence of it and would for the rest of her life.

Her father had cheated on her mother in the aftermath of both her pregnancies with younger women whose bodies were lithe and perfect. And her father had supposedly loved her mother! How could Flora's body not repulse Ramos?

She couldn't allow there to be intimacy between them. She just couldn't.

She didn't dare.

As if sensing her gaze on him, he raised his stare to her and the swelling of her heart almost choked her.

He met her at the bottom of the stairs, hooded eyes drifting over her, taking everything in.

'You look beautiful,' he said simply.

Blushing furiously at the compliment, she shrugged and strove for lightness. 'It took me long enough.'

Tonight, she'd chosen a black dress with red polka dots that had a kimono-style neck and short sleeves, and a puffed-out skirt that disguised her bum and hips. She'd held her breath when Madeline did the zip up for her, certain it would get stuck halfway up her back, but it had fastened easily. For her feet she'd selected a pair of elegant black pointed shoes with only a small heel, and twisted her chestnut hair into a loose chignon.

He chuckled. 'It has been a long time since you last went out?'

'My last date was with a midwife, so yes.'

'Then I hope you find this evening makes up for all you have missed out on.'

'Where are we going?' When she'd sought him out earlier to ask him, he'd refused to tell her, saying only that she should dress up.

His mouth widened into that devastating smile. 'For dinner and then the ballet.'

Flora turned her head for one last glimpse of the villa as the driver left Ramos's grounds.

'He will be fine,' Ramos said, reading her mind. 'Madeline has three children of her own and eight grand-children.'

'I know,' she sighed. 'It's just that I've never left him before.'

'He won't even know we have gone,' he promised. 'And we'll only be a fifteen-minute drive away. Now tell me, have you seen *Giselle* before?'

'Yes.'

He grinned. 'How many times?'

'Only three. What about you?'

'I've never been to the ballet in my life.'

'Why not?'

He shrugged. 'Never thought it would be my thing.'

'Then why take me there?'

'Because I know how much you enjoy it.' His phone rang. He pulled it out of his suit jacket pocket and sighed. 'My Vegas lawyer. My apologies. I left before we could get everything wrapped up. Let me take this and then I'll turn it off.'

While he took his call, Flora gazed out of the window at the late summer sun fading to a pink ember on the horizon, and thought back to the time he'd bought her tickets to the ballet before.

It had been a present for her twenty-first birthday.

She hadn't expected a gift from him as he'd offered to host the party in one of his Mayfair hotel casino's function rooms free of charge. She hadn't wanted to accept his generous offer or invite him to it, but her mum had been recently diagnosed with cancer and her mum considered Ramos a second son. So she'd felt obliged.

She'd been obliged to kiss his cheek in greeting, as she had everyone else too, when he'd arrived with her brother. Her lungs had filled with the spicy scent she so hated. Hated because it was wonderful. It was one of the many things she'd hated about him as an adolescent; hated the near-constant urge to trail in his wake and sniff him.

She could smell it now. Every inhalation came with a dose of his scent.

She remembered how her friends had flocked to him like a pack of gulls around a discarded sandwich. She'd wanted to smack the lot of them, something that had *really* disturbed her.

And she remembered catching his eye from the other side of the function room. He'd been in mid-conversation with her brother and he'd cut himself off from whatever he'd been saying and just stared at her. It was the first time in her life Flora had met Ramos's stare and held it…held it because she'd been unable to drag her gaze away. She'd been trapped. That awful sticky sensation had crashed through her, her breaths shallowing to nothing.

For all she knew, she might still be there now, spellbound in his gaze, if her friend Molly hadn't thrust a drink in her hand.

He'd approached her a short while later and asked her to dance.

The excitement that had thrummed through her veins and the rapid pounding of her heart…she'd never experienced anything like it. It had been the single most frightening moment of her life, and she'd danced stiffly and held her breath to stop his spicy scent filling her lungs for the entire song, then walked away without a word, all without looking into his eyes. She'd known she must never make that mistake again. Never.

In the morning, the day of her actual birthday, there had been a knock on the door of the suite Ramos had put her and her mum in. A bellboy had handed the gift box to her with birthday wishes from the owner. In the box had lain tickets for that evening's performance of *Cinderella* in Paris. Included were first-class return flight tickets for her and her mum, and a note stating a suite had been reserved under her name in his Parisian hotel.

His generosity had thrilled her mum but terrified Flora, who'd still been able to feel the imprint of his arms around her from when they'd danced. It had been a generosity that couldn't go unacknowledged though, and she'd handwritten a short letter from her Parisian suite after the performance, thanking him.

'I have been thinking,' Ramos said, breaking through the memories and putting his phone back in his pocket, 'and now that you are rejoining the world, it is time for us to employ a nanny. Madeline is happy to babysit for us tonight but she has her own family and it is not fair to expect her to extend her duties.'

'Getting a nanny seems a bit excessive for just the odd night out,' she said doubtfully. Flora had only been comfortable leaving Benjamin in the housekeeper's care because Benjamin was comfortable with her and, for all that Flora had issues with Madeline, she didn't doubt she would look after her baby as well as she would her own flesh and blood.

'It will be more than the odd night out and it will make life easier to have someone on site. I am thinking of you too. I know you haven't said anything about starting your business up again, but I remember how much you got from it and if you feel you want to start it up again at some point in the future—we can turn one of the guest rooms into a studio for you—then you won't have to worry about him.'

She met his stare, wishing her heart weren't swelling again for him.

Flora ran a small business from the home she'd bought herself with her share of her mother's inheritance, designing and creating bespoke embroidery patches that could be ironed onto clothing and creating embroidery prints from clients' photographs. Her website currently informed potential customers that she was taking a sabbatical.

Since Benjamin's birth she felt that all her creativity had deserted her and she'd hardly given any thought to starting up again. But Ramos had. Already that sharp brain was thinking ahead to the day she might feel ready to give her creativity an outlet and was making plans to accommodate it for her.

Oh, how could one man have so many different facets to him? Thoughtfulness and empathy versus vengefulness and cruelty. How masochistic was she to wish for him to show more of the vengefulness and cruelty to her because those were the traits that made it easier to dislike him?

But they had never stopped her wanting him, had they? His abhorrent treatment of her after their night together hadn't stopped her dreaming of him. Hadn't stopped the constant ache in her chest.

The car came to a stop.

They'd arrived at the opera house.

CHAPTER SEVEN

THE RESTAURANTS IN and around the opera house were heaving with people dining and drinking before the evening's performance. Ramos led her past them all and through to a nondescript, narrow side street that looked as if its better days were centuries ago.

Flora wrinkled her nose at the peeling door of the terraced house he knocked on.

He caught her expression and winked.

The door was opened by a tiny, wizened old man who greeted them both as if they were his long-lost children. Not understanding a word he said, a bemused Flora followed Ramos's lead and stepped inside. And then she gasped.

This must have been how the kids felt when they opened the wardrobe door into Narnia.

The whole street must have been knocked into one vast building to create this magnificent space.

Glass tables were strategically placed around an elaborate glass water fountain, all of which were underlit with burnished orange lights that cast the restaurant in a golden glow that managed to be opulent and showy without being gaudy. The trickling from the fountain perfectly complemented the low-level background music and hum of conversation. As they walked the quietly busy room to their table, their silhouettes cast shadows along the walls.

'What is this place?' she whispered.

'The best kept secret in Barcelona,' he murmured, leaning down to speak into the top of her hair.

With the warmth of his breath soaking through her skull, Flora gratefully took her seat.

Menus were placed before them with a flourish. There was the grand total of one item for each course displayed on it.

'We have the performance to watch soon so are eating from the quick menu,' Ramos explained. 'It just tells us what we are going to be served with. If you like it here, we can make a night of it another time soon—they do a twelve-course tasting menu that changes daily and is always excellent.'

A bottle of white wine was brought to their table. Flora allowed the waiter to pour her only a small amount. She'd never been much of a drinker even before she found out she was pregnant. She took a small sip of it and then their first course of almond gazpacho was placed in front of them. It was so fresh and silky smooth she would have gladly buried her face in it. All too soon her bowl was empty and all that was left were tiny crumbs of the fluffy warm roll it had been served with.

Relaxing into the luxurious environment, she took another tiny sip of wine and said, 'What you were saying about hiring a nanny… Knowing you, your mind is already made up…'

He grinned at her observation.

'But I'm happy to go along with it on condition that I'm involved in the hiring process.'

'That is as it should be. What kind of person do you have in mind?'

'Just someone nice. And preferably young. Someone who could be a friend.'

His eyes narrowed a touch.

Uh oh. That meant he was thinking.

'A word of advice,' he said. 'Whoever we choose, don't get too close.'

'What do you mean?'

'You will be their employer. Mixing business with pleasure is a recipe for disaster. Now that you are coming out into the world you will make friends. We have been invited to a party on Saturday night. You will meet people there. Many of my friends have young children—'

'Do they?' she asked, surprised. Ramos and Justin's circle of friends had been kindred spirits to them, hedonistic party animals.

He obviously guessed what she was thinking for he drily said, 'People do grow up, you know.'

'Not everyone does. My father never has. He's still the same pound shop playboy he's always been.'

'My father too…although he is more of a yacht shop playboy,' he added with a wry smile as their next course of pork tenderloin was presented to them.

'Am I ever going to meet him?' she asked, cutting through her pork as easily as if slicing through butter.

'When he finishes his latest holiday,' Ramos said.

'He's been on holiday for five months?'

'He has a new wife.'

'Really? Since when?'

'A few weeks after we married. She's your age.'

'You never said.'

'She's his fourth wife since my mother died. It won't last. They never do.'

Unsure how she was supposed to respond to this, Flora decided silence would prevent her from saying the wrong thing, and popped a cube of jellied apple into her mouth. A taste sensation exploded on her tongue.

'He's retired and has a few billion in the bank,' he explained. 'What better way to spend it than with the latest model of your preferred type of woman?'

A roll of nausea sloshed through her belly as she imagined herself years from now—a few years maybe, or maybe longer—pushed aside for a younger, prettier version of herself.

But she could only be pushed aside if she became his lover as well as his wife.

'Isn't he even curious about meeting his grandson?' she asked.

'Oh, I'm sure he's curious. Just not curious enough. I told you before—he's selfish. He's always been selfish but age has made him worse. Once I came of age he decided his presence in my life was no longer required and has done exactly as he pleases since.'

Whispers of a remembered conversation floated in her head and before she could stop herself Flora blurted out, 'He went to Martinique.'

'Sorry?' he asked.

'Your father. Years ago. Justin invited me to stay at yours for the weekend but Mum would only let me go if you weren't there—she loved you to pieces but she knew when you and Justin got together, trouble followed. You were supposed to spend the weekend with your dad in Barcelona but when you got there he'd flown off to Martinique instead so you came back to Oxford.' And hooked up with a lady friend.

He simply stared at her.

'What?' she asked.

'That must have been ten years ago.'

'Eleven. Nearly twelve,' she added helpfully.

A slow smile spread across his face. 'That is some memory you have.'

No way was she admitting why that particular weekend had stuck in her memory so she gave another shrug, and hoped it covered the disquiet racing through her as, for the first time, she considered that Ramos's father had stood him up that weekend. His own father.

'Was a lady involved in Martinique?' she asked in the same light tone, being careful to sound conversational rather than probing.

'With my father, there's always a lady involved,' he answered wryly. 'My mother never trusted him not to stray—when I was a child she always insisted we travel with him.'

'Did that stop him?'

'I don't know. His opportunities to stray were limited.'

'Why did she stay if she thought he would cheat?'

'For me.' He raised a shoulder. 'She believed children do better living with both their parents and she was right. We had a good life together, the three of us.'

She caught a momentary trace of wistfulness on his face and gently forked her last croquette to stop herself from extending a comforting hand to him.

'I'm sorry you lost her so young,' she said quietly. 'That must have been devastating.'

Losing her mother at twenty-two had been devastating, but trying to imagine going through that at the age of ten when the worst nightmare she'd ever had was of being in a department store and losing sight of her mum, a dream she'd woken from sobbing… It would have ripped the soul from her.

'It was.' His eyes narrowed and flashed. 'But it toughened me up. When you lose the person you love most in the world at a young age, you learn that nothing can beat that. Nothing. There can be no greater pain. The worst thing that can happen to you has happened. There is nothing left to fear and nothing can hurt you again.'

Flora's throat had closed up and she had to work hard to open it enough to swallow her last mouthful.

Ramos took another drink of his wine then bestowed her with the devilishly handsome smile she hated and adored in equal measure. 'Seeing as the show will start soon, why don't you tell me the storyline so I can know what's going on?'

She knew a deliberate change of subject when she heard one, and she was grateful for it. Imagining Ramos as a vulnerable, heartbroken boy filled her with too much compassion for him.

The seats Ramos had got for them were in a private box. It was clearly one of the theatre's most exclusive boxes as they had their own bar and a private usher to cater to all their whims and needs throughout the performance. The usher hung Ramos's jacket up for him and poured them a drink each before bowing his head and slipping out of the box. If they needed him, they had only to press a button and he would come running.

'Is this yours?' Flora asked, delighted with such an excellent, unrestricted view of the stage, but with a stomach full of knots at the intimate space they would share for the next few hours.

They would be sharing a much more intimate space when they returned home, a thought that only tightened the knots.

'No. A friend's.' He sat next to her and stretched his long legs out. 'But, as I know how much you enjoy all theatre productions, I have set the ball rolling for a box of our own.'

Her eyes widened in disbelief. 'Are you serious?'

He gave a wolfish grin. 'Always. Did I not tell you I could be generous?'

Overwhelmed that a man she knew cared nothing for the theatre was preparing himself for a future of plentiful theatre visits, she gazed at the handsome face, at the straight patrician nose and the closely shaved jaw and felt something in her heart sigh…

An alarm went off in her brain and she quickly pulled herself together to drily say, 'Generosity is your middle name, Ramos.'

And it was, she realised. Ramos had an intrinsically generous nature, not just with his money but with his time too.

'It is,' he agreed smugly, 'and I have told you many times to call me Alejandro.'

She adopted her most innocent face. 'Sorry. I occasionally suffer from amnesia.'

The roar of laughter that burst from his mouth had the audience below craning their necks.

The auditorium lights dimmed. The brief flare of shared amusement dimmed with it.

Settling back in her seat, Flora crossed her legs away from him and folded her arms across her chest so there was no danger of any part of their bodies touching. Mercifully, the seats in the box were much larger than ordinary seats.

The lights on the stage went up. The orchestra played its first beat.

Flora took a deep breath, fixed her stare on the stage and waited for the magic to transport her.

But the magic never came.

Here, in the privacy of their darkened box, she was far too aware of Ramos for anything else to properly penetrate. The distance she'd put between them was too slight to be effective.

As the first act went on, the awareness prickling over her skin deepened. Slowly but surely, he leaned closer to her. If not for the armrest separating them, their arms and thighs would be touching and it was taking everything she had to hold her position, keep her eyes glued to the stage and not move so much as a fraction of her body. Pretend she couldn't feel the burn of his stare on her.

And yet, although the dancing itself passed in a blur, the sweeping music seeped into her, and as the end of the first act approached she could feel the madness of a betrayed, heartbroken Giselle in the pounding beats of her heart…

They were the same pounding beats that had bruised her chest when she'd realised Ramos had severed himself from her, and she knew beyond a shadow of a doubt that if she succumbed to the desire that burned so deep inside her for him, her heart would once again open like a flower and leave her vulnerable to being hurt again.

When the lights came up for the interval she held her position a moment longer before facing him.

He hadn't moved. His melting eyes gleamed and a knowing smile played on his lips. 'Enjoying it?' he asked lazily.

She pulled a wide smile on her face. 'It's great. What about you?'

He raised the shoulder furthest from her. 'I will have to watch it again.'

'Why?'

He dipped his face a little closer. 'Because I have been watching you.'

The sticky heat of arousal rushed through her again, and she reflexively tightened the cross of her legs.

Thank God the usher chose that moment to enter their box.

Flora snatched at the opportunity and fled to the sanctuary of the ladies' bathroom.

The ladies itself was a plush, intimate space for the female occupants of the private boxes and had an array of toiletries and cosmetics for patrons to use. Spotting a cooling mist, Flora pulled the front of her dress out and sprayed the mist between her cleavage. Too late she noticed its seductive scent and almost stamped her feet to curse herself.

Ramos would probably assume she'd sprayed it for his benefit.

She dawdled returning to the box and then avoided conversation with him by keeping the usher busy making her a variety of mocktails to enjoy. She managed to play the charade right until the lights dimmed again.

Retaking her seat, Flora determined that in this, the second act, she would tune him out properly.

Her resolve lasted as long as it took for the first dancer to enter the stage.

This time, not even the music penetrated. Ramos didn't stare at her. No, he leaned his head right against hers so they were a whisker from touching. His soft hair tickled her forehead. His spicy scent floated in and out of her airwaves. His arm rested on the barrier between them, his long fingers hanging over her side of it. She tightened her arms around her chest and buried her hands in her sides so her tingling fingers couldn't reach for them. She crossed her legs so tightly that she wouldn't be surprised if she cut off her blood supply.

But nothing she did worked to stop the assault on her body from the man who wasn't even touching her.

'*Querida?*' he whispered after she'd sat frozen for what felt like fifteen hours.

She had to swallow hard to reply. 'What?'

'You need to breathe.'

Her face turned to him before she could stop herself making the movement.

The tips of their noses made contact.

She was breathing now. Shallow, ragged breaths.

She was helpless to stop her eyes lifting to meet his gaze, shadowed in the darkness but still filled with that hooded, hypnotic power that so easily caught her in its trap.

A finger brushed lightly over her cheekbone.

His breath was warm against her tingling lips.

She was locked in his hooded and, oh, so seductive stare; the cavity in her chest filled, a swelling that pushed into her throat making it impossible to speak…impossible to pull away.

The finger drifted down her neck and then skimmed back up to take gentle hold of her chin. Her heart was thumping so hard she thought…

His lips fused against hers and sucked out any thoughts she had.

Languidly, his mouth moved…and hers moved with equal languidness. Their lips parted slowly as his hand cupped her cheek tenderly.

The tip of his tongue darted against hers.

A moan echoed in her ears… It came from her.

With the same torturously slow pace, the kiss deepened. Slowly, his fingers tiptoed to her ear and traced the contours, burning her with shivers of delight, then dipped behind to thread into her hair…

A loud burst of applause cut through the sensory pleasure.

In an instant, Flora yanked her hand from the nape of his neck—when had she put that there?—pushed at Ramos's chest and jumped to her feet.

She clapped and cheered and hollered until her hands were raw and her throat hoarse.

Flora kept her arms firmly crossed on the short walk back to their waiting car.

She couldn't believe she'd let him kiss her.

She couldn't believe she'd kissed him back.

What was *wrong* with her? Had she taken leave of her senses? She must have done.

In the back of the car, she huddled herself against the door, trying to create as much distance from Ramos as she could.

She could still taste him on her tongue. Her lips still tingled manically. The hot, sticky sensation…it still simmered in waves.

'Something troubling you, *querida*?' he asked lightly.

'No… Yes!' Taking a deep breath, she faced him. 'That was a mistake.'

'What was?'

'You know what.'

He pulled an innocent face. 'The ballet?'

'Stop playing games,' she cried. 'Our kiss.'

His eyes gleamed. 'Ah, *that.*'

'Yes, that. I don't want you getting the wrong idea.'

He leaned his face closer and dropped his voice to a husky drawl. 'Are you trying to tell me that I shouldn't build my hopes up and expect you to throw yourself into my arms the minute the bedroom door is closed?'

Her skin danced just to imagine it. 'Exactly.'

'Then consider your message understood.'

'Thank you.'

'What we do in our bed will be up to you. If you wish to do nothing but sleep beside me then that is your right and I will respect your wishes.' Nostrils flaring, he shifted ever closer so that his cheek was a tissue away from touching hers and whispered, 'But just think, what we found the night we spent together... We can have that again, *querida*. And more. Much more.'

CHAPTER EIGHT

THE BEATS OF Flora's heart were weighty as she climbed the villa's stairs, Ramos close behind her.

His bedroom door loomed large.

Her bedroom door now.

Theirs.

She swallowed. 'I'm going to check on Benjamin.'

Not waiting for a response, she opened the door opposite and tiptoed to the cot that had pride of place next to the king-size bed Benjamin would one day upgrade to.

He was fast asleep.

The urge to lift him into her arms and hold his comforting, solid weight to her chest was almost overwhelming but, knowing it would be pure selfishness to wake him, she settled for lightly stroking his soft hair.

She couldn't use her son as a human shield against his father… No, not his father, she admitted painfully, but herself.

Benjamin's cherubic sleeping face reminded her that she'd found the strength needed to carry her through a time when she could have easily crumbled under the weight of her fears and worries. In comparison to that time, sharing a bed with Ramos was trifling. Even if it didn't feel trifling.

All she needed was to find her zen.

Breathing deeply and slowly, she willed her mind into a state of calm.

Only when her heart had slowed to a vaguely regular beat did she leave the nursery, filled with resolve that she could act and behave as if sharing a bed with her husband meant nothing more than the sleepovers she'd had with her school friends.

She entered the room her son had been conceived in for the first time since his conception. There was no sign of his father.

'Ramos?' she called out.

'In the bathroom,' he called back.

She remembered his majestic bathroom suite all too well. They'd shared a shower before he'd given her a lift to her hotel and asked if he could see her again that night.

She walked as far as the archway that led into it and, without actually looking into it, said, 'Where's my stuff been put?'

Seconds later, Ramos's towering figure appeared wearing only a dark blue towel around his snake hips.

Her zen practically flew out of the window.

Painfully aware her cheeks were burning with colour, Flora took a hasty step back and averted her eyes from the muscular bronzed torso that had plagued her thoughts every night before she drifted into sleep for years.

A gleam flickered in his eyes before he inclined his head. 'I will show you.'

With long, languid strides, he led her past the humongous bed, the tight muscles of his buttocks clearly outlined beneath the towel. She only just managed to avert her eyes when he stopped at an archway and turned to her.

He swept an elegant arc. 'Your dressing room.'

Flora had thought her last dressing room was big. This one could rival a department store…okay, a slight exaggeration. But, still, wow.

'I'm going to take a shower,' Ramos informed her. 'So I will leave you to it…unless you wish to join me?'

She answered with a glare that had him sauntering off chuckling.

Managing to stop herself ogling his backside again by a breath, Flora dragged the heavy drape across its rail to give herself privacy, but, instead of changing into her pyjamas, sat on the red velvet chaise longue and buried her face in her hands.

So much for her zen.

Why, oh, why had she kissed him? Her awareness of him had been bad enough before but now it was all a hundred times worse.

After changing into her pyjamas, she hung around in her dressing room until she was certain he'd left the bathroom and had had time to get into bed.

She counted to ten then darted across the room, not looking at him.

The first section of the bathroom suite had vanity units running along opposite side walls. Her toiletries had been placed neatly on one of them and she cleaned her face and brushed her teeth, then brushed her hair, dragging out the process as long as she could and searching desperately for her zen.

Ramos, lying on his side of the bed staring up at the ceiling, turned his face at the sound of her footsteps. 'Did you find everything, *querida*?'

'Yes, thank you.' Cheered that she'd managed to sound normal, she lifted the sheets and slid under them.

The double emperor bed was so big she had acres

of space to call her own. Ramos was far enough away that they could both stretch like starfish and not touch.

After they wished each other a polite goodnight, Ramos deactivated the lights.

It was one of the longest, most torturous nights of Flora's existence.

The sleep Flora had rediscovered had been snatched away from her again, this time by a six-foot-three hunk who slept nude in the same bed as her. Slept soundly. Three nights she'd lain awake burning inside, her mind consumed with the hunk beside her, knowing all she would have to do was prod him with a finger and he would wake up and put her out of her frustrated misery. And then her mind would go into overdrive imagining all the things he would do to her, pushing sleep even further away. After all that torture and the long days of his gregarious company, she now had to deal with the torture of sitting by his side on the leather sofa of his home office interviewing potential candidates for the role of nanny for their son. It was the closest they'd been in a physical sense since the night of the ballet.

'Which one did you prefer?' Ramos asked once the final interview was done, twisting to face her.

None of them.

They'd interviewed five women for the role. She had no idea how Ramos had been able to organise it all in such super-quick time but, as she had learned, when Ramos had an idea in his head he was single-minded until it was accomplished. Unfortunately the potential candidates made her feel a little like the children in *Mary Poppins* looking out of the window with dread at all the stern-faced women lined up, knowing one of them would be tasked with caring for them. Except none of the nannies they were interviewing were in the slightest bit stern-faced. On the contrary. They were all smiley, fresh-faced and, without exception, beautiful.

Flora hated herself for it, but her imagination ran riot whenever Ramos was away. How would she cope with a beautiful woman sleeping under their roof with them?

'They all seem nice,' she said truthfully.

Nice and smiley and young and beautiful and without a single stretchmark between them. Not one of them would look out of place on Ramos's yacht.

'You must have a favourite?' he said.

'Do you?'

'It doesn't matter what I think. They're all equally well qualified and all have impeccable references, but you are the one who will spend the most time with them so it should be your decision.'

She twisted her wedding ring they'd bought two days ago. She couldn't seem to stop herself from twisting it. Ramos had surprised her by buying himself a matching one. It was a public proclamation that he was a married man.

Oh, she was being *ridiculous*. Ramos wouldn't have an affair under his own roof. He just wouldn't, especially since she'd asked him to be discreet in his affairs.

Oh, *why* had she practically given him licence to sleep with whoever he wanted when the thought of Ramos with another woman had made her feel violently sick since she was thirteen and unwittingly caught that glimpse of him naked?

That made her straighten.

Oh, God, had she actually fancied him all that time? Was that what it had all been about? Had it all been jealousy?

No *way*. That was ridiculous. She'd felt *sorry* for all

those women. The sickness in her stomach whenever she thought of them was empathy for the heartbreak she'd assumed was heading their way when Ramos quickly bored of them.

Liar...

'Are you okay, *querida*?'

Realising she'd fallen into a daze, Flora blinked and rubbed her arms and generally tried to look as if there were nothing wrong and that she hadn't just had a frightening epiphany.

'I was just considering the options,' she said quickly. 'And I'd like to employ Sinead.'

'The Irish one?'

'Yep. She seemed the nicest and friendliest of all of them.' The most genuine too.

'Just remember what I said about not getting too close. You will be her employer, not her friend.'

'Is it your experience with Justin that makes you say that?' It was a question that had played on her mind numerous times these last few days.

His features tightened but he gave a sharp nod. 'I gave him the job because he had the qualifications and he's damn good with numbers. I trusted him.'

The job in question had been Finance Director for the Ramos Group, the company Ramos formed when he graduated from university. His billionaire father had given him a huge sum of money as a graduation present, which Ramos had promptly used to purchase run-down properties in central city locations and convert them into his chain of hotel casinos. He'd brought Justin on board four years later and paid him handsomely for it.

'When the theft from my Athens casino was discovered and brought to my attention, Hillier was the last person I suspected. He told me someone must have hacked into his computer and stolen his passcodes and I believed him because we had been friends for thirteen years and I'd thought of him as a brother.'

Watching his face go through a contortion of emotions, she instinctively reached out a hand to cover the fist he'd made but pulled it back before making contact and held it tightly on her lap.

'He really hurt you, didn't he?' she said quietly.

His eyes flashed dangerously. 'No, *querida*, he didn't hurt me—nothing has had the power to hurt me since I was ten years old—but he did abuse my trust, and trust is not something I give easily.'

'But don't you miss him?' she probed, searching his handsome face intently.

'No.'

She didn't believe him. She only half believed him about Justin not hurting him, but no way did she believe that he didn't miss him.

'I think back on how close you two were...' She sighed. 'I was jealous of you.'

His brow rose. 'Jealous of what?'

'Your closeness. I thought you were stealing him from me,' she admitted. 'I was eleven when he went to university and I missed him terribly. I was so excited about his visits home and when he brought you back with him...' She shrugged. 'I hated you for stealing what I considered to be *my* precious time with him.'

'Is that why you always stuck your nose in the air around me?'

She smiled, remembering her skinny little self back then. 'I was used to it being just him and me...and Mum, of course.'

'And I was the interloper?'

'In my mind, yes. I was too young to think of what

it must have meant for you to give up your weekends of wild partying on the student campus to stay in our little home.' Until that moment, it had never occurred to her what a big thing that must have been for an eighteen-year-old boy, and she gazed into his eyes, suddenly wishing she could go back thirteen years and welcome the motherless Spanish young man into her home with the same embracing generosity her mother had. 'You were generous with your time when Mum was ill too,' she whispered. All those visits that had brought such a smile to her mother's face.

His face inched closer to her. 'You are thinking maybe I am not so bad after all?'

'I learned that the day our son was born,' she whispered. 'I couldn't have got through it without you.'

Suddenly realising she was in danger of falling into his eyes again, Flora jumped up. 'Right, that's enough compliments for one day. Your head's big enough as it is—I don't want you getting stuck in the door. Do you want to call Sinead and tell her she has the job or shall I?'

'I will,' he said, following her lead and rising to his feet. 'You go and get yourself and Benjamin ready. I'm taking you shopping.'

'For what?'

'Clothes and jewellery for my beautiful wife's enrolment into my high society life, and if I am lucky she will let me spy on her in the dressing rooms.' Then he cupped her cheeks, planted a smacker of a kiss to her lips, and sauntered out of the office like a strutting peacock leaving Flora not knowing whether to laugh or cry.

Flora gazed out of her dressing room window the next day watching Ramos and Benjamin in the swimming pool. She couldn't hear Benjamin's happy squeals but could see them, and the joy on Ramos's face.

She'd been preparing to take Benjamin for a swim herself when Ramos had appeared in the nursery wearing only his swimming shorts and announced he'd be joining them.

As the thought of wearing a swimsuit around the man she lusted after with more desperation with each passing day, knowing most of her own body would be on show for him to sweep his expert eye over, made her feel as if she were coming out in hives, she'd quickly handed the change bag to him.

'Do some daddy-son bonding,' she'd told him brightly, relieved she hadn't changed into her own swimsuit at that point. 'I'll help Sinead get settled in.'

In typical Ramos fashion, he'd arranged for their new nanny to move in and start her employment immediately.

His returning stare had been scrutinising but he'd shrugged his broad shoulders and lifted Benjamin into his arms.

She was looking at those broad shoulders now. The strength in them. The smoothness of them. Ramos wasn't particularly vain—she supposed when you were God's gift to women you took your gorgeous face for granted—but he worked out. The end result was right there in the distance, and she soaked it up in a way she never did when alone in the room with him. The way she never *dared* to do when alone with him.

The muscles on his back bunched as he lifted Benjamin into the air.

Stop looking at him, she beseeched herself.

She might as well tell her heart to stop beating.

How much longer could she bear it?

Seeing him now, striding around in nothing but a pair

of short swim-shorts, reminded her all too much of that night of his pool party.

She hadn't wanted to go. She'd turned down so many invitations from him. They'd all come after her twenty-first birthday, delivered via her brother along the lines of, 'Me and Ramos are going to Cannes to watch an awards ceremony. He can get you a ticket if you want to join us?' The birthday pool party had been the only one she'd accepted and that had been because Justin had asked her in front of their mum who, having recently completed her second round of chemotherapy, had been of the opinion that life was for living and insisted that she go. At that time, Flora would have jumped off a cliff if it had made her mum happy.

She'd been taken through the villa to the pool area and had caught her first glimpse of Ramos semi- naked since she'd seen him nude when she was thirteen. Her body had reacted in the exact same way it had then ex-cept this time there had been no bed for her to hide in.

She'd shrunk in on herself, feeling desperately out of place amongst all these rich, semi-naked, beautiful men and women who all knew each other well and were all laughing and drinking and throwing each other in the pool. Music had pounded out, competing with the screams of laughter, and she'd been so aware of the bi-kini-clad women flirting with Ramos. He'd been hold-ing court like a king in his castle. It had made her sick to her stomach and she'd left his present, a handstitched embroidered portrait of his childhood dog she had spent hours making, on the table with all the other presents rather than approach him with it directly. She hadn't known what else to gift him. After all, what did you get the man who had everything?

He'd spotted her within minutes of her arrival, which

was pretty impressive considering the huge size of the garden and the size of the posse surrounding him and considering that she'd been trying to blend in with one of the garden statues. His smile when he'd seen her… It had almost made her heart explode. He'd pointed at the changing rooms, indicating that was where she should get changed, but right then Flora had felt she would rather die than parade her body surrounded by all those perfectly formed glossy women.

She'd spent the next twenty minutes hiding in the changing rooms then feigned illness to Justin. Except it hadn't been fake. Her whole insides had cramped and for some stupid reason she'd been fighting back tears.

Ramos had followed her.

She hadn't expected that.

'You're not leaving already, are you?' he'd asked, eyes bright, teeth gleaming, tall, tanned, virile, half naked. 'You've come all this way.'

'I'm not feeling well,' she'd replied, avoiding his stare and walking quickly to the waiting cab to take her to her hotel. Justin had laughed when she'd booked the hotel, she remembered. Everyone would crash at Ramos's, he'd said. She thought now she'd already known how her evening would end.

Ramos had caught her hand. The smile had left his face. 'If you're not well, you shouldn't be alone.'

'I'll be fine,' she'd muttered and yanked her burning hand out of his and thrown herself into the cab.

The next time she'd seen him had been at her mother's sick bed. He'd visited many times but she'd never allowed herself to be alone with him. The only reason she'd hung around during those visits was because she hadn't wanted to miss a minute of what was left of her mother's life.

He'd tried to engage Flora in conversation at the wake, she remembered. Asked how she was holding up. Asked if she was okay for money.

She'd barely been able to look him in the eye to politely tell him she was holding up fine and also fine for money.

'If you need anything, I'm always here,' he'd said.

Flora had bawled her eyes out during the funeral but that was the closest she'd come to tears at the wake. She'd had no idea why a touch of humanity from the man she despised had made her want to cry, but it had. She'd managed to compress her lips into something that was supposed to resemble a smile and said, 'I've got Justin, but thank you,' before turning her back on him and going to sit with her grandfather.

The next time she'd seen him was the night they'd conceived their son, and she watched him lift Benjamin in the air again and place a kiss to his plump belly.

What was she holding out for? she wondered despondently. Night after night, sharing his bed, torturously aware and aroused.

She was scared. Admitting to herself that she'd essentially fancied Ramos since she was thirteen had been a huge thing, but to feel herself falling for him now, knowing that to give her body to him would be to give her heart…

If she could separate the physical from the emotional then she would be fine, but their one night together had proved she couldn't.

He'd crushed her heart the first time. Even if he hadn't misinterpreted her brother's message, he would have crushed her eventually, trading her in for the next pretty woman who caught his eye.

Ramos was a playboy. She believed he'd never cheated

but he'd never been in a committed relationship before so how would he know how good his staying power was? How did he know what he'd do when his fleeting lust for her was spent and the next pretty thing came along?

And what if it never went that far? Her body had changed so much since their night together. What if it repulsed him? How could she bear it?

When Ramos crushed her heart again it would hurt much more than it had the first time because she was growing to like him. A lot.

If she wasn't careful, she would come to adore him.

Her heart did a sudden triple salchow when she noticed he was looking right back at her from the swimming pool.

He lifted a hand then took Benjamin's wrist and waved for him too.

She swallowed hard and waved back.

CHAPTER NINE

THAT NIGHT, EXCITEMENT and fear thrummed through Flora's veins as she dressed for the party they were going to hosted by an old friend of Ramos's. She hadn't dared ask if the friend had been at the pool party she'd run away from after thirty minutes. Or if any of the other guests had been there too. She doubted she would recognise them, not with their clothes on.

Ramos had said it wasn't a pool party, just a party-party and to dress accordingly, and she'd spent ages choosing an outfit from the beautiful array of couture clothes he'd insisted on buying her the other day. She could only hope she'd chosen a dress that wasn't going to make her feel like a frump in comparison to every-one else.

Not knowing which shoes to match with her outfit, a white, high-necked dress that landed below her knees and had the most fabulous floaty sleeves, she decided to bite the bullet, picked up two pairs and carried them through the main bedroom to his dressing room.

'Ramos?' she called from the archway.

He appeared and, for the longest time, did nothing but look her up and down.

'Do I look okay?' she asked anxiously, feeling even more insecure because he was dressed in a snazzy grey suit with an open-throated black shirt that only enhanced his fabulous physique.

'*Querida*...' His eyes glimmered. 'You look beautiful.'

Blushing, she held the shoes out. 'Which pair should I wear?'

His gaze drifted to her feet. She'd painted her toenails cherry red. 'I think you look damn sexy as you are.'

A flush coursed through her right from her painted toenails and rose up to the roots of her hair. 'I don't fancy getting cut feet,' she said, attempting lightness, 'so, please, which pair?'

His eyes swept from the shoes in her hands to her dress. 'Try the red pair first.'

Padding into his dressing room, she sat on the red velvet chaise longue and slipped her feet into the high red sandals, secured them, then stood up and held her arms out in a *'well?'*.

'Perfect,' he said.

She bit into her lip before blurting out, 'Does this dress make me look fat?'

Her question made his eyes narrow before dipping to her belly.

His chest rose, lips pulling together before he strode decisively to stand behind her, put his hands on her shoulders, and frogmarched her across the dressing room.

'What are you doing?' she asked.

'Making you look.'

'At what?'

He brought her to a stop in front of the walled mirror. 'At you.'

'I know what I look like.'

'Do you? Because that is not what your body language tells me. Please, *querida*, open your eyes and look.'

Sighing, trying her best to appear nonchalant that he was pressed lightly against her back, she raised her gaze to their reflection. 'There. I'm looking.' Looking at Ramos. The extra inches from the sandals had elevated her so she now reached his throat.

He rested his chin on the top of her head and, his reflected eyes glittering, moved his hands to hold her biceps.

'Do you know what I see?' he asked quietly.

She shook her head, suddenly unable to speak. There was an expression in his eyes that made her feel all choked.

'A beautiful woman. That's what I see,' he whispered. He ran his fingers through the ends of her hair loose around her shoulders. 'A woman with hair like silk.' He brushed his thumb at the small section of flesh exposed on her neck. She shivered at the sensation. 'A woman with skin like silk.'

His fingers tiptoed across her collarbone to reach the base of her throat. His hands flattened against the top of her chest. Slowly, he drew them down, over the swell of her breasts, and gently cupped them.

A tiny gasp flew from her mouth. Tiny because all the air had left her lungs.

His nose buried into her hair. His breath swirled through the strands and penetrated her skull right through to her rapidly dizzying brain. 'A woman with breasts that are every bit as plump and beautiful now as they were the night we conceived our child.'

Flora tried to shake her head but the arousal flooding her overrode everything. All she could do was squeeze her eyes shut, grit her teeth, and fight desperately against the desire firing through every cell in her body.

His hands drifted to her belly, his mouth finding her

ear. 'A woman with a stomach that carried and nurtured our child.'

The material of her dress swished around her knees, brushing against her increasingly fevered skin.

She needed to stop him…

Oh, God, he was gathering it together and pulling it up.

'Look, *querida*.'

Don't look. Whatever you do, don't look.

Her eyes flew back open.

The hooded sensuality in Ramos's reflected stare stole the last of her breath.

'Look,' he breathed.

One hand was flat against her pubis, the other holding the material of her dress at the top of her hip, exposing her belly.

She barely registered her stomach, too intent on the gorgeous man gazing at her as if *she* were a thing of wonder.

'I see a woman,' he said hoarsely, his eyes taking her belly in before rising back up to gaze into her eyes. 'A sexy, beautiful, feminine, curvaceous woman who has given me the greatest gift a man can receive. Wear your curves with pride because you earned them and because they are as sexy as hell.'

Flora gazed, trapped and helpless, into Ramos's eyes. She needed to push his hand away and scream at him to stop but the heat bubbling inside her was too needy, too strong, melting her from the inside out.

His fingers slowly dipped under the band of her knickers.

Her knees buckled. Only his strength kept her upright.

She couldn't breathe. No matter how hard she tried, she couldn't draw in breath.

His fingers dipped lower.

Dear heavens, the sensation…

Her breath came back to her in shallow inhalations that turned into pants when a finger pressed gently against her swollen nub.

She was burning. Aflame.

He increased the pressure against her nub, just a little, but enough for…

Flora was losing herself. Losing control. Terrified, she struck out wildly behind her only for her hand to clasp tightly onto Ramos's hip, and then his mouth buried into her neck and she was lost.

Flopping her head back onto his shoulder, she closed her eyes and let herself go.

Moving her pelvis, she found a rhythm with the fingers doing such magical things to her. The pleasure was impossible to contain, escaping her lips in wanton moans as the pressure built up and up and she held on for dear life, writhing against him, suffused with his breath on her skin and in her hair and the whispers of his inaudible voice until, with a loud cry, the explosion came and shattered her into a million pieces.

'Flora?'

She didn't dare open her eyes.

Her dress had been released and gently swooshed back to her knees. Two strong arms were wrapped around her waist holding her upright. Ramos's nose was nuzzling in her hair. He must be able to feel the thuds of her heart bashing through her.

She could still feel the zings of ecstasy that had split her body into mere atomic parts.

He whispered her name again.

But she couldn't respond. The second she opened

her eyes or mouth, reality was going to hit her and then she would be confronted with the humiliation of how she had just come undone with nothing more than Ramos's touch.

He twisted her round to face him. Her legs obeyed his ministrations even if her brain tried to remain stubborn.

Warm hands cupped her cheeks.

'Flora, look at me,' he breathed.

She took a long breath, opened her eyes and met Ramos's melting stare.

She'd expected to find triumph there but what she found made her heart sigh and the potential for humiliation evaporate. There was no triumph, only wonder.

Incredibly, a tiny swell of laughter rose up her throat. 'That wasn't supposed to happen,' she whispered, half smiling, half trying not to cry.

His lips curved and a low burst of laughter left his mouth before he lowered his face to hers and kissed her. It was the lightest brush of his lips against hers but, oh, thank the Lord he was holding her up or she would have swooned to the floor.

His hands skimmed from her cheeks to thread through the strands of her hair.

And then he kissed her again, harder, with a greedy possessiveness that knitted all her atoms back together and pulsed them back to glorious life.

This time Flora accepted the loss of control and melted into the heady heat of his hungry mouth.

A loud noise cut right through them and, eyes locking back together, both pulled their faces away so only the tips of their noses touched. Ramos's ragged breath was warm against her sensitised lips, and her mouth tingled for more of his kisses, her skin burning for more of his touch...

More of everything.

The loud tune continued its incessant hum until Ramos stepped back and pulled his phone out of his pocket. He swiped it without even looking at the screen and threw it onto the sofa.

His chest rising and falling in great heaves, he held his hand out to her.

Feeling as if she were in the midst of a dream, Flora threaded her fingers into his and let him lead her into the bedroom. There, he pushed her gently on the bed.

He stared at her for the longest time and for a moment she was taken back to the look in his eyes the moment before their lips had brushed together for the very first time.

That was the night she had gone to him pleading for his mercy.

She'd looked in those spellbinding dark eyes and had run out of words. She'd lost the power of speech. In that moment, the only thought in her head had been that Alejandro Ramos was beautiful.

Alone as they had never been alone before, there had been no one to distract her, no one to rescue her.

She hadn't needed rescuing from Ramos. She'd needed rescuing from herself.

Trapped in the swirling depths, her heart a sharp, painful tattoo, she'd been overcome with the need to feel *his* heart and had placed her hand on his chest before she was aware of what she was doing. He'd sucked in a breath at her touch, she remembered. The hard beats had thumped against her palm. Spellbound, she'd cupped his cheek. He'd been unshaven. The look she could see in his eyes now had rung out starkly when he'd whispered her name. Slowly, his mouth had inched closer and at that very first brush of his lips to hers, she'd been lost.

And now she was caught again and she no longer had the strength or the will to fight it.

She no longer *wanted* to fight it.

Ramos shrugged his jacket off and let it drop on the floor. Eyes not leaving her face, he undid the buttons of his shirt and let that drop too.

Flora, her heart beating fast, unashamedly drank him in.

Hadn't she known since that adolescent glimpse of his nudity that Alejandro Ramos was the epitome of masculine perfection, the physical standard for which she put all men but which no other could live up to?

He wore his rampant sexuality like a cloak, his melting eyes hypnotising and luring. Hadn't that been why she'd always avoided looking in his eyes? Hadn't she instinctively known as a young adolescent the danger that lay for her in those depths, known that they were a trap, just as she'd know his very scent was a trap to entice her too?

His hands went to his chinos.

His erection was clearly delineated beneath the fabric.

The pulse between her legs throbbed.

God, she wanted him. Desperately. A wanton craving that existed only for him.

She put a hand to the bulge in his chinos and traced the hard length.

His strong throat swallowed.

Tilting her head back to gaze up at his gorgeous face and to revel in the desire blazing from it, she undid the button of his trousers.

Working quickly, jaw clenched, he removed the rest of his clothes.

His erection sprang free, as huge and glorious as she

remembered, and the pulse between her legs throbbed even deeper.

He stepped to her and put his hands to her thighs. And then he parted them. Kneeling on the floor before her, he slid his hands under the skirt of her dress and up, over her hips to catch the band of her knickers in his fingers.

The beats of her heart now smashing against her ribs, her breaths coming in quick bursts, Flora lifted her bottom to help him tug them down. Knickers removed, he unbuckled her sandals and threw them behind him with the other discarded clothes…and then he kissed a cherry-red painted toenail. And then his lips pressed over the arch of her foot to her ankle, brushing up her calf and over her knee, the marks of his mouth and tongue leaving a scorching trail of lightning in their wake, up the highly sensitised flesh of her thighs, hands gripping her dress and pushing it up, exposing her pubis…

She flopped onto her back with a gasp when his tongue found the sweet spot his fingers had so recently brought to a peak.

Alejandro had a magical power over her, she thought dreamily as she willingly submitted to the unrelenting pleasure. He could melt her insides with nothing but a look and turn her into a mass of nerves and sensations with only the lightest of touches. His magic was stronger than her defences and when it felt this good, this essential, she could think of no good reason to fight it any more, not when surrender felt so incredible.

The sensations building deep inside her were coiling together, swelling and thickening but, just as stars were starting to form behind her eyes, he moved his mouth from her heart and up, over her belly, pushing her dress as far as it would rise.

Feeling drugged on lust, craving the feel of his skin

pressed tightly against hers, Flora undid the clasp at the neck of her dress. Working together, they pulled it off before he deftly unclasped her bra and replaced the lace with his mouth. With sounds of greedy appreciation, he sucked and licked, traced his tongue around the peaks, making her head flop back again at the intoxicating pleasure of it.

It was *all* pleasure. The magic of his mouth. The magic of his hands exploring the contours of her body. The magic of his smooth skin beneath her own exploring hands. The softness of his hair and the hardness of his body. The musk of his skin and the spiciness of his cologne. It all infused her senses and fed her increasing desperation for his possession, and when he snaked his tongue up her neck and pinned his elbows either side of her face to gaze down at her, Flora saw the passion burning her matched in his liquid stare.

His hooded eyes were eating her alive.

Suddenly desperate to be as one with him, Flora clasped the back of his head and lifted her head to fuse her mouth to his.

He groaned, and kissed her back so ravenously she could taste his hunger for her. Tongues clashing and dancing, she wound her legs around his waist and arched upwards at the same moment he thrust himself deep inside her.

The sensation was so incredible that stars flashed behind her eyes.

There was a long moment of stillness before he raised his head. Breathing deeply, he gazed into her eyes. The emotion pouring from his stare penetrated her as deeply as he was buried in her.

Please, let it feel as magical for him as it does for me,

she prayed. *Let Alejandro feel all of this as deeply and as profoundly as I do.*

He kissed her.

She wound her arms tightly around him and closed her eyes.

Breasts crushed against chest, they drove the pleasure higher. In and out he thrust, each movement taking her closer to saturation point, closer still, until he clasped her bottom, fusing their groins together, and she shot past every peak he'd taken her to before and, with spasms of pleasure exploding through her, she soared high into the sky, over kaleidoscopic stars, his name falling from her tongue, her own name shooting from his lips a distant echo caressing her ears.

Slowly, so slowly, Flora floated down from the stars.

Alejandro was slumped on top of her, breathing heavily into her neck. The thuds of his heart beat through her skin to her own cantering heart.

Alejandro was the star, she realised as she landed like a feather back on the earth rotating around him. She was the earth unable to escape his gravitational pull.

Was she in love with him? Or was it just lust?

The answer made her heart clench.

She'd been in some form of love with Alejandro Ramos for half her life. It had been a form of sickness, a violent tempest of emotions she'd been far too young to handle or understand. It had stopped her ever looking at other men. Until the night they'd conceived their child, her only kiss from a boy had come from a game of kiss chase in primary school.

She thought back to their first night together. He'd made love to her with a tenderness that had filled her chest with so many emotions it had turned her into putty in his hands.

She'd wished many times that he'd been a selfish oaf of a lover because then it might have made the pain that had lanced her when he'd stood her up the next night and then cut her so effectively out of his life easier to bear.

An icy sliver of panic washed through her now. What if this had all been an elaborate hoax to reel her back in one more time before he discarded her again?

'Say something,' he whispered, raising his head and lifting much of his weight off her.

Afraid to look in his eyes, more afraid not to, Flora plucked up the courage to gaze into the swirling depths. Whatever the emotion she was looking at was, it melted the icy panic.

Because there was emotion there. She could see it. Deep emotion.

But hadn't she seen it that night too? Wasn't that why his cruel treatment of her had cut so deeply?

Things had been different then, she reminded herself. Very different. They had a child now. They were married. He wore a ring on his finger that told the world he belonged to her.

'Say something,' he repeated. 'Please. Tell me what you're thinking.'

Exhaling a slow breath, she smiled. 'Who was on the phone?'

His brow furrowed and then his mouth widened into the heartbreaking smile she'd always hated because of what it did to her heart, and he chuckled lightly and kissed her.

'I've no idea who called me. Now, tell me what you're really thinking,' he insisted, smoothing his thumbs over her forehead.

He was still inside her.

'We didn't use protection?' she suggested as an alternative to the truth.

His eyebrows rose and then he chuckled again. 'See what you do to me, *querida*. You make me lose my mind.'

'Good,' she whispered, the feigned nonchalance deserting her. 'Because you make me lose my mind too.' He made her lose her mind, her inhibitions and all her sensibilities. Barely an hour ago she would have freaked out at the very thought of having unprotected sex with Alejandro.

And that was what he did to her and why she'd fought her desire for so long. One burst of uncontrolled passion and already she was imagining the beautiful baby they might have created through it. He made her want…no, crave…so much. All with him.

He kissed her again, more deeply. More possessively.

She wanted to cry when he broke the kiss and then broke the other connection between them to roll onto his back.

Turning his face to her, he took her hand and brought it to his lips. She rolled onto her side facing him and threaded her fingers through his.

'How would you feel if we have made another baby?' he asked, his expression serious.

Wondering if he could read her mind, she nudged her face closer to his. 'Not unhappy.' She was quite sure she should be unhappy about it but in this post-coital haze—and she was glad she had enough wits about her to know it *was* a post-coital haze—the thought of having another baby, and this time going through the whole pregnancy with Alejandro at her side, made her heart feel as if it could burst. 'What about you?'

His lips quirked. 'Not unhappy.'

'You want more babies?'

'Sure. You?'

'Until about a minute ago, I hadn't really thought about it.'

'I have.'

She hesitated before asking, 'With me?'

He kissed the tips of her fingers, his gaze not wavering. 'Only you.'

Her heart swelled so much she really thought it had burst.

'You're serious?' she whispered.

'Flora…' He sighed and closed his eyes. When he opened them back onto her, he let go of her hand and twisted onto his side. Pulling her flush against him, he stroked her hair and said, 'You are my wife. Whatever the reasons for why we married, I chose to marry you.'

'Because you didn't want me to keep Benjamin from you or poison him against you,' she reminded him.

His smile was rueful. 'I don't think I believed even then that you would do that.'

'You didn't?'

'No woman who could devote such time and love to her sick mother would treat her child like a weapon.'

Hot tears welled and stabbed the backs of her eyes, but she didn't know where they came from. The tenderness in his voice? The memory of those dark days when Flora wouldn't leave her mum's side? She hadn't wanted strangers, no matter how compassionate and lovely they were, doing her mother's intimate care.

Swallowing back the tears, she said, 'So why did you marry me if you knew I wouldn't keep Benjamin from you?'

He stared silently at her for so long that she wondered if he was trying to read her innermost thoughts, but then he shook his head and grimaced. 'It is done. We are here, we are married and we have a son. If you are happy to have more children, then that is great. I don't want Benjamin to be on his own like I was.'

Now she was the one to stare into his eyes and try to read his mind but her mind-reading skills were poor, and she didn't want to ruin the moment by forcing a confession of something that would probably hurt her. Back then, he'd hated her. What else was there to know?

She saw no hate in his eyes now. 'Do you believe me now?' she whispered. 'About our night together?'

His mouth formed a tight line before loosening. Closing his eyes, he pressed his forehead lightly to hers and kissed the tip of her nose. 'Yes, *querida*. I believe you.'

The relief at this was overwhelming and, for the second time in as many minutes, she had to swallow back tears.

Flora hadn't realised how much it had eaten at her that Alejandro had convinced himself that she'd only slept with him for her brother's freedom.

When she was certain she'd contained the emotion bubbling inside her, she softly said, 'What you said about not wanting Benjamin to be on his own like you were... did you want a sibling?'

'Yes.'

'Were you a lonely child?'

'Sometimes. Because my father travelled so much with his work and we travelled everywhere with him, I didn't go to school until I was ten.'

'That was because of your mother's death, wasn't it?' she asked, and had to swallow back another swell of emotion.

Was this what it was like for all women after sex? Did it send their emotions all over the place too? Or was it just the effect Alejandro had on her?

He nodded. 'I had nannies and an English tutor until then.'

'That must have been a hard adjustment to make. Going to school, I mean.'

His face creased with surprise. 'Not at all. I was glad to go. It is hard for a child to make friends when they are never in the same place for longer than a week.'

'But if you'd never been to school before, that would have been a brand-new environment for you. That would have frightened the hell out of me at ten.'

His voice was steady but she thought she heard an edge to it. 'I watched my mother's coffin be buried in the ground two weeks before I started school. I told you before, nothing has frightened or hurt me since and nothing ever will.'

She stared at his face, noting the underlying hardness that had just formed in his expression. It was similar to the hardness she saw whenever her brother's name was mentioned.

Palming the side of his neck, she brushed her thumb over his smooth skin and wished she could dive into his heart and smooth out the suffering he'd lived through.

For the first time she understood him. Truly understood him.

Alejandro had lived through a child's worst nightmare and survived it, but it had damaged a core part of him. He was like those deep-sea squids she'd read about who, when feeling threatened, attacked the predator and then pulled away breaking off the tip of their own arm. Except, in Alejandro's case, it wasn't predators he attacked, it was people who hurt him, his attack a defence mechanism crucial to his survival.

He'd ruthlessly severed Justin from his life without seeking or wanting an explanation for his out-of-character behaviour, just turned his back on thirteen years of close friendship and gone full steam ahead on the attack. Whatever Alejandro said to the contrary, Flora was certain that on some fundamental level Justin's theft—more likely the situation that had led up to it—had hurt him.

What had the cost of severing his closest friend been to himself?

He'd cut Flora from his life too. Made love to her with such tenderness and then, believing she'd used him, deliberately and remorselessly dropped her from a great height.

She'd heard other stories of his hard-heartedness too, like the one of the good friend for whom Alejandro had been best man at his wedding, who had been suspected of tipping off the press about minor stories of him and cut from his circle and discarded without afterthought for it.

When Ramos cut someone from his life, there was no way back. Flora was the only exception to this severing and that was only because of Benjamin.

When emotionally threatened, he was ruthless. And remorseless. She must never forget that.

The hardness in his stare softened. 'You are beautiful, did you know that?'

She tried to smile.

He inched his face closer to hers. 'Very beautiful. I remember seeing you at your twenty-first birthday...' He brushed his lips to hers. 'Hillier's annoying little sister all grown up.' He kissed her again. 'You took my breath away.'

'I did?'

'You still do.' Tongue sweeping into her mouth, he rolled back on top of her and sent her back to the stars.

CHAPTER TEN

Two and a half hours after they were supposed to set off for the party, they got in the back of the car. Alejandro was unperturbed about their tardiness, pointing out that most parties took a few hours to warm up and that no party really got going until he arrived. The latter was a point she was not going to argue with. She couldn't really argue about the former either. Flora had never been a party animal, not even close, had always preferred nights out with her small group of close friends to raucous shindigs.

Now wearing a black wrap dress—when they'd finally dragged themselves out of bed she'd found the white one scrunched on the floor—and with her hair now tied into a loose bun, Flora resisted attaching herself to him like a limpet and satisfied her body's craving for him by holding his hand.

The post-coital bliss of their second lovemaking still thrummed in her veins but the barriers she'd worn around him for so many years were refortifying themselves.

She no longer denied that she was in love with him but she wasn't so far gone that she couldn't protect the last part of her heart from him. So long as she kept a degree of detachment, she could survive marriage to a man who could never love her.

Love involved risk. It involved hurt. Alejandro would never allow himself to love anyone because the risk of hurt was too strong a deterrent for him.

He had feelings for her. Strong feelings, she was certain.

But they weren't strong enough for him to take the risk of love and if he ever found out how deeply her feelings for him ran, the tipping point of power in their marriage would fall even more heavily in his favour.

The party was in a traditional Spanish villa that matched Alejandro's for size and elegance, their hosts a wildly glamorous couple called Juan and Camila who greeted Flora with enormous kisses to her cheek and a large glass of champagne.

Having only had that tiny glass of wine over dinner the night of the ballet since Benjamin's conception, Flora knew she needed to take it easy with the alcohol. The problem was, Alejandro had been righter than even she had suspected that the party wouldn't start until he arrived, and no sooner had they entered the vast party room than all the beautiful, glamourous guests clamoured around him. Although most spoke in Spanish, she could tell by their tone and body language that they were chiding him, and guessed it was because he'd been off the party scene for so long. With everyone wanting a piece of the only person she knew there, and feeling the weight of a hundred pairs of curious eyes and so many introductions made and kisses planted on her cheeks, Flora kept sipping at her champagne out of nerves and before she knew it, she'd finished two full glasses.

'Let me show you our new swimming pool,' her hostess insisted, taking the empty glass from her and handing it to a passing waiter. Camila then slipped her arm through Flora's and bore her away.

Flora looked over her shoulder at Alejandro and her stomach settled a little when she immediately caught his eye and received a faint, knowing wink from him.

The far end of the party room had no wall and led straight onto the terrace, which acted like an extension of the party room and was filled with numerous people enjoying the humidity of the hot evening. After the air conditioning of the villa's interior, Flora felt the heat, and when Camila snatched another glass of champagne for her, she took a large mouthful of it without even realising.

'You are Justin's sister?' Camila said as they walked down marble steps to the large kidney-shaped swimming pool.

'Yes.'

'I remember you.'

Her heart sank. 'Do you?'

'A party at Alejandro's a few years ago.'

'You have a good memory.'

'You were the only one wearing clothes,' Camila pointed out with a cackle of laughter that made Flora grin. 'My sister was hoping Alejandro would notice her but he only had eyes for you.'

'Hardly,' she demurred, feeling a blush crawl over her face. 'I was only there for thirty minutes.' And most of that had been spent hiding in the changing room.

'He didn't want her after you went.' Camila nudged Flora's side with her elbow. 'That was very unusual. It is why I was not surprised when I heard he had married you, even though you are Justin's sister.'

She didn't have the faintest idea how to take that or how she should respond.

They reached the water's edge.

'I miss your brother,' Camila said. 'We were lovers many years ago.'

'Maybe a bit too much information?' Flora suggested. 'I am his sister.'

'It is okay, I will not give you details of his lovemaking. How is he?'

'Lonely. Guilty. Ashamed.'

Camila gave a nonchalant shrug. 'He should be ashamed. He screwed his best friend.'

'I know.' Justin would live with the guilt and regret for the rest of his life.

She sighed. 'But I still miss him. I bet Alejandro does too.'

Flora would bet on it too.

'And it is good that he is here tonight. We have all missed him.'

'Sorry.' She had no idea why she was apologising. 'We've been a bit busy with Benjamin.'

'It has been much longer than that since he stopped seeing his friends.'

'What do you mean?'

'A year? Longer, I think. A little after we learned Justin had stolen all that money from him.'

Around the time of Benjamin's conception, then? Coincidence?

'What are you two gossiping about?' a deep voice asked from behind them.

'You, of course,' Camila answered with a cackle while Flora hastily downed the rest of her champagne.

Alejandro noticed and raised an eyebrow.

Flora shrugged in a 'no, I don't know why I did that' manner.

He smirked before turning his attention to Camila. 'I hope you haven't been telling my wife too many horror stories about me.'

'I haven't had the time, so if you could leave us alone a bit longer…'

'No.'

'It's okay,' Flora piped up. 'I've already heard most of them.'

Camila cackled even louder, and said something to Alejandro in Spanish before heading back, still laughing, to the other revellers.

'What did she say?' Flora asked.

'That she likes you.'

'Really?'

'Yes.' He wrapped his arms around her and pulled her flush to him. 'Tell me the horror stories you have heard about me.'

'I didn't hear *about* them. I *heard* them.'

'What do you mean?'

'When you used to stay at our house, you and Justin would often go out for the night.' Whenever Justin brought Ramos home for a weekend they would be inundated with party invitations from Justin's old school friends. 'I would listen out for you to get home and then sneak out of my bedroom and sit at the top of the stairs listening to you discuss how the night had gone.'

He winced. 'Really?' he asked doubtfully.

She hooked her arms around his neck. 'Sometimes when I was feeling *really* brave, I would sneak down the stairs and hide behind doors.'

'Even when you were young?'

'I was thirteen when I started eavesdropping on you.'

A faint look of alarm flickered over his face. 'So I would have been twenty?'

'Yep.' She raised herself onto her toes and grazed her teeth over his chin. 'You were a bad boy.'

'You shouldn't have been listening, not at that age.' He shook his head. 'I didn't know.'

'I was very quiet.' She dropped her voice to a whisper. 'Like a little stealthy mouse.'

His eyes narrowed but there was amusement in them. 'How much have you had to drink?'

'Three glasses of champagne. Why? Am I drunk?'

'Do you feel drunk?'

'I don't know. I've never been drunk before.'

'Never?'

'Uh-uh.'

'Why not?'

'I didn't want to be one of those women.'

'What women?'

'You know. *Those* women. The kind who threw themselves at you.'

'Did you think you would be like them if you had a drink?'

'Alcohol makes you love…lose…your inhi…' She hiccuped. 'Inhibitions!' she finished triumphantly.

'Did you think you would throw yourself at me?'

'Not saying.'

'Why not?'

'You'll get a big head.'

'What were you scared of?'

'Falling in love with you, silly.'

Her eyesight had become a bit blurry but she thought she saw the amusement fall from his face. Her sight wasn't quite clear enough to see what replaced it.

'Come on,' he said, brushing a gentle kiss to her lips, 'let's get you home.'

'But we've only just got here. I'm having a lovely time.'

'There will be other parties.'

'Promise?'

'Promise.'

'Alejandro?'

He sucked in a breath. 'Yes, *querida*?'

'I don't feel very well.'

Someone had inserted a hammer into Flora's head and was merrily smashing it into her skull.

She opened an eye. The room was dusky.

There was movement beside her and then Alejandro sat on the bed. He was fully dressed.

He touched her forehead. 'You okay?' he murmured.

'No.'

He grinned. 'There is water and painkillers on the bedside table.'

'Thank you,' she whispered. 'What time is it?'

'Eight.'

She tried to lift her head, but, ow!

He chuckled.

The noise made her wince. 'Don't,' she moaned.

'Sorry,' he said in a completely unapologetic tone.

'Where's Benjamin?'

'With Sinead.'

'I should get up.'

'You should sleep more,' he said firmly. 'Water and sleep are the best cures for hangovers.'

'Thank you for looking after me.' She had vague memories of him helping her to the car, helping her into it, helping her crawl out of it, helping her navigate the stairs to their room, then helping her undress.

'*De nada.*'

She bit her lip as another vague memory filtered through her heavy head of trying to get him to make love to her and him kissing her forehead and telling her to go to sleep. 'Did I embarrass you?'

The grin returned. 'No.

She sighed. 'I'm sorry.'

He leaned over and kissed her. 'Don't be.' Then he grinned again. 'Twenty-four and suffering your first hangover.'

'And my last.'

Still grinning, he gave her another kiss. 'I have to go.'

Her mood went from hungover but happy to hungover and miserable in an instant.

'Now?' she asked, trying not to sound too forlorn about it.

This was his first business trip since his early return from Las Vegas.

'I have meetings in Athens at midday.'

But it's Sunday, she wanted to howl.

Hotel casinos didn't have the same working days as normal businesses.

'I'll be back Saturday. Friday if I can.'

'Call me when you get there so I know you've arrived safely?'

He stared at her with the strangest expression on his face before bowing his head. 'Of course.'

Flora concentrated very hard on not crying when he closed the door softly behind him.

The days without Alejandro dragged by.

Flora had thought herself accustomed to him being away so much but, having had him to herself for a week and with the closeness and intimacy that had developed between them in that time, she felt his absence in Athens starkly.

If not for Benjamin, she feared she would have cracked and begged him on one of their evening calls—he now called every night—to let her fly out to him, which would have been the worst thing she could have done and just reeked of desperation and exposed herself to him far more than their lovemaking had done.

But she did have her bundle of joy and it was impossible to mope with Benjamin's happy little smiling face loving her and needing her. Other than Hangover Sunday, when Flora finally managed to drag herself out of bed at ten a.m., poor Sinead hadn't had much to do apart from flirt with Mateo.

Flora also thought she had found a friend in Camila. The glamourous Spanish lady invited herself over for lunch and turned up with her toddler, an adorable little girl called Ava whose curly golden hair Benjamin kept trying to grab. He seemed smitten.

Camila was great fun and wildly indiscreet, and when she left, she extracted a promise from Flora to join her and some other 'girls' on a night out soon.

It was the evenings she most missed Alejandro. Benjamin filled her days but he was always asleep by seven, which left hours to fill before she could find sleep of her own. She bought some embroidery supplies but inspiration and creativity had still deserted her. She tried to read a book but her attention span was decimated.

Thursday evening, the same day Camila had come for lunch, she gave up trying to do anything that involved concentration and, after putting Sinead in charge should Benjamin wake up, headed to the roof terrace.

The roof terrace was something she'd only had a curious look at before. Enclosed by a waist-height white wall, it had a seating area and a dining area and a fully stocked bar, but it was the L-shaped swimming pool she'd come up here for.

Making sure her phone's volume was high, so she'd hear it when Alejandro called, she placed it on her towel then lowered herself into the underlit water. It felt deliciously cool in contrast to the humid heat of the evening, and she kept her head above water and swam a couple of lengths of the longest part, then hugged the edge as she trod water and gazed out at the spectacular view of Barcelona by night. The city's skyscape, somehow surrounding her but feeling as if it was far away too, was a golden silhouette. Shining above it all this moonless night were so many stars it made her feel dizzy to imagine their numbers.

It made her feel dizzy, too, to remember how her mouth had run away with her at Camila and Juan's party. She'd forgotten all about it until long after Alejandro had flown to Athens and her cheeks had gone so red she could have used them as handwarmers.

Her refusal to partake in more than a small glass of wine before that night had been down to Alejandro. And her brother. Eavesdropping on their drunk talk about conquests and the wild things the girls at parties had done had been a more effective alcohol deterrent than any lecture by an adult. Until Saturday, she'd never been drunk. The thought of being picked apart and rated had revolted her.

So why had she listened in; hidden behind doors like a miniature spy, hardly daring to breathe for fear of being discovered? More than once Alejandro had strolled past her hiding space without noticing her.

Camila's indiscretions that day had been mostly about Justin. Alejandro had been mentioned too but she'd had a feeling Camila had made a conscious effort not to speak of his dalliances with other women to her. Justin had been the focus of her talk, making Flora wonder if she still hankered after him.

All Camila's indiscretions had made Flora rethink the drunk conversations she'd avidly eavesdropped on.

Justin had been the one to do all the rating, she remembered. Alejandro had laughed along with it, but Justin had always been the instigator of those conversations.

He'd been trying to impress him, she realised.

And she realised too that it had been easier on her heart to blame his behaviour on his Spanish friend rather than confront the brother who'd always adored and looked out for her for being a sexist pig.

Alejandro had been wild too but he'd never boasted about it. He'd never strung women along or messed them around or made promises he wouldn't keep. She supposed he'd never needed to.

Or maybe he was just a damn sight more respectful than she'd given him credit for.

She'd childishly hated him for stealing Justin from her and then she'd seen him naked and hated him even more for the terrifying feelings his nakedness had awoken in her.

He'd deserved none of her misplaced hate. He'd been a red-blooded young man playing the field, partying and enjoying his life. He couldn't help that he was drop-dead gorgeous, filthy rich, and that women salivated over him.

She rested her chin on her hands with a sad sigh.

She missed him. That was the truth. Even when the only emotion she'd dared allow herself to admit to feeling for him had been loathing, his presence had always energised her. The world always felt a little flatter without him in it.

It felt a lot flatter now.

'There you are.'

A short scream of fright escaped her throat before the joy of recognition thrashed through her and she twisted round to see Alejandro silhouetted on the poolside.

CHAPTER ELEVEN

IT DIDN'T EVEN cross Flora's mind to play it cool. She couldn't have stopped the beaming smile from forming even if she'd tried. 'You're back!'

Pushing her feet off the pool's side to propel her, she swam over to him. The water's depth there came to her breasts and she put her feet on the bottom and her hands on the edge of the pool, and gazed up at his gorgeous face. 'You've grown a beard.'

He stroked it. 'You like?'

'It's okay.' She grinned. It was more than okay. It made him look even sexier, something she would never have thought possible. 'How come you're back?'

He leaned over and removed his shoes and socks. 'I cancelled the rest of my meetings.'

She drank him in. 'Why?'

He straightened, fingers on a shirt button, his eyes capturing hers. 'I missed my family.'

Her heart swelled. 'You should have told me you were coming home.'

'I wanted it to be a surprise... Is it?'

'Well, duh.'

'I mean, is it a good surprise?'

'It's okay.' Her mouth forming another beaming smile totally negated her efforts at nonchalance.

His teeth flashed, eyes crinkling. His shirt went flying behind him. 'You have missed me?'

Desperately. 'It's…different when you're not here.'

His naked chest rose and his glimmering gaze stayed on her even as he undid his trousers. 'I missed you.'

Her heart swelled so much at this admission that it stuck in her throat.

Now fully naked, his discarded clothes scattered all around him, Alejandro dropped himself into the water next to her and put his hands on her hips, twisting her round to face him.

'*Did* you miss me?' he asked, sliding his arms around her back to hold her closer.

Winding her arms around his neck, she tilted her head back and sighed her pleasure at being back in his arms, then raised herself up on the tips of her toes to kiss him.

He moved his head back before her lips could connect and fixed a stern stare on her. 'Did you miss me?'

Flora stared into the dark, melting eyes she had missed more than she'd believed was humanly possible but something held her back from making that confession.

Alejandro had so much power over her. More power than he knew. Emotional power.

He was Flora's one and only. Her feelings for him ran so deep they were an intrinsic part of her, but for her to admit any part of it would be to hand him even more power. To admit to any part of it would be to put it out in the open. Would make it real.

Words that were said could never be unsaid.

The sternness dissolved, replaced by a knowing gleam, and he clasped his hands to her waist and lifted her high off her feet.

Instinctively, she wrapped her legs around his waist

and was rewarded with the hard tip of his erection jutting against the fold of her sex. Only the material of her swimsuit stopped him diving straight into her.

He carried her up the gentle slope of the pool's floor until he found the perfect height to sit her on the pool's edge, groin to groin.

Only then did he kiss her, and, dear heaven, what a kiss it was, a slow fusion of lips and the slow stroke of his tongue against hers, as seductive, sensual and perfect a kiss as it was possible to have.

When he broke it, she whimpered at the loss of the pleasure.

He gazed back into her eyes and growled before spearing her hair to clasp her head and devour her mouth again.

Flora tightened her hold around his neck and revelled in the taste of his mouth and all the heady sensations fizzing and bubbling through her veins, her skin, every component of her. And then he danced his lips across her cheek to lick the lobe of her ear and bury his face into her neck. His beard scratched deliciously against her sensitised skin and she moaned, digging her nails into his skull until he put a hand to her chest and gently but firmly pushed her back so he had better access to assault her with his mouth while tugging her swimsuit off her shoulders.

Impatient to be as naked as him, she pulled her arms free and pulled her swimsuit down to her waist.

'Did you miss me?' he asked.

'Just kiss me,' she said, throwing her arms back around his neck and crushing her mouth to his, pressing every inch of her that she could to him.

Alejandro was much stronger than her and easily

slipped a hand between their conjoined chests to gently push her back again.

Eyes ablaze with sensuality, he gripped hold of her swimsuit with one hand, raised her bottom with the other, and stepped back to pull it down to her thighs. In seconds she'd kicked it off and hooked her ankles behind his muscular butt to reel him back to her.

He growled again and dipped his head to take a breast into his mouth.

Heavens, that felt so…

Flora closed her eyes and let the sensations infuse her, crying out when he cupped her other breast and kneaded it with just the right amount of pressure, straddling the line between pleasure and pain but never letting it spill over to anything that wasn't bliss.

His touch set her on fire.

He set her on fire. Stopped her seeing straight or thinking clearly. Turned her into a mass of nerves that cried out for him.

'Did you miss me?' he asked again, dragging his fingers down over her belly. She would have blocked out the question, but there was something about the hoarseness in his voice that made her open her eyes. What she saw in the tautness of his face had her slide her hands over his chest, skimming her fingers through the fine dark hair to rest them at his throat.

He must have drugged her with his kisses and his touch because she stared into his eyes and whispered, 'Yes.'

His chest and shoulders rose slowly and heavily and then he kissed her with such hunger that any fear of handing him the power of her feelings was consumed in the headiness of his passion, and she was consumed too, with the need to taste and touch him.

Trailing her fingers down his muscular arms, she ran her tongue down the column of his throat, bringing her hands onto his chest, flattening them, dragging them down his hard abdomen as she lowered her head to take a flat, brown nipple into her mouth.

He groaned and fisted her hair. His erection was jutting into her thigh, just out of reach of where she most wanted it, and, biting gently onto his other nipple, she dipped her hand further down, through the coarser dark pubic hair, and took hold of it.

His grip on her hair tightened.

She looked up, into his eyes. 'Show me how,' she whispered.

'Flora...'

She bit his nipple again, felt the shudder that rippled through him, and looked back up at him. 'Show me,' she commanded with all the sensuality she possessed.

He swallowed, then his much bigger hand covered hers.

Glazed eyes locked on hers, he adjusted her hold around it then slowly began to move her hand, first down his rock-hard length to the base, and then back up to the head, down then up... And then he released her hand and closed his eyes as she continued the movements exactly as he'd shown her. When she gripped it a little tighter, his mouth opened but the only sound to come out was dim, shallow breaths.

'Am I doing it right?' she whispered huskily.

His eyes opened.

He snatched her hand away from him and held it tightly at her side as he brought his face to hers.

For the longest moment he did nothing but gaze at her, gaze so intensely it was as if he were peering down into her soul.

'You are beautiful,' he growled.

And then Alejandro plunged into her and Flora fell into the melting swirl of his eyes.

It was too late for rescue, she thought dimly as she drowned in the intensity of his lovemaking.

She loved him. Loved him, loved him. With her heart, her body and soul.

She held him tight, infusing herself with his scent and the taste of his skin. The pleasure he was giving her filled her completely, soaked into every hidden part, then, as his thrusts deepened and his mouth captured hers, their eyes locked back together and she flew over the edge. Spasms pulsated in waves through her, and she let them carry her over the mountainous crests, staring at Alejandro's face as it tightened then contorted and a roar was buried into her neck as his release came in wild, convulsive bucks.

Flora tried not to flinch or laugh. She tried really hard. Really, really hard.

Her thighs flinched at the same moment she grabbed hold of her pillow and giggled into it.

The bedsheets around her waist flew back and Alejandro's stern face appeared from between her legs. 'Why are you laughing?'

'You're tickling me.'

'You said you weren't ticklish.'

'How was I supposed to know my thighs are ticklish? No one's ever tickled them with a feather before.'

Smugness replaced the sternness.

'What's that look for?' she asked, suspicious.

His stare was lascivious. 'I like knowing there has been only me for you.'

She scowled and threw her pillow at him.

'Hey, what was that for?' He chucked the pillow on the floor and crawled up to hover over her.

'When you say things like that it reminds me that I'm not the only one for you.'

'Do you see anyone else in this bed?' he deadpanned.

'Ha, ha.'

'You are jealous of my past?'

'Don't be ridiculous,' she lied primly. 'It's just not… very gentlemanly to remind me of it.'

He stroked her hair from her forehead and smiled. 'I like it when you're jealous.'

'I'm not jealous, but why do you like it?'

'It shows you feel something for me.'

'I do feel something for you, Ramos. Lust.'

Now he was the one to scowl. 'When will you call me Alejandro?'

She shrugged. 'Our tenth wedding anniversary?'

'Ha-ha,' he mimicked. Then he grinned again. 'And you feel more for me than lust. You miss me when I'm away, just as I miss you.'

'I miss your lovemaking.' There. She could admit that to him.

Truth was, she needed their breaks from each other to recover herself. The urge to tell him she loved him and confess every hidden depth of her feelings for him often came close to overwhelming her.

The times he spent away from them had decreased dramatically since they had become lovers two months ago. Now he was only away a couple of nights a week, three at the most. He said it was because he couldn't bear being parted from his family any longer than that, and she couldn't do anything to stop the leap of hope that he meant her as well as Benjamin.

He told her he missed her but never had he suggested

she join him on his work travels. So she didn't suggest it either. She didn't believe he was seeing other women though, not when he was always so hungry for her.

To think she'd worried he would find her body repulsive!

It wasn't just in the bedroom that he showed he cared. He liked to surprise her with trips away. There had been a long weekend in Ibiza with a meal at a restaurant that was like no restaurant she'd ever been to; a futuristic sensory experience that had blown her mind. A weekend shopping in New York. A trip for her birthday to Niagara Falls. A week sailing the Caribbean. And so much more besides, all with Benjamin and the nanny in tow, a family unit.

But for all that, never did he ask her to accompany him on his business trips.

'Is that all I am to you?' he demanded, eyes glittering. 'Your stud?'

She cupped his cheeks and rubbed her nose to his. 'Don't be offended. You are a most excellent stud.'

He snatched her wrist and bared his teeth, but then the playfully sensual mood was broken by her phone ringing.

He kissed her. 'Ignore it.'

'I can't.' Flora's phone was on silent so only her emergency contacts could get through, Alejandro, Sinead and her brother. Alejandro was on top of her, Sinead was in her room adjoining the nursery, so the caller could only be Justin, who usually waited for her to call him when she wasn't with Alejandro.

Wriggling out from under Alejandro, she scrambled to her bedside table to answer it. Her worries that something was wrong were quickly dispelled and she ended the call inordinately proud of her big brother for all the effort he was making with the wreckage of his life, but apprehensive too for what Alejandro's reaction to her brother's intrusion would be.

He'd sat himself back propped against the headboard. All his former playfulness had gone. His arms were folded across his chest, the expression on his face the one he always got whenever the ghost of her brother appeared before them.

Her heart sank.

Would he ever forgive him or was this how it was going to be for the rest of her life, the two men she loved the most estranged for ever?

It didn't have to be like this.

Taking a deep breath for resolve, Flora shuffled over and sat in front of him, crossed her legs and took hold of his hand.

Looking him steadily in the eye, she said, 'Today it has been exactly fifteen months since Justin last gambled.' Exactly fifteen months since Alejandro lured him to Monte Cleure on a business pretext and promptly had him arrested.

His already tight features looked as if they could snap.

'He goes to Gamblers Anonymous meetings three times a week. He has a job as a barista in a coffee shop. He is doing everything he can to be a better man. He will never have the money to pay you back—the money he stole from you was used to pay his gambling debts, as you know—but he is desperate to make amends with you.'

And for all that her brother was turning his life around, the only way he would find peace in himself would be through Alejandro's forgiveness.

'Impossible,' he bit out.

'Why? He spent ten months in a prison cell. He has

lost his home, the job he loved, his friends, his self-re-spect and, most importantly, he has lost you. Is that not punishment enough for you?'

His lips formed in a snarl.

'I love my brother.' She gently massaged his hand, re-fusing to let his simmering anger divert her. 'I love him and I want Benjamin to get to know and love him too.'

'Over my dead body.'

Flora closed her eyes and took a deep breath. 'I know you miss him.'

He snatched his hand from hers. The words that flew from his mouth were definitely Spanish curses.

'How can you not?' she asked. 'The two of you were as close as brothers.'

'Which makes what he did even worse,' he snapped, throwing the sheets off his lap and climbing off the bed.

'From your perspective, yes.'

'He should have come to me when he first got into trouble.'

'Agreed, but you have to remember his state of mind. All those years he'd known you and you were the golden boy. You had the money, the fame, the first pick of the women... He hero-worshipped you and couldn't bear to tell you how badly he'd screwed up.'

'Yes, he was so worried about losing my respect that he stole my money instead.' He was pacing the floor, clearly agitated.

Was his agitation because she was getting through to him?

She could only hope.

'He stole it stupidly thinking he'd be able to win it all back before you noticed. *That's* how out of his mind he was. Please, I am begging you, let him say his piece to you, and see if you can move on and forgive him.

Please, for Benjamin's sake if not for mine or his, and for your sake too—'

'Enough!' he roared, spinning around to face her.

Flora reared back, more shocked at the rage on his face than the fury in his voice.

It had been a long time since she'd seen such anger from him and it hurt her heart to see it.

Visibly composing himself, Alejandro took a deep breath and gritted his teeth. 'I have made my feelings on the subject perfectly clear and I will hear no more about it, and I will thank you to keep the promise you made and keep my son away from him.'

Then he took four paces, snatched his robe off the hook on the bedroom door and, without looking back at her, walked out of their room.

Flora had no idea what time Alejandro came back to bed. He simply slid under the covers and turned his back to her.

He'd never done that before.

She drifted in and out of sleep, the wretchedness in her belly too strong for her to settle.

Since they'd become lovers, they'd bickered but never argued. Not like that. Alejandro had never raised his voice to her.

She just wanted her family to be together again, for her husband and her brother to be friends as they used to be and for her son to know his uncle. She would exchange all the wealth and trappings if she could have that.

All she could hope was that, once his anger faded, Alejandro would think on what she'd said.

It was for his sake too that she wanted bridges to be

built. He missed her brother. She was as certain of that as she was certain of her love for him.

The sound of metal wheels rolling over the oak floor woke her with a snap from the latest doze she'd fallen into.

The room was dusky, the early morning sun still rising.

Alejandro was showered, groomed and dressed in a business suit, suitcase and briefcase in hand, ready for his trip to Paris.

'I am going now,' he said stiffly.

Flora's stomach lurched miserably. His anger didn't seem to have faded a jot.

'Safe travels,' she whispered as she always did.

His chest rose and then he inclined his head and left the room.

For the first time since they'd become lovers, he left for a business trip without kissing her goodbye.

CHAPTER TWELVE

IT WAS LOOKING to be another beautiful early autumn day in Barcelona. Flora was glad that she'd arranged to meet Camila for an early coffee. It meant she could walk there. Hopefully the fresh air would do some good in clearing her head. If it was too hot when they were done, she'd get her driver to collect her.

She checked her phone. Still no communication from Alejandro. He hadn't messaged to let her know he'd arrived in Paris safely—although he had responded to her message asking if he'd got there okay with a simple yes—or called to wish her a goodnight.

The longer his silence went on, the angrier she could feel herself becoming at his stubbornness, so she took a handful of deep breaths for some zen before putting Benjamin in his pram and calling out to Madeline to let her know she was leaving. She got a cheerful shout back.

Things had changed dramatically between Flora and the staff. It was as Alejandro had suggested, although she didn't think the change in their demeanour towards her was entirely down to them sharing a bed but more to do with them being a proper couple and the respect he showed towards her. Respect begat respect. Flora was the master's wife and they now treated her as such.

Before opening the door, she checked her phone again. Still nothing.

Her bodyguards were waiting for her on the doorstep. One carried the pram down as if it weighed nothing more than a bunch of flowers. They still spoke in grunts to her but she now suspected that was because grunts were their language.

Before they reached the gate, her phone pinged. It was a message from Sinead who'd taken the week off, saying her flight had landed.

Flora smiled, pleased to know her son's nanny was safe and well. She was careful not to overstep their professional relationship but Sinead was such a sunny presence that it was impossible not to care about her.

She returned the message with a smiley emoji and put her phone back in her bag just as the gate opened.

A swarm of journalists was waiting for her.

She barely had time to draw breath before she was enveloped in a cacophony of noise as questions were hurled at her and cameras were thrust in her and Benjamin's faces.

Her bodyguards sprang into action. Within seconds they were standing in front of the pram, not allowing the gathered press to step even a millimetre over the threshold of Alejandro's land.

Flora backed away, then turned the pram around and raced a screaming Benjamin back to the villa.

The front door flung open before she reached the steps. Madeline hurried down and helped her carry the pram indoors.

'What's going on?' Flora asked as she lifted her distraught son into her arms. Heavens, she was shaking.

'I not know.' Madeline's obvious worry only made

Flora's nerves more shot. 'Security not see them. Must have hidden.'

Flora swallowed and nodded her understanding. The gate opened onto a wide pathway. The road lined one side, huge trees the other. It would have been easy for the press to keep out of sight of the security cameras until the gates opened and then ambush her.

The house phone rang. Madeline hurried off to answer it.

Holding Benjamin securely with one arm, Flora dug into her bag with her free hand and grabbed her phone, using the voice activation to call Alejandro.

It went straight to voicemail.

Speaking over Benjamin's sobs, she said, 'Ramos, it's me. Something's going on. The press have just ambushed me. I hope everything's okay your end. Call me back as soon as you can.'

The house phone was ringing again.

Flora carried her son into the main living room and sat with him on one of the velvet sofas, trying her best to soothe him, trying not to let her imagination run riot as to why the press would be back when they'd not been anywhere near the villa in months, or worry why the house phone was ringing for a third time.

Once Benjamin had calmed down, Flora called Camila.

'I was just about to call you,' Camila said. 'Are you okay?'

'I think so. I couldn't leave the villa because of the press. What is going *on*?'

She sensed the other woman's hesitation.

'Camila?'

'Have you not looked at any gossip site today?'

'No.' She never did. Not since those pictures of her

brother and Alejandro on Alejandro's yacht with all those beautiful women. That had cured her of seeking out his name.

Madeline appeared, pale faced.

'Hold on a minute,' Flora said to Camila before addressing the housekeeper. 'What's wrong?'

'Do I have agreement to pull telephone from…?' As she mimed disconnecting it, it rang again.

'Who keeps calling?'

Madeline made a rude sign that signified it was the press.

'Okay,' Flora agreed, then returned to her call with Camila. 'What's on the gossip sites I should know about?'

'I am sure it doesn't mean anything.' Her friend sounded genuinely distressed.

'What?'

'Alejandro.'

'What about him?'

'He was photographed going into Aimee's apartment last night.'

Flora paced her bedroom.

She'd tried calling Alejandro again a number of times but with the same result.

Her phone vibrated in her hand. She swiped and stuck it to her ear. 'Hello?'

'Hi, Flora, it's Eloise Jameson from the *Daily*—'

Flora swiped again and threw the phone on the floor as if it had scalded her.

She pinched the bridge of her nose and fought back tears. She felt under siege. And alone. Very alone. As if she were in the midst of a horror story. Or a nightmare.

She took a deep breath to try to calm herself before

picking her phone up. There was a nice new hairline crack on the screen but it seemed to be working fine. It rang in her hand and she just managed to stop herself from dropping it. Not recognising the number, she refused the call, then diverted all calls to voicemail and fired a message to Alejandro asking him to message her. Only then did she finally pluck up the courage to do a search of his name.

The first thing that came up on her feed was a salacious headline. Swallowing hard to keep the bile at bay, she clicked on the link and was confronted with a set of pictures of her husband. The first had him looking over his shoulder as he approached a doorway. The second had him unlocking the door with his own key. The third had him stepping over the threshold. The fourth was an older picture of Alejandro and Aimee leaving through that door together, used as a comparison to show the reader it was the same apartment building.

Alejandro's beard gave no room for doubt that the first three pictures were recent, taken after they'd become lovers again.

She couldn't hold it back any longer. Running to the bathroom, she vomited until her stomach was empty.

Benjamin was finally asleep. The day had unsettled him enormously and he'd been as fractious as when he was teething. For now, though, Flora's beautiful boy was calm and hopefully dreaming lovely thoughts in the cot she'd bought for him when she'd been six months pregnant and expecting to raise him alone in London.

Closing the bedroom door softly behind her, she sank slowly to the floor, put the baby monitor on the carpet, and hugged her knees to her chest.

Once she'd emptied her stomach of all its contents,

the only thing she could think of was escape. Luck had shined on her. She'd managed to book herself and Benjamin onto the next flight to London.

Ignoring Madeline's protests and the ashen faces of the other household staff, she'd ordered her driver to take her and Benjamin to the airport and within two hours of booking the return flight had been in the air.

Barely twelve hours had passed since the villa's gates had opened and her world had imploded.

She'd spent the day fighting to keep her demons at bay for Benjamin's sake and it had exhausted her. She felt so hollow, as if her heart had been carved out of her.

The stairs creaked. Justin appeared at the top of them and sat beside her.

After a long period of silence he sighed and ran his fingers through his hair. 'He'll go mad when he knows you've brought his son here.'

Flora had already explained everything that had happened these last two days. Justin had listened without speaking, taking it all in.

'I know, but where else could I go?' Who else could she turn to but the rock who'd always been there for her?

There was another long silence before he said, 'Let's hope he sees it like that. And for what it's worth, I don't believe he'd cheat on you.'

'Really?'

He nodded.

'I want to believe that too,' she whispered.

'Look, he's an unforgiving bastard but he's never been a cheat, and he's liked you for a long time. Do you really think I'd have encouraged you with him otherwise?'

She remembered when she'd finally plucked up the courage to tell Justin she was pregnant with Alejandro's child and that Alejandro had cut her off. He'd said nothing, just hung his head in his hands, his devastation obvious. Their marriage had been like a weight off his shoulders. She'd assumed that was because the threat of prison and all the financial burden had been taken care of. Justin had been in such a bad place that she'd taken great pains to hide the blackmail aspect of it and make it sound like marriage to Alejandro was what she wanted too. She hadn't wanted to add to her brother's guilt.

'Are you serious? Did you *want* us to get together?'

He suddenly smiled. 'I'll be honest with you, Flo. I thought he had no chance with you. Not the way you hated him. But I always knew that if he won you round, he'd look after you. You're my sister and our mother's daughter. There was no way he'd have shown an interest if he wasn't serious about you.'

Flora hugged her knees even more tightly. She desperately wanted to believe Alejandro hadn't cheated on her. Desperately wanted to believe that history wasn't repeating itself. But those pictures of him entering Aimee's apartment…all those fears she'd had before, it turned out they hadn't gone, had simply been buried under the bliss of what they'd found together and now they had reared back up; her worst nightmare coming viciously to life.

The last two months had been so good between them that it hadn't even occurred to her to worry about him being in Paris when she *knew* that was where his old mistress lived.

Justin nudged her. 'Get you a drink?'

She tried to smile and managed a nod.

Her return flight was in two days. She would get home around the same time as Alejandro. She would sit down with him and confront him over the pictures.

She knew him well enough that she would know if he was lying to her.

She'd never known him to lie, she thought starkly. Or cheat.

What was she supposed to do if he *had* cheated? She couldn't leave him or he'd launch the prosecution against Justin again, and, while she had enough money saved to form a strong defence for him, there was no way Justin would avoid serving prison time.

If Alejandro hadn't cheated, she was in no position to demand future fidelity from him, she thought miserably. No position to demand *anything* from him.

It just went to prove that without Alejandro's love, their marriage was a house built of sand. One hit of a wave and it would come crashing down.

In the kitchen, she found she'd forgotten to switch the plug on when charging her phone earlier after the battery had drained. She sighed and turned it on, then waited for enough charge to go through it to bring it back to life.

Nausea sloshed in her belly. Had Alejandro finally tried to make contact?

Or would she still be met with a wall of silence from him?

'Lemonade in your wine?' Justin asked.

'Yes, please.'

'Fancy watching a film?'

Life flickered on the screen of her phone.

She tried another unsuccessful smile. 'You choose something. I'll join you in a minute.'

Her screen showed she had twenty-four missed calls, eleven voicemails and eighteen text messages.

She clicked on the call icon and her heart jumped. The last missed call had come from Alejandro. He'd tried calling her seven times. The others were from Camila, a couple of her old English friends and numbers she didn't recognise. Alejandro was responsible for only one of the text messages, a short, Call me back as soon as you can.

She went into her voicemail. The first three were messages from the soulless journalists who'd upset her baby so much. The fourth was from Alejandro and her heart clattered to hear his deep voice speak her name into her ear. Before she could hear the rest of it, a loud rap on the front door made her jump.

Some sixth sense kicked in and, her blood turning to ice, she knew immediately who the visitor was.

Justin reached the door before Flora had passed the kitchen threshold. He swung it open and instantly stilled.

Alejandro loomed menacingly in the doorway, still in a work suit despite the late hour, a head taller than her brother. His eyes zoomed over Justin's head and locked onto hers.

Barely a second elapsed before his gaze left her, but the fury in the dark depths was strong enough to land like a punch.

With a withering stare at Justin, he said, 'I am here to speak to my wife. Your presence is not welcome. Leave.'

Justin darted his gaze to Flora. She swallowed hard then nodded. His presence could only make matters worse.

He grabbed his jacket off the coat rack, mimed a 'call me' gesture at Flora, and slipped out of the door.

The atmosphere in the narrow house turned frigid. Flora rubbed her arms for warmth then pressed a hand to her chest in an effort to temper the loud thuds of her heart.

An age passed with Alejandro's coldly furious stare on her before he spoke. 'Where is my son?'

'Sleeping,' she whispered.

His shoulders rose slowly in a deep inhalation. 'Then let us speak where we will not disturb him.'

Somehow she managed to force her shaking legs into the kitchen, take hold of the baby monitor, and then open the integral door that led into the garage she'd had converted into a studio for her work when she'd bought the house two years ago.

Alejandro's eyes flickered around, no doubt taking it all in.

He'd never been in her home before. She'd never invited him.

Flora's studio was a small space but worked perfectly for her. She had a large table at one end with stacks of her designs, her sewing machine and other paraphernalia on it, and wide shelves filled with rolls of fabric and fat rolls of thread lining the walls either side of it. On the other side was a small sofa she often sat on when curled up hand-stitching.

She sat on her desk chair, leaving the sofa for him.

He hooked an ankle to a thigh and contemplated her with the imperious expression that took her back seven months to the day he'd blackmailed her, married her and then been the most supportive birthing partner a woman could have. The day he'd shown the best and the worst of himself.

'Let's get this over with, shall we?' she said shakily, unable to bear the silence any longer. 'I'm sorry for bringing Benjamin to London but I needed to escape Barcelona for a couple of days. I couldn't leave him behind because Sinead's on holiday.'

Barely a muscle flickered on his face. 'Why didn't you wait for me to call you back?'

'I waited two hours. Why didn't you answer my calls and messages?'

He unhooked his ankle, rested his palms on his thighs and stared her right in her eye. 'One of my casino managers had a heart attack during our breakfast meeting.'

The shock of his answer made her gasp.

'I performed CPR while we waited for the paramedics to arrive, then travelled with him to the hospital. His wife met us there. I stayed with her until the surgeon finished operating on him because she was in no state to be left alone.' Something dark flashed in his eyes. 'I don't suppose you can imagine it, but she was distraught. I didn't think it right to check my messages while she was out of her mind with fear that she would never see her husband again.'

Flora covered her face then dragged her fingers down it, utterly wretched for the poor man but even more so for his wife. She could hardly bring herself to imagine the agony she must have gone through knowing the life of the man she loved was hanging in the balance.

'How is he?' she asked hoarsely.

'Stable.'

'You saved his life?'

'The doctors saved his life,' he corrected before his lips curled. 'When I left the hospital I saw all your messages but I could not get hold of you. I spoke to Madeline, who filled me in on what had happened and told me that not only had you left the country and flown to England but that you had taken my son with you.'

His voice dripped with barely concealed fury.

Flora held his stare and swallowed back a swell of nausea. 'You were at her apartment last night.'

'*My* apartment,' he corrected. 'I kicked Aimee out after that little stunt she pulled for the paparazzi when Benjamin was born. I am selling it. I've had it refurbished and wanted to check the workmanship before I give the go-ahead to put it on the market.'

The relief that should have come at this explanation refused to form. Her heart was beating too fast for relief. It was Alejandro's demeanour. The iciness in it. 'Why didn't you tell me any of this?'

'I didn't want to upset you. I know you hate my past. I was going to sell the apartment and then that would be it—the last link of any woman in my past gone. You know why I was doing that?'

She shook her head.

'For you.' He smiled. It was the coldest smile she'd ever received. 'And you assumed I was cheating on you, didn't you?'

'I didn't know what to think.'

'Yes, you did. At the first sign of trouble, you assumed the worst of me and took my son and ran away from me, and ran away to the one man you knew I didn't want Benjamin anywhere near.'

'It wasn't like that. I didn't run away from you. I ran from the situation.'

His disbelieving icy stare made the knots in her stomach tighten. 'The press, the pictures...' She took a deep breath, trying her hardest to speak coherently. 'We never made the usual promises married couples make. You never promised to be faithful—if you had, I would have known there was more to those photos than what the press were implying because I know you don't lie or make false promises, but it was understood that you would still take lovers if you wished.'

'Understood by you. Not me. Just because your jealousy made you act perversely and give your blessing for me to have affairs did not mean I would act on it, and I cannot believe you think so little of me that you think I would leave your bed in the morning and be in another woman's bed that same night… No, actually, I can believe it.' Alejandro's eyes glittered, his handsome features contorting into bitterness. 'You think all men are cheats.'

'No!' Flora bowed her head and let her hair fall like a stream over her face.

The beats of her heart had become the beats of doom.

'I was *scared*. You left on an argument and without kissing me goodbye. You didn't call to wish me goodnight, and then the press ambushed me and I saw those pictures and I couldn't get hold of you and all I could think was that I needed to escape to somewhere safe.'

'You described yourself as an expert on men's infidelities,' he said flatly. 'You said you didn't think a leopard could change its spots. Isn't this what you've been waiting for? Have I made you so damn miserable that you've been waiting for the first opportunity to leave me?'

'Don't be so ridiculous. I couldn't leave you even if I wanted to!' she cried, stung that he could think such a thing after everything they'd shared.

For a long time he just stared at her, firm lips tightening, the darkness in his eyes turning into granite. 'So you do want to leave me?'

'I didn't say that! I said I couldn't leave you *even* if I wanted to, and I can't, can I? Not with the threat of you reopening my brother's prosecution hanging over my head.'

Slowly, he lifted his hands from his lap and placed them behind his neck, his granite eyes not leaving her face. Then he lifted his chin and said, 'If I took that threat away and asked you to choose between me and your brother, who would win?'

'I…' She shook her head, caught off-guard.

'It is a simple question, Flora. Me or him. Because it is a choice you have to make if our marriage is to continue.'

She stared at him. Was he really saying what she thought he was saying? He wouldn't. No. She must be misunderstanding him.

'I need to know your loyalty is with me, so make your choice. Him or me.'

Dear God, he was being serious.

'Do you *want* me to hate you?' she managed to choke.

'I want a wife who I can trust. Last chance. Him or me. Make your choice and make it now or I will take your silence as a choice for him.'

Her head was spinning. It wasn't possible that he could make such a cruel ultimatum. 'It's an impossible choice. How am I supposed to choose between you? *I can't.*'

He got to his feet and wiped the sleeves of his jacket. It wasn't just his eyes that were like granite. His features were the hardest she had ever seen them, set like stone.

'Then I have my answer. You can consider our marriage over.'

The dizziness that rent through her was so strong Flora had to grab hold of her desk to stop herself falling off her chair.

Almost too late, her eyes focused through the swimming haze in her brain to see Alejandro was heading for the studio door, and her legs suddenly propelled her to her feet, and she threw herself in front of him, blocking his exit.

'You are not seriously going to do this, are you?'

He looked over her head. 'Get out of my way.'

'Don't,' she beseeched, grabbing his arm. Flora had sensed Alejandro hardening his heart against her from the moment he arrived but now she feared he had shut it down completely. 'Please, Alejandro, I know you're angry with me but you don't have to do this. Please, we can—'

His mouth formed a snarl. '*Now* you call me by my name? Now? When you have spent *months* refusing?' He covered her hand and prised her fingers off his arm, face right in front of hers, eyeball to eyeball. 'There is no "we" and never has been. You share my bed but give no more. You don't care when I leave, you never ask to travel with me. You have no loyalty to me. I did everything in my power to make you happy but the only thing you wanted me for was sex. To you, I'm just your *stud*. Now get out of my way.'

CHAPTER THIRTEEN

'I SAID, GET out of my way,' Alejandro said coldly when she didn't move, his gaze now fixed over her head.

'No.' Needing to douse the rising panic, Flora folded her shaking arms tightly over her chest, protecting her thumping heart from flying out of her ribs. 'I'll move when you've listened to what I have to say.'

His tone was contemptuous. 'There is nothing you have to say that I want to hear.'

'I don't care if you want to hear it, I'm going to say it and then you can go on your merry way and leave me to pick up the wreckage, just as you did last time.'

That made him look at her.

'You cut me out so effectively I had to show you I was pregnant with your child in a public forum. I went through the whole pregnancy alone. That was a wreckage of your making, and I had no one. I couldn't turn to my brother for help because he was fighting for his liberty.'

'A consequence of his own actions,' he corrected harshly.

'He was your best friend. You knew his theft was completely out of character. You knew how much Mum's death had screwed with his head—'

'I told you before, do not use your mother's death as an excuse for him.'

'Why not when you use your mother's death as an excuse for your own despicable behaviour?'

The look on his face could have turned lava to ice. 'How dare you?'

Flora was in no mood to be intimidated. This day had been a roller coaster of emotions, a fitting end, she thought bitterly, for a marriage that had started life on its own emotional roller coaster of a day. 'You threw away thirteen years of friendship over one mistake. Justin abused your trust but he hurt you too, but you can't bring yourself to admit that, can you, not the great Alejandro Ramos who's unable to be hurt and isn't afraid of anything? Instead of admitting that he hurt you, you packed more ice around your heart and sought vengeance, and now you're doing the same thing to me, and not for the first time— you read my brother's message and assumed what it meant, and now you're preparing to cut me out again.'

Alejandro was breathing heavily through his nose, his jaw clenched, his gaze unseeing.

'You blackmailed me into this marriage. Or do you forget that? You forced it on me, but despite it all, I tried, for Benjamin's sake, and because you showed the most wonderful side to yourself when he was born…' She gritted her teeth and took a deep breath. 'I knew the danger you posed to my heart and protecting it against you is a battle I've fought every single day of our marriage. It's a battle I've fought for years.'

She thought she caught a flicker in his distant, unseeing gaze.

Dropping her voice, she said, 'That weekend when you came back to Oxford early because your dad had gone off to Martinique… I saw you naked. Just a glimpse through the gap in my bedroom door. I was thirteen years old.'

His eyes suddenly regained their focus and widened in shock.

'You woke something in me,' she confessed, 'and I haven't looked at another man since. I have spent over ten years insanely jealous of the women in your life and comparing myself to them. The only reason I gave you my blessing to have affairs was because of my stupid pride—I was *terrified* you'd see how deeply my feelings for you ran. I've been running from them for *years*. All I have ever known is men who cheat and lie and discard women when the next pretty thing comes along… You knocked my barriers down, but I got too close, didn't I? That's what this is all about, isn't it? I got close enough to hurt you.'

His throat moved and he shook his head. For a short moment she thought he was going to say something but then the moment was gone.

Flora filled her lungs with air and her heart with resolve. 'It *is* the truth. You're not incapable of being hurt like you pretend to yourself. You're scared of it. You have the most wonderful side to you, Alejandro. You're fun and considerate and affectionate and incredibly loving, but the second someone hurts you, you shut down. You twist the pain of their hurt into anger and strike back.

'You lost the most precious person in your life far too young but pain and hurt are facts of life. Grief is too. There were days I thought the pain of losing my mum would kill me. That pain was the price I paid for loving her, but I wouldn't trade a single day of her life to have erased that pain. You were a child when you went through that grief and I get why you shut down emotionally from it, but you're an adult now, with a child of your own. What are you going to do when Benjamin hurts you? Because one day he will. Are you going to turn that pain into anger and strike back at him? Will you shut him out of your heart too? Your own flesh and blood?'

The baby monitor suddenly came to life. The sound of their son's cries cut through the toxic atmosphere swirling around them.

Feeling sick, Flora stepped forwards and placed a hand on Alejandro's frozen chest.

Staring hard into his eyes, she said, 'When you're old and lonely and thinking back on our marriage, remember you were the one who threw us away. Despite all the odds, you did make me happy; very happy. I fell in love with you and I think a part of you fell in love with me too. We could have had something good but you were too scared to take it. You gave me the cruellest ultimatum you could and you made it because you knew I would never turn my back on my brother. You *wanted* this outcome and, in all honesty, I'm glad of it. Anyone who can make an ultimatum like that and try to force someone to give up someone who means so much to them doesn't deserve love, and you don't deserve mine. Now, I'm going to see to our son. You can see yourself out.'

And then, she turned around, opened her studio door, and walked away from him.

Benjamin's bright red cheeks and high-pitched wails told Flora he was teething again. Her battered heart ached for him. Every time she put him down, he started crying again and she ended up settling with him on her bed and letting him fall asleep in her arms. A good hour passed before she remembered to message her brother and tell him he was safe to come home.

A short while later there was a tap on her bedroom door and her brother's worried face emerged.

She swallowed hard and shook her head.

He closed his eyes briefly before padding over to perch on the side of her bed. 'I'm sorry,' he whispered.

A tear fell down her cheek. 'So am I.'

He kissed the top of her head and left the room, closing the door softly behind him.

Flora kept a tight grip on the swell of emotions battering her until she put Benjamin back in his cot beside her bed and he stayed in peaceful sleep. Only then did she crawl under her bedsheets and sob until her throat was raw and her insides battered and bruised.

Justin was already in the kitchen when Flora carried Benjamin down for his breakfast.

'You look exhausted,' he observed, taking Benjamin from her and putting him in his high chair.

'Thank you.' She tried to sound bright but her vocal cords obeyed only to a 'listless' level. It had been the longest night of her life. Every time she'd drifted into sleep she'd had dreams of Alejandro walking past her in the Monte Cleure court, looking straight through her, not hearing her pleas, Flora a ghost he could not see. She'd snapped herself awake from all of them, frozen in her chest and her face soaked in tears.

'Why don't I take him out for a walk?' Justin said once she'd fed Benjamin his cereal and given him his bottle of milk. 'You go back to bed.'

'I don't need—'

'Yes, you do. Go and get his change bag for me and I'll take him to the park.'

Oh, but she felt wretched. She hadn't told Justin that the prosecution against him would be reopened...although, now she thought about it, she didn't remember Alejandro mentioning it, but it must be a given...and she opened her mouth to deliver the heartbreaking news, but what came out was, 'Are you sure?'

'He's my nephew. Of course I'm sure.'

She closed her eyes and smiled wanly in thanks.

Let her brother spend some time with his nephew in the fresh air before she gave him the news that would destroy his life again.

Soon, Benjamin was secure in the pram that had been sat in the understairs cupboard since she'd bought it all that time ago, and she was kissing them both goodbye.

The house felt so silent without them.

Dragging her weary legs back to the kitchen to get herself a glass of water, Flora found herself staring at her studio door. The space she'd created, her happy place, now tainted for ever.

Would she ever be able to enter her studio without thinking of him and remembering how he'd ripped the heart out of her?

She couldn't take any pleasure at getting the last word in or from the image of his ashen face when she'd told him to let himself out.

Her words had wounded him, she was sure of it, and, like a wounded animal, it would only make him more dangerous. She should be frightened at where this could lead but her heart refused to accept how far he would go. She didn't believe for a second he would ever try to take Benjamin from her, not even out of vengeance... He hadn't mentioned custody either.

She didn't have the strength right then to pray she wasn't mistaken in this, not when her heart was so bruised with grief at how it had ended between them, because that was what it felt like. Grief.

But she had to be strong. She had her baby to think of and her brother's future to deal with and could not afford the luxury of wallowing over a man who, however happy he had made her, didn't deserve her love.

Rubbing away the fresh tears that had let loose, she was filled with resolve and she marched to her studio door and threw it open...and almost screamed when she saw the figure on the sofa, doubled over, head slumped forwards on his lap, hands clutching his dark hair.

Certain she was hallucinating, Flora blinked a number of times.

'Alejandro?' she whispered.

Slowly, the head lifted.

She covered her mouth in horror. The beautiful, meltingly dark eyes were puffy and bloodshot.

Frightened, she took a tentative step towards him.

A contortion of emotions danced over his haggard face. He held out a hand to her. It was shaking.

She took another step and touched the tips of her fingers to his. He sank to his knees and wrapped his arms around her, holding her so tightly all the breath was pushed from her lungs.

'I'm sorry, I'm sorry,' he sobbed into her breasts. 'So sorry.'

Utterly thrown, her heart ripping at the animalistic sounds coming from this most arrogant and prideful of men, Flora instinctively cradled him tightly and kissed the top of his head.

When the shudders wracking his powerful body abated, sense came back to her and she let go of him, but before she could step away from his hold, he lifted his head to stare into her eyes. 'I...'

He swallowed and squeezed his eyes shut. Then he took a long breath before fixing his desolate gaze back on her.

'I tried to go,' he said hoarsely. 'But I couldn't. I couldn't make my body leave. I couldn't stop the thoughts…' He grimaced tightly and loosened an arm from around her waist to tap the side of his head. 'So many thoughts. Memories. The people I have cut from my life. I thought life is too short to give second chances. Not everyone deserves a second chance. Hillier didn't but he deserved the chance to make amends. I denied him that. Worse… I used him as a weapon to get to you.'

At her shocked stare, he smiled grimly. 'I think…' He swallowed again and took her hands in his.

'Let me start from the beginning because it all starts with you. *Querida*, I have been in love with you for years. Your twenty-first birthday, that's when I fell for you. I looked at you and what I felt was like nothing before it. Hillier's little sister all grown up and so beautiful it hurt my heart. One dance was all you let me have. You trembled the whole time.' He pressed her hand to his chest. She could feel the strong thuds of his heart against it. 'I could feel your heart beating against me like a little hummingbird… And then you ran away like a frightened mouse.'

Flora's heart was beating like a hummingbird now.

Was she dreaming? Had she not actually woken up at all?

Alejandro only opened himself up to her in her dreams.

The eyes gazing into hers were swirling with more emotion than she'd ever seen in her dreams.

'After that night, I couldn't get you from my mind,' he whispered. 'For months I tried to entice you to me. I would get your brother to invite you to functions with us but you refused them all, apart from my birthday party but you ran away again.' Sadness shadowed his face. 'And then your mother's condition deteriorated when things had been so hopeful. When I visited... I had so much admiration for the way you cared for her. You were like an angel watching over her.' He smiled wistfully. 'An angel making jokes that kept a smile on your mother's face until the end. Hiding your pain for her sake but never hiding your love. And you have so much love in you, *querida*.

'When she died, everything changed. The house I had always been welcome in was sold and for a year I saw nothing of you...and then you turned up at my home a week after your brother's arrest...' He shook his head, self-disgust emanating off him like a wave. 'I knew you would come to me to save him. Believe me, please, it was not done on a conscious level, but something was driving me to take the actions I did against him and when I look back I can see that was you. I knew you would come to me.'

She *must* be dreaming...

'That night with you blew my mind. To know I was your first...' He closed his eyes and inhaled deeply before locking his stare back to hers. 'Turning my back on you is the cruellest thing I have ever done and I do not seek your forgiveness. What I did to you was unforgivable. That night...how you looked at me the next morning... I had dreamt of you looking at me like that for so long. But I am everything you accused me of being. Scared of feelings. Like a child trapped in a man's body.

'I went to great lengths to stop you making contact with me again. I told myself it was because I hated you for using me and for snubbing me all those years and only wanting me so you could save him, but it was because, that night, you made me feel too much. You are my one weakness, *querida*. My Achilles heel. And for all my efforts, I could not stop thinking of you. You were a plague in my head I had no cure for.' He inhaled deeply and brushed his lips as lightly as a feather over the tips of her fingers. 'I was your first and you were my last. There has been no one but you since that night.'

Flora's hummingbird heart jumped into her throat. It wasn't just the words he was saying but how he was saying them, the fluency of his English more jumbled, his accent more pronounced. Agony and sincerity vibrated in every syllable.

'I didn't sleep for weeks before the court case. I knew you would be there and I would see you again and that you would hate me... Deservedly.' He inhaled through his nose. 'I had much guilt. Much vengeance but much guilt too. I had pushed the situation with your brother so far—too far—and my conscience was not happy with me. I had nightmares of him as an old man in jail. You were in those dreams too, crying and pleading with me.

'You carrying my child was the dream I never knew I had come true. I could end the prosecution of your brother without losing face but, more importantly, I had the means to tie you to me for ever, and I took it. I wish I could call it madness, the thing that gripped me and forced you to marry me, but that would be kind. It was monstrous. *I* was monstrous. All night I have been going over that day and asking myself what possessed me to do that to you and I will not insult your intelligence by calling it love. I was in love with you but my actions were not those of a man in love. They were the actions of a monster. Real love came later. It grew in me. Every day it got deeper, but the demons that have lived with me for so long, they were still there. I tried to forget how our marriage was forged. I tried to forget my actions, but just as it is impossible to forgive my actions, it is impossible to forget them too, and deep down I never believed you could forgive or forget them or love me because of them, so when you fled to England and to your brother...

'*Querida*, that is when I realised just how much power you have over me. The self-protection that has shielded my heart from hurt since I was a child did what it always does.'

He brought her fingers to his mouth again then smiled tightly and released them. Rising, he sat back on the sofa and rubbed the back of his head before looking back at her. 'You were right to call it like packing my heart with ice. I don't know how to be any other way. But I must learn, for Benjamin's sake. I see that.' A small, sad smile played on his lips. 'But I think he will melt the ice like his mother does.'

Alejandro's eyes squeezed shut and his throat moved. His gaze when he opened them was utterly desolate. 'Losing you...how I'm feeling now...is the greatest pain I have ever known and there is nothing I can do to stop it. I have to find a way to live with it and accept it as due punishment. When I leave here, I will have the prosecution file on your brother shredded and I will instruct my lawyer to contact you—give him your terms for the divorce and custody of Benjamin. I will not fight you.' His lips tugged into another small, sad smile. 'You think I had the power in our marriage? *Querida*, you had it all. You have complete power over me, and I want you to know the months of our marriage were the best of my life. You are an incredible woman and I will regret the pain I have caused you until my dying day.'

The pumping of her freshly swelling heart was so strong blood rushed to her head, dizzying her.

She felt as if she'd just been spun a thousand times on a Waltzer.

All this time. All these years.

When Alejandro rose to his feet and bowed his head to her, she followed him with her eyes as he walked stiffly to the door, a thousand thoughts filling her head.

All this time…

Snapshots came to her, one after the other, a picture reel of images.

That look between them on her twenty-first birthday. The thrills and terror to be held in his arms when they danced.

The joy on his face when he'd spotted her at his party. The concern when she'd fled so early from it.

The tenderness and compassion in his eyes at her mother's funeral.

The hunger and need etched on his face the moment before their lips fused together that first time.

The icy fury in his eyes in the court waiting room. The triumph when she agreed to marry him. The flash of panic when he realised the birth was imminent.

The tender encouragement throughout the birth.

The swirl of pride, relief and happiness that had lit his face when he first held their son in his arms.

Love had been there in every one of those images. Love for her.

Hadn't she known it? His feelings for her?

And she'd run and run and run.

She'd been right to run, but not for the reasons she'd told herself. Alejandro would never cheat on her. He would never lie, not consciously. But she'd been right to run because the Alejandro she'd been running from hadn't been capable of fully opening his heart and letting her inside it, not with the monsters that had plagued him for so long.

The monsters he'd just spent a long, lonely night torturing himself over. Admitting them. Banishing them… maybe not for good, but Alejandro's determination meant he would succeed in banishing them completely. He would do it for her and their son.

He loved her. Truly loved her.

And she loved him.

Flora's feelings for him had always been so rabid and greedy and *terrifying*, but as the picture reel faded and her eyes soaked in the proud but broken flesh and blood man who'd just opened his soul up to her, her heart bloomed like a giant rose and for the first time she realised all her fear had gone.

'Wait,' she called out to him as he reached for the door handle.

His back muscles tensed before he slowly turned back around to face her.

'How long do we have to wait for the divorce to go through?' she asked.

'In Monte Cleure, divorce is allowed after a year of marriage,' he said hollowly.

'Is there a separation period?'

He winced but didn't drop his stare. 'No.'

'So we can divorce in five months' time?'

He inclined his head curtly.

'And then can we remarry immediately after?'

He froze.

'But somewhere nicer than Monte Cleure,' she added. 'And in a church. And I'd like to wear a wedding dress. And have a honeymoon. Do it all properly.'

His mouth moved but nothing came out.

'And I suppose I'll have to let my dad give me away. Unless you agree that Justin can do it?'

Flora held her breath while she waited for him to respond.

Alejandro attempted to clear his throat a number of times. He shook his head. 'No. Your father will have to do it. Hillier will be my best man.'

For the longest time nothing more was said. Not verbally. Their eyes though... Flora could feel the emotions flooding Alejandro as vividly as she could feel the emotions flooding her, all warm and joyous and ballooning into her every crevice.

And then he moved.

In three long strides he was hauling her into his arms and holding her tightly enough to squeeze all the air from her lungs again. When his mouth found hers, his kiss was the most passionate and reverential she had ever tasted, leaving her clinging to him weak-kneed with giddiness as much as with need for him.

'I love you,' she said when he finally pulled his mouth from hers to rain kisses over her cheeks. 'I love you so much.'

He cupped her face. 'How?' he asked simply.

She smiled and stroked his cheekbone. 'Because when you're not being a vengeful bastard, you're actually pretty wonderful, and you make me feel *everything*.'

He gazed at her with wonderment. 'You're my life, do you know that?'

Yes, she thought dreamily, she *did* know that. 'And you're mine.'

He kissed her. 'I love you.'

She kissed him back. 'Always.'

'For ever.'

EPILOGUE

THE CATHEDRAL SHONE brightly under the summer sky. With her father's help, Flora got out of the limousine, being careful not to trip over the train of her ivory wedding dress. Camila, dressed in a baby-blue bridesmaid dress, got out of the car behind with Benjamin and her daughter Ava, who were pageboy and flower girl, and somehow managed to herd the two toddlers to the cathedral door to wait for the bridal party's cue to enter. Only Ava reacted to the flash of the paparazzi cameras, cheekily sticking her tongue out while simultaneously waving at them.

Flora's divorce two weeks ago had been front page news in the Spanish tabloids and the top trending item on social media. She was quite sure her subsequent remarriage that day to the same man would beat it for coverage. She might even buy some copies of the papers and magazines herself, for posterity. Something to show the grandkids.

The cue came.

Flora took hold of her dad's arm and planted a kiss to his cheek. He might be a useless, cheating deadbeat but he was still her dad and she now lived in hope that one day he might become less of a cheating deadbeat. If her brother could turn his life around then anyone could.

And there was her brother, right beside the groom, waiting for her. The path to forgiveness had turned out to be surprisingly easy. Alejandro being Alejandro, when he set his mind to something he didn't stop until he achieved it. His mind had been set on finding forgiveness and understanding of his old friend. They would never have the friendship they'd once shared—and Flora wouldn't want them to have that one, thanks very much!—but it was a friendship all the same and for that she was content.

As she walked down the aisle, giving a discreet wave to Louise, Justin's pregnant fiancée, she felt a kick in her belly. It was such a special moment that she stopped and put her hand to her stomach so she could feel it under her palm.

It happened again.

She hurried her movements to Alejandro and, as soon as she was standing beside him, she forgot all propriety and put his hand to her belly so the man she loved could feel their child kick for the first time too.

* * * *

CROWNING HIS
LOST PRINCESS

CAITLIN CREWS

MILLS & BOON

CHAPTER ONE

DELANEY CLARK RAN the back of her hand over her too-hot brow, frowning at the clouds of dust in the distance.

Someone was coming up the long dirt drive toward the rickety farmhouse and the tired old barns and outbuildings. In the middle of the afternoon. And that was unusual, because no one was expected.

She glanced over toward the old farmhouse, where her mother had raised her the way she'd been raised in turn. The way Clarks had raised their children here since the land was first settled. But she didn't need to walk inside from the vegetable garden to see what Catherine Clark was doing or whether she was expecting anyone. Her mother didn't get out much any longer, and any visits were planned well in advance—usually through Delaney, who hadn't planned a thing for her this week.

Delaney's confusion only grew when she saw what looked like a fleet of gleaming black SUVs roaring up the quiet lane.

Pickup trucks would have been one thing. This was Kansas. Right smack in the middle of the great prairie. Pickups were the preferred mode of travel, because everything was farmland or farmland adjacent. She would have been surprised to see a line of pickups barreling her way, too. But she could come up with a number of reasons why her neighbors might show up together.

She could not, however, think of a single reason that five extremely fancy-looking SUVs should come out to the farm at all. She couldn't even imagine who might be driving them—or where they would get such vehicles this far from anywhere. Her closest neighbor was a fifteen-minute drive away. The nearest town around was Independence, but calling it "close" was pushing it. It was half a day's drive south.

Well, missy, I expect you'll just have to wait and see what's going to happen, won't you? came a familiar wry voice inside her. Her beloved grandmother's voice. Delaney still hadn't fully accepted Mabel Clark had passed. It had been some five years ago, but the pain of it still walloped her when she least expected it.

Even now, with the memory of her grandmother's scratchy voice in her head, she could feel the hit of grief. She tried to shake it off.

Delaney walked across the yard, wiping the dirt off her hands on the bib of her worn and torn overalls. She wasn't dressed for company, but she supposed that folks who turned up out of the blue shouldn't expect much more than the dirty overalls she was wearing and the faded bandanna on her head. She stood there, frowning a little, as the gleaming black vehicles came to a stop before her, kicking up dust in all directions. She counted five in total.

And for a moment, she thought that maybe they'd realized their mistake. Maybe they were all peering out their dramatically tinted windows at her and realizing they'd taken a wrong turn somewhere.

Because nothing happened.

It was just Delaney, out beneath the endless bowl of

a Kansas sky, corn stretching in all directions. It was a pretty day, not too warm or too cold, and she supposed if she had to stand around in her own yard waiting to see who'd taken it upon themselves to show up here today, she ought to be grateful there wasn't a rainstorm. Or a tornado.

Thank you, Grandma Mabel, she said in her head.

She was grinning a little when the door of the vehicle that had stopped in the center of the other four opened.

By this point, Delaney could admit, she'd let anticipation get the better of her.

But it was only a driver. Though that, too, was fascinating. Who had a *driver*? She supposed she'd become her mother's driver, in these last few years since Catherine's arthritis and heart trouble had robbed her of so much. But she did not make her mother ride in the back seat. Nor did she wear a uniform. Unless her overalls counted.

Somehow Delaney knew that her overalls did not, in fact, count. Not to the sort of people who rode about in fleets and had uniformed drivers to open up their doors.

And it was an otherwise ordinary Tuesday, so she found herself far more interested in who, exactly, those sorts of people might be than she might have otherwise. She was really bemused more than anything else when the driver nodded at her as if she was exactly who he'd come to see, which was both laughable and impossible, then opened the back door of the SUV.

Some part of her was expecting trumpets to sound.

But there was still no particular sound, so there was nothing to distract her from the way the breeze danced in from the fields, or the sound of the wind chimes that made her mother happy, and then, there before her, the most beautiful man she had ever seen in her entire life…

unfolding himself from the back of the SUV that seemed entirely incapable of holding him.

Because what could possibly hold…*him?*

He was otherworldly. Almost alien, so little did he belong here in the middle of this rolling prairie, where the farmhouse and the red barn stood exactly as they had for ages and yet, she was sure, had never borne witness to anything like him.

Even the tornadoes would find it hard to top this man.

She knew exactly where the sun was above her, and yet Delaney felt certain that it had shifted. The better to beam its golden light all over this man. As if the sun itself wanted nothing more than to highlight him as best it could.

Delaney found she understood the urge. She felt it herself, everywhere. When she could not recall a single other time in her twenty-four years that she had ever had any kind of reaction to any kind of man. The boys she'd grown up with had been nice enough. They still were. And if she'd wanted, she had always suspected she could have gotten close to one of them and settled down the way so many of her high school classmates had.

It had never really occurred to Delaney to do anything of the kind. Because there was the farm. There had always been the farm. There was Grandma, and her mother, and Delaney took very seriously the fact that she was the last Clark. This land would be hers—was already hers in all the ways that mattered—and while she didn't intend to farm it alone the way her mother had done since Delaney's father had died before she was born, she also knew she had to make sure she picked the right kind of man.

She had yet to find a man around here who came close to her idea of the right kind.

It had never crossed her mind that the reason for that might be because none of them were *men*. Not like this man was.

As if he was redefining the term.

Delaney was always solid on her own two feet, planted right where they belonged in Kansas soil, and yet she actually felt dizzy as she stared up at the man before her. As if he was doing something more than simply standing there next to that obnoxiously glossy SUV that still gleamed as if the country roads hadn't dared get any dirt on it.

It wasn't that she thought the creature before her was the right sort of man. It wasn't like that, no matter that her body was doing all kinds of bizarre things. Too hot. Too cold. Fluttery, for some reason. As if he was so beautiful that human eyes were not meant to behold him.

Maybe she was coming down with the flu.

Besides, she doubted very much a man like *this* even knew what a farm was. He likely looked down the not inconsiderable length of his own body and saw nothing but dirt. Delaney had no use for such people.

She told herself that. Repeatedly.

Still, she couldn't seem to bring herself to look away from him. Maybe it was the loving way the sun fell over him, calling attention to the crisp black suit he wore that should have made him look as if he was attending a funeral. Yet it did not—or not the sort of funeral Delaney had ever attended around here, anyway. Maybe it was the way he held himself that made her think of the neighbors' prize bull. Never quite at rest, always rippling with that ferocious power right beneath the surface that could erupt at any moment…

Though she associated the sort of suit he was wearing with men in magazines, always too angular and wee to her mind, he wasn't either of those things, either. He was powerfully built, a symphony of lean muscle in a tall frame that made her breath feel a little short.

She had the sudden, strange conviction that this was a man who was well used to people looking up at him the way she was.

He was wearing dark glasses, but as she stood there gaping at him, he shifted them from his eyes. He did not shove them on the top of his head, or even on the back of his head, the way folks often did around here. He slid them into the lapel pocket of that suit of his, a small, simple gesture that made clear the breadth of his sophistication. She couldn't have said why. Only that it was as obvious as the width of his shoulders, the power in his chest, all the rest of him cast in stone and dark glory.

And Delaney should have laughed at herself for even thinking something like that. *Dark glory.* It was so melodramatic. It was so unlike her.

But then, it was almost too much to look upon his bare face. It was almost *too much.*

It was as if he'd been carved, not born. As if he'd been sculpted in a fury, bold lines and a forbidding palette. She thought of stone again, immovable. The harnessed power of great, wild animals. And some kind of hawk, too, fierce and commanding as he peered at her.

The man was…a lot.

"Wow," Delaney said, the word coming out of her mouth of its own accord. "Who are you? Are you lost?"

That was the only thing that made sense. That he was lost, out here in the prairie in his conspicuous caravan to God only knew where. That he'd turned in to ask for directions, perhaps—though that was hilarious in its own way. Since he looked like a man who would *know* where he was, always. As if he was his own compass in all things.

She was vaguely aware that other doors were opening, and other people were coming out of the gleaming vehicles, but she couldn't seem to look away from the man before her. She felt as if she was caught, somehow. As if he was deliberately holding her where she stood. There was something about his burnt gold gaze that nailed her to the spot. And though it wasn't even warm, she could feel herself heat up—even as a strange shiver worked its way from the nape of her neck all the way down her spine.

Dark glory was the only term that fit.

"You are called Delaney Clark," the man said.

"I am," she replied, because it seemed important that she answer him immediately. And only when she had did it occur to her that he hadn't actually asked her a question.

That had been a statement. As if he already knew her when she knew she most certainly did not know *him*.

That should have been a huge red flag, but all Delaney could seem to think about was *dark glory* and the way he spoke. That was certainly no Kansas accent. It was as if his words had a particular spice to them, and the way he said her name—

Get a grip, girl, she ordered herself. *Before you start drooling on the man.*

She was embarrassed at the very idea.

But she didn't step back.

"I see it," the man pronounced. And Delaney was aware, then, that he was making some kind of declaration. More, that all the people he brought with him were making murmuring noises as they gazed at her, as if that declaration meant something to them. Something intense.

"The cheekbones. The mouth. And of course, the eyes. She has a look of the Montaignes."

Again, there were more murmuring noises of assent. And awe, if she wasn't mistaken. And Delaney was still standing there in her overalls, with dirt all over her, allowing this strange moment to drag on. Because she didn't know quite what to do. Or what to say.

Or maybe because this man was too darkly beautiful and it turned out she was a silly little farm girl after all. That was how she felt, which was novel in its own right, because she had never been *silly*. Surely she could come up with something to say that wasn't *dark glory* or the neighbors' bull.

"Who *are* you?" she asked again.

Not exactly an improvement, though not as bad as it could have been. Delaney realized how dazed she was when the men flanking him stepped forward. Because she hadn't even seen them fall into place like that. But there they were, clearly...*bodyguarding* him.

In response, the man himself...barely moved. He did something with his head. Maybe inclined it slightly. Maybe shook it? But either way, the men froze on either side of him, as if he'd stopped them with his own hands.

"I am Cayetano Arcieri," he replied.

And then waited, as if his name itself tolled across the field like deep and terrible bells, calling down storms from above.

But it was still the same old Kansas sunshine. Delaney blinked. "I can tell that I'm supposed to recognize that name."

The man before her was hard and fierce, yet the way his brow rose was nothing short of haughty. "Do you not?"

"Well. No. I can't say that I do. I'm guessing you're not

a salesman. I doubt you're here to see about the tractor, which is a pity, because it's nothing short of poorly these days. And to be honest, I'm pretty sure I would remember that name if I'd ever heard it before." She shook her head sadly. Because she actually was sad that she was who she was and always had been—and that, therefore, there was no way on earth this man could possibly be looking for *her*. It felt a bit like grief, but that was crazy. "I thought you were lost, but now I think maybe you have some bad information."

He no longer looked haughty. Or not entirely haughty. A weather system moved over his face and what was left was a glinting thing that made her feel entirely too warm.

His hard mouth curved. Slightly. "If you are this Delaney Clark, and I can see that you are, I am afraid, little one, that I'm in exactly the right place."

No one had ever called Delaney *little one*. She had the sense she ought to have been offended.

Yet that was not, at all, the sensation storming around inside of her.

"I really don't think so," she said, because it felt critically important to her that she set the record straight. It didn't matter that every part of her *wanted* to be this man's *little one*. She would have to investigate that later and ask herself some hard questions. Probably. But she couldn't cope with extending this misunderstanding.

She had the oddest conviction that humoring this man not only wouldn't work, but that going along with him only to discover that she was not the Delaney Clark he was looking for would…*bruise* her, somehow.

And merely being in his presence felt bruising enough.

The more he looked at her, the more she began to feel as if the burnt gold of his gaze was somehow…*inside* her. She could feel the flames. And that delirious heat.

Cayetano seemed impervious to the dust beneath him, the breeze, the typical Kansas spring carrying on all around. He seemed to grow broader and taller the longer he stood there before her…and Delaney had never considered herself a whimsical person.

It was difficult to be too whimsical on a farm. There were too many chores.

And yet that was the only word she could think of as she looked at this man. *Whimsy.*

Except a lot hotter.

"I come from a country called Ile d'Montagne," Cayetano said. He paused as if he expected her to react to that, so she nodded. Helpfully. His mouth—a thing of wonder itself, stark and sensual at once—curved faintly once more. "It is a small place. An island in the Mediterranean to the north and east of Corsica. And it has been ruled for many centuries by false kings and queens."

Delaney felt as if she was outside herself. Nodding along while this man who could have stepped out of a Hollywood movie talked to her of kings and queens. *Kings and queens,* of all things, as if *royalty* was something he thought a great deal about. In his day-to-day life. So much so that there was a difference between false and un-false kings and queens.

Maybe she was actually still in her vegetable garden. Maybe she'd toppled over and hit her head on her loop hoe and was dreaming all of this.

That made a lot more sense than this conversation.

With this impossibly magnetic man.

Out here in the yard, talking of *royalty* and Mediterranean islands.

"For almost as long, there has been a rebellious faction," Cayetano told her. "The mountains that form the spine of the island have been contested since the first false king attempted to claim it. Just because a man comes along and calls a bit of land his, that doesn't make it so. There have been skirmishes. What has been called a civil war or two, but for that to be the case, all involved would need to be citizens. Subjects. When those who fight do not consider themselves either. Between these conflicts there have also been long stretches where those who reject the false kings merely…wait."

"Wait?" Delaney repeated. Hoping she sounded like something more than a mere parrot.

But what else was there to do but squawk?

"Wait," Cayetano agreed, his gaze dark and intent. "Have you never heard the proverb? Wait long enough by the river and the body of your enemy floats by."

That seemed to take an unnecessarily dark turn, in her opinion, in an already notably violent little tale this stranger was telling her. Out here in the yard where she should have been alone with her plants the way she was every other day.

"I can't really speak to rebellious factions hunkering down in contested mountains," Delaney said. Nervously. Her hands suddenly felt like they might betray her in some way. So she shoved them into the pockets of her overalls. "Or waiting by rivers. You do know that this is *Kansas*, don't you? We don't really have mountains. Though there are some big rocks."

Was it her imagination or did Cayetano move closer? Whether it was or not, she found she was having trouble breathing, and instead of being alarmed by that…

She kind of liked it.

Obviously she was not well.

But still, she couldn't seem to move.

"For centuries, my people have waited to claim what is theirs," Cayetano told her, and his voice was low now. Almost quiet. And yet it was as if all the fields in all directions went still. As if the sky paused, the better to listen. To *wait*. "For an opportunity. A chance. My grandfather negotiated our current peace, which has held far longer than anyone thought might. Yet still we believed that any chance we might get to reclaim what is ours could only come with bloodshed."

Bloodshed.

And…there it was at last. That alarm that Delaney should have been feeling from the start. It washed through her in a torrent then, so electric she was sure she could feel every hair on her body stand on end.

"I'd like to come down firmly against bloodshed, if that's an option," she said, as carefully as a person could when talking about…whatever it was they were talking about here. This very serious nonsense the man with the burnt gold eyes seemed so intent on sharing with her.

"I am a warlord," the forbidding man before her told her. "I earned my place in blood and fire."

"Metaphorically?" Delaney asked with a nervous little laugh.

No one echoed that laugh.

The men arrayed behind him were stone-faced. Cayetano himself appeared to be fashioned *from* stone.

"I have found a far better way to reclaim my ancestral lands than any war," he told her, his gaze never wavering. "A foolproof plan, at last."

"Oh, good." Delaney was beginning to feel something like lightheaded. Or maybe it was more of that dizziness. "That sounds much nicer than bloodshed."

The look on his face changed, then. And if she hadn't been so overwhelmed she might have thought that, really, it looked a lot like amusement.

Assuming a man like this was capable of being amused.

"That depends on how you look at it," Cayetano said. Distantly, Delaney registered the laughter of his minions, indicating that they were capable of it. "You and I are to marry."

Had he said that he planned to ride a dinosaur down to Independence and back, or perhaps catapult himself high enough into the air to swat down the sun, that would not have been any more astonishing.

"I...what?"

"You are the key," Cayetano Arcieri, self-styled *warlord* of a country she'd never heard of, who had earned his place in *blood and fire*, assured her.

Delaney's throat was upsettingly dry. "I feel pretty sure I'm not."

"You are the lost heiress to the crown of Ile d'Montagne, little one," Cayetano informed her. "And I have come to take you home."

He said that the way something as over the top as that should be said, really, all ringing tones and *certainty* and that blaze in his burnt gold eyes. Delaney thought the corn bowed down a little, that was how impressive he sounded.

But all she could do was laugh.

CHAPTER TWO

THIS WAS NOT the response Cayetano had expected.

An offer of marriage from him should result in exultation and gratitude, not laughter. He could think of any number of women who would have fallen to their knees and praised the heavens had he indicated he wanted a second night, much less a lifetime.

This woman was baffling.

More to the point, she was not what he'd expected, either, and he had pored over all the photographs his spies had gathered for him. He had looked for every possible clue to determine that she was, in fact, who he hoped she was. She should not have been a surprise in any way. On balance, she was not—the pictures his men had obtained of her were accurate.

But that was all they were. A picture could only show her features. It could not capture the warmth of her. The way she drew the eye without seeming to try. The brightness that seemed to light her from within—when he had long since accepted that the Montaignes were a clan of darkness and bitter cold, every last one of them.

Not this lost one, it seemed, with all this American sun in her hair.

And more, in her very eyes somehow, so that that famous Montaigne blue was neither cold nor fierce, but bright enough to make a man think of little but the kinds of summers other men enjoyed. On tropical beaches far away from the concerns of a contested throne.

He had seen her standing in the dirt, dressed like a peasant—and despite these things, had been shot through with a hunger unlike any he had ever known. He had sat in his car, waiting for the intensity of his hunger to pass, yet it had not.

Even now, her peals of laughter still ripe in the air between them, it only grew.

Cayetano blinked at the direction of his own thoughts. Since when had he considered himself nothing but a mere man? He had never had that option. Not for him the call of flesh and sin. Not for him the comforts of oblivion. His entire existence had been honed and focused to a hard shine.

And yet here he stood in this foreign place, thinking of sunshine and excess, and the sweet oblivion of flesh and desire.

But the unexpected lost heiress of Ile d'Montagne was still laughing. As if, truly, she had never heard anything more preposterous than what he had told her. As if anything he had said to her was funny.

As if he, Cayetano Arcieri, sworn enemy of the Montaignes no matter the two generations of uneasy peace, was given to telling *jokes*.

Cayetano could see the way his men began to scowl at the insult, but he waved them back as they started forward. He told himself he was letting her go on merely to note how long it took her to collect herself, and then to understand the discourtesy and disrespect she showed, but he had the sneaking suspicion that, actually, it was simply to watch all of that light dance around her—

You must stop this, he ordered himself grimly. *There is more at stake here than your* hunger.

"It is a lot to take in, I grant you," he said stiffly when she wiped at her eyes.

"It's just so silly," she said as if she was agreeing with him. "What a story. First of all, I'm not lost. I'm right where I'm meant to be, right here where I belong. And there are certainly no crowns involved. Or *princesses.*"

And that set her off again, tossing her head back to laugh straight up toward the endless sky.

Cayetano could admit that he had not given this part of his mission as much thought as the rest. Finding her had been the hard part. It had taken time and patience, when he was famous for ignoring the first when it did not suit him and exhibiting very little of the second when he pleased. The task before him had been immense and overpowering.

He'd had to believe the impossible. Then prove it.

That he had done so beat in him, a dark drum of victory, even now.

It was, perhaps, not unreasonable that he had thought collecting her would be the easy part. What he wanted to do was simply toss her over his shoulder, throw her in the car, and start the journey home. He wanted to focus on what came next. How and when he would finally disrupt the line of succession and take back what had been stolen from his people so long ago, not so much breaking the peace between the factions in his country so much as obliterating the need for it. Both the peace and the two factions, in one fell swoop.

It had never occurred to him that he would have to *convince* his Princess to reclaim her place.

Though diplomacy was not his strong suit, Cayetano

endeavored to make himself look…nonthreatening. Understanding and inviting, if such a thing were possible.

He did not think he achieved anything like it.

"Perhaps this is too much to take on faith," he said, trying to sound sympathetic. Though the edge he could hear in his own voice suggested he was not successful. "But you're not required to believe me. The science speaks for itself."

"The science?" She repeated the word, then started laughing again. "What science could there possibly be to lead a *warlord* to a quiet old farm in the middle of nowhere? I'm telling you, I think you took a wrong turn. Maybe back in whatever mountains you're from. I'm not the Princess you're looking for."

But the more she insisted, the more he saw the truth of her parentage. The absence of doubt. The deep belief in her own discernment above all else, when surely it should have been clear to her that a mere farm girl could not possibly have access to the same information as a man of his stature. It should have been glaringly apparent.

Cayetano was not conversant in Americans or farm girls, it was true, but he felt sure that without the Montaigne blood in her veins, this one would have quaked before him, as was only right and proper.

"It did not begin with science, of course," he told her, shifting as he stood.

He was not accustomed to having his commands and wishes dismissed, but he was also aware—on some distant level—that it would not serve his cause to take this woman against her will. It would only muddy things, and he needed clarity. Rather, he needed to appear to act with clarity and sensitivity, the better to fight the right battles.

Probably it would not kill him. He attempted a reassuring smile, but she only frowned.

"There were whispers," he told her, still trying to exude something other than his usual forbidding intensity. "There are always whispers around any throne, but perhaps more so in Ile d'Montagne, where the ruling family has been contested for so long. Mostly these are rumors that come to nothing. Just malicious little tales told to pass the time between spots of civil unrest. In this case, someone began telling a story that Princess Amalia was a changeling, almost from the moment of her birth."

His lost princess blinked. "A changeling. Like in a fairy tale."

She sounded doubtful. And if he wasn't mistaken, that look on her face was a clear indication that she did not find him a trustworthy source.

But he didn't have time to revel in that novelty.

Delaney was wearing a pair of coveralls that should have offended him on every level, so common were they, marking her as some kind of farmhand when she would be his bride. But she stood in them with such confidence that he noticed her lush form instead. There were freckles across her nose, but they only drew attention to the perfection of her cheekbones. And her hands looked capable and strong, not merely delicate appendages suitable only for the hefting of fine jewels. To think—all this dirt, all these fields, and she was nonetheless the true heir to the kingdom.

She pleased him more than he'd dare imagine.

As did the fact that whether she believed it or not, she would be his.

"There's no particular reason that such a fairy story should come to my attention," Cayetano told her. "I do not make a habit of listening to the dark fantasies of bored aristocrats. Yet in this case, the story did not die out quickly the way the most outrageous usually do."

"At least we can agree that the notion of changelings is outrageous," Delaney offered. Almost helpfully.

Did she intend to be provoking? He could not tell, so he pushed on. "I could not get the idea out of my head. And the more I considered it, the more it seemed obvious to me that Princess Amalia was not who she pretended to be. Dark-haired and light-eyed, yes. But too many other curiosities that had never before appeared in the Montaigne line throughout history."

"I think you'll find that's called genetics."

This time Cayetano had no trouble recognizing that she was, almost certainly, provoking him. Or, at the least, defying him in what small way she could.

He opted not to react to these affronts the way he normally would. He inclined his head instead. "When there arose an opportunity to test the genetic material of the current Princess against that of her supposed mother, I had no choice but to take that opportunity."

"You took blood samples from princesses and queens?" Delaney shook her head as if she hadn't meant to say that. "This is an entertaining story. Really. I always had a soft spot for fairy tales. But the more outlandish this all gets, the less and less I believe it. And I didn't believe it to begin with."

Cayetano waved a hand as if it was nothing, her disbelief. He would not tell her, then, the lengths he and his men had gone to. The risks they had taken. The potential penalties had they failed.

None of it mattered, for they had not failed.

"But the tests were conclusive," he told Delaney quietly. "Princess Amalia of Ile d'Montagne bears no genetic relationship to the Queen. She is not Queen Esme's daughter."

"Okay." Delaney wrinkled up her nose. "You do know

that people are complicated, right? There could be any number of reasons for that."

"Indeed. And we have explored them all. But I will tell you the most astonishing thing. Are you ready to hear it?"

"Is it more astonishing than all the other things you have said?" she asked.

Rather aridly for his tastes. And yet his hunger to taste her continued unabated.

"Queen Esme suffered from a particular cocktail of ailments while pregnant," Cayetano told her with a quiet ferocity. "Because of them, she was taken to a specialist hospital in this vast country of yours. A city with the unlikely name of Milwaukee."

"Yes," said Delaney, her eyes narrowing. "I was also born in Milwaukee. As were a great many other people, I think you'll find. This is absurd."

But Cayetano looked behind her. An older woman had come to the door during their conversation and was standing there on the other side of the screen, listening to him tell this story.

Not just listening, he corrected himself. Frozen into place.

He pushed on. "There were twelve babies born in that hospital on that particular day. Only two of them were girls. One was the Crown Princess of Ile d'Montagne. The other, a farm girl from Kansas."

"And you think…what?" Delaney demanded. She was frowning even more deeply now, which Cayetano hoped meant she was also beginning to take the truth on board, however unpalatable to her. "That somehow, a princess and a perfectly normal girl from Kansas were—"

"Switched," came the older woman's voice. She pushed open the screen and stepped through it onto the porch. Her expression was taut, but her eyes were bright. "There in the hospital. On the third day."

Cayetano already knew he was right, but that didn't prevent the surge of triumph that raced through him then. A deep and satisfying roar from deep within, because the throne of Ile d'Montagne was in his grasp at last.

He had succeeded.

Finally.

He studied the girl as she turned, jerkily, as if her mother had taken a swing at her. And had made contact.

"Mama?" Her voice sounded too soft now. Almost plaintive. "What are you talking about?"

"I knew," the older woman whispered, loud enough to carry across the cornfields. There was a fierce look on her creased face. "I knew they brought me the wrong baby. I said so, didn't I? The nurses all laughed. They told me I was a new mother, that was all. Drunk on hormones, no sleep, and whatnot. But I knew."

"Mama?" Delaney's voice was thicker now.

More panicked, Cayetano noted, and that couldn't be helped.

"For a time I thought something was wrong with me," the older woman continued, her voice stronger with each word. Only then did she look at the girl she'd raised into a woman. The baby that wasn't hers. "And it didn't matter, because I loved you. With everything I am, Delaney, switched or not. But the switch explains too many things that have never made sense. That you can carry a tune, for one thing. There's not a Clark stretching back into the old country who was anything but tone-deaf."

Delaney was full-on scowling now. "Mama, this is ridiculous. Babies aren't switched in hospitals. You're as likely to have a child snatched by the fae folk and I hope we all know *that* is pure fantasy."

"I know what I know, Delaney. No matter how addled you think I've become."

"I don't think you're addled, Mama," Delaney retorted. "But I know you're weak. This sort of melodrama can't be good for you."

"I know what I know," the older woman repeated, looking mutinous. She nodded at Cayetano. "And so does he."

"There's an easy solution," Cayetano interjected, at his ease now, because as far as he was concerned the truth was already out. "We can perform a quick genetic test here and now. No need to debate *what-ifs*. This is not about feelings, you understand. It is about facts."

And it was a fact that the way his future wife looked at him then should have set him alight. Cayetano found he liked the burn of it.

Something in him shifted. Readied itself.

He liked that, too.

Delaney's fierceness faded a bit when they moved inside, her expression changing into something closer to apprehension. Cayetano sat there in the tidy, cozy sort of living space that looked the way he supposed he'd imagined an American farmhouse would. Having never entered one before. When he would have said he took in very little foreign media.

But this room felt familiar to him just the same, down to the stitched sampler on one wall.

He stared at it as his doctor administered the tests quickly. The results were nearly immediate. The man cleared his throat and made the expected announcement, there in the homespun room.

And then there was no further need to argue the point. Delaney Clark was not related to her mother. She was, however, possessed of nearly fifty percent of the DNA of Queen Esme of Ile d'Montagne.

The facts did not lie.

"This can't be happening," Delaney said. More than once.

In a voice that sounded less and less like the one she'd used at first outside.

"As I have told you," Cayetano said mildly, for he was at his ease now. All that was left was convincing her to do what he, for one, already knew she would. Because it could be no other way. "It is only science."

He found himself unprepared when her bright blue eyes shifted to him, wide and accusatory. "It is not just science," she whispered. "This is my *life*."

Cayetano did not have it in him to understand the lure of farmland when kingdoms awaited. But then again, who more than he understood the connection one had to the place they called home?

He settled himself in the chair that, for all it looked worn and tired, likely rated as among the most comfortable he'd ever sat in. He attempted to arrange his features into something...understanding.

Failing that, he attempted to look less forbidding.

Because now that the tests had been administered, he needed to present himself as less of a warlord, if possible. And more of a bridegroom.

He wasn't sure it sat easily on him, but he attempted it all the same.

"It is time for a new era in Ile d'Montagne," he told her quietly, holding that blue gaze. "For too long it has been a country torn in two. For too long it has been brother against brother, no one safe, no one trustworthy. There is no way to build a future in these conditions. There is only war and uneasy treaties in between. There is only loss, fighting, and generations of waiting for the next blow. It must end."

Delaney was breathing roughly, but she did not speak. Cayetano looked over at her mother, sitting near her on the couch, but the old woman had her gaze lowered.

"You may think that I have come to find you to advance my own interests above all else," Cayetano said gruffly.

"Because that's why you came, didn't you?" she asked, and something flashed in her gaze before she, too, dropped her focus to her lap. "You want that throne."

"I am the leader of one half of my country, it is true." Cayetano was not ashamed to admit this. Still, he did not love the way his words seemed to hang in the air between them. "I wish to marry you not only because it will grant me access to the throne, though it will. But because you represent the other half of my country and I wish our union to unite all of Ile d'Montagne's people."

"Your people, you mean," she said, more to her lap than to him. "People who have nothing to do with me."

"I do not want revenge, Delaney. I want renewal. My country needs it. And you are the only one who can make this happen." She did not respond to that, though her chest moved as if she was breathing heavily. "I don't know what you think it is a princess does."

She lifted her gaze to his. It was not a friendly look, but something in him sang nonetheless. And that hunger inside him bit deeper. "I have never given the matter the faintest shred of thought. I have been too busy planting. And farming. And a great many other tasks princesses are not known for, I'd guess."

Cayetano waved a hand. "It is irrelevant in any case. What matters is what you and I will do. We will create a bright and gleaming future. Your blood and mine will pave the way to the future, together. Gone will be the bitter, bloody factions of the past. Together, you and I will remake the world." It was a ringing speech and all the better because he meant it—though he had prepared it before meeting her. He had prepared it for the idea of her. He couldn't have said why that felt wrong, now. He shook off the strange notion. "All you need do is say yes."

She did not even need to do that, but this was America. Cayetano paid little attention to the doings of the place as a whole, but even he knew that Americans deeply prized their sense of freedom, however elusive it might prove in reality. No need to tell his farm girl that her acquiescence was merely a formality. There was no earthly reason to tell her that he, the warlord of the Ile d'Montagne hills, would be only too happy to toss her over his shoulder and handle the situation in the time-honored fashion of his people.

He did not think she would react to the news well.

It was another indication of how sheltered she was, out here surrounded by her corn and her vegetables. It had yet to occur to her that a man on a mission that was intended to remain wholly peaceful did not turn up with a battalion.

Though he did find that he was suddenly far more intrigued by the notion of his people's marital wedding practices, which he had always considered archaic, than he ever had been before.

Delaney stared at her hands for a long while, though the ragged movements of her chest gave away her continued rough breathing. She lifted her gaze again, her blue eyes seemed almost tortured, and Cayetano felt...

Not regret. Not quite. But something in him twisted, all the same.

"I wish you the best of luck, then," she said, almost

solemnly. "But this sounds like your fight, not mine. Even if I was remotely interested in some far-off place I've never heard of, it would be impossible. I belong here. This is my home."

She held his gaze as she said it. She looked at him steadily, as if wishing him on his way even now. She was dismissing him, he thought with some amusement, and that was certainly not the way he was normally treated.

It was so unusual that it was almost…nice.

"Delaney," he began, trying to sound…reasonable.

"There's no possible way," she said, shaking her head as if the matter was decided and she had moved on now to be faintly sorry about it. "I can't even consider it. Maybe you noticed the whole farm outside. It can't take care of itself."

The older woman stirred herself then, there on her end of the couch she shared with Delaney. Her eyes were grave as she gazed at Cayetano, then back at Delaney. She looked as if she was taking her time coming to a decision. Then she nodded, slightly.

"I'm needed here," Delaney said, her voice urgent. And cracking around the edges, to Cayetano's ear, the longer she looked at her mother—who wasn't truly her mother. "You can't do this alone, Mama, you know that. You *can't*."

The old woman smiled, and something in it made Cayetano's neck prickle.

"I do know that," she said softly, and the softness was not for him. Her gaze had been shrewd when she took him in. The softness was for Delaney, and she smiled when she turned to the daughter she'd raised. And loved, he saw, just as she'd said. "But nonetheless, Delaney, I think you should go."

CHAPTER THREE

DELANEY COULDN'T STOP shaking. She couldn't remember ever actually *shaking* before in her life, and now it was as if she was little better than a leaf in a swift wind. She was actually *trembling*.

And she would have hated that she was so weak, but she couldn't seem to focus on her body or the things that were happening in it. Not beyond noticing what was happening.

Not when her world had fallen apart.

Cayetano murmured something and left the room, taking his men along with him. She hardly knew the man who had turned up here and set everything spinning madly out of control, so she shouldn't have been surprised to see him show a little compassion. But she was anyway. Or maybe it was the opposite. Maybe it was a performance of deep cynicism, because he had somehow known what her mother would say. Maybe he was simply, politely, leaving the two of them to talk now that all his *facts* were laid out.

Not that it mattered, because the shock waves from her mother's surprise statement were still rolling through *her*. And Delaney knew without having to ask that for all his apparent compassion—or whatever it was inside a man made of stone—he was not going far.

She couldn't think about that, either. Or any of the implications when she didn't hear any car engines turning over outside.

Because now was simply her and her mother, here in this room, where she'd spent the whole of her life. Where she knew every picture in every frame. Where she'd played on the floor as a child, there on the thickly woven rug. Where she and her mother—*not your mother,* came that terrible voice inside her—sat in the evenings and worked on their sewing, their knitting, and other projects while the light was good.

This farm, this house—this was her *life.*

How could her mother possibly tell her to go?

"You can't think that any of this is real," Delaney said furiously. "No matter what it says on a test that he could easily have doctored—"

"I know that you're upset," Catherine said. And she suddenly seemed imbued with the strength Delaney hadn't seen in her in ages. It made her heartsick that it was only now. Only under these bizarre conditions. "I understand. I'm upset, too."

Delaney couldn't keep herself on her end of the sofa any longer. She moved toward her mother, reaching out without thought and making a little sobbing sound when her mother grabbed her hands.

It was hard to tell who held on tighter.

"Listen to me," Catherine said, her voice as fierce as her grip. "You are my daughter. In every way that matters, *you are my daughter.* I took you home from the hospital. I loved you. I raised you. We're not debating whether or not you are mine. You are, Delaney. *You are.*"

"But you said…" Delaney croaked out, horrified when she realized the water splashing on her hands was coming from her eyes. Clarks didn't cry. Clarks didn't make scenes. Clarks endured. But this Clark felt as if she'd already been carried away in a tornado. "You told him…"

"I had a funny feeling," Catherine said quietly. "And was quickly told it was my hormones, that was all. Over time I would sometimes remember that feeling, when you would sing, perhaps. Or when I would think about the fact that you don't have the Clark chin. All Clarks have the same pointy chin." She tapped the end of hers, round and stubborn. "You don't even have mine. Still, these are little things. I love you, Delaney. I find myself interested in meeting the child I bore in my body, I won't lie. But that will never change my love for *you*."

Delaney couldn't let herself think about that other child. That *princess*, if Cayetano was to be believed. And how could she possibly believe a word he'd said? How could her quiet life have anything to do with *princesses?* It made no sense.

She knew about corn. Not thrones.

"Even if it's true," she said, after a moment—though she didn't think it was. But Catherine clearly did. "Even if somehow it's actually true, that doesn't mean that I need to go off somewhere with this man. This *stranger.* It certainly doesn't mean I should *marry* him."

"Weddings don't necessarily happen overnight," her mother said, an odd gleam in her gaze. "No need to rush into anything, I would say. But I think what we have before us is an opportunity, Delaney."

"An opportunity for what?" Inside, she thought, *to question everything? To find out I'm not who I thought I was?* She could have done without the opportunity, thanks.

All she'd ever known, all she'd ever wanted, was the farm.

"I know you love this land," her mother said quietly.

Almost as if it hurt her to say. "But I have agonized over it. As my own strength wanes, I've watched you try to work with your own two hands what it took my father and a full set of workers and family to maintain. How can you possibly stand up to it? How can anyone?"

"It's Clark land," Delaney protested. "I'll find a way. That's what Clarks do."

"I'm an old woman now." And Catherine sounded firm now. She patted Delaney's hand in the way she'd always done. A quiet *chin up, child*. "I have tended this land since I was little more than a girl. Sometimes I think I'd like to live in town, in the time I have left. It would be nice to walk somewhere, if I wanted. Be easy, if I wish. Sleep in late and leave the cows to do their business with someone else."

Delaney's heart was kicking at her, some whirl of fear and panic and too many other dark things she couldn't name. Or breathe through, really.

She made herself focus on her mother, not whatever was happening inside her. "Mama, if this is how you feel, why have you never told me?"

"How could I tell you?" Catherine asked quietly. "You've already given up so much for this farm. You are young, Delaney. You shouldn't be here, isolated and away from everyone. You have more in common with a vegetable patch than people your own age. It's not natural. And it's not good for you."

Delaney sat back, pulling her hands away. "But you think some stranger showing up and saying he wants to spirit me off to play some sort of political game is better? How is that natural?"

"What kind of life will you have if you never leave the farm?" Catherine retorted. "I could never think of a way to tell you what I thought you should do. You have always been so determined. And you never asked. But it seems fate has taken care of it, doesn't it? You have a birthright, Delaney. You already know what this one looks like. Why don't you go and see what this new one is about?"

"Because I don't want to go!" Delaney cried, and she didn't care if Cayetano with his burnt gold warlord eyes could hear her. "I don't want to go anywhere!"

Her mother—*because she is still my mother, I don't care what that test said,* she told herself—reached over and patted her hand again. She had that canny look about her that Delaney had always rued. It was too much like her grandmother. It always led to truths she'd have preferred to ignore. "Is it because you truly don't wish to go? That's fine. No one will make you go anywhere if you don't want to go. I don't care how many cars he has."

"Thank you," Delaney said in a rush—

But Catherine held up a hand. "I wonder, though, if it's more that you're *afraid* to go?" She shook her head. "Because if that's the case, my dear girl, then I'm afraid I will have to insist."

It took Delaney two days to answer that question.

And she wasn't happy about it. Any of it. She spent forty-seven hours talking herself around and around in circles. And a lot of those hours succumbing to emotions unbefitting a person who had been raised in the Midwest.

Emotions were for high-strung coastal types. Midwesterners were made of sterner stuff. Salt of the earth, in point of fact. She would pull herself together as quickly as possible, reminding herself that *salt of the earth* did not mean sobbing into her pillows.

But then she would remind herself that she wasn't made of anything Midwestern at all. Because the DNA test didn't lie, much as she wished it did. She'd researched it. Delaney was a good Kansas girl who'd been raised up right on a farm—but now she was a *princess*.

It felt *wrong,* that was all. There was no other word for it.

Except embarrassing.

A man had showed up in the yard one day and the life she'd thought had been built on a solid foundation, generations deep, turned out to be nothing more than a row of dominoes.

None of them hers.

The truth was, she blamed said man for those dominoes. She'd researched him, too. It didn't take much. It seemed that most papers' coverage of Ile d'Montagne and its current rebel leader were nothing short of fawning. All papers, in fact, save those actually in his country.

Delaney held on to that like it was evidence.

Or maybe because it was all she had to hold on to.

Because everything else seemed to be rolling downhill, and fast.

Catherine was moving into town. She intended to sell the land to the neighbors, to keep the farm in good hands. But when Delaney had argued that she should stay and oversee the move and the sale and the unfathomable life changes she hadn't even realized her mother desired, Catherine had waved her away.

You've been seeing to me for far too long, she had said, again and again, until Delaney was forced to accept that she really, truly meant it. *It's time you go out and live.*

So this was Delaney living.

Against her will.

The fleet of glossy SUVs came back up the lane far

too early that morning. And this time, only Cayetano emerged.

They stared at each other, he from beside the muscular vehicle that, if anything, looked glossier and more pristine than before. She stayed where she was—on the step where she had taken herself after saying her goodbyes to her mother, red-eyed and cried out and wondering how on earth she was supposed to *live* through this.

And how exactly she could prove that she'd lived enough so that she could come back home.

Assuming there was any *home* to come back to, without the farm.

Not to mention, she isn't your mother, came that same insidious voice inside her, forever telling her things she didn't want to hear. Not her grandmother's voice, sadly. She would have welcomed Grandma Mabel's observations, however dry.

This particular voice sounded a lot more the way she imagined gold might.

If it was burned half to ash.

"You do not look excited, little one," Cayetano said from his place beside his enormous SUV, in that voice of his that seemed to change the weather. She felt a breeze that hadn't been there before dance over her skin.

"That's because I'm not," she replied, scowling at him for good measure. "Would you be excited to be torn from everything you know and forced to march off to a foreign country because someone thinks your blood will… *do* something?"

"Focus less on blood," Cayetano suggested, with a faint curve to his hard mouth that she ordered herself to stop looking at. "And more on what pleasures await."

Delaney didn't much care for the way the word *plea-*

sures burst open inside her. Like a water balloon against the side of the old barn.

"If you're talking about the whole marriage thing, forget it." And she couldn't understand why she wished, immediately, that she hadn't said that. That she hadn't heard the word *pleasures* and mentioned the marriage that was never going to happen. It was…unseemly, somehow. She hurtled on, her cheeks hot. "My mother thinks that I need to go and see my birthright. I keep telling her I'm happy with the one I already have, but she insists."

"Are you refusing to marry me?" Cayetano asked, but not as if the prospect made him angry. There was none of that haughtiness. Or even a particular sense of the threat he posed. Instead, he looked as if her refusal amused him.

It was disconcerting.

"I am." She said it as bluntly as possible, so there could be no mistake. "I am absolutely refusing to marry you. Because the very idea is absurd. I don't know you."

And again, that little tug in the corner of his mouth sent a terrible heat, far more intense than the flush on her cheeks, cartwheeling through her. Once again this man felt like a fever.

She ought to tell him to do something about his infectiousness, but she didn't quite dare. Or maybe the truth was that she liked all that cartwheeling.

"Allow me to tell you something about me, then," he said, as if he could see her turning cartwheels inside. As if he knew. "I love a challenge, Delaney. I have yet to meet a challenge I couldn't get the best of. Better you know that now."

That was an unambiguous warning.

And there was a flash in his gaze that made the skin over her bones seem to draw tight. She was suddenly aware of herself in a way she never had been before. Right there on the porch steps of the comfortable old farmhouse, she felt…*lush,* somehow. Her breasts ached and felt heavier than before. There was a shivery sensation that started at the nape of her neck and wound its way ever lower, down the length of her spine, spreading more of that shimmering lushness as it went. Strangest and most wonderful of all was that between her legs, she felt hot and bright.

Maybe it wasn't her fault that she'd never paid much attention to the boys she'd grown up with. Maybe the problem was that none of them had ever looked at her and made her feel like a whole weather system.

As if, that voice inside her whispered, *the moment you met this man you became someone else. Not because of your blood. But because he changed you from a farm girl into a princess with a glance.*

And she *felt* it. She felt different, down deep in her bones. As if no matter what happened, even if she returned here the way she wanted to, she would never be the same.

But Delaney also knew, in a flash of insight that felt like truth no matter how odd, that she must not, under any circumstances, start talking to this man about *weather.* Whatever she did, she needed to keep how profoundly changed she felt to herself.

"I expected your mother to see you off," Cayetano said, and there was a note in his voice that made her wonder how long she'd been standing on the porch like this. *Gazing* at him.

It must have been at least a minute or two, because he was no longer standing beside his vehicle. He was standing in front of her. She was sure that if she inhaled, his scent was there, a faint hint of spice and heat that made her…*want* things.

Mostly Delaney wanted to lift her hand to her cheeks, to test the heat there, but she thought that would be a dead giveaway. And she was not going to tell him about *her* weather issues. No matter how close he was.

She scowled at the bag Catherine had insisted she pack, there at her feet. "We've already said our goodbyes. We don't need to perform them out here for you to see it."

"I understand," he said smoothly. "Parting must be difficult."

It might kill her, actually—but Delaney refused to cry anymore. And not where Cayetano Arcieri could see it. She focused on him instead. Today he was wearing another one of those suits that made her reconsider her stance on suiting altogether. Because on him, there was no denying it looked good. Even out here on the farm, where he should have looked silly wearing such formal clothes.

Nothing about this man was silly.

But, no matter how good he looked, he was still the reason that she was being forced to do this. She picked up her bag with very little grace, and then practically bit her tongue to keep from reacting when he simply…took it from her hand. Then dropped it back on the ground.

"My woman must necessarily carry many burdens," he told her in that way he had, like he was inscribing stone as he spoke. "Such is my lot in life, and thus hers. But she does not carry her own luggage as long as I am alive."

He moved to usher her toward the vehicle, lifting a finger in the direction of one of the other tinted windows. And that lifted finger was a call to action, clearly, because another car door opened immediately. When she glanced back over her shoulder, her bag was being loaded into one of the other SUVs.

But there was no time to concentrate on such practical matters, because Cayetano was closing her inside the vehicle he'd exited. The interior was dark. Cool. And noisy—

Until she realized that the racket was inside her. It was the thunder of her pulse through her veins. It was her heart, deep and loud.

And when Cayetano swung into the deep seat beside her, that didn't help.

I've made a terrible mistake, Delaney thought in a panic.

She only realized she'd said that out loud when Cayetano shifted in the leather seat beside her. He reached over and took her hand in his, a nurturing sort of gesture that astonished her. She was...floored. So much so that she couldn't seem to do a thing save freeze in response.

He didn't squeeze her hand the way her mother might. In fact, the longer he held her fingers in his, the heat of his palm skyrocketing through her, the less nurturing she found the whole thing.

She expected him to say something. To make another one of those statements of his, so matter of fact, as if the world would arrange itself before him as he willed it. Simply because he wished it.

But he said nothing. It was only when she heard her own breath come out in a long sigh, from somewhere deep inside her, that she recognized the uncomfortable truth. The simple act of him holding her hand was... calming.

It wasn't only calming. It was a great many other things and a significant number of weather changes, but above and around and in all of that, it was *calming*.

Nothing could have confused her more. How could anything about a man so elemental be calming? How was it possible?

It took her a long time to lift her gaze to his, but when she did, she caught her breath all over again.

Cayetano's burnt gold eyes blazed. And there was something about the hard stamp of his mouth that made everything inside her feel overly fragile. Perilous, even. As if she wasn't sitting down in plush leather but teetering over the side of some great height, so high she didn't dare look over to see the ground that must surely be rushing toward her—

He dropped her hand, but it was not until he pulled a buzzing cell phone out of his pocket that she understood why. Even then, she had the most bizarre urge to protest. To reclaim his hand. To touch him as if this was something she did, leaping into strange cars with strange men who wanted impossible things from her. Dark, overwhelming things involving thrones and vows, no less.

And maybe a weather system or two, came that voice.

This time sounding amused, the way her grandmother would have been if she'd been around to see her usually unflappable granddaughter so…*flapped.*

Cayetano called out something that made the car begin to move, and then directed his attention to his call, stretching out his long legs before him as he sat back.

And Delaney could not understand a single word he said, rapid-fire, like poetry at top speed. French, she thought, though she'd only ever heard French spoken on television. Or no, possibly Italian. Because she sometimes watched cooking shows.

But she couldn't help feeling, now that the urge to protest the loss of his attention was mostly gone, that his attention being directed elsewhere felt like a reprieve.

She needed that as the SUV turned around, then headed back down the lane. She needed to be herself again, even if it was for the last time.

Because this car—this man—was taking her away from everything she'd ever known.

You can't really want to sell the farm, she had protested.

I would have sold it after your grandmother died, Catherine had replied with that steel that had reminded Delaney of when her mother hadn't been the least bit fragile. *It was all you had. But I want you to have more, Delaney. You deserve more.*

It's because I'm not yours, she had dared to say. Earlier this very morning, standing stiff and feeling unwelcome in the same kitchen that had once felt like an extension of herself.

You are mine, Catherine had replied fiercely. *You will always be mine. But I will not let this cursed farm stand between you and an opportunity like this.*

I have no interest in being some kind of trophy wife, Delaney had protested. *You should know that.*

Then don't become one, Catherine had replied. She had even laughed, like a fist to Delaney's heart. *Be whatever and whoever you wish to be. Just promise me you will give this adventure a chance, Delaney. That's all I ask.*

She'd had no defense against that. Against her mother's heartfelt plea—even if Catherine wasn't technically her mother. In all the ways that mattered, she was and always would be. How could she say no? Until Cayetano had showed up here, she had assumed she would never leave the farm. And so she'd often been wistful, watching far-off places on television, trying to imagine what it would be like to sink her toes deep into exotic white sand beaches. Or climb distant mountains.

Or just…*be somewhere else,* where no one knew anything about her unless she told them.

And every time Catherine had caught her being wistful, Delaney had always assured her that she was all about the farm. Always and forever about the land. Because what good was wistfulness when there was a growing season to consider?

Someday, her mother had liked to say, *you're going to see the world, Delaney.*

And they'd both laughed, because the only world Delaney had ever been likely to see was on television.

Until now.

Just promise me you'll give it a chance, Catherine had said this morning.

I promise, Delaney had whispered, because how could she do anything else?

And then she'd sobbed when her mother had hugged her, as if it was the last time. As if this was a kind of funeral. Hers.

Giving up something when you don't know what it is isn't much of a sacrifice, Grandma Mabel had told her once in her usual crisp, knowing manner. *And the truth is, it's only the choices that hurt a little that make us any better.*

Well, this hurt.

A lot.

Delaney could repeat those things to herself over and over. She could even accept, somewhere deep down, that they were true, and maybe—in time—the acceptance would bring her solace.

Maybe she was setting off on an adventure and the real reason she was so unnerved was because, deep down, she was as excited as she was apprehensive. Maybe she thought admitting that was a betrayal.

She didn't know.

But the grief sat on her all the same, heavy and thick, until the farm was out of sight.

CHAPTER FOUR

THAT THE LOST Princess of Ile d'Montagne might not wish to marry him after he had spent all this time tracking her down had never crossed Cayetano's mind.

He found the very notion of her refusal preposterous. For it was normally he who was forced to crush expectations, maintain boundaries, and make certain that none of his lovers ever got the wrong idea. He had never intended to marry. He rarely intended to spend more than a night or two with a single woman—it was too tempting for some of them to imagine that it meant something it could not.

Because Cayetano was not meant to be like other men. He could sample pleasure, and he did, but his was a life of duty. Responsibility. And the great weight of his people's destiny.

It was only his country that could inspire him to take vows, and he had made those vows long ago. It was only his country—and the sure knowledge that because his sacrifice was for the island, he would never commit the sins his own parents had. His father by dying too soon and too badly and leaving a mess in his wake. His mother by losing herself and her purpose entirely.

He didn't like to think of such things. It was too tempting to allow his memory to take him to places far too painful. When he had been a boy, powerless and far away from all the things that mattered to him. Cayetano had vowed then that he would never be so powerless again.

Never for him the betrayal of his duty for love, no matter what it looked like. He would not make the mistakes his parents had. He would not allow emotion to poison him as it had them.

Ile d'Montagne came first. Always.

He had comforted himself with the knowledge, as his obsession with finding the lost Princess grew, that he was not focused so intently on the *woman*. That would be unacceptable. That would put him on a level with his mother and he could neither accept nor permit such a thing. Cayetano was fixed on her *function*, that was all.

As they drove away from her farm, he told himself that keeping her functional so that she could play her part was all that mattered. And was why he had…held her hand, as a lover might. That was why he had attempted to give her comfort.

He, who had been bred for war.

Never in his life had he been so pleased to take an irritating call that he barely had to pay attention to as the car pulled away from the farm. He should never have taken hold of her hand in the first place.

It was better that he pay less attention to the woman beside him. Better that he make certain his armor was in place and the vows he'd made to himself when he was young still held true, no matter how perfectly her hand had fit in his.

Or how that hunger within him raged on.

As a set of his advisors tried to one-up each other on the call, Cayetano found himself toying with old memories, frayed at the edges, as they made it to the private airfield. Memories he preferred to believe he had ex-

cised. The last time he had seen his father, so distant
and remote, the way a warlord ought to be in Cayetano's
estimation—far above the petty concerns and mawkish
sentimentality of normal people, surely. And then later,
lost beneath the weight of his dismay and powerless-
ness after his father's death, chafing at the restriction of
his age. Unable to go home and take his rightful place.

He had vowed to himself that once he was old enough,
he would make himself the perfect warlord.

No emotions allowed.

But there was no use reliving the past. What mattered
was that he had wrested back control of his people. And
together, they had all moved on.

There was enough history to fight over when it came
to the crown. Cayetano did not care to add his family's
history to the list. Especially when he had handled it all.

The way he handled everything.

As an instrument of his people, stripped free. He concentrated instead on the future. He loaded his precious
cargo onto the jet that waited at the airfield, prepared
to take the lost Princess back home. Where a new life
awaited them. Both of them, and his country, too.

Finally.

His men dispersed as they boarded, taking up their
usual positions throughout the plane. Cayetano led Delaney to the area that functioned as a lounge. And watched,
with some amusement, as she looked around, her eyes
wide.

"Have you ever been on a plane before?" he asked,
amused by the notion of such newness. But then, why
should a farm girl fly?

"Never." She blinked, taking in the quiet luxury that
surrounded them. And finding it overwhelming, if the
way she curled her hands into fists at her sides was any

indication. "But I'm pretty sure that any plane I might have gone on would not look like this."

"You may wish to brace yourself," Cayetano said, almost idly. "Because you're a princess, Delaney. You're going to have to get used to the royal treatment."

The look she threw him then would have been comical, had she not looked so genuinely horrified.

"I don't know a thing about that," she protested. "I don't *want* to know."

But he was already getting to know this woman, whether she liked it or not. And having nothing to do with his body's response to her. Or almost nothing, he amended. He had studied her in advance and meeting her in person had only added to his arsenal. He knew her tells. Like the mutinous look in her blue eyes just now. And a set to her jaw that spoke of stubbornness, not overwhelm.

He found it cute, really. He liked to watch her spark. Because whatever stubbornness she might possess, it was of no matter in the long run. And certainly no match to his. It might even serve her well in the days to come.

She had wrestled crops, perhaps, in this wholesome life she'd found herself in by accident. But it wasn't who she was. And he could assume, from the redness of her eyes, that she had a wealth of feelings about her change in circumstances. But Cayetano had been born to a calling. And he had been shaped since was small to be nothing short of the weapon that could finally topple a throne and restore his kingdom.

She could be as stubborn as she wished. It would change nothing.

But he knew better than to say so now.

He took his time settling himself in his preferred chair, then indicated that she should take the one opposite him. And was not surprised when, instead, she sat on the leather couch that put her farther away from him. As far as she could get while remaining on the same plane.

It was hard not to admire these little rebellions, however futile. At heart he would always be the rebel he'd been raised to become. Even now that he had secured a different future for his beloved island.

"I sympathize with your situation," he told her when they were both seated, though only he was anything like relaxed. And it was not entirely untrue. "It cannot be easy to learn that you are not who thought you were."

She blinked a few times, rapidly, then scowled at him. "If you sympathize, you wouldn't have turned up out of the blue, dropped a bomb, and then taken advantage of the mess you made to push your bizarre agenda."

"You misunderstand me." He inclined his head. "Sympathetic as I might be to your plight, that does not change the facts."

He had grizzled old advisors who dared not argue with him. But this little farm girl crossed her arms, tilted her chin up higher, and dug in. "The facts as you see them, you mean."

Cayetano smiled. Patiently. "Facts do not require a certain perspective to be true, though I know many people these days like to pretend otherwise. Facts, you will find, are true whether you like them or not."

She only sniffed. "You can keep making pronouncements all you like. It's not going to change the fact that regardless of what any test says, there's not one single cell in me that is in any way *princess material*."

He did not say what he could have. That the only material that mattered was her DNA, it was inarguable, and her feelings were irrelevant. Somehow he knew that would not land well—and it seemed almost churlish to belabor the point when he'd already won.

"I understand that this is difficult for you," he told her as the plane began to taxi. He saw her look of panic, quickly hidden, and the way she reached out to grip the arm of the sofa. Though she never made a sound. Not his Princess. "I admire your bravery, little one. To charge headlong into the unknown takes courage, whatever your reasons."

"I don't really think I'm charging anywhere," she told him, still arguing though her voice was a bit higher than before. "For one thing, I don't have a passport. So at some point or another, you're going to find that your big plans are destined for—"

But she stopped midsentence as he drew an American passport out of his breast pocket. "I took the liberty of arranging one for you." He flipped it open so she could see that it was, in fact, a picture of her.

She did not look pleased at his forethought. "How is that possible?"

He lifted a shoulder. "You will find that a great many things are possible when you are willing to pay for it."

Delaney's scowl deepened. "I don't understand. I thought you were some ragtag band of freedom fighters, off in the hills somewhere. How do you have private jets? And enough money to do things that shouldn't be possible?"

The plane leaped into the air then and she let out a soft gasp that she clearly tried to muffle.

Cayetano extended her the courtesy of ignoring it. He furrowed his brow as if lost in thought when really, he was allowing her a few moments to look out the window and pretend she wasn't panicking.

"The Ile d'Montagne crown has spent a great deal of

time and effort attempting to dismantle the wealth and status of those they like to call rebels," he said when the plane leveled out and her cheeks took on some color again. "And for a long time, they succeeded. We used to have to hide ourselves and the truth about our capabilities. There were sanctions, embargoes, and cruel laws that targeted only our part of the island. We built a castle hidden in the side of a mountain so that only we would know it. Many of these things changed with the last peace accord. We no longer have to pretend. And because my family has always taken care to hide our resources outside the reach of the grasping Montaigne family, we did not have to build ourselves up from scratch."

He knew this personally. He had been one of those resources—deemed too precious to the future of the country to be permitted to grow up there, no matter how peaceful things were meant to be in his lifetime.

Cayetano could still remember with perfect clarity his first trip to cold, drizzly England. His father's gruffness as he was dropped off at boarding school, left in the care of his ever-present and always watchful guards. Because he was an easy target. Everyone agreed. There was a security in the fact his whereabouts were known by the international press, but all it took was one overambitious Montaigne to shrug and decide the global condemnation was worth it and he'd have been done for.

His visits home had always been more stealthy. It was always best that the Queen not know precisely where the rebel faction's hope for the future was at any given moment, particularly not on the island where she claimed her sovereignty. It was healthier.

And he was as educated as any Montaigne princeling had ever been when he finally returned home to claim his birthright at twenty-one. To wrest it back from his unscrupulous would-be stepfather and try to find it in him to forgive his mother her betrayal. He still tried. Because he understood loneliness, after all his years in the north. He had never taken part in the heedless, reckless shenanigans of the careless students around him in the places he studied. Not Cayetano. When he was not studying, he was fighting. Or learning all the things he might need to know should he do what no one else had done and break, once and for all, this Montaigne stranglehold on his island.

Because the peace might still hold, but everyone knew that the Montaignes could renege on their part at any point.

Cayetano had been raised to act as if there was no peace. As if he was as ancient as the wrong done to his people, a warlord from long ago, prepared to battle with his hands if that was required. Any time he might have been tempted to waver, he needed only to remind himself of those who waited. His people, who waited and prayed and supported him, even when he was far away on that cold island so unlike his own.

A pity that his own mother had not managed to do the same.

But he had handled her as he handled everything. It was his duty. And Cayetano Arcieri always, always did his duty.

"And when you speak of the grasping Montaigne family, you mean…my family," Delaney said, snapping him back to the present. "*My* grasping family, according to you."

"I do not know if you are grasping or not." Cayetano kept his voice mild despite the unpleasant memories kicking around inside him. "How could I? But I can think of no other way to describe the work our false kings and queens have done for centuries."

"If it is so terrible, and has gone on for so long, how do you hope to change it?"

He studied her for a moment. He did not expect such cynicism from an American. Were they not a country raised on hope? Yet he could see the flush in her cheeks and suspected she spoke not because she was particularly hopeless, but because she was out of her depth.

Cayetano told himself he was not imagining other ways he could put that flush on her lovely cheeks. He told himself his hunger for her had abated. Even as he had to adjust the way he sat.

"I do not believe that a lie can flourish when faced head-on by the truth," Cayetano told her, with perhaps more ferocity than necessary. "And you, little one, are the embodiment of that truth."

"I'm just a farm girl," she said, but her chin lowered a notch. "I don't embody anything. Unless it's Kansas dirt."

"But you see, the DNA you care so little about will do it for you." Cayetano was keeping his voice soft, but still she sat up straighter. He reminded himself that she was not one of his people, used to ages of struggle. Moreover, she was not one of his men. She would likely respond better to honey than salt. It was on him, then, to find some honey within. However scant. "It matters not what you believe, or who you think you are. Your blood tells the truth."

"Maybe it's different where you're from," she said with a quiet hint of steel. He liked that, too. He wanted to explore all her possibilities, when it had never occurred to him that she would interest him like this. It would take getting used to—he had only thought of what she would do for his people, not what she might do for him. Though his sex was interested in little else. "But I've never found truth treated as much more than an opinion."

"I am Cayetano Arcieri," he replied, with his own suggestion of steel. Or perhaps it was more than mere suggestion. "In some places, the very hint of my opinion is treated like a commandment."

She blinked at that, but she didn't alter her expression. Or attempt to curry his favor in any way. She only gazed at him, looking faintly censorious.

That, too, was new.

"That isn't the least bit healthy," she chided him. *She* chided *him*. "If that's true."

And Cayetano had the strangest urge to truly laugh then, when he was not given overmuch to the practice. Still, he found he wanted to throw back his head and let go…when he never let go. That wasn't who he was. Far too much was riding on this for levity—

But still, the urge was there, making its own ruckus inside him.

"The door to the left leads to a guest room," he told her when the urge within him subsided. He indicated the door he meant with a nod. "Feel free to make it your own during the flight. If you find you need anything, you can find me either here or behind the door on the right."

And if he had been an insecure man in any regard, the face she made then would have cut him straight through.

"I can't think of any reason I would need you," she retorted.

Much too quickly.

And he waited until she disappeared behind her guest room door, locking it loudly and ostentatiously, to grin.

But the grin soon faded and once it did, he could hardly recall how it had happened in the first place. He called in his men, and tried to get his head back into the business of this thing they were doing here. This glorious thing, this marvelous enterprise, that would finally restore his kingdom.

His life's work, the work of so many lives before his, *this close* to fruition.

Yet he soon found that when he should have been thinking critically, planning out how best to launch his lost little princess on the world—with the proof of who she was so there could be no debate, and the inevitability of her ascension, and thus his, secured in the minds of all the world—all he could think about was the scent of her hair. Like sweet almonds. Or the strength in that hand of hers that he'd held in the car. It was no princess's hand, that was for certain. Her nails were cut low and he had felt the work she'd done all these years in the roughness of her skin.

He should have been thinking of strategy. Instead he thought, *It suits her.*

And more, he found himself wondering how those hands would feel on his skin. His sex.

Cayetano, who preferred his women draped in silks, round and lush, found himself growing almost uncomfortably hard at the very notion. Of a peasant's hand on a princess, but then, he knew the truth about her. Even if she did not.

There was nothing common about her at all.

He nodded at something one of his men was saying in support of Delaney.

"She will make us a fine queen," he agreed.

Yet what he thought was, *She will make me a fine wife.* Having nothing at all to do with her strategic importance and everything to do with that hunger in him that only seemed to grow—even as he sat with his men. The people who depended upon him to be rational.

He tried to call on that rationality now.

"Her unusual upbringing is a gift, I think," he said now. "As we know, the Queens of Ile d'Montagne are not known for their work ethic."

"Their treachery, more like," one of his men said with a snort.

"And pretenders to the throne all the while," growled another, setting off the predictable calls for the end of the reign of the Montaignes, once and for all.

The calls had a different flavor this day, Cayetano thought. Now they were so close to their goal.

Yet he wasn't basking in their triumph the way he should have been. Instead, he found himself thinking about how, when his men had made their discreet inquiries and pretended to be looking for farmland to buy, the first thing anyone had to say about Delaney Clark was how hard she worked. She had put her heart and soul into it, as if it had been her mission since birth to save that farm. Most of her neighbors thought that if anyone could, it was her.

Imagine, what could a woman like that do for my country? he asked himself.

Or for him, not that he chose to accept he needed anyone.

But as a warlord turned king, he would. He would need a queen who could support him, not defy him. Instead of a woman like his own mother, so bitter and resentful. Focused on the past, on avenging any and all historic wrongs, and never what might come next unless it suited her ambition. It was a fine line to walk. History must never be forgotten. He lived that truth. The history of his people and the island animated all he did. But it was far too easy to sink too deep in it and risk losing everything.

This had been his mother's downfall. Therese Arcieri had imagined herself a kingmaker. Her family's roots were sunk deep into the island, just as the Arcieris' were. And she had imagined that after Cayetano's father died, her favor alone could elevate the man of her choice to the position of warlord.

But Arcieris did not sit idly by while other men attempted to rule their people.

Even if standing up against his own mother had killed something in him, something he doubted he could get back. Something he'd told himself could not matter when his country was on the line.

Cayetano had taken his rightful position by the ancient rites. He had defeated his mother's lover with his sword, and then had showed him mercy. His people had risen up and called him warlord when he was little better than a lad. A mere twenty-one, but he had stepped into his destiny.

He had showed that same mercy to his treacherous mother, little though she deserved it. And she might have railed against the manner of his mercy, but yet she lived. When he would have been well within his rights to show her the harshest possible justice.

Many had called for it. Some still did.

But on some level, Cayetano understood her. He too thought only of the country. How could he blame Therese for doing the same?

Liar, came a voice from deep inside him. *You cannot bear to part with your last remaining parent. You are as sentimental as anyone.*

That snapped Cayetano back to the plane he flew on and the men who surrounded him. Because he was no pathetic child. He had never been given the opportunity.

His mother lived because he was merciful. She remained locked away because she deserved to live with what she'd done.

Sentimentality had nothing to do with it.

But when his men left he settled in on the bed in his own state room for the rest of the flight. And he found himself thinking that Delaney Clark was nothing like Therese Arcieri, the would-be Queen of Ile d'Montagne. For one thing, Delaney wanted no part of this. She'd had no wish whatsoever to leave that farm.

To his way of thinking, that already put her head and shoulders above any other pretender to the throne. For anyone who aspired to rule should be prevented from doing it, Cayetano had long believed. He would include himself among that number, save for one thing. He did not want the throne for his vanity. He did not want the power for its own sake.

He wanted what he had always wanted. What he had been brought up to want. And had then interrogated from every possible angle while he'd studied abroad, looking for the lies inside himself.

In the end, it was simple. He wanted Ile d'Montagne to be a country torn asunder no more. He wanted his country whole. And that could not be accomplished, no matter his strength, by a simple show of force. All that would do, if successful, was switch the positions of the two factions. He needed Delaney to bring the country together.

For as long as there was a Montaigne on the throne, the royalists in their seaside villages would fall in line. But only if an Arcieri was also on the throne would his people from the mountain valley do the same.

This was the opportunity his people had been waiting for since antiquity.

She was.

Cayetano would do everything in his power to make certain he finally delivered what no other ever had.

And possibly enjoy his little farm girl more than he'd expected he would, while he was at it. Maybe that was a good thing. Maybe that would make this all the sweeter.

Because she might not think she wished to marry him.

But Cayetano knew she would.

CHAPTER FIVE

DELANEY WOULD HAVE denied it if asked, but she did feel the faintest stirrings of something like excitement hours later as she peered out the window during the plane's descent, much as it shamed her to admit it.

Surely she should have been in tears, so far away from home and with no home to return to anyway, with Catherine resolved to sell.

Not that it was her home anyway, really, since she wasn't a Clark after all.

She'd spent the whole of the flight hiding away in her room, giving herself a crash course in all things Ile d'Montagne. She'd done some research in the days since Cayetano had appeared in the yard, but then, she'd mostly been looking for things to refute Cayetano's claims. Or *him*, if that was even possible. Instead she'd seen pictures of a princess who looked...not unlike her, once she looked beyond the fancy dresses and actual tiaras. It had been too much for her, fast. She'd found she had a deep and instant aversion to looking any further into the actual human woman who she'd been *swapped with* in a Milwaukee hospital.

Because Princess Amalia hadn't chosen this, either.

It was like someone walking on her grave. It had made Delaney shiver.

But she'd sucked it up on the flight today. She'd re-pressed that shiver. And she'd done a deep dive into the road not taken these last few hours.

She'd looked at pictures of the Princess she wasn't. She'd studied the other woman's face, and she didn't think she was kidding herself when she saw the Clark chin. Right there for all the world to see.

The one that wasn't on *her* face and never had been.

It had made her feel a little dizzy.

It made her curl up in a ball and fight to breathe evenly again.

And for a while there, she hadn't been sure she could. She felt as if she was cracking wide-open, falling to pieces, there on an ostentatious plane flying her off into a future she couldn't begin to imagine.

Delaney hadn't had to imagine her future, ever. She'd always known what it would hold. The seasons would change. There would be good years and bad. Drought and blight. There were a thousand things that could dis-rupt the yield, including bankers. But she knew where she'd be.

Her vegetables would grow without her now, and for some reason that was the part that made her throat tight and her eyes burn. She'd stayed where she was, curled up in a ball fighting hard to keep the tears inside, for longer than she thought she should have.

When she got herself back under control, she'd stopped thinking about her garden and had returned to piecing together the life Cayetano seemed to think she'd be stepping into. She hadn't come that close to crying again, but she had found herself…panicky at the notion that *she* might be expected to do the things a princess did. That Cayetano might expect her to do those things.

And more panicky still when she imagined how she

would go about telling him she would be doing none of them. That she was here for the adventure, nothing more.

But that wasn't why her heart skipped a beat or two in her chest now. It was because, down below her, she could see the sea.

An actual *sea*.

The first she'd ever seen outside of a television screen.

Delaney could see the waves, topped with the occasional bit of white here and there. She knew it was a part of the greater Mediterranean, and even their likely location on a map. But what caught at her was the color. She'd always known that oceans were meant to be blue, but she'd had no idea what that meant. Not really.

Nothing she'd read had prepared her for all the layers of that blue. Aquamarines and blues and deeper navies, rivaling the sky above.

Needless to say, there was no sea of any kind in Kansas.

She wasn't sure there was even any blue, comparatively speaking. Not on this scale.

And then the plane was flying in over an island that looked like make-believe to Delaney. It was too perfect. Too pretty. She saw those white sand beaches that looked too pristine to touch and then built up into the hillsides, gleaming small communities in whites and more blues and deep terra-cottas. But the plane kept going, circling around until it began a breathtaking descent into a high, green valley. She saw fields, though none of them like the ones she'd left behind. Still, the presence of crops—even if it wasn't corn—made her feel less…adrift, maybe.

Though she suspected she wasn't going to feel like herself for some time.

Because she quite literally *wasn't* herself, and she didn't have the slightest idea how she was meant to deal with that truth.

Her breath seemed to tangle in her throat then, but she swallowed hard. And maybe concentrated that much more fiercely on the fields and villages below her.

She refused to cry again. She was filled with horror at the very idea of *showing* someone else—especially burnt gold and ferocious Cayetano—her emotions. And she couldn't help feeling something more than the mess of loss and uncertainty. It was another hint of that same excitement, and it made her feel worse.

Surely she shouldn't like a single moment of this charade.

Delaney hated herself that she did.

She forced herself to concentrate as the plane descended even further.

And she didn't need to ask. She understood without being told that the fortress she could see on one end of the valley, built into the side of the mountains, was where Cayetano was taking her. The castle he'd mentioned.

Because where else would Cayetano Arcieri, the warlord of the north, rest his head? Of course it was in a forbidding stone citadel with the rest of his world at his feet.

Delaney's reading, all the way across the Atlantic, meant she knew more about him now, too.

Some factions online referred to him the way he'd referred to himself, as warlord.

But others called him the rightful King of Ile d'Montagne.

Delaney didn't know what to call him as they disembarked, particularly as she recognized—without him having to say a word to her in explanation or defense—that he was immediately different here. It wasn't so much that he held himself differently, or even acted differently, it was more that he made sense. The exquisite suit seemed to match the ancient stones, somehow.

As if they both grew bigger, brighter, when connected.

As if they were made of the same material.

She had to fight back a shudder at that.

And another wave of grief at what she'd lost when he'd come to tear her away from the place where she'd made her own kind of sense.

Out on the tarmac, the men who had escorted him in Kansas were joined by even more men, all cut from the same solemn, dangerous cloth. They all spoke the same language that she did not share, but lest she think no one was paying attention to her and make a break for it, Cayetano himself herded her toward another waiting vehicle.

Just as glossy and impressive as the SUVs back home.

She braced herself for another one of his deceptively mild interrogations as the car set off, but he only cast an opaque glance her way—leaving marks behind, she was fairly sure—before taking to his phone again. And though she still couldn't understand a word of what he said, she was certain she recognized that tone.

Commanding. Powerful.

Delaney thought again of the long, in-depth article she'd read on the plane that talked so lyrically about the true King of Ile d'Montagne. The true heir to its long-contested throne.

It turned out that the man who had turned up in the middle of her cornfield was something of a pet cause around the world. The plight of the Ile d'Montagne rebels was discussed in papers and symposiums across the globe. While the peace of some seventy years was lauded, most of the articles suggested it was destined for a bitter, bloody end. Delaney had thought she might ask him about his celebrity—and not his plans for possible bloodshed, as that seemed impolite at best—but she bit the urge back. Because somehow, she doubted very much that his international stature was accidental. She might not know anything about would-be kings or contested land or conflicts stretching back into the Dark Ages, but she knew, with a deep certainty, that Cayetano was exactly the person the articles had made him out to be.

Canny. Deliberate. And more sympathetic. Persuasive in ways his ancestors had not been.

He was, all the articles claimed in one way or another, the greatest threat to the Ile d'Montagne royal family since the last civil war that had killed so many in the late eighteen-hundreds.

And Delaney felt certain, as her heart kicked at her and the blood in her body seemed to heat whenever he was near, that he posed no lesser threat to her.

It was another thing that should have upset her, when instead it made a different kind of anticipation drum through her. Like her blood flowed to a beat.

Instead of concentrating too closely on what that must mean, she looked out the window at the lush green all around, fields and vineyards in the spring sunshine. And at the pretty villages, clustered here and there and certainly not hidden, as they moved ever closer to that fortress carved into the mountain.

It took her some time to realize that Cayetano was no longer on his cell phone.

She snuck a look at him and found him regarding her with that burnt gold consideration that made her shiver. The goose bumps seemed to take on a life of their own, marching down her arms and her spine with a certain resoluteness that made her…breathless.

Just a little bit breathless. Just breathless enough to notice it—and notice him.

Because when he looked at her it was as if she fell forward when she knew she stayed still, toppling out of her seat and catapulting deep into all that gold and heat—

"How do you find my home?" Cayetano asked, in a tone that suggested there was only one answer.

Luckily enough, it was also the only answer she wanted to give.

"It's beautiful." Delaney sat back in her seat, gripping her hands together in her lap and hoping it looked as if maybe she was being whatever *ladylike* was. Not her wheelhouse. "But surely, if you are forever at war yet live out in the open, it would be easy enough to simply come to this valley and get rid of you all."

The gold in his gaze warmed several degrees and she did, too, as if they were connected as surely as he was to this place.

"How bloodthirsty you are," he murmured.

But as if he liked that about her.

It was…disconcerting. It made the beat inside her brighter, somehow. Faster and hotter. "Not at all. I just got the impression that rebel armies usually spend their time hiding in underground tunnels or something."

That impression did not come from any of the articles she'd read today. She was fairly certain it came from the action movies she and Catherine had watched together over the years. But Delaney found she really didn't want to think about things like that. It sat too uneasily in her belly, like the memories themselves were fragile.

Like he could take them from her, too.

Cayetano shifted in his seat to look at her more squarely and that was better, in a way. She felt less fragile. But everything else was…*more.*

"It is no longer the Dark Ages, Delaney." She almost thought he smiled, and a prickle of heat moved over her, washing its way down from her temples to her toes. "We are no longer required to hide ourselves away and pray for deliverance, especially not when a peace has been declared and held for so many years. And, of course, there are no longer pockets of this world where atrocities can be committed without consequences. The internet is everywhere."

Delaney tried not to look as dubious as she felt. "I'm not sure I'd trust my safety to the internet, of all things."

"It is the internet, yes," he agreed after a moment. "For good or ill. But part of why these eyes upon us work is Queen Esme's vanity, far greater than her father's before her, hard as that is to imagine. She wishes to be known as a good queen, you see. I believe Britain's Elizabeth has left an indelible mark on her peers. How can they achieve her longevity or be even a fraction so beloved? Yet Esme has aspirations, almost all of them European. She would find the price too high were she to let her temper take hold."

"I suppose that's something." And better than nothing.

"It is what we tell ourselves, in any case." Again that ghost of a smile. "And as yet, we are still here."

They reached the base of the great fortress and Delaney expected that they would have to get out, and clamber up into it, somehow. She couldn't decide if she welcomed a climb or feared it. But instead, the road led straight into the mountainside.

And when the car did not stop, did not so much as brake, she braced herself—

Only to let her breath out in a rush when she realized that the shadow before her was not shadow at all, but a tunnel.

"It is an optical illusion that has served us well," Cayetano said from behind her, as the interior of the car was cast into the dark of the tunnel. "It is less effective on automobiles than horses, I grant you. But we make it work all the same."

Before Delaney could think of something to say in response to that, the car was barreling back out into the light. And it took her much longer than it should have to realize that they were now in an internal courtyard.

Not a tiny little courtyard, like the ones she'd seen in picture books about castles and keeps. This courtyard was much bigger. Surrounded on all sides by tiers of stone, some with windows cut into the rock, others with open galleries, the whole thing climbing up toward the sun far above.

She was sure there was some militaristic reason for the different levels. She was sure it was all about armies and wars, as her research told her so many castle-ish places were in this part of the world.

But that didn't mean it wasn't beautiful. That didn't keep the Mediterranean sunshine from cascading down, highlighting the fountains, the greenery, the thick vines dotted with joyful flowers in an astonishing array of colors.

The car finally stopped in front of the grandest of the many entrances around the courtyard, and once again Cayetano was there to usher her from the vehicle. He did not pause to look around or make speeches or whatever it was warlords usually did when returning home. Instead, he swiftly led her inside. She had the impression of graceful archways and cool floors, light-filled rooms and walls filled with the kind of art that only rich people seemed to have. Not something pretty that a person might like to look at every day, like Grandma Mabel's sampler, but dark, dreary paintings of off-putting scenes that no one would ever want to look at too closely or for too long.

That probably means each one is worth its own fortune, she told herself.

Though from her reading, Cayetano didn't need any extra fortunes to go along with his.

It was all dizzying, really. The space. The stone. The obvious grandeur at every turn. She walked and walked, trying to get her bearings, though it proved impossible. Every hallway looked like the one before. And more distracting, Cayetano guided her along with his hand in the small of her back.

It felt like a hot coal, melting off her skin and making her whole body hum.

Making it hard to concentrate on castles and art and directions.

She felt a bit shocked when he took that intense heat away, and was taken back to find herself in a happy little room a few levels up. An elegant sitting room, by the look of it, with more of that sunshine pouring in.

Delaney had seen *Downton Abbey*. She recognized the sort of small couches and meticulously placed tables that she associated with fussy places and the people who inhabited them.

"I must attend to some matters," Cayetano told her, and she understood, then, that he'd been playing a role in Kansas. That the man she'd met there had been accessible in comparison. She caught her breath, even as everywhere else, she burned.

His gaze swept over her as if he knew every flicker, every flame. He ignited her anew, and then he was gone.

Leaving her to run a hand around to the small of her back to see if she could feel the scorch marks he must have left behind.

But the door swung back open almost at once, and she found herself surrounded by a group of chattering women who exclaimed over her, pantomimed things with their hands that made no sense, and then disappeared again.

Though unlike Cayetano, who she suspected could always find matters to claim his attention and no doubt too many of them, she did get the impression that the women would return.

Delaney took the opportunity to take stock of her surroundings in what little time she had to herself. She was standing in the center of a cheerful room, as bright as all the ones they'd passed, which made no sense to her. Weren't they packed in beneath thick walls of stone?

Something about the stones stuck with her, though when she pivoted around in a circle there was nothing offensive anywhere. The paintings were lovely landscapes. The room was done in pale yellows and sweet blues. The walls were stone, yes, and so even though it was not cold outside, Delaney was grateful for the thick rug beneath her feet. She had the feeling it would be much colder in here without it. There were various chairs and fancy little couches and end tables scattered about, all of them loosely grouped in the direction of a big fireplace that looked far too clean to have ever been used.

Was she supposed to sit down? Was this a cell of some kind? Should she go over and test the door to see if she was locked in? Or perhaps gauge if she might need to climb out a window?

Not that she felt as moved toward her escape as she should. She pressed a hand against her heart, but she already knew it was still drumming along, telling her truths she would have much preferred to ignore.

She was still debating what she should do when the door flew open again. Another group of servants streamed in, this time bearing platters of food and a rolling trolley.

And behind them came Cayetano.

Suddenly, it was as if that fire between them was lit

in the grate. The room was too hot. Too close. She worried she was suffocating.

Delaney was still where he'd left her, there in the center of the room. And she discovered, as his gaze punched into her, that she was unable to move. She watched, in a kind of panic, as the servants laid out all the dishes they'd brought with them on the largest of the small tables, and then, one by one, disappeared back out into the hall.

Leaving her alone with this man.

She knew her reaction didn't make sense. She'd been alone with him now for hours and hours. She'd willingly gotten into that car in Kansas. She'd boarded that plane. She'd let him carry her off to this fortress and had walked into the stone enclosure on her own two feet. She'd assessed potential escape routes in theory, though she hadn't tried any out.

Yet it only occurred to her now to question what on earth she was *doing*.

"You look like a terrified rabbit," Cayetano informed her, standing some distance away.

Looking almost idle.

A kind of alarm began to beat in her then, for this man was many things, but she was certain that *idle* wasn't one of them.

"Thank you," she squeaked out. She cleared her throat, furious with herself for betraying her internal struggle. "That's not at all condescending."

"It is an accurate description, nothing more."

"What do you intend to do with me?" Delaney demanded, the way she should have before. Long before they landed. Maybe before she'd gotten in his car. "Is this supposed to be a cell? Am I to be locked up here until you wear me down and I agree to marry you just so I can get a glimpse of the sky?"

She got considerably more melodramatic as she spoke, which was shocking, given how little she'd ever given herself over to melodrama before. But all he did was lift one of his dark brows and she forgot to be embarrassed. This wasn't the Midwest. And extraordinary circumstances required unusual responses.

"Surely you have seen the row of windows behind you." She had, of course. She could feel the warm caress of the sunlight even now. Clearly she would have to work on her melodrama if she wanted it to be effective. Assuming *effectiveness* was ever the point of it. "You need only step out on your balcony and look up, Delaney. The sky is where it always is."

"I think that qualifies as avoiding the question," she said primly.

"Why didn't I think of a cell?" he mused, as if to himself. "I believe the castle we stand in is possessed of a dungeon, now that you mention it. I'm sure something could be arranged."

Delaney stood a little straighter. "So you do intend to lock me up until I do what you want?"

He thrust his hands into his pockets, which somehow made the suit he wore look better. Less perfect, yet more rampantly masculine. And it made him look more idle and more dangerous, all at once.

Surely that shouldn't have been possible.

But she was more concerned with how nonchalant his expression was. "Allow me to assure you, little one, that it is unnecessary for me to lock anyone up."

"Let *me* assure *you* that whatever you think that means, it's not exactly comforting on this end," she shot back at him. "It's also not a *no*."

"Delaney. Please." He did something with his chin that

somehow swept over the small feast laid out on the long, low table between them. "I thought you might be hungry."

"Why would you think that?" she demanded, as if he'd mounted an attack.

"Because I am hungry." His mouth stayed in that straight line, but still, she had the unshakable conviction that he was laughing. Just somewhere she couldn't see. "A not uncommon occurrence after I travel."

She swallowed, hard, not understanding why she felt so…fragile. Though that wasn't quite the right word.

Upended, maybe. Caught out.

But she didn't know what to do about any of the things she felt, so she went and sat on one side of the table in a stuffy sort of chair that made her question her posture. She ignored her sudden debutante concerns and tried to focus instead on the many small plates laid out before her, all laden with things she had never seen on a table in Kansas, yet all smelled and looked wonderful.

Yet the only thing she was really aware of was Cayetano. What he was doing. Or not doing. When he chose to move. When he settled himself opposite her, clearly not concerned that the furniture might be judging him. How he sat and how he looked at her and even what plate he appeared to be eyeing—

That was how she felt, she realized then. Uncomfortably *aware*. Of everything.

Including that spot in the small of her back where he'd touched her, that pulsed like its own flame.

The table was laden with more than enough food for the two of them. There were sweets and cakes on one end. Trays of vegetables, raw and cooked alike and smelling of new and different spices, took up real estate in the middle. And on the other end were cold and roasted meats that smelled so good her belly rumbled. There were what looked like baked casseroles, but with ingredients she could not begin to identify. And the longer she stared, the more she accepted that she didn't have to know what it all was to find it tempting.

And more, that she really was hungry.

She opted not to think about why it slid around inside her like a new heat that Cayetano, a stranger to her in all the ways that mattered, had known that when she hadn't known herself.

Delaney picked up a plate and then set herself to the important task of tasting everything. She barely glanced at Cayetano while she helped herself, then commenced the tasting. It wouldn't help her any to get mixed up in all that dark glory while she was eating, and anyway, she was too busy filling her belly.

When she was deliciously, extravagantly full, she sat back to find him watching her.

Maybe, she admitted to herself, she'd known full well that he'd had his eyes on her all along.

"I imagine those aren't good enough manners," she said when he seemed content to do nothing more than study her. The way he had since he'd stepped out of his car, now that she considered it. "For either the real or fake royal households on this island."

Again, the sense of a smile when there was none. "I see you've been doing your reading."

She was full, pleasantly so, and that made her feel... expansive. Delaney settled back in her own seat and regarded him, for a change. And took her time about it as she studied him. Unapologetically.

This isn't the time to get lost in how starkly beautiful he is, she cautioned herself when her contemplation of his sensual mouth threatened to overtake her.

"I read quite a few articles," she said when she thought

she could speak without the fire inside her taking over. "All about Cayetano Arcieri, beloved by celebrities and charities and protesters the world over. They all take turns gushing about your contributions to this island and to the planet. In various interviews."

"The plight of my people moves many," he replied. Easily enough.

"They made it sound as if you fought a war or two to get your position. That's not exactly true, is it?"

His gaze gleamed and she found herself repressing a shiver. "It is not untrue."

"The Arcieris have been a particular thorn in the side of the royals for as long as anyone can remember." She wanted to say that it reminded her of the longstanding feud back where she came from, between Jean Lynnette Baker and Lurleen Snyder about the origin of a potato salad recipe, but thought better of it. She regarded this intense man before her instead. "Haven't you?"

"It is the duty and privilege of the name."

"And all because, a million years ago, there were twins."

He nodded, and now she was sure that there was a definite curve to his mouth. But she had the strangest notion that it was a kind of pride. In her. "Identical brothers. So identical that when the younger twin stepped in and took his older brother's place at the coronation, no one recognized the switch."

"The royal family swears this never occurred."

Cayetano only shrugged. "They would."

"There was a war, led by the twin who claimed the throne."

"The false king." Cayetano shook his head. "Because he believed that if he went on the offense immediately, he could end the argument. By killing anyone who dared stand against him. As tyrants do so like to do."

"The other side was formed by the supposedly deposed twin, who began calling himself one of the family names. Arcieri."

"Indeed."

"So really, give or take a few centuries, you and I are related," Delaney pointed out.

Helpfully.

She thought she saw the flash of his teeth. The gleam in his gaze was brighter, that was a certainty. "If that is how you wish to think of it."

"Well," she said, and managed to make herself sound regretful. "We certainly can't marry if we're related, can we?"

He actually did laugh then, a bark of a sound that made her breath ache a bit. It was so *male*. "It would take a lot more than a tiny drop of shared blood, generations behind us now, to put me off marrying you, Delaney."

"I really think—" she began.

"But no matter how much I might wish to marry you, I won't," he told her, smoothly. "Not at this moment."

That should have been music to Delaney's ears.

Instead, she found herself scowling at him. She did not choose to ask herself why. "Why not?"

If that amused him, too, he didn't show it. Instead, he leaned back in his seat, cocked his head to one side, and merely gazed at her. Then, making sure she was aware he was doing it, he took his time looking her up and down.

And despite herself, Delaney found herself sitting up straighter. Her hands moved to her lap, as if to brush off crumbs she knew weren't there on her favorite pair of jeans. Because she was suddenly much too aware that she was in this make-believe realm of princes and princesses, royal houses and one true kings. And more, she was supposed to belong here by blood.

Maybe, just maybe, her beloved T-shirt that read "MIDWEST IS BEST" was not the appropriate thing to be wearing here.

Cayetano aimed all that burnt gold at her, and looked, if anything, almost sorrowful. Pitying, even, and no one liked to be *pitied*.

So, really, there was no reason at all that look should make her feel lit up, from the inside out.

"Because I am the true King of Ile d'Montagne," he told her, in that way he had. As if, were she to look closely, she might find these words stamped into her bones. "That is why not. And you are the true heir to the current throne. And the future Queen of this island might very well be the farm girl you call yourself, Delaney. I like that this is how you see yourself. I like the look of your Kansas all over you."

What she felt all over her then was him. That look he was giving her. The fire inside her, crackling higher all the time.

As if she'd never heard of Kansas.

"But no matter how much I might like my farm girl as she is," he said in that same stamped-into-bone way that made her want to sigh and blush and whisper things like *your farm girl*. "I am afraid that here, on this island where you will soon be hailed as the Crown Princess in front of the world, you cannot *look* like one."

CHAPTER SIX

SHE LOOKED SO affronted that Cayetano rather thought she might snatch up one of the small plates and throw it at him. Or a great many of the small plates.

He could admit that no small part of him wished that she would. Because an explosion on that level would require an appropriate response from him.

And he would love nothing more than to...respond.

At length.

The hunger in him felt like a fever. Like a calling. He had no idea how he would hold himself back if she burst into a flame of temper before him.

But all Delaney did was glare at him.

"That is very rude," she admonished him, and to his astonishment he found himself feeling...ever so slightly abashed. Or he assumed that was what the unfamiliar sensation was. "I did not come to you, claiming a throne or whatever it is people do in situations like this. You're the one who appeared in the middle of my life. And ruined it. If you don't like how I look, well. That sounds a lot to me like a *you* problem."

And he liked the way she looked at him as she said that. As if she were prepared to launch herself over the table to make her point and was only *just* holding herself back.

Just as he was.

Perhaps for the very same reason.

"But you are in my valley now," he replied, leaning back as if he was perfectly at his ease. He should have been. He had been navigating far more treacherous waters than this for the whole of his life. Why should a girl who didn't know who she really was get beneath his skin? "My problems are your problems, you will find. My problems are everyone's problems."

"You are not *my* warlord, Cayetano."

And she made an emphatic little noise when she said that, like punctuation.

He should not have found that charming. If it had been anyone else, he knew he would not have. He would have been far more focused on the disrespect. "I think you will find, little one, that soon enough I will be your everything."

She didn't like that. She sat straighter and she glared at him—but then again, her cheeks warmed.

"That is delusional." She even pointed a finger at him, and it took him a moment to recognize that she was *admonishing* him. "I came here because this is an adventure for me, whatever it might be for you. And I decided it might make sense to meet the people I'm actually related to."

"Yet you have not so much as asked after them."

"I'm hardly going to ask *you* about them." Her chin rose. "You are their sworn enemy, by all accounts, including yours."

"I had no idea genealogy intrigued you so." He fought to keep the smile from his face and did not think too hard about how unusual an occurrence it was that he should wish to smile at all. "You seemed uninterested in it back in Kansas. Your blood was of no matter to you. I am sure you said as much."

"People who can trace their ancestors back several centuries shouldn't comment on those of us who learned we were an entirely different person only days ago," Delaney retorted. "Of course I want to meet my…the woman who actually gave birth to me. Eventually."

He did not miss the way she looked away when she said that. As if she was in no rush to meet Queen Esme, and not for the usual reasons. He suspected that if she thought too much about the Queen, this might become real to her.

Clearly, she didn't want that.

"I was under the impression you came here because your mother told you to," he said. "No more and no less."

"Thanks to you, I now have to grapple with the fact that—biologically speaking—she's not my mother."

And she said that tartly enough, but there was something about the way she held herself that made him regret… Well, he couldn't regret what he had done. He could never regret something that would shortly put him on the path to finally right such an ancient wrong. But he regretted, more than he would have thought possible before this very moment, that finding her and telling her who she was had hurt her.

It changed nothing.

But still, he felt it.

And he did not like such things. *Feelings.* He had been avoiding them for most of his life. Feeling anything at all made him certain he was on a collision course with the fate that had met his parents. Death. Dishonor.

He refused.

"I think you're laboring under a misconception," he said, in a more repressive tone than he might have used had she not inspired him to *emote*. "I did not ask you for your hand in marriage and then wait, filled with a trembling hope, for your answer. I informed you that our wedding would take place. I imagine you think that a display of arrogance."

"Extreme arrogance," Delaney agreed too swiftly, color high. "Appalling, rude, delusional arrogance."

"Little one, that is merely me," Cayetano replied, and lifted an unconcerned shoulder. "What you should concern yourself with are the ancient laws of this island, in which I very much doubt you are conversant no matter how many internet articles you read."

She had gaped a bit at the *that is merely me* bit. Now she snapped her mouth shut and glared at him. "Let me guess. You can lock a girl in a tower and everyone shrugs and says, *Oh, well, I guess you get to keep her.* Like women are nothing more than fireflies you can collect in a jar."

Cayetano could not remember the last time he had stopped to appreciate the fireflies that heralded the summers here. When as a small child, he had delighted in them. He could recall running, barefoot, through the fields while his parents walked behind, trying to catch the little bursts of light that popped in the air all around them—

The memory fell like ice water through him, horrifying him. He was not a man given to nostalgia. It smacked of those emotions he abhorred.

"This is not a jar," he replied with what he thought was admirable patience. "It is Arcieri Castle, built with painstaking care across the ages. First hidden, its residents and servants risking death if they were discovered here. Sometimes its own kind of cell, because my ancestors weathered many a siege within these walls. Now open to celebrate the peace. But never a mere jar."

Naturally, his farm girl did not look impressed by anything he said. He had never encountered another human so devoutly unimpressed, in fact. She sat there on a priceless settee in jeans and a T-shirt, in an ancient castle renowned for its beauty, and dared to glare at him as if he was the offending party here.

"None of that makes it any less of a cell," she told him, in a tone he could only call *mulish*. "Whether it was built in two days or two millennia, and no matter what it means to you and your people, it amounts to the same thing."

Cayetano sighed. "There is no need for cells. Still, as I said, there are old ways. This is a very old place."

"I may be American, but I'm capable of understanding dates. And history."

He found her tone excessively dry. But once again, the problem with his lost princess was that he found himself fascinated by her total lack of awe in his presence. He had seen a hint of it in that dusty yard in Kansas, but it had faded. Quickly.

It was the novelty, nothing more, he told himself. Any moment now, he would stop thinking about her as a woman, as an individual, as *his*. And get back to thinking about her role here and how best to deploy her upon the unsuspecting House of Montaigne.

Before he'd gone to Kansas, that deployment had been his fondest fantasy.

"Some of our old ways are enshrined in law as well as custom," he told her, maintaining his posture of seeming ease when he did not feel easy. He was not making up the old ways here. He could marry her in the morning if he chose, ending this farce that she had a choice in the matter that quickly. Cayetano liked that notion. A lot.

But it did not strike him as particularly strategic. He reminded himself that he had already won—she was here. What would it hurt to attempt to woo her a little?

Or, at the very least, not rush her.

"Let me guess," Delaney said in the same dry way. "The men in charge forgot to update things around here because why bother? They like it medieval."

Cayetano ran his tongue around his teeth and abandoned any *wooing* plans. "It is not necessary to imprison you, Delaney. I need only keep you for a night, then claim you in front of my brethren come the dawn. Only one, if I like, though at least three is more traditional."

She stared at him as if waiting for more, then scowled when no more was forthcoming. "That's barbaric."

"It was necessary in a certain era." Cayetano waved an idle hand. Mostly to infuriate her. A success, if the look in her blue eyes was any indication. And he should not have taken such pleasure in these games. This woman was a means to an end, not a pleasure. He could not fathom why he kept forgetting that. Or why, despite himself, the way he wanted her felt more like a roar within him every moment. "There was a time when this island was far more lawless than it is now. Times were perilous and lives were short. Men in need of wives took them where they could, and it became necessary to make sure that their children were legitimate."

"You can't *take* me," she said. And it took tremendous control on his part to refrain from pointing out that he had already done just that. That she had packed for the privilege. "I demand that you release me."

"Little one," Cayetano said, his voice rich with amusement, "where do you think you are? This is not the American Embassy. The only person who can intercede on your behalf with me…is me."

Her breath left her in an audible rush. Her mouth opened and shut more than once, before her cheeks flushed red and she snapped her teeth closed. It took her a fair few moments to gather herself once more.

"You cannot think that this will actually work," she seethed at him.

He found himself caught, anew, at her reaction. There was no hint of fear on her face, which would have stopped him at once. Or made him approach this differently, at any rate. But she didn't look remotely uncomfortable. If anything, she was ablaze.

At the *injustice,* unless he missed his guess.

And Cayetano was very rarely wrong when it came to reading people.

Though he was finding it difficult to read himself tonight. Why should her reaction, whatever it might be, make his body tighten with desire? He was not used to this intensity. Not for anything but his purpose, his promises.

He hated the very idea that a person could turn him from his lifelong path. Was he no better than his parents after all?

The very notion appalled him.

"I do not wish it to work," he told her, more severely than was necessary. Perhaps he was directing that at himself. "I would far prefer that you decide, of your own volition, to marry me. Freely. Who would not wish this? I do not want a prisoner for bride, Delaney. But you should know this about me now. I will always do what I must. When it comes to this island, and my people, I always will."

She seemed almost electrified, as if a current ran through

her. She shook slightly—but with temper, he thought, still not fear. Then, suddenly, she shot to her feet, her hands in fists at her side that suggested that he was right. "None of this is okay."

He might not understand himself this day, but he did like to be right.

"I do not think this the tragedy you're making out to be," he countered, and it was easy, in the face of her outrage, to sound very nearly lazy again. "Please bear in mind that in order to achieve my goals, I am forced into the match as much as you. There are worse things than wedding a stranger, Delaney. Trust me on this."

Her blue eyes were a storm. "That's easy for you to say. You're the one doing this."

"Because I must," he said again. With finality.

"But *why*?" she threw at him, as if the query was torn from somewhere deep inside her.

He would not have responded to temper. He would have laughed at a demand. But he found he couldn't ignore a plea like this, as if it hurt her.

"This is a fractured place," he told her, and this was no prepared speech. The words simply welled up from within him. "It has been broken for so long that the people here have come to imagine that they are broken, too. And nothing will fix it. No talks. No treaties. No wars. As long as there are two sides, there will be conflict. It is my job—my calling—to do what I can to dispel it. Not because I do not have the same urges as the rest of my people, to rise up and take what was taken from us. Of course I do. But I know that in these skirmishes, we all lose. I am so tired of loss, Delaney."

He had never said such a thing out loud before. He had not known the words existed within him.

He wasn't at all sure that he liked knowing that they'd

been there all along, but he pushed on. "But there is only one way we can do away with these sides. Not so that I can win a throne, but so all of us can win back what was taken from us so long ago. So that we can move forward without this loss that marks all of us, royalist and rebel alike. We can only be whole if we come together."

She stared at him, round-eyed. "You truly believe this."

"I do."

And he had made a great many vows in his life. To himself. To his people.

This was not a vow, but it felt like one. Like bright, hot steel pressed into flesh.

He could feel it in his skin. Directly over his heart, a terrible, marvelous brand of truth.

Cayetano hardly knew what to do with the storm in him then. Instead, he watched as she blew out a breath, punched those fists of hers into place on her hips, and began to pace around the room.

"I don't understand this...sitting around in pretty rooms and *talking*," Delaney seethed at him, her blue eyes shooting sparks when they met his. "I like to be outside. I like dirt under my feet. I like a day that ends with me having to scrub soil out from beneath my fingernails."

She glared at the walls as if they had betrayed her.

Then at him, as if he was doing so even now.

For a moment he almost felt as if he had—but that was ridiculous.

"When you are recognized as the true Crown Princess of Ile d'Montagne, the whole island will be your garden," he told her. Trying to soothe her. He wanted to lift a hand to his own chest and massage the brand that wasn't there, but *soothing* was for others, not him. He ignored the too-hot sensation. "You can work in the dirt of your ancestors to your heart's content."

Delaney shot a look at him, pure blue fire. "Even if I did agree to do such a crazy thing, you still wouldn't get what you want. It doesn't matter what blood is in my veins. I am a farm girl, born and bred. I will never look the part of the Princess you imagine. Never."

She sounded almost as final as he had, but Cayetano allowed himself a smile, because that wasn't a flat refusal. It sounded more like a *maybe* to him.

He could work with *maybe*.

In point of fact, he couldn't wait.

He rose then. And he made his way toward her, watching the way her eyes widened. The way her lips parted. There was an unmistakable flush on her cheeks as he drew near, and he could see her pulse beat at her neck.

Cayetano was the warlord of these mountains and would soon enough be the King of this island. And he had been prepared to ignore the fire in him, the fever. The ways he wanted her that had intruded into his work, his sleep. But here and now, he granted himself permission to want this woman. *His* woman. Because he could see that she wanted him.

With that and her *maybe,* he knew he'd already won.

"Let me worry about how you look," he said as he came to a stop before her, enjoying the way she had to look up to hold his gaze. It made her seem softer. He could see the hectic need all over her, matching his own. "There is something far more interesting for you to concentrate on."

Delaney made a noise of frustration. "The barbaric nature of ancient laws and customs?"

"Or this."

And then Cayetano followed the urge that had been

with him since he'd seen her standing in a dirt-filled yard with a battered kerchief on her head and kissed her.

He expected her to be sweet. He expected to enjoy himself.

He expected to want her all the more, to tempt his own feverish need with a little taste of her.

But he was totally unprepared for the punch of it. Of a simple kiss—a kiss to show her there was more here than righting old wrongs and reclaiming lost thrones. A kiss to share a little bit of the fire that had been burning in him since he'd first laid eyes on her.

It was a blaze and it took him over.

It was a dark, drugging heat.

It was a mad blaze of passion.

It was a delirium—and he wanted more.

He drew her closer to him, then hauled her up into his arms, letting the fever take hold of him, a delicious madness. He kissed her again, then again. Delaney made a low, broken sort of sound and he made as if to retreat, but she threw her arms around his neck and held on.

And then there was nothing at all but the pounding of his heart, and the hard pulse of need in his sex. The slick fire with every angle, every dance of his tongue and hers.

The glory of it. The desire.

He found his hands moving over her, wild with need. As if they moved of their own accord, and ached to glance over each and every part of her—

My God, you're losing control—

That voice inside him shocked him into stillness.

Cayetano set her aside abruptly, his breath hard and raw.

And almost lost control of himself again when he saw that her blue eyes were two shades darker. While her pretty mouth was faintly swollen from his.

Not reaching out for her again felt like a blow.

"Is that reason enough?" he managed to grit out. "Do you think that happens every day?"

Delaney blinked at that, then swallowed hard. She looked vulnerable for a moment, and that clawed at him, but then she straightened her shoulders and lifted that stubborn chin. "Speak for yourself. It happens three times a day for me. Sometimes more."

He moved away from her, because it was that or continue as he had been and take her right there against the wall, and he couldn't allow that. He needed to figure out how it was he had lost his composure here. He had to make sure that he was in control of himself the way he always, always was.

Because this flirtation with chaos could never happen again.

"You have two choices," he told her when he could speak without shouting—another red flag—and he was aware that his voice had gone arctic. There was no helping it. Everything inside him was on fire, but God only knew what would become of him if he showed her that. If he allowed himself such a display. The very idea chilled him to the bone. "You may agree to marry me. If you do this, our wedding will take place in one month. It will give us time to prepare the perfect way to launch you and what you mean upon the House of Montaigne, and the world. Because it must be perfect. Meanwhile, you can study up on your relatives, if you wish. We have a great many books on the topic in our libraries, plus any number of personal experiences. And while you are learning where you come from, we will prepare for where you're going. We'll make you the Queen my country deserves."

"And the second choice?" she asked without missing a beat.

Her eyes were glittering with temper now.

Cayetano inclined his head. "The second choice is simple enough. My men will stand guard outside your door. Come the morning, I will gather my people in the courtyard and claim you as mine as if it is still the Dark Ages. It will be done, and we will spend the same amount of time readying ourselves for our unveiling. But you won't be trusted, and I fear that you might find Arcieri Castle more of a cell than you might otherwise."

"So the choice you're offering me is really no choice at all."

There were too many competing shadows inside him, and he did not have the grip on himself he should. "If I were you, my little farm girl, I would count myself lucky I had any choice at all."

"And do I get two different marriages to choose from, too?" she asked, folding her arms in front of her. As if she had all the self-control he was appalled to discover he lacked.

"I beg your pardon?"

"Does a barbarous beginning lead to brutality?" she demanded. "Is that what I have to look forward to?"

She could not have said anything that would have cut him more.

"I would never lift my hand to a woman," Cayetano bit out, though even as he did, something in him pointed out that if she thought otherwise she surely wouldn't have said such a thing, and so baldly. Maybe that was what spurred on the words that came out of him then, as if the desire in him had taken him over completely. "The only battles you and I will have will be in bed. But both of us will win. And the only question will be how much you can take."

There was something about the stunned sort of way she stared back at him that got to him. That made him think she was not necessarily as sophisticated as she pretended in the midst of her defiance. And that would mean...

But he dismissed it.

And then Cayetano forced himself to leave her in that sitting room before he could think better of it.

Before he could show her what he meant, there and then.

Before he betrayed himself any further.

CHAPTER SEVEN

DELANEY HAD NO choice but to pick the first option. Because she certainly wasn't prepared to find herself barbarically married tomorrow morning.

What else could she do in the wake of that kiss? Of that…hurricane that had swept her away before she knew what was happening to her, making a mockery of any *weather systems* she thought she knew before?

Her body was no longer recognizable to her. She no longer felt like herself, as if he'd taken her from the uncertain ground of learning she wasn't a Clark head-on into the sea she'd seen out the window, shifting and moving and no ground at all beneath her feet. There were too many wild sensations simmering inside her. Too much longing.

As if all that was left of her—the only part of her that was *her*—was that blooming, near-incapacitating ache that suffused her as he left.

What would you have done if he hadn't stopped? she asked herself after he'd gone and she was left to try to find her breath, her own ragged breath loud in the quiet room.

But no matter how many times she asked herself, it was always the same unsatisfactory answer.

Surrender.

Delaney tried to ignore the heavy heat that rushed through her every time she thought that word. Every time she imagined what surrendering to a man like that, stone and fire, might do to her…

What was the matter with her that some part of her craved that kind of immolation? She wanted him to kiss her again. She wanted to lose herself in it, and then find herself there in his arms. She had the half-mad notion that it was only there that she might feel like herself again. Only there she might truly come *alive.* She wanted—

A servant stepped in while she was still standing where Cayetano had left her, clinging to the wall. Delaney was sure he must have been able to see how red she was. How disheveled. How off-balance. Though if he did, no trace of his reaction showed on his face.

"The warlord wishes to know your choice," the man said with great dignity.

Delaney wanted to pretend she didn't know what he meant, but that felt a bit beneath her.

"The first one," she told him, trying to match his dignity with some measure of poise and grace—or at least calm. "Thank you."

It was a month. A lot could happen in a month. He might come to his senses, for one thing. She told herself that was what she wanted. Meanwhile, she would use the library he'd mentioned to educate herself on what she'd walked into here. Not only about her biological family, but about the Arcieris and their castle, too.

She'd hardly had a chance to breathe, much less think. Her new reality had been thrust at her, and now she was in this strange and overwhelming place, and Cayetano had kissed her like one or both of them were dying—

You're all right now, she told herself. *Perfectly alive and well and* yourself. *You can start using your head again.*

Relief flooded her. She pressed her feet into the floor

beneath her, assuring herself that she stood on her own two feet, as always. It would cost her nothing to stay here. She could go along with Cayetano as long as it suited her and gather all kinds of information before she was forced to face the Queen who was, apparently, her mother. Or the Princess who had taken her place on this island—yet belonged back home in the Kansas that Delaney loved.

She told herself this was nothing more than a delaying tactic. And more, that she was in control.

Weddings don't necessarily happen overnight, Catherine had said. *No need to rush into anything.*

That was what Delaney was doing. Not rushing.

After Cayetano's man left, she moved away from the wall. She frowned at the feast still laid out on the table, trying to decide if she was actually hungry or just feeling the very real need to eat all her feelings. But before she could get to repressing with pastries, the original trio of female servants swept back in.

They carried her battered old duffel bag with them. They were bright and chattery, like three happy birds, and they didn't appear to require any response from Delaney.

That was a good thing. Delaney was still having more trouble standing on her own two feet than she cared to admit.

"Are you well?" one of the women asked, possibly noticing the way Delaney wobbled.

"Jet lag," Delaney said with great authority for someone who had never been on a jet before today.

But she knew it wasn't *jet lag.*

It was that kiss. It was Cayetano. It was that part of her that thought surrender sounded terrific and why not go ahead and marry the *dark glory* that had come for her like a tornado, lifted her up and out of Kansas like she was Dorothy after all, and brought her here?

Because that's what happens in books, Delaney lectured herself, though her attempt to sound internally stern was a bit stymied by all that delirious sensation she could still feel inside her, lighting her up. *Real life is different.*

Though it was, admittedly, hard to cling to her idea of what reality *ought* to be when she was standing in an actual *castle.*

The trio of servants threw open a pair of doors that Delaney hadn't even known were there. She'd thought they were part of the wall. But it turned out that she was already in a kind of apartment, equipped with everything from her own kitchenette to a vast bedroom that opened up onto its own balcony that overlooked the sweep of the valley.

The bedroom alone, she was pretty sure, was bigger than the farmhouse.

The entire farmhouse. And the bed looked about the size of her vegetable patch.

She felt itchy. The whole thing—the pageant of it, the obvious wealth, the fact that there were *servants* who treated her with a sort of brisk deference—made her deeply uncomfortable.

A lot like she was coming out of her skin, she thought, as she was led on a tour through one beautiful room after the next, all apparently a part of her guest quarters. It was a far cry from the inflatable mattress on a floor that had served as the farm's guest accommodations. All the smug paintings and complacent vases. All the self-aggrandizing rugs, so thick and pristine she very much doubted anyone else had walked across their intricate designs. Even the parade of carefully chosen colors seemed condescending to her. Who would ever choose a mint green? A pale yellow? Then anoint it all with gleaming gold and silver and sanctimonious furnishings?

She longed for the simplicity of her real life. The demands of crops, livestock. The inevitability of the seasons. Rain. Sun. Storms. Drought. Those were the things that mattered, not a castle on a mountain above an island she'd never heard of before. Not all these trappings of a kind of moneyed life she couldn't even begin to understand.

Maybe she didn't want to understand.

One thing she could tell she most certainly did not wish to understand was servants.

She'd never had a servant in her life. Clarks did for themselves or they did without.

"I know I'm not a Clark," she muttered, before she felt compelled to remind herself, and smiled when the servant with her in the bedroom—flinging open curtains and doors and bustling this way and that—looked at her quizzically.

Maybe if she kept saying that, it would start making sense. And maybe if she did it enough, she would believe it.

And maybe you're happy at the notion of hiding away here, researching and reading and distancing yourself in all your not rushing, *because you don't want to face the truth,* came a voice inside her, tart enough to be her grandmother's. *You want to put off reality as long as possible.*

What she wanted, Delaney thought then, was not to collapse on the floor and cry.

Because she was afraid that if she started up again, she might never stop.

Delaney squeezed the bridge of her nose until the heat

there dissipated. But then she didn't know what to do with herself. There appeared to be nothing for her *to* do but stand about as the women breezed around her in the overlarge bedchamber, chattering brightly as they unpacked her clothes and set out her few personal things. Her attempt to help was swiftly rebuffed with a laugh, so she…stood there near the gigantic four-poster bed that she worried she'd need a ladder to climb into, feeling awkward.

So awkward that it took her a moment to realize that they were speaking to each other, and sort of *at* her, in English.

"I thought everyone spoke French here," she said.

A tad too bluntly, she realized, when all three women—who she was only now realizing were probably about her own age, a fact she probably shouldn't have found so astonishing—stopped what they were doing and gazed at her.

"French, yes. Also, Italian," one of the women said. "But the world is big and speaks more than two languages. So, also Spanish. German. And, yes, English."

"I have a smattering of Japanese," another woman boasted.

But the third one laughed. "Knowing how to say thank-you in Japanese is not a smattering," she said. "It's one word. *Arigato.*"

Delaney felt as if she ought to apologize for speaking only the one. But didn't.

"Also," the first one said as the other two glared at each other, "the warlord insisted that only English-speaking servants wait on you. It caused quite a commotion."

"I'm not surprised," Delaney said. "I can't imagine who would want to wait on a farm girl from Kansas."

All three women looked confused. They looked at each other, then back at Delaney.

"Everyone wanted to wait on you," the third girl said, as if she didn't understand why Delaney had uttered such blasphemy.

"It's an honor," agreed the second.

"You are to be the warlord's bride," said the first. Rapturously. "What greater honor could there be than to attend you?"

Delaney did not have an answer to that. Her body seemed to respond on its own. She told herself it was shame and horror, that thick current of sensation that coiled low in her belly as the words *the warlord's bride* chased around and around in her head. She told herself her body was staging a revolt at the very idea.

But she knew better.

She remembered that kiss too well, and she knew better.

Still, she didn't have a lot of time alone to sit and brood about it.

Because the three servants moved on from the awkward moment, getting down to business quickly. They unpacked everything from her duffel, and then examined it. Critically. One of them pulled out a tape measure. Another produced a pad and pen and noted down the numbers. And only smiled when Delaney asked why.

After they finished whirlwinding around her, they delivered her to another servant waiting for her outside her guest apartment. He wore a uniform that even Delaney's untutored eye could identify as fancy. Fancier than the women, certainly.

And significantly fancier than Delaney in her jeans and T-shirt.

"I am the majordomo," the man intoned.

Then waited for her to reply to that in a proud manner that suggested a bended knee on her part might not be out of the question.

When Delaney did not alter the position of her knees, or change expression at all, he sniffed. Then proceeded to take her on a tour of the castle, stopping along the way to point out objects of note, paintings of historical figures—most, if not all, of the Arcieris—rooms wherein great moments in Ile d'Montagne's history took place, and, at every window, a detailed description of the view. What lands, buildings, villages were before her, their significance, how they had disguised their true purpose during periods of conflict, and so on.

It took her longer than it should have to realize that this was not a tour. It was a lesson.

She blamed the jet lag again, but once she caught on, she paid much closer attention.

And chose not to ask herself why, when she was obviously not going to stay here, she felt it necessary to learn anything about this place. She told herself she was listening so intently because this was, in its way, a story about her family, too. Who better to tell the story than her family's enemies? After listening to a litany of complaints against the Montaigne family across the ages, she could surely only be pleasantly surprised by Queen Esme one day.

She took in all the commentary about the Montaigne line, filing it all away to look up on her own later. To see how the story changed depending on the telling. But she couldn't help but notice that, somehow, she was also interested not only in the details of the castle they stood in, and the valley she could see on the other side of the windows, but of Cayetano himself.

Knowing the enemy, she told herself stoutly. That's

all this was. She was *gathering intelligence,* the way people did when embroiled in games involving castles and queens.

"The Arcieri family have controlled the castle almost without interruption since its inception," the majordomo told her while standing in front of a portrait of a long-ago warlord, clearly taking great personal pride in both the image and the Arcieris. "They have been the heart, soul, and conscience of this island these many ages."

Delaney could see Cayetano in the portrait of his ancestor. Stone and fire. Eyes like a hawk.

She could still feel his hard mouth moving on hers.

"It does make a person question what the royal family actually wants, though, doesn't it?" she asked.

The majordomo looked at her as if he'd never heard such blasphemy. "It is abundantly clear that what the Montaignes want is power."

Delaney nodded at him. "But if this one family—" *my family,* she thought, to try to get used to it "—has been the problem for generations, why didn't they just take out the family instead of all these wars and skirmishes and whatever else?"

The way the man looked at her reminded her that she was standing there in another gleaming room, this one a gallery, with the smell of the farm all over her. In her T-shirt and jeans, which were as comfortable as they had ever been but really didn't match her surroundings. And the way he was looking at her, she was tempted to look and see if, in fact, she was also covered in dirt.

"They have tried, madam," said the man before, frostily. "They have tried and tried."

"It's really amazing, then," Delaney said hurriedly, "that the Arcieris have managed to stand against them all the while."

Them in this case being the bad guys whose blood ran in her veins.

When all she'd ever wanted was Kansas dirt and a long, fruitful growing season.

Her words seemed to mollify her companion, though the look he gave her was still ripe with suspicion. "It was not so long ago that we were certain the great cause was lost," he told her, straightening the resplendent coat of his uniform as if it had somehow become imperfect during this lesson. When it had not. "Our current warlord's parents…" But he stopped himself. "I do not wish to speak out of turn."

Delaney wanted nothing more than for him to speak out of turn. At length.

Because she was buying time and collecting information, she assured herself. That little leap inside at the mention of Cayetano was nothing to worry about. Maybe it was heartburn after whatever she'd eaten earlier. She'd never had heartburn before, ever, but these were extraordinary circumstances. If it persisted, she thought as serenely as she could, she would have to ask for the warlord version of antacids.

"It is only history, surely," she said mildly now, keeping her eyes on the picture of the historical warlord before her. He was very impressive, but not as impressive as the current version. But she was quite sure that if she showed even the slightest bit of prurient interest, the already-not-so-sure-about-her majordomo would go silent altogether.

She must have showed the appropriate amount of respectful disinterest, because he continued. "Our warlord's father died when he was quite young and Cayetano became the hope of our people. But for a time it seemed that hope was to be dashed. His mother ruled our people in Cayetano's stead, for he was underage. Some factions believed that she was Arcieri enough, having been married to the previous warlord, and could lead us where we needed to go. But then she considered remarrying, and things became more complicated." He shook his head. "Her choice of a potential husband was no Arcieri. I will leave it at that."

Delaney snuck a look at his expression then, and found it…troubling.

And she didn't like that at all. Because all the things the majordomo did not say seemed thick in the air then, and it made her feel more sympathetic to Cayetano.

When she had no desire to feel the slightest hint of sympathy for him.

Not when she could feel the aftereffects of that hurricane, still kicking up a fuss inside her.

"That must have been hard for the warlord," she said anyway. From some unknown place inside herself, where she was gentle and not the least bit stormy.

"Our warlord is a great man," the majordomo told her, in unmistakable tones of awe. "What would bring other men to their knees only makes Cayetano stronger."

She was still mulling that over when he delivered back to what he called her *rooms* with Ile d'Montagne history in her head and a strange worry for Cayetano in what she was terribly afraid was her heart, to find the same three servants buzzing around. They were laying out garments and if she wasn't mistaken, that was a curling iron she saw being plugged in.

"Surely it's time to rest," she protested.

Because she had never been so tired. She wanted to *droop*.

This is maybe real jet lag, a voice inside suggested. *Because it's an actual thing, not just an excuse.*

"Don't be silly," one of her servants was saying gaily. "We have to get you ready for dinner."

"The warlord regrets that he is unable to dine with you this evening," said another, with the kind of giggle that Delaney associated with memories of middle school. As if Cayetano was some kind of boy band singer.

"You will be dining with the Signorina instead," said the third.

"The Signorina?"

Delaney didn't know what to do as they swarmed around her, so she stayed still. She didn't object when they started looking at her clothes as if they meant to remove them right there where she stood in the middle of the bedroom floor. Or even when they did.

She was so exhausted and overwhelmed it didn't seem real.

And they were so matter-of-fact about the whole thing that it felt perfectly acceptable, in this strange, unreal place, to find herself surrendering. They tugged everything off and whisked a silk bathrobe of sorts into place so seamlessly that she had the possibly half-hysterical urge to ask if they had choreographed it. Then they spun her around, making clucking noises as they sat her in front of a mirror in what she hadn't recognized was a vanity table in the separate apartment that was her bathroom. Though calling it a *bathroom* didn't really cover the many rooms, nooks, and walk-in closets that were each bigger than the farmhouse's whole attic.

Delaney couldn't really process anything, it turned out. So it seemed reasonable enough—or almost—to let someone work on her hair while the other two kept holding different garments that weren't hers in the mirror's reflection, then conferring.

Why not? something in her asked.

After all, she had a whole month. Surely she could effect her escape later—or rather simply leave without all the melodrama.

Not tonight.

"The Signorina is the foremost expert on manners and customs in the valley," Delaney was informed. The girl applying the hairbrush and curling iron to her hair looked very serious as she said this. "She has dedicated herself to the Arcieri family. She has been the governess not only for the warlord, but for his father before him. It is a great honor that she has agreed to this."

Once again, Delaney was aware that she was being studied. For her reaction.

She made what she hoped were noises that suggested she felt appropriately honored.

After they finished fussing with the hair she usually paid no attention to, or put into braids to really ignore, she was packed into a dress that was finer than any other single garment she'd ever beheld. It was soft. It seemed to *whisper* at her, little secrets about its own finery.

Delaney wanted to hate it on principle. But she couldn't.

When they angled her so she could look at her full reflection, something in her…seized, maybe. Or went so still it amounted to the same thing. The woman looking back at her from the mirror wore a dress that belonged behind glass somewhere, maybe in Hollywood. The rope of pearls wound around her neck felt silky against her skin but looked impossibly elegant—a word that had never been used in reference to a girl who spent most of her life in dirty overalls. Never, ever. And it was all topped off with the kind of sophisticated twisty updo that made her look like a complete stranger.

She understood, then. This was a dream. Or it felt like

a dream, and that was why she was simply going along with the whole thing, because that was what a person did in dreams. What did it matter that none of this made sense? It didn't have to.

Because in a dream, it wasn't necessary to check with her feelings of dislocation and despair on the one hand and something too much like desire on the other. It wasn't necessary to untangle that knot. Or face this shocking joy in things she would have said repulsed her, like a pretty dress that moved around her legs like it was made of light. If it was real life, she would have had to square up to all the things that were happening to her and had already happened. In a dream, she might as well decide to give herself over to the sheer madness all around her without complaint. So that was what she did.

And a person who was wide awake might have objected to being marched down to what the majordomo had told her was the private wing of the palace, where she was shown into a dining room. But the dreamer in her simply went along with it.

There were only two places set at one end of a glossy table in this new room, packed to the ceiling with the kinds of priceless artifacts she'd been told so much about today, but what caught her attention wasn't more vases and candelabras. It was the tiny woman with an enormous beehive hairdo who waited, peering at Delaney through a pair of spectacles.

Delaney had the strangest urge to curtsy.

When she wasn't sure she even knew *how* to curtsy.

The doors closed behind her, and then there she was. Shut in yet another room in this castle, this time with a diminutive woman who emanated a certain intensity that made Delaney feel...

Well, unfortunately awake, for one thing. But also as

if she didn't quite fit in her skin. As if everything about her was *wrong*.

And she realized with a start that she hated it.

More than hated it.

Because Delaney was used to feeling personally comfortable in her own skin. She was used to feeling grounded. Centered. She knew who she was. She knew what her life held and would always hold.

She'd taken pleasure in those things. She'd enjoyed them.

And now she was standing here in clothes that weren't hers, her hair twisted beyond recognition, while a strange woman eyed her down the length of a strange room as if *she* was somehow the problem.

"I take it that I'm supposed to be intimidated by you," Delaney said.

The tiny woman moved only one eyebrow. It rose up, edging toward her towering beehive that made up the better part of her height. "Are you not?"

Her English sounded precise, but with a hint of an accent. Only the barest hint.

"I'm used to a farm," Delaney told her. "The livestock does get a little fractious and plants are known troublemakers, but you learn to deal with it. But no, I wouldn't say that I'm ever intimidated by posturing."

She expected temper. Or more of that haughty affront she'd seen from the majordomo.

But instead, the older woman cackled.

"Marvelous," she cried, clapping her hands together. "You're wildly inappropriate and borderline offensive, and that's what makes you perfect. This will be fun."

She waved Delaney to the seat at the head of the table, still laughing, and settled into the other seat. "Come," she urged Delaney when she hung back. "Everything must be quite strange to you here, myself included, but the food is phenomenal."

And she waited so expectantly that Delaney found herself moving to sit down. Then, not knowing what to do with herself, she watched as the other woman rang the bell beside her dramatic place setting. Vigorously. The sound was still hanging in the air as servants swept in, laden down with trays of food.

"Tonight, we eat," the Signorina said as Delaney blinked down at the array of utensils and piles of plates heaped before her. "We will concern ourselves with the stuffy rules of etiquette tomorrow."

Delaney was shocked to find that she spent a surprisingly enjoyable evening in the Signorina's company. It wasn't until she was in her absurdly oversize bed, finally alone, that she remembered that she really wasn't supposed to enjoy any part of this.

Why not? a voice inside her asked. Sounding a lot like Catherine, who was merrily not taking Delaney's calls— the way she had the summer Delaney had gone to camp for one miserable week.

"You're supposed to be trying to figure out how to *not* marry that man," she told herself sternly. "Or at the very least, discovering things about the Montaignes. And therefore, you."

But she dropped off to sleep before she could start coming up with a plan to do just that.

And as one day became several days, then a week, Delaney realized two things. One, that she didn't seem to be in any hurry to come up with a plan, and she probably ought to think about why that was. And two, that she knew how Cayetano expected to wait out his month.

He'd put her on a schedule.

Because the days followed a sort of pattern. During

the day, there was usually some time dedicated to wardrobe concerns and somehow this led to more and more items in those spacious closets that went on forever. And her three bright and cheerful servants never seemed to be able to find the clothes that Delaney had brought with her, so sorry, so they used the new clothes instead. They dressed her for every meal save breakfast, which she was allowed to eat in her bathrobe while they bustled around her, telling her what her day would hold.

Delaney told herself she hated these things, but the truth was that she quite liked the clothes that were picked out for her. She liked the hair, the makeup, which she would never have done for herself. She was getting more and more comfortable with the stranger in the mirror.

She told herself that it was in her blood, the inner Princess she'd never known was there.

Even though, if she was honest, her blood scared her a little. Maybe more than a little. Not the battles recorded in musty old books. She figured that was history. Packed full of events no one wanted to happen to them—but then, history was a lot closer on this side of the Atlantic. People here spoke of the fourteen-hundreds as if they were last Tuesday. What scared her was that the old books with the gold-edged pages weren't filled with tedious facts she would need to regurgitate for some test.

They were records of things her family did.

Mostly to Cayetano's family.

And she didn't want to feel connected to either part of that equation. She was supposed to be having an adventure, not finding herself in history books. Especially not when what she should have wanted was to find her way back home.

But sometimes, late at night in her bed, she admitted another truth.

If Cayetano had kissed her like that in a "MIDWEST IS BEST" T-shirt, what would happen when he saw her like this? Dressed like she belonged here? Could it get better than a hurricane?

Yet even as she wondered about kissing him, she couldn't help wondering if, for all his talk about healing the fractures on this island, he wanted to marry her because she looked too much like all the paintings she'd seen reproduced in his books. Of his enemy.

Sometimes the notion made her sad. Other times it made her shiver.

Still other times, she questioned why she was focusing so intently on Cayetano at all when her family tree was just down the side of the mountain…

Each night she would fall asleep resolved, planning to wake up and demand to be taken to Queen Esme. Because she wanted to look in the other woman's face and *not* find herself there.

Yet every morning she woke and made no such demands.

Possibly because, deep down, she was terrified that what she'd see in the Queen's face was the inarguable evidence that they were mother and daughter.

And she already had a mother. Even with Catherine's blessing, it felt like a betrayal.

She spent the bulk of her time with the Signorina. There were usually lunches and teas, during which Delaney learned comportment and manners and customs, and, if it was only the two of them, dissolved into cackles more often than not. When there were others at these meals, Delaney practiced all of the above plus what the Signorina called the *art of conversation*.

"Everybody knows how to talk," Delaney said the first time she brought this up.

"And all they do is talk," the other woman replied. "Talking, talking, talking while the world spirals into wreck and ruin. *Talking* is not an art. It is merely moving your lips so that sounds may escape and collect them into sentences. What you and I are concerned with is conversation, which is not only an art, but a rather underestimated and lost one, in my opinion."

"We're having a conversation right now," Delaney retorted.

The Mediterranean sun streamed down all around them as they sat out in a lush garden, tucked away in one of the private courtyards. Birds sang above them and bees hummed along merrily.

The Signorina set down her teacup and smiled. "And would you categorize the conversation that we're having here as *artful*, dear?"

Delaney was forced to concede the point.

"At the sort of events you will attend in your formal role, one does not talk about oneself," the Signorina told her, holding her teacup aloft.

That was how she liked to refer to Delaney's supposed upcoming wedding. Her *formal role*. And maybe it said something about Delaney that she didn't correct her—but this wasn't the moment to talk about herself, was it?

"It is not the time for personal revelations, confessions, or monologues," the Signorina continued, as if she could read Delaney's mind. "None of that is artful conversation. That is what one saves for one's diary or inflicts upon one's intimates. The point of a good conversation is to engage. The point of the kinds of conversations you may find yourself in, with so many agendas and competing interests, is to entertain without revealing anything you do not wish to reveal. While at the same time trying to make whoever you're speaking to reveal too much. It is very much like a dance."

"I don't dance." Delaney brushed the crumbs of her scone off a dress that probably cost more than her entire previous life. She looked back at her teacher sheepishly. "Maybe that's obvious."

"It is one more thing you and I shall have to remedy," the Signorina said with a laugh. "But first, we will converse, you and I."

And the more they practiced, the more Delaney understood why. It wasn't about the talking. It was a skill, and one she would be expected to use once the world found out who she was. She had no illusions that Cayetano would keep those DNA tests to himself. Whether she married him or not.

She had told Cayetano that she didn't understand the point of pretty rooms filled with all that talking, but now she understood it was in those pretty rooms that a great many decisions were made about what went on outside them. The Signorina was merely teaching her how it was done.

Very much as if she really would be a queen someday.

Her stomach twisted a little more every time she thought such things.

Though she couldn't quite tell if it was panic…or a complicated kind of excitement.

And no matter what it was, it never propelled her into actually *doing* something. She never demanded that she be taken to Cayetano so she could tell him how *she* would like to handle *her* family situation. She never took the opportunity to tell him what he could do with his threats of marriage.

The marriage the Signorina prepared her for every

day, as if she wanted to make herself into the warlord's perfect bride.

Sometimes she was tempted to imagine that was what she truly wanted. That she could let herself be swept away by his will alone, and let that be enough, because if she couldn't go back to Kansas and unknow what she'd learned about her parentage…why not be the princess bride of a man who looked at her with burnt gold eyes, dressed her like a queen, and kissed her like a hurricane?

Maybe he was the adventure after all.

One night, two weeks into her time at the castle, Delaney walked to dinner with one of the servants. She knew all their names by now and knew that this one, Ferdinand, was far too overawed by the castle to talk much. She kept catching glimpses of herself in the various mirrors they passed, and it was different, now. *Of course* she had no intention of going through with anything like a wedding, or so she was telling herself tonight, but she no longer saw a stranger in her reflection.

She saw the future Queen all these people were trying—trying *so hard* and she didn't always help, she could admit that—to make her into.

And on nights like this, she thought she could see it, too. She really could almost see it. Because that woman in the mirror looked as alien to a Kansas cornfield as Cayetano had. Delaney thought that really, she looked a bit regal.

She wasn't surprised when Ferdinand led her into a new and different room this particular evening. The Signorina liked to keep things fresh, always moving to a new room, a new group, a new scenario. Training Delaney to stay forever on her toes.

Not that she cared to admit it, but she'd come to like the game.

Delaney was already halfway through the room, the doors closed behind her, when she truly took in the fact that the figure waiting for her tonight was not the diminutive Signorina.

It was Cayetano.

At last.

As if she hadn't learned a thing. As if she was back in that dusty yard, mystified and too hot, his dark glory almost too hot to bear.

And that suddenly, she was nothing but a farm girl all over again.

CHAPTER EIGHT

CAYETANO COULD SEE the exact moment Delaney registered his presence, because she actually stopped still. Her eyes went wide. It was charming, really. A doe in headlights right here in his private dining room, and his body reacted in what was becoming a predictable way to the little puzzle that was Delaney Clark.

His farm girl who insisted she was no princess when tonight, she looked like a goddess.

That red gown was a wonder, sweeping from one shoulder as if she was competing for a spot in the pantheon. Her black hair was set in a complicated French twist with hints of something sparkly to catch the light.

God, how he wanted her.

That ill-considered kiss had set off a wildfire in him, and even though he'd kept his distance these last two weeks, the sparks remained. One look at her and he could feel them all begin to smolder.

He liked the way she flushed at the sight of him. He liked that he could see exactly how aware she was of him. And he suspected that he was not the only one remembering how that kiss had tasted. And the heat.

That silken, delirious heat that had nearly made him forget himself.

But there was more to concern himself with tonight

than the memory of that kiss. For one thing, she no longer in any way resembled that farm girl he'd encountered that day, dirt on her cheeks and all over her clothes.

Her attendants had worked the precise miracle he had entrusted them to perform. There was no hint of overalls and kerchief about her tonight. Her gown skimmed over her figure and made her skin seem to glow. Her hair was not left to the weather and its complex elegance highlighted the fine, inarguably royal features she'd inherited from a long line of Montaignes. That sophisticated nose. Those soaring cheekbones.

He wanted her. This was true. It was always true. He had become uncomfortable with how true it was these last weeks, but tonight it was on another level. She took his breath away.

Because tonight he saw the diamond, not the rough.

And it was a complicated triumph that pumped through him then. Because Cayetano was attracted to her either way, and the man in him wanted nothing more than to explore her femininity with all the tools at his disposal. His mouth. His hands. His sex.

Until they were both weak with desire.

But the warlord in him, who meant to be King at last, saw his Queen.

And it took more willpower than it should have to stay where he was. To stay put, there at the far end of the room, waiting to see if she would continue to come to him or stay frozen where she was.

Waiting to see what he would do if she stayed put, staring at him as if he was an apparition.

But one that made her cheeks red and her eyes overbright.

He wasn't sure which he would prefer, now that he considered it. Because looking at her was no hardship.

Neither was imagining what he would do with each and every version of her. Farm girl. Vision. Princess. Queen.

And all of them his.

All of them as wild and hot as she'd been in his arms.

It seemed to take her a lifetime or two to straighten her shoulders, then find a practiced sort of smile that he knew came straight from the Signorina. He recognized the particular contours of what the old woman had called her *company smile.*

But he had never wanted to lick a smile like that off anyone's face before.

"This is very disappointing," Delaney said, but she sounded arch and amused, not disappointed. And not really like *Delaney,* either. "The Signorina has been at great pains to tell me that you're an excellent conversationalist. Yet all I get is glowering."

"I'm looking at you, this is true. But I am not glowering."

"Did you know that conversation is an art?" Her smile deepened. "It seems you and I have something in common after all. We are both of us artless."

And that caught him so completely off guard that he laughed.

But, however surprised he might have been at his own laughter, that was nothing next to Delaney's clear astonishment that he was even capable of making such a sound.

She looked...spellbound.

He had not intended to move from where he stood and yet he found himself crossing the room. When he reached her side he took her hand, perhaps because the last time he'd done so, she had looked equally astonished. In the same way she did now, shot through with heat and awareness and the same kind of wonder he could not help but feel when he looked at her.

He led her not to the table that waited for them, but out through the doors to the wide balcony that let in the cool spring night. The stars were already out, thick in the night sky. The valley was inky black below them, the lights in the villages soft, buttery clusters against the dark. The air was not warm, but it was soft as it moved over them.

Usually, Cayetano took this view as seriously as he did everything else. Every point of light he saw before him represented a swathe of people. His people. He had spent years standing here, renewing his commitment to them. Night after night, he had rededicated himself to the cause.

But tonight he let himself marinate in the sweetness of this moment he had often worried would never come. His very own princess in his castle, his wedding in a couple of weeks, his future finally secured.

And through him, his people's destiny forever changed.

Justice was winning. After all these centuries. And it was all because of her.

He had been delighted to find his lost princess, particularly when so many had been certain she didn't—couldn't—exist. He would have brought her here no matter what. But tonight Delaney had transformed herself. She had made herself his dream come true.

Cayetano doubted that had been her goal, or if she'd even had one, but she had done it all the same.

He could not help but take a moment to bask in it. In her.

There were lanterns lit all around, and he liked the way the soft light played over her face.

"What I cannot understand," he said quietly, as if not

to disturb the dark, "is how no one in that cornfield of yours recognized the fact that you could not possibly be one of them."

That was as much a statement of fact as some kind of compliment, so he was unprepared when she frowned. "I don't know what you mean."

"Look at you." He was still holding her hand as they stood there against the railing. He indulged himself with his free hand and traced the curve of her cheek. "Your sculpted and aristocratic lines. The House of Montaigne is in your face. It is unmistakable."

"The funny thing about that," she said, in a voice that made it very clear that she did not think anything was particularly funny, "is that what I look like is a Clark. Salt of the earth. Kansas through and through. The freckles on my nose come from working in the Kansas sun. I have calluses on my hands that are there thanks to Kansas dirt and stubborn Kansas fields. Until you showed up, anyone who'd ever known me would've laughed at the notion that I could ever be anything but a Clark."

Cayetano managed to keep his sigh in check. "I understand this is difficult for you." He did not, in fact, understand. But what could it harm him to say otherwise? He was not precisely lauded for his empathy, but he cast about for some now. "It cannot be easy to be so far from your home, thrust into unfamiliar surroundings, and expected to behave according to others' wishes. I do not envy you."

Her frown eased somewhat. But then it turned speculative. "Is that what it was like for you? When you were sent off to boarding school at a young age?" He must have stared, because she blinked. "The majordomo told me all kinds of history. Some of it was yours."

Cayetano felt himself tense, but tried to dismiss it.

"If there were hardships, they pale in comparison to the hardships my people have suffered."

Normally when he said things like that, anyone who heard him started nodding vigorously, because the cause was always paramount—and especially for him. No one actually said *amen,* but it was implied.

Delaney did neither. If anything, she looked quizzical. "It's not like suffering is a pie and if one person gets a piece no one else can have some. Tragically, there's always enough to go around."

Cayetano felt something inside him…tilt and go precarious, suddenly. He didn't understand what it was. "I don't believe I attempted to quantify suffering."

"It's what you do, though, isn't it?" She phrased that as a question, yet did not appear to actually be asking. "You never actually talk about your feelings. You talk about your country."

"My country matters," Cayetano retorted. His fingers tightened, ever so slightly, on hers. "My feelings do not."

She looked down at their joined hands as if there was some significance there that he had missed. He found himself looking, too, and was furious with himself.

"Is it that your feelings don't matter or that you don't know how to identify them?"

"What is the Signorina teaching you?" And he recognized the new sensation rising inside him. It was as if he was preparing for battle. He felt the way he sometimes did, honed and ready, as if at any moment he would be required to fight to the death.

Not the physical battles of his ancestors, swords and blood. His battles had mostly been in the press. But the preparation within him was the same. And he always landed his blows.

And there was a very specific battle he wished to undertake with this woman—but it was not this one. And it was not about blows, but passion.

"You look angry," Delaney observed with maddening calm.

"I doubt that very much," he managed to reply, with a reasonable facsimile of calm. Through his teeth. "I cannot get angry. As policy."

"Says the man who identifies himself as a warlord, angrily."

"Warlord is a title." Cayetano made himself smile. Or curve his lips, anyway. "A title I take seriously. A warlord cannot afford anger. Not in these uncertain times."

She tilted her head to one side, her blue eyes seeing far too much. "Do you actually know when you're angry?"

And it was suddenly as if everything inside of him was jumbled all around and out of place. He felt out of control again, and he wasn't even touching her the way he wanted to do. He could not abide the *mess* of it.

Or the fact that it was more than that madness that had overtaken him when he'd kissed her before. It was as if she'd reached inside him and threw everything out of place, and he couldn't understand how that could be. He was a fortress. And while this was an odd conversation, it was innocuous. Surely it was no more than idle talk.

Yet inside him, the call to battle kept sounding.

Cayetano attempted to settle himself down in the usual way, by thinking about their upcoming wedding. Because nothing mattered but that. All roads led to that ceremony.

"Plans for our wedding are well underway," he told her. Gruffly.

And only when she drew her hand from his, then crossed her arms, did he understand that he had deliberately changed the subject so that she could be the one on the defensive here.

He couldn't say he liked what that said about him.

"The wedding of the warlord would normally be an international affair," he said, pushing forward despite the way she was regarding him. "We have many allies in different countries and we usually like them to take part in our rituals. It legitimizes them. Not that we require legitimacy, but it does make claims to the contrary from the palace below more difficult."

He trusted that the majordomo had done his job and Delaney knew that *the palace below* was how his people had referred to the seat of the Montaigne family's power, sitting pretty in its own rocky cove on the island's prettiest beach.

Because of course it did.

"No one's consulted me about any wedding plans." And while her tone was still calm, Cayetano could easily read the temper in her gaze.

"Why would they?" he asked, finding it far easier to make himself appear at ease now that it was her temper on the rise. "You have far too much on your plate as it is. Learning to accept your new role. Exploring your new home."

Becoming his Queen.

She glared at him. "I think that if there are wedding plans, they should include the bride. That seems reasonable, doesn't it? Otherwise it starts to look a lot like you're hiding something. Or plotting something."

"Anyone can be a bride, Delaney." He was enjoying himself now, even if, somewhere deep inside, where everything seemed to have found its place again, he questioned himself and his motives. And deeper still, he wondered why it was that only she managed to penetrate all the shields he'd spent his whole life nailing into place. "All a bride need do is appear at the wedding. But not everyone can train to become the next Queen of Ile d'Montagne."

Then he watched as she clearly wrestled with her reaction to the idea of becoming Queen. Very clearly. Very obviously.

He found it more intriguing than he should have.

"One thing at a time," she said after a moment, though her eyes darkened. "First I need to become a bride. I should focus on that. Something that would be easier to do if I was actually included in my own wedding plans."

"And by *focus on that* do you mean you wish to actually plan our wedding?" He wanted to touch her again, so he did, reaching over to run his hand down the length of one bare arm, delighting in the way she shivered at the contact. And the goose bumps that marked the path he'd taken. "Or do you mean you would like to obstruct any wedding plans so that they never come to pass?"

He hadn't intended to accuse her, or not so directly. It had been more of an idle question, really, because he knew what she did not—that nothing would stop their wedding. This was Ile d'Montagne and he was the warlord. It was his vow that made them one, not her compliance.

But he opted not to share that nugget of ancient law with her. Because it made sense to wait, to create a scene that could be extensively photographed and beamed around the world. To make sure valley artisans made a dress that was worthy of a queen.

To make sure that she was already considered a queen before he made it clear to everyone that she would be the next one here.

Yet her response showed him that the question was

not idle at all. Her cheeks bloomed a new red. And she looked as guilty as if he'd caught her in the middle of a desperate act.

"I'm shocked," he drawled. When, in truth, he was charmed. Captivated. It should have worried him more than it did. "Do you truly imagine you can scheme against me?"

"You said I had a month. It's been two weeks. Barely."

"I said the wedding would be in a month and so it shall be." She made as if to argue and he shrugged. "You knew the choices before you, Delaney. Perhaps I should remind you that at any time I can make my claim upon you. We do not need to plan a wedding at all."

"No," she said hurriedly, and maybe there was something wrong with him that he took such pleasure in the panic in her gaze. "I want to plan it. That's all I meant."

"You're a liar, little one."

But he couldn't muster up the sense of outrage that should have accompanied a statement like that. He, who prized honesty so dearly. There was something about the genuine distress in her blue eyes that made it impossible.

"Cayetano," she said, sounding as if she was working very hard to consider each word carefully. Or maybe she wanted to taste his name as much as he liked to taste hers. "I don't want you to get the wrong idea. I'm not lying. Or I don't mean to lie. But you want me to accept two overwhelming things, and you want that acceptance immediately."

She paused, as if waiting for him to argue, but all he did was incline his head.

Delaney let out a shaky breath, then continued. "One overwhelming thing is that I'm not the person I thought I was my entire life. That instead, I'm this completely *other* person, who is meant to live in places like this and has to worry about *artful conversation* as a potential weapon of diplomacy when what I know is corn. And the other is your apparent belief that it's perfectly reasonable to marry a total stranger. It's only been fourteen days, Cayetano. That's not enough time. For acceptance. For anything."

He settled in against the railing, studying her lovely face. She didn't need the cosmetics she wore, but he liked the way they enhanced her natural beauty. The truth was, he liked every version of her that he'd encountered so far. Including this one tonight.

The one who spoke of needing more time when the Signorina reported that she came to her daily lessons eagerly. And enjoyed herself, by all accounts. Almost as if she'd already accepted more than she wanted to admit.

To herself.

"And what amount of time do you imagine it would require for you to make yourself easy about both of these things?" he asked her.

She dropped her arms and opened her palms to the sky. "A year? Five years? A lifetime?"

"I sympathize." And the strange thing was that he did. But it would not save her. "And yet you must know that these things cannot wait."

"Maybe not forever." Her voice was a whisper. Her eyes had gone big in the lantern light as she pled her case. "But surely they can wait a little while."

The strangest sensation washed over him then, more shocking to him than if he'd suddenly lost his footing and plummeted over the steep side of the castle walls. It was something about how plaintive her voice was. Or how wide her eyes were. Maybe it was her voice. All of it. None of it. How could he tell?

Maybe it was the simple fact of her, so unlike any

other woman he'd ever known, with her talk of dirt and calluses on the one hand and her interest in his bloody feelings on the other. When what he was used to was simpering and flattery and attempts to spend more time in his bed than he wished. From women who apparently failed to comprehend that he was actually a man, flesh and blood and possessed of a few stray thoughts that did not involve the cause.

His own people had never seen into him like this woman did.

No one ever had.

It should have been dizzying. Perhaps it was. Perhaps that was this new sensation inside—a kind of mad intoxication that would lead to peril, whether he toppled over the walls or lost himself the way his parents had.

But he rather thought instead it was something far more curious.

There was a part of him that wanted to give her time. That wanted her to find her way into this. To meet him here.

Yes, they were strangers. Yes, this was swift, and there were a thousand reasons not to marry in haste and only one reason to go ahead—a reason that had nothing to do with her, save a trick of DNA and a careless hospital.

Yet the part of him that wanted to give her time was the part that didn't care about any of that. It cared that at the root of it all, he wanted her.

He had set eyes on her in that yard, before he'd even exited his car, and he'd wanted her.

The way normal men must want, he'd thought at the time. With so much desperation and uncertainty when he should have been filled instead with purpose. Because she was the answer to generations of prayers.

She was his endgame.

And still he wanted to wait. Not so he could stage a wedding that would captivate the imaginations of the world as he was doing now. What he was doing now made sense. This urge in him to let her find her way to him was a traitor.

Because you want her to want you, came a voice within. *Not the warlord of this valley, the true King of this island. But you. Cayetano. The man.*

But that was a treachery he did not intend to allow this night. It was far too seismic to take on.

"I'm sympathetic to the whiplash you must feel, given your change in circumstances," he told her, hoping he gave no hint of his inner turmoil. Or how desperately he wanted her in all the ways he shouldn't. "It cannot be easy to have the world you know swept from beneath you so swiftly. I cannot apologize for it, but I do understand it can't be easy."

She looked at him for a long while, there in the darkness with only the lantern light between them. It made everything seem closer. Warmer.

It made him wonder if *feeling* was not so terrible after all.

"I suppose I am trying to think of it all as a gift," she said, as if she was confessing. As if it was not easy to get out the words. "It's not a gift I would have chosen. But it's better to know the truth than live a lie, right?" She let out a laugh, though it was rueful. "That's what my grandmother always said."

"She sounds a wise woman," Cayetano said.

He chose not to point out that her actual grandmother had been the icy Queen Carlota, notable for both her cruelty and her voracious appetites. Not a font of wisdom, the little-mourned Carlota.

But he kept that to himself.

And felt virtuous in his restraint.

"I can't say that I'm coming to terms with it, exactly," Delaney told him in the same confessional tone. "It helps that every time I try to call my mother, she's too busy setting up her new life to talk to me for more than five minutes. And she sounds happy. Two weeks ago she barely had a life. For that alone, I guess I'm grateful."

"Then perhaps, little one, you do not need so many years after all."

"Accepting that it's true isn't the same thing as accepting it's who I am." Delaney pulled in a breath and straightened her shoulders, and the way she looked at him changed. Intensified, maybe. "But it's the other part that I'm more worried about. Because what I accept or don't accept doesn't have a time limit, does it? But this wedding of yours does."

"You said that your primary objection is marrying a stranger," Cayetano reminded her. "But I'm not so strange, am I?"

That fine line between her brows made an appearance. "I don't know you at all."

"You know the most important things." He inclined his head. "You know that I need you, which gives you power."

If he'd expected that to make her easy, he was disappointed. She scowled at him.

"When my grandmother used to talk about falling in love with my grandfather, she talked about a lot of things. How quiet he was with everyone except her. How he looked at her as if she was prettier every day. The nicknames that were only theirs. She never once mentioned *power* unless it was a story about waiting out a tornado." Delaney shook her head. At him. "Weirdly, she was much more focused on love."

Once again, he was struck by how much he liked the sheen of temper in her gaze. He wanted to taste her fire. He wanted a woman who could handle his own. He could not help but think this all boded well.

Despite this talk of feelings.

"Love is a wondrous thing, or so I'm told," he said dismissively. "But it is not all things. Love is blind, but with the power you already possess, you also know certain truths. I cannot harm you, for how would that look? The eyes of the world will be upon us the moment your true status is known. That makes you safe. I assume it is why you came with me so easily."

She did not nod along enthusiastically to that. On the contrary, her eyes narrowed, and she looked at him as if he didn't make sense. "It hadn't actually occurred to me to be worried about my safety. Until now."

"Then you are even more sheltered than I imagined." He could hear that his voice had gone rough. "What could possibly be more important than your safety?"

Delaney laughed a little, and looked something like dazed. "When you put it that way, it does seem silly. But I've always felt safe." She shook her head slightly. "Even though it's very clear to me that you are by far the most dangerous man I've ever met."

There was something so innocent in the way she said that. It nearly unmanned him. Because she did not seem to understand the great compliment she was giving him.

And he could not bear to tell her.

Though turned out, he could not bear to let it slide by unremarked, either. "I will never hurt you, Delaney," he managed to grit out. "Know this, if nothing else."

She nodded, slowly, as if she was busy considering him. "Cayetano. Why would you think that my expectation is that you would hurt me?"

Once again, this all seemed to be inching a little too close to topics he did not discuss. Ever. "I only wish to make you feel easy about the choice before you."

"Is that it?" That blue gaze seemed to see straight through him, again. When he had always considered himself opaque. He had reveled in it, in fact. "Because this is starting to seem as if it's a great deal more personal."

But Cayetano thought only of the history of his people. Not his history. Not his family.

Not the choices that had been made when he was too young to have a voice.

Not the things that had happened that he'd been unable to prevent. The wild, raging displays that were his legacy—the legacy he had decidedly turned his back on.

All in the name of one love or another, so that the word itself was suspect.

He spoke of none of this.

And still his heart hammered against his ribs, as if he was that young boy once again. Trapped in the decisions of others so far away from home.

"I'm glad you've given no thought to your safety," he told her silkily. "That either makes you very foolish or me very trustworthy. I choose to believe it is both."

"Wait—" she began.

"The fact of the matter is this," he said, cutting her off, no longer worried that he might sound too forbidding. Too ruthless. He was both. "It is not that I dislike the modern take on marriage. I am modern myself in many ways. But falling in love, getting to know another, and wasting so much time… These might seem like virtues, perhaps, on a farm. In this Kansas of yours. But here we speak not of cornfields, but kingdoms. And you already know all you need to know. I am not brutal. I have vowed not to harm you and I have not. In cases like ours, this should be enough."

"Maybe that's enough for you. It's not enough for me."

And she lifted her chin while she said that, clearly not recognizing that doing that only made her more beautiful to him. Because he was not brutal, that was true. But he was still a warlord. He liked the battle. It was only that the battleground had changed in this modern era. He did not intend to fight Queen Esme on horseback, surrounded by warriors. He did not intend to use his hands. But his future wife?

Well. He would use the weapons he had.

"Do you want romance?" he asked her. "Love?"

He had been taking care not to sound mocking, but she still jerked her head away as if he'd slapped at her. "And if I say yes?" Her eyes flashed. "What then? Will you start spouting poetry?"

"I have already given you a sample of the only poetry I know," Cayetano told her, dark and low. "And if memory serves, my little farm girl, you loved it."

"You have never given me a poem." She glared in that way that sent a bolt of pure desire straight to his sex. "I think I would remember."

"Memories are so fickle," he murmured.

Cayetano reached over and hooked his hand around her neck. He pulled her close, taking a deep pleasure in the way her lips parted immediately. The way heat and awareness bloomed in her gaze. And the way she melted into him as if this edgy, encompassing wanting was in her, too. As if it had claimed them both.

"Pay attention, Delaney," he told her. "This is a sonnet."

And then he fit his mouth to hers once more.

CHAPTER NINE

DELANEY HAD STUDIED poetry in high school like everybody else. She wasn't any kind of expert on the subject. But one thing she did know was that no poem she'd ever read for English class had exploded inside her like this.

It was different from that kiss her first afternoon here. Better. Wilder.

He kissed her and he kissed her, his hard mouth making her feel fluttery, everywhere. Parts of her that shouldn't have fluttered at all couldn't seem to stop. Maybe she was the flutter. And maybe she didn't care. She felt reckless and sure as his hard mouth claimed hers again and again.

She meant to push him away, because surely she should *want* to push him away, but instead her hands got tangled on him. Lost somewhere in the sweep of his wide, hard chest. Her fingers curled around the lapels of the suit he wore, and she relished the fact that she could cling to something. Anything.

Because everything else was a storm of sensation. It pounded through her. It stole her away and redeemed her anew as his tongue stroked hers. It was all pulse and heartbeat, sensation and need.

She hadn't known that a person could ache like this,

filled with an almost pain for something she couldn't even name. It felt like a prayer.

Delaney kept thinking, when she could think at all, that she hadn't known what she was missing.

On and on he kissed her with what she could tell, even half out of her mind, was both consummate skill and an edgy sort of passion. Something in her recognized it. Thrilled to it.

Wanted it—and him—all the more.

Something in her cracked open, wider and wider with every touch of his tongue to hers.

As if this was her true homecoming. His hands on her neck. His mouth on hers. And the storm that she thought she'd be perfectly happy to see rage on forever as long as he kept kissing her like this.

Like he might die if he stopped.

His scent was all around her now. It was indefinably male and entirely him. She wondered if later, if she survived this, she would be unable to breathe without the scent careening through her.

And even imagining that made it better. The intensity seemed brighter.

She shuddered, low and long.

And for some reason, that made him laugh in much the same way.

For a moment, she remembered herself. Her goals—or the fact that she ought to have had goals these last two weeks. She should have demanded to be taken to meet her biological relative at the very least. But she hadn't. Every day she'd meant to make that stand, but she hadn't.

Maybe this was why. She could see only Cayetano, and beyond him, the stars.

She could only see him and ever since she'd laid eyes

on him at the farm, he was all she wanted to see. Here, now, she could finally admit that.

This was what she wanted. Or no matter what Catherine had said to her about *adventure,* she would never have gotten in that car.

There were more complicated reasons she hadn't forced the issue of meeting the Queen. That hadn't changed.

But there was also this.

There was Cayetano.

And this magical, marvelous fire between them that burned hotter by the moment.

When he pulled her close again, then hauled her up even further so he could hold her in his arms, all she could do was melt.

This time, he kissed her with all the wondrous desperation from before. She met him with the same yearning, the same fire.

But this time, as their lips tangled, the hand that wasn't gripping her and holding her to him…traveled.

Down her bared shoulder, then to the bodice of her dress, unerringly finding her breast and lifting it out. He broke off from the kiss again, but before she could think to protest the loss, he bent his head. Shifting her as he held her there—outside, where presumably anyone could see them if they had a view of his balcony, and why didn't she care?—he bent his mouth to her breast instead.

And when his lips closed on her nipple, proud and taut, it was as if all the stars in the sky above her crashed into her.

She let her head fall back. Her hands were fists on his shoulders.

But Cayetano…slowed down.

He slowed down, and then, if she wasn't mistaken and it was her own pounding heart, he growled.

Then he did it again, and there was no confusing it. It was a profoundly male sound. It seemed to crash through her like so many stars, but they all landed deeper. Lower.

And one by one, began to burn there, low in her belly.

She had the notion, intense and beautiful, that he was devouring her. Eating her alive where they stood.

His mouth kept working at her breasts, and she arched her back so she could better offer herself to him. So she could be certain that he didn't miss a single part of her.

Because she would have sworn in this moment that she had been born for this.

For him.

She was so consumed with what he was doing that she almost missed the way his hand tracked lower, finding her hip and the outside of her thigh where the fabric of the dress parted. His mouth moved against her nipples, one and then the other, but his hand found the roundness of her bottom and squeezed tight.

That, too, was a storm.

Too many storms to name.

And then everything felt tinged with red, hectic and stunning at once, as that same hand reversed track, but this time beneath the skirt of her dress.

It seemed as if she couldn't quite take in the sensation that moved through her. She couldn't catalog it. She could only ride it out. His wonderful, devilish mouth. The arm that held her up and the hand that gripped her side. And below, his marvelously strong fingers as they traced a path—slowly, agonizingly, beautifully—up along the inside of her thigh.

She thought she might die when he finally reached the soft heat between her thighs.

But she didn't. Delaney had never felt so alive.

Bristling with need, beautiful and impossibly lush—

Cayetano continued into her wet heat, circling the center of her need until she found herself making the strangest keening noises. Then, with a twist of his wrist, he plunged deep within.

His thumb found her outside while his finger stroked deep within. His mouth stayed busy at her breast. Everything was fire and a tugging wet heat, and then she had absolutely no choice.

No choice and no fight in her.

Delaney didn't so much fall apart as fly.

She became stars, all of them at once, and it was hot and, oh, so bright.

It was him, Cayetano, in all his dark glory.

And she was certain of only one thing as she burst bright and then became so many torn apart pieces that she felt she was made of stars herself.

She would never be the same again.

But he gave her no time to contemplate what that might mean. She was dimly aware that he set her back on her feet. Even tucked her breasts back into place with a surprising gentleness, and then, without a single word from her—because she could hardly speak and wouldn't know what to say—he ushered her back into his dining room. And seated her. So that they shared the corner of the table.

And by the time she blinked herself fully awake and aware again, the food was served.

Delaney hardly knew what to do with herself. She hadn't noticed the servants' arrival and was only dimly aware when they withdrew. And Cayetano seemed not to notice that she merely sat there, undone. Completely and totally undone. Or maybe he did notice, she amended a moment later, because he served her as well as him.

And everything on her plate made her mouth water,

but how to concentrate on food? That wasn't what she was hungry for.

She still felt as if everything in her was simmering along, coming closer and closer to a boil. Her body felt like it no longer belonged to her. As if the way he had touched her, so masterful, so certain, had altered her. Inside and out.

Her thoughts spooled out in her head like songs. Like a melody she couldn't quite catch. The burnt gold of his eyes. What he'd said about her safety when she worried about his. That impossible storm he brewed in her, and how eagerly she'd leaped over an edge she had never known was there.

There had been no edges in Kansas. No cliffs.

She watched him eat in silence, the heat in her rising and rising, cresting toward that boil as her own body seemed to work against her—or maybe with her—

But when he looked over at her, his gaze was darker. Knowing. And that mouth of his that she'd now tasted and learned and craved…curved.

She felt as struck as if he'd hit her. She wanted to jump to her feet and announce what was so obvious to her. That she wasn't the same woman who'd walked into this room feeling like a queen. That her entire *being* was different. That she had changed, profoundly, and how could he *eat dinner*?

This was yet another edge and she'd already gone hurtling off the side. He should have seen her, catapulting out into space.

Delaney thought she might explode. Or maybe she already had. Maybe that was the trouble. Maybe that was where all the commotion inside her came from.

Her problem was, she had no idea where it was going to go.

"I've never actually had sex," she announced.

Which summed up everything and nothing. It was just awkward and embarrassing. When inside her, what she'd wanted to say was all elegance and lyricism.

She instantly wanted to snatch those words back, particularly when they seemed to land with such a loud *thunk* in the middle of the brightly tiled mosaic table.

But then again, perhaps not, because the heat in Cayetano's mythic gaze…shifted.

And Delaney felt a different sort of warmth move through her, almost as if this bizarre night had turned… affectionate.

Don't kid yourself, she lectured herself sternly. *You know exactly what this man's interest is in you.*

"You have my condolences," Cayetano said after a long moment that felt breathless to her. "That seems an unfortunate oversight."

"If I had a boyfriend at all, it was the farm," Delaney told him, still trying to find her feet beneath her. She was glad she was sitting down. "And besides, I never understood how my friends from high school were suddenly able to overlook the fact that the boys in our class when we were seventeen were the same boys in our class from when we were six. With much the same issues in the way of personal hygiene and questionable behavior." She wrinkled up her nose. "It seemed like everyone had amnesia, but I didn't."

Cayetano did not comment on the dearth of acceptable suitors back home. Instead, he filled her wineglass with something rich and red, that smelled to her of currants and honey. The one other time she'd tried wine it had been from an illicit box at a high school friend's bachelorette party, and it had been notable for its grittiness and sour taste. But when she pressed this glass to her lips, the kiss of his wine warmed her almost the way he did, leaving a kind of yearning on her tongue.

"I don't drink much, either," she said very solemnly over the rim of her glass. "So if this is an attempt to loosen me up, well… It's going to work."

"Excellent."

His intense eyes crinkled in the corners and that made her feel as if she was turning cartwheels when she knew she was sitting still. He reached across the corner of the table that separated them and pulled on one of the tendrils that had fallen free from the rest of her hair, tied back in such a complicated arrangement it had taken all of her servants to make it work.

And she probably shouldn't have allowed him to toy with her hair. Or with her. But she was still hot and molten between her legs. There were still all those sensations charging around inside of her. Her breasts were so oversensitized that she felt shooting streaks of electricity every time she breathed. So all she did was cup her wineglass between her hands, take another, deeper sip, and carry on talking.

"I expected to get married someday," she told him. He was curling that strand of hair around and around his finger, tugging it slightly, and somehow that made everything between them just that little bit dizzy. "But all I cared about was the farm, you see. So it couldn't be just anyone. It had to be another farmer, and how do you find a farmer who's willing to farm your land, not his?"

Again, that lift at the corners of his eyes. As good as a belly laugh from another man. "I am afraid, little one, that I am not conversant on the intricacies of farmland dating in the American heartland."

She registered his dry tone, and for some reason that made her laugh. "But don't you see? I grant you, the scope is different. But at the end of the day, both you and I want to marry for land. You just think yours matters more."

Cayetano stilled. This close, she could see an arrested sort of light dawn in his eyes. And it was so strange how actually reading him made all these various sensations inside her seem to pull tighter and tighter.

As if this was what she'd wanted from the start.

To know the impossibly beautiful man, sculpted to perfection, who never should have set foot on the farm. To *know* him in every way a person could know another.

He stared back at her for a long while. Then his gaze shuttered, and he shifted to pull one of her hands into his. It felt new and almost sacred to sit there, hushed like this. Hot. To watch as he bent his head, his gaze on their linked hands while his thumb made slow, sweet sweeps against her skin.

"You're quite right," he said, and when she felt a jolt deep inside her she realized that this was a surprise, too. That she'd expected him to argue. To rant and rave about history and Montaignes and false queens.

"I beg your pardon?"

He looked up then, his expression rueful. "I said you were right. You are. It is not for me to decide the importance of the things that matter to you. My understanding is that this farm of yours is being sold."

Her throat was much too dry, suddenly. "It seems my mother found it a burden."

"And you did not?"

Delaney sighed. She hadn't been gone from Kansas long, she knew that. And yet still, the fact that she was gone at all made everything different. That was the thing about perspective, she supposed. You only recognized how little you'd had when you happened upon some.

"I would never have called it a burden," she told him, and she was aware that she had never been this honest before. Not with anyone. Not even with herself, because it would have felt like a betrayal. "It's just… That's what love is, isn't it? You put in the work because it's worth it, because you love it. Not because it will ever love you back. You work the land because that's what you do. Because you're a farmer who lives on a farm. And nothing could ever change that, or so I thought, so it never occurred to me to think in terms of whether or not it made me happy. How can you know that you're carrying a burden until you put it down and see how much it's weighed all this time?"

Again, that arrested look. And she could see something, there on his face of stone, but it was gone in the next instant.

But she knew what she'd seen. For a moment he'd almost looked…raw.

"There's absolutely no reason that you can't hold on to that land if you wish it," he said, roughly. His attention was on her linked hands again. "I will instruct my people to buy it tomorrow. It is easy enough to hire someone to tend to it."

"But it's not mine," she said quietly. And then, though it hurt, "it was never mine. If my mother doesn't want it, then it must belong instead to Princess Amalia."

Cayetano let out a derisive sound. "There is no possibility on this earth that a spoiled princess like Amalia will ever wish to dirty her hands. And certainly not somewhere so far away from the beaches of Positano or St. Tropez."

"Perhaps a princess would not." Delaney kept her gaze trained on him. "But she's not a princess, is she?"

And something seemed to swell between them. It

wasn't as simple as heat. She almost wanted to call it something else, something more like *vulnerable*—

But Cayetano made another noise, this one a deep rumble of need that seemed to lodge itself deep inside her. And then he was moving from his chair, sweeping her up from her seat and into his arms, pausing only to fuse his mouth to hers once more.

There was a part of her that wanted to protest, because she was sure that something momentous had happened here. And that if they only stayed *right here*, in this odd little moment where she was sure she could see parts of him he normally hid, they could make something kindle to life—

But his kiss was hard and hot, demanding her focus. Commanding her full attention.

She hardly knew what was happening when he began to move, carrying her out onto the balcony again. But he didn't stop there. He continued walking, still holding her aloft, before shouldering his way in through a different set of doors.

His bedroom, she understood in a haze as he laid her down on the high, imposing bed, and settled himself half beside her and half on top of her.

And then he kissed her more. Deeper. Harder. In a way that made it clear that he'd been holding himself back before.

This was different. This was raw, unchained.

Beautiful, something in her whispered.

And he built the same storm, leading her even more quickly this time toward the same edge.

Delaney had some faint presence of mind as he helped her out of her dress, growling in deep male appreciation as he found her breasts, then slipped her panties from her hips. She was aware of every moment, of every part of her that he bared with his hands, then gazed at with such delicious possessiveness. He lavished her with heat and need, stirring her to a fever pitch. Then he tossed her over the side again, this time not waiting for her to shudder back to earth.

Instead he moved further south to settle himself between her legs.

That time she screamed when she flew apart, as the warlord ate her alive.

He rolled away from her then to strip out of his own clothes, and she felt almost uncomfortably torn. There was the spectacle of his beautiful male body, somehow even more glorious out of his clothes than in them. But at the same time, she couldn't help thinking how mad this was. How unlike her.

Was she really about to do this thing that for twenty-four years had never been so much as the faintest blip on her radar?

Yes, he was beautiful. Yes, he seemed like more of a man to her than every other man she'd ever met, put together.

But this was so out of character.

He stood over her, there by the side of the bed, his eyes blazing and every line and muscle of his body held taut.

"You are already mine," he told her, his voice low and dark, like a stirring deep inside her own soul. "You are the answer to prayer. The hope of a people. This is already so, little one. But tonight, you understand, the gift of your innocence and the fact you give it to me changes everything."

"You're too late," she whispered, and it was odd that she had no sense of shame. No urge to cover herself when she had always been so modest. On the contrary, she felt wild with her own power and sat up, offering herself to him even more fully. "Everything is already changed. What's one more thing?"

And finally, Cayetano laughed. He laughed and laughed, and she understood with a deep kind of shock, a wild sort of thrill, that she had known this man so short a time. Almost no time at all, and yet would do anything for that laughter.

Anything for him, something in her whispered.

But maybe she already knew that.

Or she never would have come here.

And she certainly never would have found herself naked with this man.

She felt as unsteady as she had on the plane, but this time, he was with her. This time, she could reach and touch him, and that made all the difference. She didn't need ground beneath her feet, not when the burnt gold of his gaze seemed to cover her in all that molten heat.

As if she was made of the same stuff.

"I have already claimed you for my country, Delaney," he growled at her. He moved over her then, climbing onto the bed and lowering himself so that he pressed her down, his flesh against hers, and it was extraordinary. He braced his hands on either side of her head, holding her face where he wanted it. "But tonight, little one, I also claim you for me."

She felt him between her legs, huge and hard, and she caught her breath—whether to cheer or sob or laugh wildly herself, she would never know.

It was all molten and gold straight through.

Because with a twist of his hips he thrust himself deep. And she was soft and needy still, but yet she felt that sharp tug—

She gasped, but it was gone in an instant.

And his mouth was at her neck while he began to

move, inexorable, inescapable, and so shockingly beautiful that she didn't understand how anything could possibly feel this excruciatingly perfect—

But with every thrust of the hardest part of him deep into the heart of her heat, it got better.

When that should have been impossible.

She felt raw, exposed. And at the same time, closer to this man than she had ever been to another in her life.

He was inside her. But she felt as if she was inside him, too.

Cayetano held her against him, and she arched up so she could press herself against the wall of his chest. So she could take him deeper and deeper still. And the color of his eyes was as molten she felt—

And then everything was bright and too hot and shattering.

It went on forever.

But this time they broke apart together.

And it was a long while later when she found her way back to herself again, drowsy and inordinately pleased to find herself tucked up against his side. She could hear his breathing. His scent was all around her. She was delightfully warm though there were no covers over her.

It was only when she thought about looking for one that she realized he had never turned on a light when they'd come inside. That meant that she could lie there, his heavy arm around her and her head on his magnificent chest, and look out and see nothing but stars. Brilliant, beautiful.

As mysterious and unknowable as he was.

But even as she thought that a different sort of melody wound its way through her. Because everything was changed again. He was right about that. What had happened tonight had made too many things abundantly clear to her. But maybe because of that, something had occurred to her.

Because it was true, everything that had happened since he'd pulled up in the yard was out of character for Delaney Clark, farm girl from Kansas, who never had seen beyond the cornfields.

But that wasn't who she was. Like it or not, she was a princess. One day she would be Queen.

His Queen.

When he shifted beside her, she turned to find that he was wide-awake, the burnt gold of his eyes simmering.

And before he could speak she reached over and traced a finger over that hard, starkly sensual mouth.

She couldn't say what she wanted to say. What it hurt her not to say, with all her heart. It was too soon. Too new.

I love you, she wanted to shout. To cry. To sing.

But she couldn't say it out loud. Not yet.

So she said the next best thing instead.

"I will marry you," Delaney whispered. Not that he had been in any doubt, she knew that. But it was different for her to say it. And she could see the way it lit him up. She could feel the heavy male part of him stir against her. So she held his gaze, even as she reached her hand down to curl her fingers around that silken steel. She shuddered in anticipation, but held his gaze so there could be no mistake. "Cayetano, I will be your Queen."

CHAPTER TEN

THE DAY OF the wedding dawned blue and bright at last. Cayetano had barely slept.

And not for the usual reasons these days.

He allowed himself a smile where he stood, aware that such things as smiles came easier these days. He had dispensed with Delaney's guest quarters and had her moved into his the morning after the night she'd given herself to him, because he hadn't wanted to waste a single moment more. It wasn't just her body, that lush wonder, that called to him, though it did. It was her.

Cayetano hungered for the stories she told him, at first haltingly and then, when he asked for more tales of the alien place she'd come from, with a little theater. He longed for the wisdom wrapped up in the tart sayings she ascribed to her grandmother, so different from his own experience with family. And more and more he found he craved the steady way she listened and the calm way she talked, proving to him with every passing day that no one could possibly be more perfect for what lay ahead.

The future might be rocky as they claimed their rightful place. He knew that. But these last two weeks had been a revelation.

He might even call them a joy, had anyone dared to ask.

He would have married her and made her his Queen no matter what, but it pleased him that the Signorina reported nothing but stellar progress. And more, actually liked the woman she called their perfectly imperfect Queen. All the palace personnel adored her. Delaney had applied herself to her new role with all the determination she must have brought to bear back home, season after thankless season in those fields of hers.

And what time she did not spend preparing herself for what was to come when her identity was released to the world, or telling him her homespun stories because she delighted in making him laugh, she spent in his bed.

It had been only two short weeks and yet Cayetano found he could no longer recall another woman's face. Delaney's taste haunted him. He even found himself drawing the kinds of boundaries he never had before with his men, because he needed to make sure he got back to her as soon as he could. As often as he could.

Soon enough there would be nothing but the cause again, as there had always been, all his life.

And every time he tripped over his own alarms, his own red flags, he reminded himself that he was not his mother. His aim was to fulfill the centuries-long dream of his people, not pervert it to his own ends. And today, as he waited for his bride at last in the grand courtyard of Arcieri Castle, he admitted to himself that it was true. He had lost his head a little these last weeks.

Some part of him was already grieving that these heady, magical days needed to end, but they did.

You could only give yourself so fully because it was temporary, a voice in him said. He wanted to believe it. He really did.

But it didn't matter what he believed. Today was the day that everything changed.

He heard a cheer go up and he took in the sight of so many of his people packed onto all the galleries and balconies, even peering out the windows, all of them there to catch a glimpse of this moment.

This moment that was theirs. It belonged to them, after all this time. There was no foreign press, no dignitaries. There was only Cayetano, warlord only a little while longer, and the lost Montaigne Princess—who appeared in the grand entryway dressed in a snowy white that made the black of her hair and the blue of her eyes seem enchanted.

Or maybe her smile did that.

Still, there was only Delaney, who had insisted that she hold wildflowers picked from the valley floor today, endearing herself to his people forever.

Delaney, who'd given herself to him so fully, and with such innocent delight, that even thinking of her beneath him made something deep within him shudder.

But that, too, was about to change.

He had told himself repeatedly over these last two weeks that this was merely a little breath, that was all. He'd spent his whole life fighting and the better part of these last years searching for her. Today he would marry her. No one could fault him for these too-short weeks of enjoying her before the world found out about her.

But now the day had come. Now, at long last, the throne of Ile d'Montagne was within the grasp of an Arcieri.

Cayetano told himself that he was impatient with this ceremony only because it was the final necessary step before he launched himself straight on into his destiny.

But as his beautiful bride held his hands there at the altar they'd made, and repeated her vows in that lovely voice of hers—gone husky with emotion just as her eyes filled with tears—he accepted another truth, too.

He wanted the coming space between them. Because he was terribly afraid that Delaney wasn't the only one surrendering herself here.

And that was unacceptable. He could not allow himself to falter. He knew what might well become of him if he did.

As the priest intoned the words of the ancient rite, Cayetano found himself searching the windows on the highest level of the castle, looking for the blazing set of eyes he knew all too well.

His mother, trotted out today as an emblem of his enduring mercy. Allowed to attend her son's wedding, but only from afar, lest she take it upon herself to try take her son's place.

Again.

But no matter how many times Cayetano told himself that he was done with his mother and satisfied with where they had ended up, when he saw her again it was as if he'd started from scratch.

It couldn't have been more different from what he shared with Delaney, but something about his mother wedged its way beneath his armor, too.

He jerked his eyes away from hers, focused once more on his bride, and somehow controlled the pulse of impatience inside him. For he had come too far to fall now.

When it was time, Cayetano kissed her.

His wife. His Queen.

His.

And he had intended to set the necessary wheels in motion immediately, but something in the way she looked at him stopped him. Or maybe it was that blazing flame of possessiveness that moved in him. He didn't want to leave her.

It should have horrified him to think such a thing. It did.

"Everyone is dancing," she said, and he could see the delight on her face as she turned back toward the crowd.

And he didn't have it in him to stamp it out.

She looked around, lit up with wonder. Because the people were dancing, right where they stood. He took her hand, and led her to the courtyard, where the crowd cried and stamped, danced and cheered around them. Then he led her up onto the ramparts, so she could look out and see all the people lined up outside the castle. The flags waving, the cheers seeming to well up from the valley itself to scrape the sky above.

"You have not merely married me today," he told her. With a fierceness he should not have allowed. "You have set us free."

And once again she proved herself, because she took his hands in hers, fixed her gaze on his, and did not shrug the moment away. "I will do my best to be the Queen you told me I could be. A bridge between the royal family and this valley. Never a barrier."

And for a moment, standing there high above the valley, while his people danced out their jubilation and Delaney was still only his, something in him turned over.

He almost let himself wonder what would happen if he...put it off a day. This revolution that no one knew was coming. These announcements no one awaited. What if he pushed it back another week, maybe three? Surely everyone deserved a honeymoon, even the true King of a contested throne.

Especially when he'd already won. Everything now was the bitter details.

He saw his mother's face again, her eyes still so bright with resentment. The embodiment of bitterness when once upon a time, she had burned with a different kind of zealotry.

He would not succumb to the same temptations. He would not become the very thing he loathed.

But he couldn't seem to say the words. Not when Delaney was gazing at him the way she was now, her face so soft and yet her eyes so fierce. Not when everything in him clamored to wait. To hold her here. To sink into this moment.

To live for something else, if only for the night.

The treachery of that thought appalled him. He might as well be his parents all over again, giving lip service to the cause but in the end, only truly dedicated to their own selfishness. Was that what he wanted?

When he had come so far? When he had made vows to himself that he would never, ever risk his people in this way?

When he had been so sure that he would be better?

His own weakness sickened him.

"I must leave you," he told Delaney abruptly. Sternly, as if she'd tried to stop him. "There's much to do."

She looked startled. "Now? We have not been married an hour."

"My people have waited for centuries," he told her, sounding all the more disapproving because he felt much the same. "Surely they need not wait another moment."

His own gut twisted at that, because she didn't look angry. She looked hurt. But she looked away for a moment, and when she looked back her gaze was clear.

And he told himself that he had imagined it, that was all. For his Delaney was nothing if not practical.

"Of course," she said in her usual calm way. "You must do what is necessary, Cayetano. I understand."

And he didn't like how hard it was to walk away. He didn't like that when he found his ministers and they gathered together to begin this much-planned and plotted-out endgame, no small part of him wanted to turn around and go back.

The sound of his own wedding was loud inside the stone walls as the party raged on in the courtyard. And instead of feeling nothing but pride and determination as he trod up the steps that would lead him to the throne at last, he felt…a kind of hollowness.

He had no idea what to call it. No clue what it was. He had never encountered such a thing before.

Especially not when he should have been triumphant straight down to his bones.

But he encountered it a lot over the next weeks of work and strategy, worse every day until he admitted the unnerving truth.

He missed her.

Sometimes he missed her so much it neared the point of pain, but by the time he identified the problem, it was too late.

Because Cayetano had finally gotten what he wanted.

He had finally turned the Montaigne family rule on its head.

He had released news of his wedding first with the photographs of the two of them at the altar, looking, as one of his ministers liked to say, like love's young dream incarnate. He had used every media contact he'd ever made to sell the world a love story.

And the world had responded.

Loudly.

It turned out the story of a farm girl Cinderella and

a throneless king caught the fancy of well-wishers the globe over. Their wedding photos appeared on the front covers of magazines and papers in too many countries to count. Delaney was an instant icon, a title she disliked intensely—but after a particularly enterprising paparazzo dug out a photo of her in her overalls, no retailer could keep them in stock. Anywhere.

Talking heads in a slew of languages discussed her *eclectic style,* from comfortable overalls to her fairy-tale gown.

"They talk of your gravitas and they wonder what undergarments I wear," Delaney said one morning as they watched some of the coverage in his office, too many ministers about for it to be anything like the private moment Cayetano craved. "I'm sorry, but how is this a ringing endorsement?"

"It's spin," his media guru said shortly. "We want people to look up to the warlord. We want them to imagine they *are* you."

Delaney smiled politely back at the man and murmured her thanks.

Cayetano, for some reason, wanted to kill him.

He refrained.

And he waited until his first in-depth, televised interview, with Delaney at his side, to drop the bomb of her parentage.

"Imagine my surprise to discover that this perfect woman is also the true heir to the Ile d' Montagne throne," he said, as if he had happened upon Delaney on her farm and had then uncovered her parentage. He had not lied about how they met. He had simply not explained it.

Delaney laughed a bit ruefully, looking straight into the cameras. "Imagine mine," she said dryly.

And the world's love affair turned into sheer adoration.

While Cayetano sat back and let the debris fly where it would.

At first it was nothing short of a tempest. It blew and blew, and it was hard to tell if he was exhilarated by the intensity of the storm or if he wanted to it to die down. Maybe both.

It went on and on. Tests upon tests were demanded, laboratories were questioned, more tests were required. Emissaries from the Montaignes exchanged bitter words with the Arcieri representatives, and vice versa. But eventually, all the storming about in the world had to give way to the inescapable truth.

Especially in the glare of so much attention. And Delaney's rising popularity.

"I have been personally summoned to Palais Montaigne," Delaney told him one day. He had been up late the night before strategizing, and had found her in their bed, asleep. She had woken when he'd stretched out beside her and they'd come together the way they did so often these days. Wordless. Desperate.

It was never enough.

Cayetano found himself missing those weeks before the wedding, when the days had seemed to last forever and the nights twice as long. He had explored her body in every possible way, yes, but they had also had time to sit together. Sometimes he had held her in his lap, wrapped up in a blanket as they'd sat out on the balcony, telling each other silly, throwaway things while the moon rose above them.

He had never expected to miss anyone the way he missed her now, even when she stood before him.

The way she did today, and he felt another pang, for

there was no sign left of his farm girl. He hadn't been able to get rid of those overalls quick enough, the world was obsessed with them, and now he found himself missing them, almost. Because this Delaney was almost *too* polished. This was the Delaney who sat beside him in interviews and sounded cultured. Sophisticated. Royal. No trace of Kansas about her.

Today she was dressed in one of her uniforms, a quietly elegant A-line dress in a bright shade that complemented her coloring. Nothing too flashy. Nothing off-putting. Her hair was styled to casual perfection as it fell around her shoulders. She sat in his office with her usual self-possession, as if she hadn't noticed that they only really talked here, now.

She had long since far exceeded even his most optimistic hopes for her.

He had made a farm girl into the perfect princess.

Cayetano should have felt nothing but joy at his success.

And yet.

"I am not surprised that the Montaignes finally wish to see you in their lair," he said, trying to focus on the matter at hand, not these strange and unwelcome *feelings* that seemed to pounce on him at odd hours. These bizarre emotions he would have said he was immune to, for he always had been before. "They have tested and retested your blood. And Princess Amalia's. And Queen Esme's, too. It's only been a matter of time."

Once again, he thought he saw a glimpse of something too dark in her gaze, but it was gone in the next breath.

"Time has run out, apparently," she said in the same steady way she said everything these days. He found himself recalling that brash, awkward girl who had blurted out her innocence at his table.

That version of Delaney seemed like a dream he'd had.

"It is an invitation to private dinner with the Queen," she told him. "Family only. She has not mentioned you specifically, but I'd prefer it if you came."

"She's testing you." Cayetano sat back in his chair and wished his wide desk was not between them. "She wishes to see for herself how ambitious you are."

Delaney frowned and he was so pleased to see it—a *frown*, for God's sake—that it was unseemly.

"What does ambition have to do with an awkward family dinner?" she asked.

"An ambitious woman would come without her husband," Cayetano told her smoothly, but he was more focused on the novelty of seeing her frown at him to worry that she was that sort of woman. "And dedicate herself to making an ally of the Queen instead." He considered her for a moment. "Is that what you wish to do?"

Delaney shrugged, and something in him eased, because it was the shrug of that girl he'd found in Kansas, not the perfect princess he crafted here. He did not care to examine how relieved he was to see she was still in there. "I don't really see the point. She is not young. And whether she and I are allies or not will not matter in the end, will it?"

He found himself smiling at her. At that relentless practicality. "As you say."

But then his ministers were at the door again, Delaney excused herself, and it was another late night of giving interviews to different time zones. And once again he found her sleeping when he made it to their bedroom. This time she did not wake, so he lay down beside her and waited for sleep to claim him.

And found himself wondering why it was that now,

having gotten what he wanted in every possible way, he had never felt more alone.

Come morning, Cayetano was appalled at his own mawkishness. He punished himself with a brutal training exercise with his guards, then prepared himself for the showdown he'd been anticipating for most of his life.

Tonight he would face Queen Esme. And not as a rebel, but as the man who would take back her throne. But first, he took himself to see the other woman who'd influenced his life beyond measure.

His mother.

Her lover, his would-be stepfather, had left the country after Cayetano had defeated him in combat. His mother could have taken that option, but had chosen to remain instead. Even though he would only allow her to do so under supervision.

"Call it what it is, Cayetano," she said this day the way she always did. She lit herself one of the long cigarettes she favored—as much because he disliked them as anything else, he assumed. "The mighty warlord has kept his mother in jail while he makes a run at the throne. How proud you must be."

"Soon you will be as free as the rest of us," he told her, deliberately bland. Because he knew how to annoy her, too. "Tonight I dine with Queen Esme. I have already married her true heir. The deed is done, Mother."

His mother blew out a plume of clove-scented smoke. "A lost princess, switched at birth." She shook her head. "It's like something out of a storybook."

"It's science," he replied.

"Yes, yes, your precious facts," she murmured in her raspy way. Dismissively, as ever.

And when Cayetano looked at her, he hated the part

of him that was still her son. The part that was only her son, and still wished she'd been less…angular. Less ambitious. Less about power and more about him.

But he had found the lost Princess of Ile d'Montagne. A man could not ask for too many miracles. It became greedy.

"I know facts are not your friends," he said. "I came here to inform you, that is all. Because however perverse, I know that at one time, you were focused on the same enterprise."

"I wanted to cut them all down," his mother said, her eyes glittering with what he assumed was remembered fury. "As they deserve."

"You wanted to take my place," he corrected her. "Violent solutions were the excuse, not the reason."

She laughed at that, but it was not a good sound. "I pity your princess."

This was his cue to leave. He knew that. Therese liked nothing more than to poke at him. It was all nonsense and malice that he usually shrugged off as he left. But when it came to Delaney, he couldn't help himself. He couldn't let it go.

"My princess reclaims her rightful place in the world," he informed his mother. "She does so with grace and sensitivity, unlike some I could mention. She met with Princess Amalia only last week and came away the stronger for it. Save your pity for yourself."

It had been a stiff, formal meeting, entirely staged for the cameras to assuage the international interest in the story of babies swapped at birth. The sort of interest Cayetano had always craved, and yet now it was happening, he found he liked it less than he should. It was that hollowness again. But all the tests were in, and conclusive, so the meeting of the two had gone forward. And it had been a strange farce of two similar-looking women, smiling as if their lives hadn't been upended, shaking hands and then sharing a tea service while scrums of journalists hung on their every stiff and overly polite word.

Still, Delaney had told him later, *at least our first meeting is over. It was almost better that there was no chance to talk about anything.*

"She loves you," his mother said now. "It is painfully obvious. And as we know, you are your father's son. You care only for facts and figures, plots and plans. But nothing at all for the emotions that make any of this worthwhile."

He restrained himself from rolling his eyes, but barely.

"You will be set free from your remarkably comfortable prison just as soon as Queen Esme issues the proclamation we've all been waiting for. An announcement of the new line of succession. If I were you, I would take the time to reflect on the fact that you have not been, as you like to claim, imprisoned for *love.* But rather because you attempted a coup. Let us be honest about that, Mother, please. If nothing else."

He expected the cloud of smoke she blew his way. Sometimes she even threw things at him. But she surprised him by sighing.

"I loved him," his mother said, far more quietly than usual. "I can admit it blinded me. But I loved him. And a love like that, no matter how it ends, is worth anything. Even this." She blinked, and the bitterness he knew best crept back over her face. "You'll never know that, Cayetano. Because you are precisely how you were made. Cold and cruel and destined to be alone forever."

That wouldn't have insulted him a month or two ago.

He would have taken it as a compliment. But things were different now.

"If I'm cruel," he gritted out at her, "you have only yourself to blame. For I think you'll find that it's a natural response to a coup attempt. By a mother to her son. No matter how much you dress it up and try to call it a love story."

"Alone," his mother said, distinctly. "Forever."

And Cayetano spent the rest of his afternoon trying to get her voice out of his head.

With little success.

He worked up until the car arrived to take them down from the valley to the sea, where Palais Montaigne had stood almost as long as Arcieri Castle. Almost.

He fielded the usual calls as they wound through the mountains, aware that Delaney was beside him with her face turned toward the glass.

"Are you excited for tonight?" he asked, tossing his mobile aside.

She turned toward him, and he was struck, as ever, by her beauty. By the way she glowed. She looked almost ethereal, in a sparkling gown that made her look as if she, perhaps, was made entirely of froth and sparkling wine. She wore jewels around her neck that had been handed down in his family through the centuries, including the ring on her finger, the pride of many Arcieri brides before her.

Her expression was perfectly placid but still, there was something about the way she regarded him that made him regret…everything.

Cayetano was unused to the feeling. He disliked it intensely.

"It's a formality, surely," Delaney was saying. "All your

sources in her palace indicate that she will be making her announcement soon. Possibly even tomorrow."

"We do not need her proclamation," Cayetano agreed. "The laws of the island dictate that you will inherit the throne, whether she likes it or not."

"So it is done, then." Delaney's blue gaze moved over his face. "You have everything you've wanted, all this time."

And he had spent a great many years fighting. Hand-to-hand combat, martial arts, exercises like today's with his guards. All in preparation for a future that, as far as he had known, might include more coup attempts from his own mother, assassination attempts from Montaigne sympathizers, and who knew what else.

This way of winning was better than those dark imaginings that had preoccupied him for so long. But her tone of voice sent a finger of premonition down the back of his neck. "I'm sure she also wishes to speak with you." He kept his voice…careful. "She is, after all, your mother."

Something flashed in Delaney's gaze. "She is not my mother. I already have a mother."

Cayetano could hear the wealth of pain there. The hurt. The betrayal. He recognized all of it.

And for the first time in a long while, he found…he didn't know what to do.

He reached over and took her hand as he'd done before. He held it in his, though he could not have said, in that moment, if he sought to comfort her…or himself.

Delaney frowned down at her hand as if it wasn't connected to her. Or to him.

"You have everything you ever wanted," she said quietly. And before he could figure out how to answer that, though he registered the tone as dangerous but had no earthly idea why, she kept going. "But what do I have?"

Me, he wanted to say. But couldn't. Because he'd barely seen her since their wedding day. Because he had gone out of his way to make certain she had everything *but* him.

And he could spin any story he liked to anyone who asked. He did it all day long.

But he couldn't lie. Not to her. "Delaney."

Her fingers gripped his, but she lifted her gaze and it speared straight through him, pinning him to his seat.

"I love you, Cayetano," she said, but in a quiet way. A warning sort of way. "I thought you must know this, because why else would I spend twenty-four years perfectly happy to keep to myself only to fling myself into your arms with such abandon? I followed you across the world. I made myself into a princess when all I've ever loved is good, honest work in the dirt. For you."

He felt choked. He couldn't speak. It was as if there were hands tight around his throat, and he was fairly certain that if there were, they were hers.

"Little one," he began.

"I love you," she told him, with a little more intensity. "Even though you left me on our wedding day. Even though it is as if you've disappeared since."

"You knew what had to happen," he managed to grit out, and no matter that it sounded inadequate even to him now.

She smiled, but it was not that smile of hers that made the sun shine brighter. It hit him then that he didn't know when he'd last seen it.

And this one was sad. So deeply sad it broke his heart, when until this moment he would have sworn he didn't have one. That he'd lost it long ago.

That he had banished it the way he'd banished any hint of emotion within him.

The way he'd banished his own mother, too.

Cayetano didn't much care for the way that realization sat on him.

"I love you," Delaney again, her voice faintly scratchy now. "But all you love is this throne that you won't even have until an old woman dies. I love you, Cayetano. I do. But all things considered, I think I prefer the cornfields."

CHAPTER ELEVEN

DELANEY PROBABLY COULD have picked a better moment.

The car had nearly made it into the island's main city. Outside, the sun was heading toward the waiting sea, sending a lustrous golden light dancing over the white and blue buildings, interspersed with splashes of terracotta and covered in bougainvillea. As they made it further down the mountainside, the roads changed, too. Still winding and narrow, so unlike the wide-open roads where she'd been raised—but made treacherous in places by the curious spectators who'd come out to see if they could get a glimpse.

Of her. Of Cayetano.

Of the unexpected new future of their country.

She'd experienced the same thing on her way to her meeting with Princess Amalia, too. A meeting she would have put off forever, if it had been up to her. But then, nothing was. She'd handled the churning inside her by channeling it into an intense interest in this part of the island, so different from up in the valley where she had been treated more as a prize than a curiosity.

Tonight she found herself scanning the different faces, looking through the different expressions. Much as she had when she'd been unable to let herself think about her imminent meeting with Princess Amalia. The real Clark.

And she had changed so much in her weeks on this island. She had accepted that she was holding on to Kansas in ways she shouldn't. She had also accepted that falling in love with Cayetano was an excellent way to avoid thinking about all the unpleasant family things that still made her stomach twist.

She'd become okay with taking on the role of Cayetano's queen.

It was the current Queen—and the woman who'd expected to succeed her—that made her feel off-balance again. One was her biological mother. The other might as well have been a blood relation, given how much they shared, like it or not.

And the fact that it was only the two of them, princess and farm girl, who could possibly understand what had happened to them.

What was still happening to them.

I'm told I come from a long line of farmers, Amalia had said, smiling brilliantly over her tea. *How splendid. It sounds significantly more honest than royalty.*

Delaney had seen behind the smile. She'd seen the darkness lurking there. The confusion. She'd felt it herself.

Less treacherous, I think, she had replied. *But still, I wouldn't turn your back on the chickens.*

Amalia had laughed, and then looked as if the sound surprised her. *Never fear,* she'd said briskly. *I don't think that will be a problem.*

Because she likely had as much interest in farming as Delaney had initially had in princessing. And yet despite herself, Delaney had liked the other woman tremendously.

Liking Amalia felt like the one thing that was hers. There was no betrayal involved. No giving up anything.

They had been switched at a hospital when they were days old. If that didn't forge a bond, Delaney couldn't imagine what could.

On the drive back, she had found herself even more aware of the gawkers. Lined up to stare, to make up stories, to tell lies—and she'd told herself to get used to it. This was her life now. This bizarre fishbowl.

That day, she'd told herself it was worth it, because she had Cayetano.

Everything in her had changed so profoundly after that first night. Once she had let go of what remained of her old identity, she found she knew herself better than she ever had before. Part of it was him in all his *dark glory*. But part of it, she thought now, was what Catherine had been trying to tell her.

It had been what she'd been attempting to explain Cayetano about carrying a burden.

If he hadn't found her, she never would have thought of the farm as a *burden*. It brought her as much joy as it did struggle, even if the fight to keep it going had seemed to take more out of her each year.

She hadn't known how to let go of that. She'd never planned to let go. And she never would have, on her own.

The choice been taken from her and that night, she'd accepted it.

Just as she'd accepted him into her body.

And for a time, she'd truly believed that was enough. It had felt like more than enough in those first days. She'd imagined that what they were building together would bloom. That it would last.

But everything had changed on their wedding day.

Maybe it was one too many betrayals.

"I don't know what you want from me," he said from

beside her now, and when she glanced at him the look on his face seemed to scrape through her, leaving her raw.

She looked down at their hands, still joined. She wore his ring now, the ring he had not shown her himself because, of course, he'd never actually proposed. He'd left it in the care of the majordomo, who had told her, with great pomp and circumstance, the historical significance of the Arcieri diamond. Delaney had received a long lesson on the topic before the ring had been packed away, not to be seen again until Cayetano had slid it on her hand during their wedding ceremony.

Every night she slept in his bed. He usually woke her when he came to bed, later and later all the time. No matter how she tried to stay up, she always seemed to be asleep when he arrived, so her marriage so far seemed to her like little more than a fever dream.

Some parts of it were beautiful. She wouldn't deny that.

But none of it felt *real*.

"Are you threatening me already?" he continued when she did not respond. "Do you think there's any possibility I will let you leave, Delaney?"

And she wasn't sure when it had occurred to her that she couldn't leave. Not because he would stop her, though he might. But because she didn't *want* to leave. She was too invested.

I never wanted to leave Kansas, she'd confessed to Catherine, who had been almost too understanding about not being present at her wedding. She'd laughed and said it was far beyond her to guess at the reasoning of royalty. *I never had the slightest desire to go anywhere.*

And now you have the whole world, Catherine had said with all her usual warmth, as if nothing had changed when everything had. *I'm so proud of you.*

As if she knew Delaney needed that courage. Because she'd always known.

"I don't think I said I was leaving," Delaney said now.

"Forgive me." His voice was scathing. "I must have misinterpreted your loving remarks about preferring cornfields to my company."

"Cayetano." She turned toward him, and faced him, there in the back of the car. The beautiful island was putting on a show in the syrupy gold of the coming sunset, but she couldn't focus on this place. Because what was this place to her without him? "I married you. You do know that for all your bluster, I didn't have to do that, don't you?"

"I know that is what you like to think."

He pulled his hand away and she wasn't surprised to see him curl it into a fist, there on his powerful thigh.

"I like to think it because it's true," she said, her voice no longer as steady as she would have liked. "You forget, I've met your people now. They would never have cheered as they did on our wedding if I had not looked happy. They would not have supported you if you had behaved the way they believe the Montaignes have behaved for so long. I might not have known that you were bluffing about forcing me into marriage at first, but after all these weeks, how can you imagine I haven't learned the truth?"

That hard, beautiful face of his changed again, until he looked less like the man she'd come to know. Less like the lover she knew so intimately now, there in the dark of their bed. Less like the leader he was in the eyes of his people, who would follow him anywhere, willingly.

"If you do not intend to try to leave me, I do not see the point of this conversation," he bit out as if this was one of his wars. "I never made any secret of the fact that our marriage must serve a purpose. I apologize if that purpose was not made clear to you, or if you did not understand what pursuing that purpose would entail. I will have words with the majordomo."

"I understand perfectly," she retorted. "And I think you know that your majordomo would hurt himself before he would neglect his duty."

It was amazing how much affection she'd come to have for that stuffy old man and his uniform. She would hear no word against him, not even from Cayetano.

Beside her, Cayetano nodded stiffly, so Delaney continued.

"I have no problem with the purpose. Our purpose. But I want more than a few stolen hours in the middle of the night." She waited for him to look at her, his burnt gold eyes nearly dark now. So dark she had to repress a shiver. "I want everything, Cayetano. I want a real marriage. I don't see why our marriage can't be like the weeks that preceded our wedding."

"Because they cannot," he bit out, and the anguish that streaked through his gaze took her breath. "It can never be like that again. You wouldn't like it if it was."

"I don't understand," she began, though a trembling sort of uncertainty had taken up residence inside her, and surely this time, touching him wouldn't help. No matter how much she wanted to. "Cayetano, surely—"

But he sat forward, cutting her off that easily. She had started taking lessons in French and Italian, but her few hours of wrestling with two new languages wasn't enough to understand his rapid-fire instructions to the driver. She sat there, her head spinning, as the driver turned off the main road, followed a few side streets, and then headed back into the hills. But instead of taking the road that led back toward the valley, when they reached the spine of the mountain, the car went the other way.

"Where are we going?" she asked. Softly.

Almost as if she didn't want to know.

Cayetano didn't answer her. He only shook his head, staring out the window with that telltale muscle tense in his jaw.

Delaney blew out a breath, then directed her gaze out the windows, too. The car followed the narrow, twisting road that wound its way along what was nearly the very top of the mountain. It was an undeniably stunning drive, though she doubted very much that Cayetano had been seized with the sudden urge to take her sightseeing. Still, they were so high up that Ile d'Montagne looked like something out of a storybook. On one side of the car there were views into the beautiful valley she'd come to love so much these last couple of months. And on the other, down the slope the outside of the mountain, picture-perfect villages nestled with the sparkling, beckoning sea beyond.

She wished she could appreciate it all the way she wanted to, but her pulse was hammering at her. And Cayetano seemed farther away than he ever had been before. It made her stomach twist.

The car pulled out onto a kind of overlook, then stopped. For moment, nothing happened. Delaney snuck glances at Cayetano beside her, but he looked as if he really had turned to stone. Only that clenched fist and the muscle in his jaw gave him away.

After some time had passed, his nostrils flared. Then he threw open the door beside him and got out.

Delaney took a breath or two, gave up trying to do something about her drumming heart, and then followed him.

It was windier up this high, and she was acutely aware

of the foolish clothes she was wearing—all dressed up tonight to meet the current Queen. At first they'd felt like bizarre costumes, these dresses. But the Signorina had helped her feel at ease in them. She had taught Delaney to dance in them. And more than that, had encouraged her to run through the halls of the castle, play, walk outside, and fling herself messily on this couch or that as it moved her. Until Delaney no longer felt as if her chattering trio was dressing a mannequin—a mannequin who wasn't her—every time she dressed for one of her events.

But here, on this rocky outcropping with such a steep drop below, the sun dripping toward the horizon and the sea all around them like a deep blue halo, all she could think about was the absurdity. This dress with its silly ruffles and shoes better suited for circus, they were so much like stilts, as she wandered around this island playing princess games.

Yet it was an absurdity she had come to appreciate.

All because of the man who stood at the edge of the overlook, staring out into the distance.

She had the stray thought that she wished she could jump back in time to show herself who she'd become, because she knew the old version of Delaney would have laughed herself sick at the very idea.

But even as she thought that something in her rejected it.

The old Delaney was gone now. She was *this* Delaney now. Princess Delaney, the papers were already calling her. And there was no possible way she could ever go back. Cayetano was a huge part of that, but it was more than simply him.

She had gone too far from Kansas to ever imagine she could sink back into the life she'd left there. Delaney understood that she would no longer fit.

And maybe that was why, though her heart kicked at her and her stomach cramped, she was able to go and stand beside Cayetano, there at the edge. And remain calm, though the height was worrying and the look he threw her way was something like ravaged.

For a time there was nothing but the wind, and the sun painting the sky in oranges and pinks as it sank.

"I cannot allow myself to love," he told her at last, in the ringing tones he'd used long ago, there in the yard at the farm.

This time, she didn't laugh.

Though she was sorely tempted, if only for symmetry.

This time, she considered what he'd said for a moment, then sniffed. "That seems stupid," she replied, calmly. Very, very calmly. "If you want my opinion."

He turned to look at her fully then, and it wasn't that she was immune to how tormented he looked. He tugged at her the way he always did, and the way, she imagined he always would. It hurt her to see him hurt. She supposed that was what loving someone did.

But Delaney hoped she loved him enough to hold out for better than this. For more. From both of them.

Love isn't a weak little greeting card on a holiday, Grandma Mabel had told her, long ago, when elementary school aged Delaney had not received any valentines on Valentine's Day one year. *Love is ferocious. It is fearless. It is not for the faint of heart, child. It takes a warrior.*

And Cayetano was a warlord. But Delaney was prepared to be a warrior, now, when it was needed.

Whenever it is needed, she promised herself. *As long as we're together.*

She had to hope that she wore her fearlessness on her face.

Maybe she did, because at last, Cayetano began to speak.

"My father was not a cruel man," he told her, as if the words hurt him. "But he was distant. Focused. It was always clear that he had married and had a child because it was expected of him, not because he had any emotional investment being a husband or father. I was never sure if he had any emotions at all. My mother would tell you he never did."

"I'm sorry," Delaney said softly, trying to imagine growing up like that. "It can't have been easy to be the son of such a man."

"You misunderstand," Cayetano bit out. "His focus was the cause. Our people were his only concern and nothing else mattered to him. He was a hero."

He rubbed his hands over his face, and Delaney wanted, badly, to reach over and touch him. But something stopped her.

"He died when I was twelve," Cayetano said, his gaze out toward the setting sun again, all that golden light spilling over the harshness of his expression. And it was as if she could feel that same harshness inside her, like so many jagged edges, cutting into her. Making her ache. "I was in boarding school in England, so it fell to my guards to tell me. They pulled me out of class, sat me down, and called me *warlord*. I was not permitted to fly home. It was thought that having me at the funeral was a risk too great."

"That's terrible," Delaney whispered, and had to grip her own arms as she hugged them close to keep from reaching for him.

"On the contrary." He looked down at her from his great height, stern and something like ruthless—though his eyes were dark. Too dark. "My father's death is what made me. I had no choice but to jettison my emotions. My guards made it clear to me that I was the face of Ile d'Montagne, then and always. That any outbursts on my part would not only reflect badly on my people, but would be trotted out as evidence to show that the House of Montaigne's possession of the throne that was rightfully mine was warranted. Even at twelve I was keenly aware that I could not let that happen. No Arcieri has been born in centuries without accepting that it was more than likely that his attempts to regain the throne would fail. I never expected to win it back, Delaney. But I would die before I made the situation worse."

Delaney could feel the ache in her grow sharper. Those edges dug in harder.

But Cayetano kept going. "It was not until years later that I understood the truth of what happened to him. It was a car accident. Here." Delaney jolted at that, and the way he slashed his hand the air, harsh and hard. "My mother, always the emotional one, had been in a rage. She wanted his attention. As ever, his focus was on bringing our people's case to the world, the better to put pressure on Queen Esme. They had a blazing row and my father took off from the castle, leaving his guard behind and driving himself to his death. They say he lost control of the car here. Because he was not perfect. He was cold and slow to anger, but when his temper finally engaged, it was catastrophic. He proved it so."

Now Cayetano was breathing hard, as if he was running. His gaze was so dark that it, too, began to hurt her as he stared down at Delaney.

"Do not apologize," he growled when she opened her mouth to do just that. "He was reckless, in the end. For all his focus, all his disinterest, he let emotions get the better of him and he lost control of his vehicle. He was a leader of men. A hero to the cause. He should have known better."

She heard the bleakness in his tone. And all she could do was whisper his name.

"But instead, he died." Cayetano looked desolate. Stark stone carved in unforgiving lines. "And that left my mother, in all her erratic sentimentality, in charge until I came of age. I know you read up on my family. I'm certain you know what this moment of recklessness cost us all."

Delaney had read the dispassionate facts of his life on the first night, after he'd showed up out of nowhere. But it was something else again to hear him tell it. And she hadn't loved him then—she'd merely been fascinated against her will. Now that she loved him with everything she was, all she could think was of the boy he'd been, caught in all these terrible forces so much larger than himself.

Not even allowed to grieve.

"She fell in love again, she claimed." Cayetano's voice was derisive. "Then she and her lover schemed to take what was not theirs. I was forced to fight him, with my hands, to claim what was already mine. And none of this would have happened if either one of my parents could truly control their emotions."

Her pulse picked up at that. She reached out, then dropped her hands before she made contact. All she could do was whisper his name again, as if maybe—if she said it the right way—he would hear her.

"I know what love is, Delaney," he told her. Mercilessly. "I know what it does. And I decided a long time ago that I would never allow it in my life. You will have to live with that."

And that should have cut her in two. She imagined it was meant to. She could see the recklessness he'd accused his father of in his gaze then, and on some level, she understood it.

He thought that if he hurt her enough, it would save him from what he must have spent all these years believing was his fate. But she knew better than most that fate was only fate until perspective shifted.

Until the truth was told.

"No," she told him, clearly. Her gaze steady on his. "I don't have to live with that. And I won't."

"I won't love you," he threw at her, as if this was a fight and he had to respond with every last bit of rage and anguish within him. "I can't."

"Cayetano," she said, with all the certainty of the ferocious heart in her chest, "I think we both know you already do."

And she watched as something immense slammed into him. It was as if she'd taken some kind of sledgehammer to the top of his head, cracking open the armor that surrounded him so that the light trapped inside poured out.

So much light that it rivaled the sunset.

He looked dazed. Then he surged forward, taking her upper arms in his hands and lifting her up to her toes.

"It is a death sentence," he growled at her. "Or a lifetime imprisonment in a cell of your own making. That's what love would do for you, Delaney. Is that what you want?"

"I want you," she threw back at him, letting herself blaze in turn. "All of you. If that ends badly, Cayetano, maybe we deserve such a terrible fate. For not loving enough. For not loving well. For letting all the rest of this twist us into pieces."

He shook his head. His grip tightened, but she melted against him and slid her palms on his chest. He was hot, hard. He was mouthwatering. He was Cayetano.

And he was hers.

Whether he knew it or not.

"I promise you that I will love you more than enough, and well," she told him then, and this time, she could see that he was riveted to these vows she made. Unlike the ceremony in the courtyard. "I will put you first. Before crowns and thrones, the reporters who follow you around, the lies people tell. Your heart and my heart, Cayetano. And what we build together. That's what I love. That's what I want. All of you." She slid her right hand up to cover his heart and held it there as she felt it pound. "And all of me. Forever."

He looked haunted. Ravaged straight through. She could see the storm that worked in him, and she almost thought she could hear it, too, like thunder everywhere.

Inside and out.

But she was from Kansas. No storm could scare her.

When he spoke, it was to whisper her name. Again and again, like a melody.

"I don't know how to do this," he told her, when the storm had faded into song, and only the thunder of his heartbeat remained.

Still, she held his gaze. She reminded herself that she was a warrior. Fearless and ferocious.

"Do you want to?" she asked quietly. "All you have to do is *want* to love me. We can build anything we like from there."

It seemed to her then that the golden sunlight of the

last of this day…changed. That it fell across him in a new way. Or maybe it was simply the way he looked at her, something so raw and intense in his gaze she wasn't certain how she could ever look away.

His hands moved on her arms, smoothing up, then down. Then he let out a ragged breath, that she knew, without doubt, was as close as this man of granite ever came to a sob.

"I want to," he whispered, his eyes dark with longing and need, and his voice rough. "Delaney… I want nothing more."

She felt moisture threaten the backs of her eyes. But she moved closer, tipping her face up so she could be closer to him. So she could see all of him.

Because he was still and always the most beautiful thing she'd ever seen.

"That was the hard part," she promised him. "Everything else is downhill."

Cayetano shifted so he could hold her face between his hands.

"I'm not afraid of hard," he told her, his eyes blazing gold once more. "Or hills. But I could not live with it if we do to each other what my parents did. If we even come close."

Delaney lifted her hands to cover his. "We get to decide. We get to choose. Destiny might have brought us together, Cayetano, but it doesn't get to decide how we stay together." Her voice was fierce. Her gaze was steady on his. "We get to choose how we live."

He made a low sort of noise, like something in him was broken. And then he was kissing her, all the heat and dark glory, all that raw desire.

But today it was so much more.

Today, it was laced through with hope.

"I will make you happy," he told her, resting his fore-head on hers as the setting sun finally made it to the sea. "I will do my best, every day. And I will love you, Del-aney. I love you now—I think I loved you at first sight, overalls and all. I promise I will love you with all that I am. And I cannot promise you that it will always look the way you wish it to. I cannot promise you that it will be the way you imagine it. But I do promise you that I will always try. So that somehow, between us, we will achieve something I have long thought was nothing more than the story. A silly little fairy tale."

"But you and I are made to do impossible things, Cay-etano," Delaney said, and her tears fell freely even as she smiled. So wide she thought she could rival horizons. "You found a lost princess who shouldn't exist. You took back the throne of Ile d'Montagne after all these years. What's happy ever after next to that?"

He kissed her again, all that heat, and all of it hers. Then he held her close as if he would never let her go.

She believed, at last, he never would.

"The happy ever after is everything, Delaney," he told her, the way some men said vows in churches. But this was their church, so high above the island they would rule together one day. This was who they were and who they would become, as long as they had each other. "You will see."

"Everything," she agreed, and the word felt like a brand, stamped deep into her skin.

Cayetano held her close as the sun sank below the horizon. As the old day ended so a new day could dawn.

But first, the riot of the stars, inside them and out.

Tonight it felt like they were filled with them.

"Everything," Cayetano repeated as the rest of their

lives began. "And I promise you, my little farm girl, it will be ours."

And then, together, in the kingdom they cared for and the children they raised, they made it happen.

Until forever seemed like not nearly long enough.

CHAPTER TWELVE

CAYETANO ARCIERI WAS a man of his word.

They never made it to see Queen Esme that day. Instead, Cayetano took his wife back home, marinated in her, and the following day, set off on a long honeymoon that in no way made up for the first stretch of their marriage.

But he hoped it was a harbinger of the joys to come.

And as months became years, and hope became truth, he liked to think that they'd built the foundation for all that would come in those eight weeks.

Because with such a foundation, anything was possible.

Delaney and Queen Esme met, and while no one would describe them as *fast friends,* they found a way forward. Eventually, their way forward involved Catherine, too.

And years later, when time began to dull the edges of old memories, he found his way back to his own mother, too. Therese left Ile d'Montagne and married her long-lost lover, and Cayetano could see that truly, they loved each other.

Though even when his mother and he found ways to sit in peace together, speaking of soft and uncomplicated things, he made sure to make it clear that their love was better blooming off the island.

"I am far too old and tired to play games with your throne, Cayetano," Therese would tell him.

"Good," he would reply.

And the more time passed, the more they laughed.

But none of it would be possible if there hadn't first been those two sweet months, just Cayetano and Delaney.

No causes, no people. Just the two of them and that farmhouse in Kansas. Walking the land. Tending to vegetables, listening to the wind in the corn, getting dirty beneath the sun and lying out at night to lose themselves in the stars.

Most future kings did not honeymoon on a remote Kansas farm, but then, Cayetano was not most kings. He intended to be the best King Ile d'Montagne had ever had. He meant to split his time between the sea and the mountains. He meant to make his people whole.

A prospect that was only possible because he had Delaney.

He never took her for granted again.

Like all the things he studied, once he'd decided to love her he threw himself into it, body and soul.

"I love you," he liked to tell her when he woke her in the mornings, even years later, whether they were in their winter palace on the water or their summer castle in the hills. "I love you, little one. More today than yesterday."

Every day it was true.

"I love you, too," she would reply, always with that beautiful smile, wrapping herself around him while the morning sun danced in and the island breezes murmured all around them.

The way they'd woken up every morning of that honeymoon, tucked away beneath the eaves in that old farmhouse.

And he took care to love her there, when it was just the two of them. Deeply. Thoroughly. Before their children came bursting in. Before the concerns of the day took hold. Before they became King and Queen again.

First, they loved each other.

Fierce and ferocious, just Cayetano and Delaney.

Forever.

Just the way he'd promised.

* * * * *

COMING SOON!

We really hope you enjoyed reading this book. If you're looking for more romance, be sure to head to the shops when new books are available on

Thursday 26th May

MILLS & BOON®

Coming next month

THE SECRET SHE KEPT IN BOLLYWOOD
Tara Pammi

It was nothing but sheer madness.

Her brothers were behind a closed door not a few hundred feet away. Her daughter...one she couldn't claim, one she couldn't hold and touch and love openly, not in this lifetime, was also behind that same door. The very thought threatened to bring Anya to her knees again.

And she was dragging a stranger—a man who'd shown her only kindness—along with her into all this crazy. This reckless woman wasn't her.

But if she didn't do this, if she didn't take what he offered, if she didn't grasp this thing between them and hold on to it, it felt like she'd stay on her knees, raging at a fate she couldn't change, forever... And Anya refused to be that woman anymore.

It was as if she was walking through one of those fantastical daydreams she still had sometimes when her anxiety became too much. The one where she just spun herself into an alternate world because in actual reality she was nothing but a coward.

Now, those realities were merging, and the possibility that she could be more than her grief and guilt and loss was the only thing that kept her standing upright. It took her a minute to find an empty suite, to turn the knob and then lock it behind them.

Silence and almost total darkness cloaked them. A sliver of light from the bathroom showed that it was another expansive suite, and they were standing in the entryway. Anya pressed herself against the door with the man facing her. The commanding bridge of his nose that seemed to slash through his face with perfect symmetry, the square jaw and the broad shoulders…the faint outline of his strong, masculine features guided her. But those eyes…wide and penetrating, full of an aching pain and naked desire that could span the width of an ocean…she couldn't see those properly anymore. Without meeting those eyes, she could pretend this was a simple case of lust.

Simon, she said in her mind, tasting his name there first…so tall and broad that even standing at five-ten, she felt so utterly encompassed by him.

Simon with the kind eyes and the tight mouth and a fleck of gray at his temples. And a banked desire he'd been determined to not let drive him.

But despite that obvious struggle, he was here with her. Ready to give her whatever she wanted from him.

What did she want? How far was she going to take this temporary madness?

Continue reading
THE SECRET SHE KEPT IN BOLLYWOOD
Tara Pammi

Available next month
www.millsandboon.co.uk

MILLS & BOON

THE HEART OF ROMANCE

A ROMANCE FOR EVERY READER

MODERN

Prepare to be swept off your feet by sophisticated, sexy and seductive heroes, in some of the world's most glamourous and romantic locations, where power and passion collide.

HISTORICAL

Escape with historical heroes from time gone by. Whether your passion is for wicked Regency Rakes, muscled Vikings or rugged Highlanders, await the romance of the past.

MEDICAL

Set your pulse racing with dedicated, delectable doctors in the high-pressure world of medicine, where emotions run high and passion, comfort and love are the best medicine.

True Love

Celebrate true love with tender stories of heartfelt romance, from the rush of falling in love to the joy a new baby can bring, and a focus on the emotional heart of a relationship.

Desire

Indulge in secrets and scandal, intense drama and plenty of sizzling hot action with powerful and passionate heroes who have it all: wealth, status, good looks…everything but the right woman.

HEROES

Experience all the excitement of a gripping thriller, with an intense romance at its heart. Resourceful, true-to-life women and strong, fearless men face danger and desire - a killer combination!

To see which titles are coming soon, please visit

millsandboon.co.uk/nextmonth

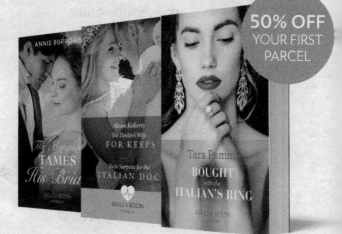

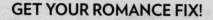

MILLS & BOON
MEDICAL
Pulse-Racing Passion

Set your pulse racing with dedicated, delectable doctors in the high-pressure world of medicine, where emotions run high and passion, comfort and love are the best medicine.